THE
SHADOW
PEOPLE

THE SHADOW PEOPLE
P.R. BROWN

DB
PUBLISHING

By the same author:

Fiction
The Mirror Men
The Treadmillers

Non-fiction
The Gods of Our Time
Dreams and Illusions Revisited
The Mountain Dwellers

First published 2019 by DB Publishing, an imprint of JMD Media Ltd,
Nottingham, United Kingdom.

ISBN 978-1-78091-602-6

Printed in the UK

Chapters

Chapter One

A Developing Constant

And here I sit, listening to the singing wires that stretch from pylon to pylon, and to the distant bleating of sheep on these lonely grassy hills once pounded by the martial tread of Roman soldiery; not so close to home to be comforting, yet not so far to feel foreign; no place this for those who yearn for the society of man, but one more fitting to remember the faces of the familiar dead.

~ ~

Amongst them the face of Adam Sedley; that poor deluded soul who dreamed he might become a fisher of men and instead was himself hooked by them and thrown back to be mauled by the creatures of the black depths. His paternal uncle, Alan Sedley, had taught General Studies in a large comprehensive school; what was called General Studies was a catch-all, which, in consequence, ended up catching little or nothing at all. And there can be little doubt that Adam looked to his uncle as a role-model, since both believed that the world was changeable if only one tried hard enough to change it. If only one could catch human fish, teach them how better to swim in this dark and difficult sea, and thereby alter the moral composition of the world! Adam was a dreamer who dreamed a worthy dream, and since the dream was worthy, his story merits a hearing, albeit muffled, before it is finally relegated to the nursery of mankind and buried deep where it can be temporarily forgotten and perhaps someday rediscovered by the uncomprehending, like some Dead Sea scroll written in an indecipherable tongue.

Adam grew up unattracted to school teaching; but he remembered his uncle's remark that a good teacher, like a good anything else, must be a 'developing constant'; a good teacher, like a good doctor or a good bus driver, may develop his talents and his skills, but his personality, his *person*, is defined by his principles, and if those principles are worth anything at all, they must remain constant and inviolable; values take first place; principles first, methodology second, and never the twain shall meet, for it was all too easy to confound them and mistake the one for the other, and easy, too, to allow methodology to overshadow principles and suffocate the very person defined by them. He remembered his uncle saying that it was important to keep one's head above water and that this was particularly difficult when others were so bent upon pushing it under. To the young Adam Sedley, this sounded like a swimming lesson, and it confused him; but as the years passed the message became clearer. The key point was that the tendency to put methodology first was rife and in every profession, and perhaps had always been so; but it had to be fought tooth and nail, even if at the expense of methodology and talent and skill altogether! Methodology in particular was particularly troublesome, because it was all-too-often surrounded with dogma or one kind or another, and dogma was the bane of mankind – or so his uncle had said.

The notion of a developing constant and memories of his uncle were as inseparable as the execution of Charles I and David Copperfield's reminiscences of Mister Dick. He even imagined his uncle passing from this world into the next with the phrase 'developing constant' on his pale lips like a deathly mantra, though he had in fact shaken off his mortal coil, utterly oblivious to his surroundings and quite incapable of uttering so much as a syllable of this delicious phrase, let alone articulating the idea for the very last time. Whether the fact – if it is a fact – that sons follow their fathers and never their mothers is the gross tragedy that Oscar Wilde whimsically records and laments, it has to be said that Adam Sedley enjoyed a kind of cerebral chemistry with his uncle that was absent with his father, James Sedley, and that he enjoyed a filial intimacy with his mother that had never been extended to his father.

The distance Adam felt between himself and his father might well have contributed to his sense of inadequacy, against which only his memory of his uncle could serve as a redeeming counterweight. The trouble was cyclical. He would build up his expectations on the persistent assumption that he was worth something and could make a real difference in this world; but then, when he met failure at every turn, he felt obliged to question the assumption, and would end up believing he was worth nothing at all. Somehow, the belief that he was worthless required too much strain to be truly sustainable, and gradually his expectations would rise again, like a phoenix from the ashes of its own demise. Then, once again, his repeated failures would bring him down to earth, too often with a crash. It was a cycle of rise and fall which promised to last his whole life through, a continual process of stumbling and falling and picking himself up and dusting himself down, and all he had to show for it was that he was still standing and making as little sense of his surroundings as ever before – battered, worn and exhausted, but not yet quite broken. Whenever a sense of failure made him feel less than nothing, he felt strangely relieved and at peace, as though a heavy burden had been cast off, having been divested, supposedly, of the need to prove his worth. But this aura of tranquillity, which felt like the calm in the eye of a storm, would pass as his expectations once again revived, to lead him astray once again. He was himself, one might say, a 'developing constant' – of a kind. These failures, it must be noted, had little to do with success or failure at school or college or work or in personal relationships, for in all these things he was admirably competent. No, it was much more a deep, internal thing; a feeling that he should *be* more than he was and therefore be capable of *doing* more – doing more than simply going through the motions of what people commonly regard as 'getting on' and 'getting settled'. Even in his late teens he felt the boredom of convention and routine.

The role his uncle played in this process of rise and fall was no doubt incalculable. Alan Sedley had about him more the aura of a philosopher than the average teacher of so-called General Studies. Those long walks they took in his childhood down nearby country lanes whenever the fancy and the opportunity arose no doubt worked their magic on this impressionable youth. His uncle replaced his father, James, on these occasions, who was invariably otherwise engaged in the attempt to feather the family nest, or else in a state of recovery from so doing, with a round or two of golf to soothe the nerves and recharge the batteries for yet another assault on the unforgiving, relentless world of commerce. But James's brother, Adam Sedley, found time for everything because he took an interest in everything, even in the grass that grew under their feet; he had made a study of grasses and would stop, call attention to a blade of grass, gently pluck it and turn it this way and that in his fingers to reveal its shape, colour and texture to his young companion who, in those early days, was quite amused by these obvious eccentricities. This kind of thing – stopping, stooping and picking up the odd bit of grass, and then talking about it as though it were a most valuable painting ... well, you wouldn't find his father, James, doing such silly things; oh no, James was a no-nonsense man who had much better things to do. But it was what Alan *said*, too. He would come out with things that seemed oracular to the ears of young Adam, like, 'What tomorrow brings belongs to tomorrow!' in response to Adam's stressful countenance when asked about an impending school test. Or, as they walked down a residential street, Alan would suddenly mutter, 'All those doors, windows and walls – hmm. I'm moved to ask who breathes, I do not say, *lives*, behind them.' Adam would just walk unquestioningly by his side, content to believe that his uncle was simply thinking out loud. Sometimes not simply content, but more than happy, for his uncle's ramblings were sometimes too much even for a child's imagination. 'You know, in Heaven, if you believe in it, no one grows older than they were when they entered it. Well, suppose you were in Heaven, being, say, middle-aged when you got there, and you looked down upon the earth and zoomed in, and you saw some old man walking there, and a voice over your shoulder said, "You see that old man down there – yes, that's right, the one with the walking-stick ambling slowly along, well, that's your grandson!" Now that would be something, wouldn't it?' It took young Adam quite a while to think this one out; thankfully, it didn't require an immediate response – it was just his uncle musing aloud again.

Such musings seemed to be his uncle's trademark, and so dear to him that they had to find expression, an expression that perhaps they could find nowhere else – not in the classroom, not amongst his colleagues, not even within the walls of his own home. Instead they were released like darts in his rambling walks, where they could do no harm, and heard only by his young nephew, who could hardly make head or tail of them. And one dart might quickly follow another, as though in competition. 'Self-interest now. Well, that's the lamest, albeit the most natural, of excuses; it is also the most powerful and enduring.' Quickly followed by, 'Power, with the greed and fear it engenders, is the worst cocktail devised by mankind, and one that will endure as long as man himself endures.' Or perhaps, in answer to Adam's enquiry whether they might find a snake in the grass, 'Don't talk to me about snakes, young man. I can tell you this much: a venomous snake carries its poison wherever it goes; like a wolf – ravenous even on a full stomach!'

The walk through the cemetery on the way home, which they might easily have avoided, occasioned a stop before a large gravestone, and a remark which stuck burr-like in Adam's mind ever-after. His uncle bent forward in a vain effort to read the inscription. 'Well, anyway, his epitaph is already written – but yours is in the making!' There was an inevitable question about whether Heaven really exists.

'Look, remember this: love one another and demonstrate your love in life; even though they may have passed, love them still. That's all. There's no more to it. That's enough, you see? As for anything else, well, it's just a wallpaper-pattern. Yes?' His uncle spoke with warm authority and gentle assurance. He didn't seem at all his old eccentric self. Just plain, simple common sense. 'Just think of all the things we do and say – all that stuff which doesn't touch the truth of things at all – and after all that, we simply sigh, and fall, never to rise again.' Here he was again, musing and talking to himself.

There can be no doubt that his uncle bequeathed something inexpressible to the young Adam Sedley. When Alan Sedley, just after his 50th birthday, suddenly passed away from a massive and irreversible cardiac arrest, his God entered young Adam's soul and fashioned it irretrievably. The boy was stuck with the God he had inherited and could not be shaken off or induced to leave. Adam was away, as a 20-year-old university student steeped in statistics on a course, much to his dislike, in finance and accounting, which his father had urged him to undertake in the interests of future job security – 'It'll set you up nicely,' his father had said. When Adam received the news about his uncle Alan, he slipped out from beneath his books, bought a half bottle of cheap whisky and sobbed his way through it; there was only one statistic that absorbed his attention now; one statistic too many.

So it was that Adam Sedley had about him a disquietude of spirit that would dog him all his days, endowing him with the notion that it was unthinkable to be born into the light of day only to spend the rest of one's life in obscurity. For obscurity was uselessness, and uselessness was abhorrent. Life was to be lived; like a theatre-production, it needed both a stage and a script; the script was already half-written, though still unread. But where would it be played out?

Chapter Two

Of Real Men

And from these hills you might see what follies pass for wisdom far below, where real men, though blind, confound the warnings of the wise and purport to teach us all, with all the common arts they can devise, pretending good sense but leaving wisdom far behind.

~ ~

The script was played out deep in the suburbia of the city; there in the well-tended gardens of the tastefully modernised semi-detached; there in the concrete wasteland of the mortgage-holder and the premium-payer; there where empty milk bottles sparkle like crystal, awaiting the milkman, who always arrives on time; there in the land of order and orderly assumption, where the baker is expected to bake, the doctor to treat if not to cure, the plumber to install and repair, the police to protect, and the clergyman to protect his flock: in short, it was there where everyone has his place and his purpose; no boat-rocking there, where everyone knows his place and must study the art of contentment. This was the commuter land of leafy suburbia, whose inhabitants tacitly, and, on proper occasion, not so tacitly, toasted their green and pleasant heritage.

There lived James and Judith Sedley, deep inside their semi-detached, cosy as mummies and as real as death.

Approaching his mid-60s, and apparently enjoying every miserable minute of it, James had, whenever the opportunity conveniently presented itself, owned to being a self-made man, and, since it was hard to imagine that the hand of the Creator had had much to do either with his advent or subsequent development, it was a claim both credible and pathetic. What to more discriminating minds might take on the character of a sad confession, is to the James Sedleys of this world a claim to considerable virtue and merit. And so it was that James Sedley regarded his progress in the jungle of personal and familial advancement a worthy conversational piece, to be held aloft and to the light, some priceless gem unveiled to furnish example to the young and validation to his peers.

James Sedley regarded himself a pillar of the establishment and was, like all such architectural wonders, endowed with an intellect hewn of rough stone, fated to remain unpolished and untouched by the insights of better men and the simple innocence of children. He was a monument to common sense, propriety, and the rule of law. And there were those who in all seriousness said of him that he was a man, a *real* man. Not a hair out of place. A man of routine. Of precision. One whose opinions were reliably respectable and respectably reliable, and one whose organisational abilities were God-given and God-blessed – after all, was he not entrusted with the priceless accounts of the golf club, a treasurer to be treasured? No, it had to be admitted he was a born organiser, an inveterate arranger, and a spontaneous hand-clapper at Conservative rallies. He was, in short, altogether a man. A real man. And real men would inherit the earth – or at least deserved to. In their own communities and on their own ground real men tend to stick loyally together, like the proverbial birds, each applauding the other's merits while at the same time secretly desiring, and on occasion actively plotting, hegemony over their peers.

And Judith? Ah, Judith! Alas, alack, she was not now what she had been when young and foolish and innocently planning her route to marital and parental bliss. A changed woman! A changed woman, indeed. Sullen, morose; of few words, and even those carefully chosen. Now she was in her late 50s and looking much older still, with the weight, not of the world, but of the world of James Sedley, sitting hard and long on her shoulders. The weight of a real man, and 30 years of marital bliss. She had long abandoned even the slightest pretence of self-preservation, rarely having a hair-do or using make-up, though she was not yet as hopelessly dishevelled as Miss Havisham. She would dress late and lounge about the house, a habit that infuriated her spouse and sent him off to the office in a silent fury, which was later to be unleashed at juniors in the game of human dice known respectfully as Life Assurance. He might have retired years earlier and devoted the rest of his life to improving his handicap on the golf course, but the prospect of having much more to do with Judith than was absolutely necessary was off-putting; this, together with the fact that he had been absorbed in statistics for so long and wedded to a routine that now served to define him, meant that the idea of retirement had been relegated to the back-burner and would stay there until it boiled over and simply had to be confronted come what might; but for now, it was out of sight, out of mind.

While James spent his day dedicated to the human lottery, Judith spent much of hers languidly and lugubriously preoccupied with her pre-marital past, or else pathetically longing for a return of the infant years of their only child Adam, whom she had long regarded the only palatable fruit of her marriage; her photograph albums were her most reassured possession, put together at times when there was everything to look forward to. In this, she was not, of course, alone in deep, respectable suburbia – transposing to her offspring all the virtues of her marriage, leaving none for the union in its own right. And when her thoughts drifted, as drift they so frequently did, to childhood, in which parents normally play a key and affectionate role, there was little consolation there: her father had died too soon; her mother had performed her motherly responsibilities with the coldness of duty and her mother still lived, herself now unwanted, slowly shuffling off this mortal coil in a geriatric hospital in a no-man's land of senility, far beyond the edge of either reason or desire, quite out of reach, and as unreachable in her dotage as she had been when a young mother, despising motherhood and holding the innocent culpable. Judith's childhood musings were naturally soured by paternal loss and maternal indifference.

When Judith became a Sedley, she expected more than a mere change of name. James would be lover, father and friend. This was her natural expectation, one that was, equally naturally, doomed to die the death of a thousand cuts, each cut deeper and more painful than the one preceding, until, finally, only the memory of expectation remained, a taunt and bitter reminder of what might have been, like a cause, now lost, over which much blood has been spilt.

James had changed, too. But they had changed in opposite directions. Judith had cultivated the notion not only that materialism and selfishness were somehow bound up with one another, but that the association was unsalutary and unsatisfactory. Such serious misgivings are unwelcome in respectable suburbia, as indeed they are elsewhere, for they tend to threaten stability and orderly assumption and are for this reason discouraged – at least in the best circles. Judith wanted to speak of loving and giving rather than of despising and receiving, of finding the best in people rather than the worst. But such ideas are considered too airy-fairy to be of much practical value; they are vague, and vagueness and logic have long been considered an unacceptable cocktail in the commuter land of leafy suburbia. As far as James was concerned, such talk sat well with dressing late and lounging about all day but was too namby-pamby for the real world and could never get anything done – though he never actually said as much. And so, deprived of a sympathetic audience, she gave up trying to communicate with her husband. Nevertheless, the desire to say something remained; she was not academically inclined, but this was her only intellectual virtue. She found it difficult to articulate her feelings, nor could she appeal much to her own reading, since there was so little of it, but she did remember being told about the life of Socrates – by Adam, who had read about such things. She remembered how Socrates had spoken in his own defence at his trial – something about his sons, and how he wanted them to grow up untarnished by the selfish pursuit of profit; how Socrates had begged his friends to look after his sons after his death and make sure that they never put profit before goodness; and then they killed him, probably because he had gone around saying things like that, and because that was what they called 'corrupting the youth' of Athens, because they didn't like stirrers, and Socrates was a great stirrer, and ... well, anyway, it was something like that. James would probably say it was all a load of romanticised claptrap. But she remembered Adam saying that Christ was a stirrer too. So it seemed that stirrers of this sort shared a common fate. To be eliminated if they were important. To be idly mocked or studiously ignored if they were not. She herself was ignored. Whenever she wanted to speak to James about Socrates, she was ignored. So she had given up trying. She consoled herself with the thought that she could hardly improve upon the words of people like Socrates and Christ, anyway; so, if they had received short shrift, well ... what was the point of talking at all? Besides, she was never quite sure what she wanted to say. Deep stuff sounded alright when Adam came out with it. But it never came from her in the same way. Anyway, she was getting older, certainly very tired, and there was so much of the past to remember. The past – the only certainty left.

James had changed, yes. He had begun deep in the countryside, where the air is reputedly more wholesome, and ended in the insurance business. Starting with an inherited but unsuccessful smallholding, he had come to believe in the business of risk as a far more reliable undertaking than the risk of business, encouraged by the fact that the business of risk is founded upon the risks taken by others. He had grasped at the easier and thicker straw of conventional wisdom that a popular notion of propriety and respectability had held out to him. It was not the meek, but those who played the game of chance that inherited the earth; but the beauty of life assurance was that it was founded upon the certainty and resulting fear of death; and so, for as long as the human race endured, for as long as babies came into the world and subsequently left it, job security was assured. James had heard the call and saw that it was good. He became progressively possessive of his enlightenment and progressively unforthcoming in either the praise or the defence of the unfortunate and the deprived. For James Sedley took the view that God helps those who help themselves, and that He is particularly fond of those who help themselves the most. Therefore, he felt bound to receive the full approbation of the Almighty if, that is to say, the Almighty existed at all. It should be noted that the word 'therefore' occupied pride of place in his vocabulary. James Sedley was nothing if not a therefore-man and a stickler for exactness and detail; not for him the filofax of the junior executive, for he carried all his memos in his head, together with all the relevant operations of financial logic.

A chasm now yawned between James and Judith Sedley. She might have guessed. She might have known what lay ahead. In the early days of courtship she had called him Jim, only to be shyly but unmistakably rebuffed. No, her man would not be abbreviated, not even in the interests of love and fond familiarity. It hardly seemed to matter at the time – in fact she managed to convince herself that the name 'James' was proper and 'Jim' was not. Yet, now she knew it had been a foretaste of the inner man, who was in residence at the outset and who would, in the fullness of time, emerge to consume her, hopes and all, like an insurance policy grown to maturity.

The chasm was unbridgeable. The man who stood before the long mirror in the hallway, brushing imagined specks of dust from the cuffs of his pinstriped jacket, grunting now approvingly, now contemptuously, had produced the woman who slouched in her dressing-gown, waiting to be alone with her memories, with her photograph albums whose pages she turned with all the loving care of the archaeologist doting on the frail leaves of ancient papyrus.

The revulsion, for that is what it had now become, of the one for the other was conspicuously silent and intensely physical, as indeed is the common run of things in the commuter land of leafy suburbia. She thought of him as the man who gratuitously brushed his cuffs. He thought of her as the woman with unkempt hair who gratuitously slouched in dressing gown and slippers. Quite simple, really. Simple, and, of course, anything but simple. No, the face of revulsion must not be confused with its source. But the Sedleys would not or could not probe below the surface appearance of revulsion to discover causes. Had they done so, they might have survived the experience and found, at last, something in each other to love. But they stopped at the threshold of revulsion and were overcome. They were charmed out of a genuine desire to communicate, charmed out of love altogether, if love had once played any part in their lives at all. Instead, they thought of each other in terms of cliché and generality, of which there is great abundance and very little else in the commuter land of leafy suburbia.

How unpleasantly mysterious the whole thing seemed to James Sedley! After all, he was respectable and industrious, and, if not at all wealthy, at least sufficiently capable of paying his way, of keeping the wolf from the door. He had always put his family first. Was that not *something*? In fact, was that not *everything*? Judith's ingratitude was unacceptable, incomprehensible, intolerable. And he was no fool, either. Oh, no! He *knew*. He knew that she despised him.

She did. She had lost respect for him, immeasurably worse than falling out of love, though often its cause. Things, objects, began to symbolise him, to stand for him, to *mean* him.

Well, there was that thing about the wall, for instance.

A low wall of brick, topped with long, rectangular blocks of cement, separated off their front garden from the road. One evening the wall was vandalised. The uppermost layers of brick and concrete were yanked off by a small band of teenagers swaggering through the neighbourhood late at night, whose appreciation of order and the rule of law was dulled to extinction by a large dose of lager. Thuds and contemptuous laughter were heard, mingling with the crash of falling masonry through the adjacent rose bushes and shrubbery. But such was James Sedley's confidence in his immunity from the crudities of ordinary life that it never once occurred to him that his domain could possibly be under attack. He was only slightly and momentarily disturbed from his slumbers, and continued to sleep soundly 'til morning.

But then, when, in the cold and revealing light of day, he first beheld the wonton destructiveness of ignorant youth, he gaped silently in shock for an instant, like one hit by a bullet. He then erupted with nothing short of volcanic might, his white hot lava evaporating everything that dared to stand motionless in its path. His initial imprecatory denunciations of youth quickly grew to embrace every living thing, and even included Judith Sedley for her general laxity and lack of vigilance – as though there were indisputable causal links between her bedroom slippers and the lamentable failings of modern-day youth. His wrath could not be cooled by his customary cup of Earl Grey, nor yet soothed by a thin count of blessings.

Then came the rebuilding. The broken masonry was replaced with painstaking care and precision, the bricks fitted together with strength of purpose and were destined to last for centuries, outlasting Hadrian's brave attempt – a wall which would stand as a monument to the supreme virtue of Right over Might. Sand was carefully proportioned to cement, cement to sand, and the spirit-level was frequently deployed to ensure that Art herself was not betrayed nor discerning Posterity disappointed. And all this done *by* James Sedley, *for* James Sedley, and to the immense credit *of* James Sedley. Immense credit, indeed. For it was not as though the wall had merely been restored to its former self – which would have been a most acceptable achievement in its own right. No, it had now heaped upon it a far greater glory. For it was now the product of Justice and Right incarnate, and stood all the stronger for that.

Next came the vigil. Each evening of the ensuing month James Sedley would stalk round the garden in the darkness of the night, in particular the hour between closing time and midnight, hiding himself in this or that bush, or behind this or that shrub, crouching low and in wait, and more than ready this time for any further assault upon the wall. He lurked in the shadows, acutely alert to every sound; hedgehogs in slippers could not have escaped his keen hearing; there he waited, ready and willing to pounce like a hungry lion with a roar like thunder upon any attempt, youthful or otherwise, to ravage his monument. And thus he stalked in the shadows, face almost hidden by his wide-brimmed gardening hat, crouching quietly like a commando, determined to smite any offender with the Sword of Supreme Justice. Nor was this sword a mere abstraction. Far from it! For close by him lay the very thing: an old dress-sword in its scabbard, ready to do the work of its wielder. He entertained a fantastical vision of how he would wield it against a horde of drunken youths, of how they would fall before him into pools of their own blood and gore – albeit the sword was entirely blunt and useless as a weapon of war; no matter, just let them lay a finger on that wall, that's all! – heads would roll and blood would spill!

Night after night James Sedley lurked in the shadows and behind bushes while indoors Judith Sedley grew increasingly contemptuous of him. Each night, getting on for the witching hour, she would lie in bed waiting for the pre-arranged signal – a sharp rat-a-tat-tat of the front-door knocker, at which she was to phone for the police quick as lightning while her brave spouse, sword in hand, confronted the offending horde, making his stand at the front gate, awaiting the arrival of the cavalry in peaked hats and panda cars.

It is no doubt just as well that the signal never came. In any case, the lion of right-over-might had at least made his presence felt, even at a distance, for no youth, monstrous or otherwise, ever so much as looked that way again. The only sound Judith heard was the nightly rattle of the sword as it was returned to its scabbard, yet undefiled by the blood of the guilty. After the Angel of Death had rattled his chains, James Sedley slowly made his way upstairs to bed, heavy footed and heavy laden, a general spoiling for a fight, but forced to quit the field in the cowardly absence of an unworthy enemy.

Long after these nights of sentry work had ended he persisted in checking his wall at the close of the day, strolling up to it and placing his hand upon it, as though in blessing or in salutation, later peering through cracks in the curtains to check that it was still there and intact.

Nor had he forgotten to inform the police. He was not one to let such an event slip by unstamped by the due weight of the law. But since the police, much to his chagrin, were not disposed to spare a whole policeman to guard the wall, it naturally fell to James Sedley himself to perform the role of Lord Protector, a role which he played obsessively and with all the precision of military strategy. In the spirit of the rugged pioneer, he did not fail to rise to the occasion with all the integrity it so clearly deserved.

Neither would he accept any social engagement during these nights of vigil, lest the heathen horde should attack in his absence and undo all his work of reconstruction; an attack *in absentia* would also deprive him of the indescribable pleasure of making a citizen's arrest – the idea that he himself would have come off very much the worse in the attempt had not of course fully dawned on him.

All normal life suffered suspension while James Sedley played the part of policeman, judge, jury and, given half the chance, executioner. Not really executioner: he found little difficulty persuading himself that the sword was merely defensive and, if not defensive, symbolic – yes, a symbol of righteous indignation; and besides, he was no spring chicken.

The wall stood and continued to stand; indeed, it would outlive him altogether and become a lasting monument to his strength of character, a totem of the inner man and thus almost an object of worship.

Judith Sedley despised it, since she thought so little of its maker, its guardian and what it stood for. How could she have married a man so solicitous of the longevity of a mere garden wall and so mindless of humanity and all things bright and beautiful? What had become of the man she had married, this monumental wreck? – and yet the answer was simple, painfully simple: Nothing, nothing had happened to him at all; he had not changed into what he was from something more noble and fine; time had simply revealed more clearly what he had been all along. Somehow she had received sight, and the gift gave her a perception of beauty, and with that, inevitably, a perception of what fell so very short of beauty.

But such reflections were hard to live with. Had he really been like this all along? She thought differently at turns. Perhaps there had once been a time when James would have rebuilt the wall without so much as batting an eyelid, without a second thought, with no fuss at all, and she had always admired people who were able to ... well, just get on with things; the ability to just get on with things was after all the mark of a 'real man', and this was one of James's favourite phrases; and as for telling the police, much less keeping a nightly vigil, perhaps he wouldn't have given it a second thought; surely, he would have forgotten the whole episode as soon as the thing had been rebuilt. Yes, perhaps somehow he had lost his sanity, somewhere along the way, and become like ... well, like everyone else in the commuter land of leafy suburbia, a kind of lost soul clutching at inconsequential straws.

But perhaps in giving him a generous appraisal she too was clutching at straws. No matter. There was no denying the facts as they stood. The wall was James Sedley – hard, precise, well-measured, immovable, untouchable without permission, and ... ever-lasting. The wall and James Sedley were two of a kind. It had become impossible for Judith to think of the one without the other.

But it was not just the wall.

There was also the box!

His box – a wooden rectangular box no more remarkable than a shoe box; James Sedley's box, which he kept in James Sedley's cupboard in the bedroom he shared with his wife. Alone in that room he would take out his box and examine its contents. Inside it he kept his best things, which meant that they would never see active service: his best wristwatch and his best pocket-watch, which would never ever be worn on this side of eternity; his best fountain pen, which would never caress paper; his best wallet, whose shiny leather exterior would never be dulled by the commerce of everyday life; his best cigar lighter, which would never be tarnished by ash – not even the ash of the un-smoked trio of best-quality Cuban cigars that lay neatly next to it inside an expensive, leather cigar-case. He would wipe each item with a small clean cloth that he kept there for the purpose. Having cleaned these items lovingly, each in turn, he would return them carefully to the box and close the lid gently, having first made sure that no item rubbed against another to cause scratch or smudge.

This curious ritual would be repeated on average once a month with the utmost care and attention. The box had of course been checked out by Judith Sedley, who at first satisfied herself that it was merely some strange masculine quirk, essentially childlike and innocuous. But after a while the box began to irritate her, and at length she longed to hammer it to pieces, contents and all, ceremoniously at the bottom of the garden. She managed to resist the temptation to commit symbolic murder, feeling perhaps that the box had come to master her spouse and that he could never survive without it – as though it were an umbilical cord that gave him life but might just as well strangle him if he refused to give it sufficient obeisance. Be that as it may, there it was. His life. James Sedley in a box.

If it wasn't the box, it was the wall. And if it was neither the box nor the wall … it was the clock.

One afternoon, in the early years of their marriage, he returned home with what he described as their anniversary present: a mantlepiece-clock. But not an ordinary, run-of-the-mill sort of clock – a special clock. An antique, no less! It was at least 100 years old, he said, and therefore proof positive that it was a genuine antique. The chimes had not worked. He had had them repaired. And so he brought it home, covered in newspaper. He placed it delicately in a place of his own choosing over the fireplace in the sitting room, and there it sat imposingly in state in its ebony case inlaid with gold flower patterns. It was faded and jaded, but that could be expected with genuine antiques, he pointed out. Having placed it, he wound it up with an equally imposing key, first the chime mechanism, then the clock mechanism, which was, said the antique dealer, the correct order of play; then he gave the pendulum a gentle prod with his index finger and, lo and behold, it began to swing to and fro by itself, thus beginning its long journey through time and tide. A journey that, unsurprisingly, James Sedley would never suffer to be interrupted for love, life or, for that matter, money. It was a clock with an eight-day winding mechanism, and James was at pains to note the date in his diary so that the winding ritual might be repeated and in the exact order prescribed.

He would glance at the clock daily, with a hardly perceptible smile of satisfaction. He would dust it lightly, and he would judge it fitting at times to readjust its position by imperceptible fractions of an inch. He would demand the silence of the grave while reassuring himself that it ticked and tocked as soundly as the proverbial bell; had he been a medical man, he might even have applied a stethoscope to the casing in times of uncertainty.

For he would, above all else, keep it going! – alive! And the chimes? Ah, the chimes! The glow on James Sedley's face when first they struck had to be seen to be believed; it was positively angelic and altogether unworldly, and more than a match for the gratification he had felt those long years ago for the loss of his virginity to an uncommonly willing girl whose face he now hardly remembered and who had had the decency, not to say very good sense, to melt away into the darkness of the night and leave the country the following day, never to return – thus saving him the prospect of an early and unwanted responsibility, the kind of thing he would, in these clock-watching days, describe as a nightmare scenario.

The chimes! He would lie in bed, late at night, and count them one by one. And if they threatened not to strike the required number, he would be ready the next hour to receive confirmation of some irregularity or reassurance that all was well. But he was always reassured. The chimes were always right, which was to be expected since they were always wound to perfection. Even so, James Sedley regularly sought reassurance. The idea that an expectation of future performance might reasonably be based on past and uninterrupted regularity was not a principle of rational thought that impressed him much; the James Sedley in James Sedley saw to that!

And Judith Sedley? Well, when first the clock was unveiled to her in all its glory with a 'Now, what about that!' her reply 'It's marvellous!' went unheard – partly due to its meekness. He never did learn what she thought of it, and in all its years on that mantelpiece in the living room, it was never once the subject of genuine communication, nor indeed of criticism.

~ ~

Since he subscribed to the principle of 'doing the decent thing', James Sedley had had no affair since his marriage. He was a master of propriety and fidelity, and although he counted jealousy as unseemly, he had also found it impossible to conceal. There were times when he had felt caught off-guard by those who had given Judith Sedley some admiring glances, usually on summer days when she wore pretty summer dresses. He trusted Judith as one business partner should trust another: implicitly, but not without some form of written guarantee as back-up. Since written confirmation was inappropriate beyond the marriage contract itself, he made do with the next best thing, which was to sulk and invite a variety of solicitous gestures which, when deemed sufficient, he would accept *in lieu*. And since he regarded himself as a businessman of consummate skill, he was not prepared to be left holding the baby, either figuratively or literally. Jealousy was to marriage what prudence is to contract, and that James Sedley regarded his marriage in the cold light of contract, as honest and as exacting in its detail as an insurance proposal, is as inescapable as the rotundity of the earth. 'What God has joined together let no man put asunder' was at least one proposition in the corpus of the Christian ethic that had won the heart and mind of this good fellow.

Indeed, he had himself insisted on a white wedding. The fact that God was in on it somehow made it a sure thing. If God backs it, it must be a good bet. It was not a case of 'God is good, and good is good enough for me'. No, not at all. It was simply that James Sedley, like anyone else in the commuter land of leafy suburbia, was attracted to anything that seemed to him to guarantee his best interests; whether that guarantee emanated from God or the International Monetary Fund mattered little. As a man well versed in the business of risk, James Sedley was unlikely to ignore the power of the Almighty; given, of course, that the Almighty existed at all, but here, as elsewhere, it was only prudent to hedge one's bets. If God is the final arbiter, the super-superbeing, more deadly after all than the Dark Lord himself, why spoil one's chances? On these grounds, James Sedley was prepared to pay occasional lip-service to the Deity on a just-in-case basis, provided, that is, that in so doing he was not thereby obliged to a clear and exacting ethic. Notions of self-sacrifice, self-criticism, let alone self-extinction, had no part to play in any of this. He had in fact nothing but contempt for the softies and wets of the clerical collar, a contempt equalled, and sometimes surpassed, by that which he felt for socialists and do-gooders; and as for Communists, they were simply beneath and beyond all contempt, the lowest of the low. He remembered once having passed a poster advertising a talk, which read, 'Jesus, the Father of Communism,' which made him cringe so much he was almost tempted to tear it down. Since then he felt much the same about them all: priests, vicars, socialists, intellectuals, radical reformers, communists and do-gooders were all tarred with the same brush, all lumped together in one contemptible heap. He never once stopped to analyse his feelings, let alone hold them up to the light of judgement. But it would have taken a very different creature altogether to do that and survive intact. He was a man of contraries, of ambivalences and contradictions, with as little aptitude for understanding himself as the composition of the universe. He just felt, more or less intuitively, that all those he counted contemptible threatened something that should not be threatened or questioned something that should not be questioned – something that was as solemn and as unalterable as his contract of marriage.

The product of that contract was Adam Sedley, recently appointed Vicar of Christ in a parish deep in the commuter land of leafy suburbia.

Adam's upbringing had been left largely to his mother, to whom his childish misdemeanours were sheer entertainment. James Sedley had assumed the role of rule maker and chastiser, and it was to his mother first, and Uncle Alan second, that the child always turned for comfort, guidance and advice. Despite his father, perhaps because of him, Adam grew up, if not entirely free, then at least deeply suspicious, of his father's cant, his niceties, his obsession with exactitude, his stifling routine and his devotion to the entire corpus of conventional wisdom. The rift between father and son was as inevitable as it was painful, thanks to the balm provided by uncle and mother.

James Sedley, the self-made man who had mastered the rudiments of monetary algebra unaided by either God or man, had stopped at nothing, save the tenets of conventional decorum, to set himself up in the world, to give wife and child all the comforts and opportunities that he believed had been denied himself. A model of the decent, respectable law-abiding citizen, he had no-one but himself to thank for it, and was at least thankful for that! Hercules had laboured, but James Sedley had laboured and had something to show for it. Yet, as he himself painfully realised, it was hard for lesser folk to comprehend the enormity of the burden of familial responsibility he carried, and especially difficult for those nearest who had stood to gain most from his efforts.

His own son, for example. His only son, whom he had laboured to bring up on the straight and narrow of stability, security and respectability – did *he* understand any of this? Apparently not. Most certainly not. He was just like his mother. No, it just went to show how little faith one could place in one's own children – so much for the theory of paternal conditioning! Yet he, James Sedley, could hardly be blamed for that. The boy's mother had been an obvious hindrance to enlightenment. Without her constant cosseting the boy might have made something of himself. He had been on course for a sound and respectable career – the kind that a good qualification in finance and accounting would ensure. Instead of which, he decided to quit finance and accounting too ... and here James Sedley could hardly bring himself to utter the words even in the privacy of his own mind ... to 'enter the church', or, as his son had corrected him, 'enter the ministry'!

And it was not, as James Sedley attempted to console himself, that his son had had a bad start. For, apart from the indescribable fortune of having James Sedley as his father, he had, as it were, been rationed into the world on the principles of cool, sound reasoning. He had, one might say, been admitted into the world as a product of James Sedley's rigid adhesion to logic and common sense. That is to say, it was most fortunate for Adam Sedley that he had been conceived at the 'right' moment, at a time when his advent fitted neatly enough into his father's plans for procreation. Judith Sedley had wanted to conceive from the very outset of their marriage, but she was argued out of it by her husband's appeal to financial constraints and the as-yet untapped possibilities of a promising career; and not too long after Adam Sedley's conception, she wanted to 'try for a girl' to make, as she thought, an ideal duo; but she was argued out of this, too – and on much the same grounds. Adam Sedley was therefore conceived, on his father's reckoning, somewhere between too early and too late – which was, his father had thought, much to his advantage.

It was a frequent source of wonder to James Sedley that a child born in conformity with the dictates of reason could possibly make career decisions so completely at odds with them. But there was much about the world that James Sedley could not understand, and the strange phenomenon of his own son was simply one more mystery to add to all the rest – but one that he was determined to live with, come what might.

Adam Sedley was, then, a man who did not know his own good luck, a true child of fortune. But if he did not know his own luck, his mother knew hers, and thanked God for him as zealously as she cursed herself for having been swayed against her better judgement, which is to say her better feeling, allowing herself to be taken for a ride down the hollow, icy roads of common sense and temporal budgeting. She had all this time felt cheated, like an animal manipulated by farmer and vet, or victim of injustice helpless enough to stand humbly before the executioner but intelligent enough to know where and why he so stands. Little wonder that Adam Sedley was one of her few remaining links with her own humanity and a living reminder of the humanity she had also surrendered and lost by giving in to cold calculation and detached logic. Adam Sedley was to her conscience what circumcision is to the Chosen. She showered her blessings upon him and prayed to receive them in return.

She discussed this with no one, least of all James Sedley. Her own feelings were as silent as the misgivings of James Sedley concerning his wife and son. And so, it is remarkable how much noise can go unheard in a relationship considered sane, normal respectable and beyond reproach, and how much heat can be generated in the absence of fire.

Feelings were expressed, if at all, only tangentially, and then only finally given direct vent in response to a specific stimulus.

James Sedley would not normally have dreamt of voicing his opinions as to the sad and bitter irony of his own son's becoming a man of the cloth; the initial shock of Adam's trading finance and accounting for theology had reached its zenith and at length faded. No, he now required a strong stimulus, and it eventually arrived in the form of his being upbraided and reproached by none other than his own son. And that was something that James Sedley could neither tolerate nor forgive; the very idea! – to be wrapped over the knuckles after all he had done for his wife and child! – to be told by his own child that he had lived wrong, thought wrong, felt wrong! There are some ironies one might live with, and there are some, like this, that are unbearable, intolerably unjust, unforgivably cruel. The fact that those fed on such fine fare should finally bite the hand that feeds them proved far too much for James Sedley. The whole thing was illogical, irrational, absurd; and if he himself had spawned such an unrepentant Judas, what hope was there for the world at large?

And on what was his son's vitriolic outburst based? Only on a further irony! Judith Sedley had been caught, well, there was no word for it but the right word, *shoplifting!* The very word was a dagger in his heart. She had denied it, of course.

She had drawers full of her own jewellery – good stuff, too, and most of it she had never worn nor ever would wear. Yes, she had denied it, denied intending to … *steal* – the dagger turned a full 360 degrees. Yet, there it was! Caught red-handed, the store detective had said, and he had been fully quoted in the local press, too. She had been let off this time pending a psychiatric report; and here again the irony was too obvious for words; she had been treated with leniency due to his standing in the local community at least, that is how he preferred to view it: despite the fact that it was clear to all and sundry that she could not possibly have taken the bracelet, a piece of fake costume jewellery at that, out of an inability to pay for it; despite the fact that she herself had an unblemished track record; and despite the fact that her plea of guilty had been advised, explained and mitigated on the grounds that her offence had been an unfortunate cry for help. But to James Sedley the irony was unendurable. When in need of money she had appealed, naturally and properly, to him, and now, when allegedly in need of help, she steals a cheap article. Bizarre. In any case, what possible help could she require? She had everything at her fingertips: money, respectability, security; James Sedley had seen to all that; he had seen the best years of his life seeing to it, and yet it all seemed to count for nothing – suddenly and explicably to count for nothing.

There had been a scene, of course. An almighty scene. It was over now. Well, not quite over. A thing like that could never be quite over. It was a scar, deep and irremovable. But at least they didn't talk about it anymore. There had been a lot of shouting – that was to be expected. But he, James Sedley, had finally sorted it out as best he could.

But to add to these layers of insufferable irony, Adam Sedley had to stick his oar in, too. He had actually blamed his father for the whole sorry episode! It was James Sedley who had to bear the brunt of all this, as if the humiliating publicity wasn't quite enough – and the looks and the stares, the mumbling in corners, to say nothing of his own inner and very private sense of despair. For he had, naturally, felt betrayed by his own wife. And now, on top of all that, his one and only son accuses *him* of some kind of betrayal. No, it had all been too much for James Sedley to bear. And no one, save one or two stalwarts in the office, had any idea at all of all the suffering he had had to endure both at home and outside it. He might have expected some word of understanding from his own son … But no, that was not somehow – and God knows *how*? – a reasonable expectation!

His son might at least have had the decency to maintain a respectful silence while his father tried to get his head around the whole thing, while he tried to regain his bearings and overcome the strain of it all. But no, James Sedley was made to face the fact that he was the victim of some kind of deadly conspiracy and that fate had dealt him a cruel and untimely blow.

Still, as James Sedley saw it, time has a strange way of levelling things out. He consoled himself with the thought that fate might also work its irony on ungrateful sons. Adam Sedley had recently married Julia Robinson. Oh, what a contrast! They had met while students and they had somehow stuck together. There was a feast of irony here. The very idea that a stunning creature like Julia Robinson should attach herself to Adam Sedley! – and remain attached even after his decision to become a clergyman! Opposite poles attract, they say. But was this not the calm before the storm? How long could this partnership possibly last? Now had Adam decided to make something of himself, were he a man of ambition and good sense … but how could a simple clergyman handle someone such as she? She had qualified in finance and accounting, and she wanted to get ahead, despite her hobby of painting landscapes in watercolour; even if she said she painted for fun, it was clear enough that she wanted to sell the products of her leisure time; no, James Sedley was convinced that she was a woman of latent talent and hidden ambitions. There was nothing save antithesis here: raw ambition *versus* a senseless form of self-abnegation. True, she had stuck with Adam Sedley even after his defection from finance and accounting. But no, this could not possibly last. She was a *man's* woman and not at all likely to be content for long with the simplicities and deficiencies of a parson's living. Oh, yes, a cold wind was blowing alright; it was only a question of time.

And James Sedley had all the time in the world. He would be there, waiting – waiting for the plea of support, and when it came he would give as good as he got. He would be full of his 'I told you so's', and he would relish every syllable. Every syllable.

Such were the occasional and meandering thoughts of James Sedley. Of course, it had occurred to him that he was not himself a malicious man, that he did not wish upon his own kin the little tragedies that beset the common run. At the same time, he drew no small comfort from the thought that those who flout the principles by which he himself had set immeasurable store were doomed, sooner or later, to decline and eventual oblivion. Such was his faith in his own nature. Such was James Sedley, an obelisk of stability in the commuter land of leafy suburbia.

To say that Adam Sedley held nothing against his father apart from his mistakes, or to say that he loved his father but not what his father did, is to under stress and miss the point. The problem for Adam Sedley was far more critical than such sentiments might suggest. The trouble is that he did not take a narrow view of his father at all. It was not simply his father that irritated him, but the fact that in so many ways his father represented in microcosm everything that seemed to him to inhibit the realisation of God's kingdom on earth. It was, admittedly, all very vague and general; but there is no escaping the fact that Adam Sedley was bedevilled by a puzzling dissatisfaction, not merely with his father, but with something much larger that materialised in his father and in all others like him. Rather as a physician might view a disease through the patient functioning as a window: curing the patient of the disease is all very well, but eradicating the disease itself is the thing to aim for. Yet there was no getting through to his father on such themes, and therefore no possibility of changing him either. It was all very confusing and disheartening. But he was convinced that he had to resist despair.

The truth is, there was much that confused Adam Sedley. There was the *institution* of the Church, for example, with its rituals, hierarchies and grand buildings, which he had long regarded as a recurrent obstacle to those teachings. But those teachings were now under attack because Christianity itself was in decline and was in danger of being eclipsed by secularism, on the one hand, and alternative religions, on the other. The teachings of Christ had to be saved. Just how they might be saved and gain a wide social ascendency became his overriding preoccupation. He compared the institution of the Church with his father: both were obsessed with internal detail, with upholding the *status quo* under a vow of political silence; they were both blocks of granite, unbreakable, immoveable – until, that is, they were eclipsed by a power they were unable or unwilling to resist. It was part of a general decline: the rise of homophobia and anti-Semitism on the back of a religion that spoke loudly of compassion yet was bereft of love and consequently of toleration was particularly disquieting. But intolerance had secular as well as religious roots. An informal vote amongst students had been taken concerning the formation of a Jewish Society on campus, with 300 votes for and 200 against; this huge number of dissenting voices was particularly worrying; and this amid the dissemination of divisive literature, which made the ridiculous claims that Jews are murderers of women and children, that they pervert democracy, and that their veins are devoid of human blood. Indeed, it was the growing anti-Semitism and homophobia, in a *university* no less, that finally made Adam Sedley not merely quit finance and accounting but the university as well , and to transfer to a theological college.

He believed that those who condemned Christianity itself by attacking the institution of the Church for its political inertia, or by appealing to occasional cases of sexual abuse, were throwing the baby out with the bathwater. The Sermon on the Mount needed to be rescued and protected from what were in essence assaults upon an institution distinct from an ethic. He decided that the Church as an institution was powerless to arrest the forces of moral retrogression, because it set such a bad example and in consequence lacked sufficiently wide public support. Like his father, he was troubled by irony. How could an institution that sought to embody Christ be incapable of doing so. And if he was incapable of reaching his father, there was little hope that such an institution could succeed in reforming itself or that it could be reformed from the outside. There is no doubt that James and Adam Sedley might have afforded one another the deepest consolations of mutual sympathy, had their ironies been of the same kind. A problem shared is a problem halved, it is said. Yet this was not a problem that could be shared between them. They were poles apart. A clear case of never-the-twain.

The conviction grew upon Adam Sedley that Christianity could be saved only by stripping itself down to the bare essentials. It would suffice if it could be made clear that the only God worth worshipping was the one defined by the Sermon on the Mount. There were many Gods, but it was a question of elevating the right one and putting all the rest firmly and irrevocably in their place. The right God could not be seen, because He was hidden by meaningless ritual, by hypocrisy and cant and because those who might yet support Him were blinded by the gall of their own invective against Him. What was needed was a kind of revelation, an eye-opening – and again this reminded him of his father.

Adam Sedley understood that his father, or any number of James Sedley's, did not directly govern the commuter land of leafy suburbia. Indeed, his father's integrity, his desire to see the decent thing done in matters of monetary detail, and the care he devoted to his rose garden – such things were counted virtues. Yet, consequentially, they were also vices, because they merely served to blind him to the bigger picture; they were dangerous diversions. What James Sedley counted as virtues and high principles of conduct were irrelevant to the kind of decline that Adam Sedley was so determined to halt; they were not merely irrelevant but helped to sustain that very decline, since they served only to detract attention away from it. If only his father had the merest inkling of what really counted; if only he could get his priorities right ... then he could never be the same again, and at last he would be reachable. It would be painful for him, no doubt; he would be like the slave who for the first time is brought to acknowledge his captivity, or the man who, having once thought himself free, now understands that the door to freedom is locked and has always been so. Yes, it would be painful, but he would at least be loved by God – the *right* God! After all, a dissatisfied Socrates, as John Stuart Mill once put it, is preferable to a contented pig.

Adam Sedley's profound misgivings concerning the institution of the Church had not prevented him from entering into a vocational career but had, on the contrary, motivated him to do so. He therefore pursued his theological studies and entered the ministry with all the dedication and decorum required. He vaguely felt that he might follow his career, minister to his parishioners, tend to his flock, and perform all the pastoral duties required of him while at the same time satisfying his deeper conscience and fulfilling the function of reformer of hearts and minds, stripping away the inessentials and the hindrances that served only to accelerate the decline of Christianity and encourage the twin demons of alien religions and wayward secularisation. The Sermon on the Mount was the centrepiece of all religious endeavour and required no trimmings, no further adornment. And in all this, he had Julia Robinson at his side, a lively and consoling counterweight to the profound matters he had in hand.

He had met her at an art exhibition. It was not a mutual interest in art that had brought them together on a rainy day in November; in fact, it was the day he had finally decided to quit finance and accounting, and the trip to the art gallery was incidental to that – he felt he had to go somewhere to think things through and ended up at the art exhibition simply by chance. Had it not rained, he might have gone to the zoo. They often joked about that, about the fact that his taste for art was somewhat climatic.

The fact that their interest in art was not strictly mutual is suggestive; for there was nothing but contrast between them. Julia was a tall, slim and shapely brunette, with black eyes that flashed like a gypsy's round a camp fire in the dead of a winter's night. James Sedley was heard to remark that she dressed sensibly and that that was one of her few redeeming features since it made her appear respectable. Not that either Adam or Julia put much store by his father's meagre acceptance of her. She could speak with sensitivity about art: past masters, old styles and new trends. But this competence was lost on James Sedley, for it was extraneous to the question of the current market value attached to a work of art; current market value took precedence over the identity of the artist, the subject rendered on canvas or the comparative merits of style; and what was more, he firmly believed that current market value also assumed first place in Julia's own reckoning despite her ramblings touching the history of art. In any event, James Sedley believed that art would play a large role in her, much larger than a mundane job as an accountant or financial adviser; he took the view, which deserves some credence, that a job is what you have to do to keep the wolf from the door, but a hobby is a matter of choice and is therefore a more accurate indication of one's true leanings and aptitude. It must be remembered that the word 'therefore' loomed large in his vocabulary and was used with a frequency and a certainty that would make more discerning minds wince with despair.

Whatever her own misgivings about her son's choice of partner, Judith Sedley could only wish them well and a finer marriage than her own. She wished them a child, and another, and then another, as though this were the only way open to her now to compensate for the decisions that had been made for her and which she could not now undo. The hopes of the mother were visited upon her only child, be they right or not, rational or not, possible or not. The hopes she entertained for her son's marriage were in any case the continuation of the hopes she nurtured for her son: for him, who, in all the barrenness that surrounded and enveloped her, carried a torch and in doing so carried forward the hopes she had once naively had for herself. What was now impossible for her might be possible for him – with just a little bit of luck.

She remembered in her reading something Abraham Lincoln had said, and she was at pains to pass it on to her son. Lincoln had remarked in the early days of his political career that it would be a sad thing for one to die leaving everything as one had found it: unimproved, miserable, unjust and uncaring, unloving. She had begun to hate the prospect of leaving the world just as it was, let alone worse than she had found it. But feelings are all she had. It was hard for her to see a philosophy in it. But she saw enough, and she pinned her remaining hopes outside herself – on Adam Sedley.

Adam Sedley shared his mother's feelings and thought them beautiful. It seemed to him ironic that his father should devote so much care to his rose garden while so evidently failing to recognise the beauty in his own wife – a reflection that was nurtured by the fact that Judith Sedley, unlike so many women in the commuter land of leafy suburbia, cared less for roses than the more common varieties of plant life that adorn the dusty hedgerows and byways of the inner cities.

Chapter Three

The Real World

And he who looks round from the hills will see one planet with many worlds upon it, all like remorseless Titans, each one vying with the rest — but who save the truly wise can tell which world is the best?

~ ~

It chimed seven times, the black ebony clock.

It chimed majestically on a spring morning, a morning that was anything but majestic to the mind of James Sedley. The majesty of the chimes was one thing, the majesty of the morning quite another.

Sioux warrior of the Great Plains might have awoken on such a morning, spread his blanket on a hill, and heaped his blessings on the Great Spirit or Great Mystery, Wakan Tanka, for the gift of life, or he might have stood outside his tepee, taken a few deep, wholesome breaths and proceeded to smoke his calumet in noble anticipation of the day ahead, ever cognisant of the wonders of Nature, ever sensible of the miracle of life. Admittedly, James Sedley's rose garden held nothing of the vast and unkempt splendour of the Great Plains. No, it was ordered and planned down to the very last shrub, each plant knowing its place in the order of things, and no weed was suffered to sojourn in the rose beds longer than its very first sighting. If the native Americans of the Great Plains marvelled at the landscape gardening of the Great Spirit, James Sedley marvelled at his own, at least on Saturdays and Sundays; but on weekdays he denied himself even a casual gloat. Simply, time would not allow it — or rather, his carefully planned routine would not.

In the commuter land of leafy suburbia, normality and sanity are measured by the degree to which routine tasks can be performed with the minimum of interference. Ask James Sedley whether yesterday morning existed and he would remember that he had brushed his teeth, organised his briefcase, examined his pin-stripes for lingering specks of dust, and, like a reflex action, checked his wristwatch with the black ebony clock — or he would recall that nothing had happened to *prevent* his brushing his teeth, organising his briefcase, examining his pin-stripes for lingering specks of dust, and checking his wristwatch with the black ebony clock. Mornings for James Sedley were simply un-extraordinary unless something happened to *make* them extraordinary. In this he was quite normal and safely beyond reproach. Birds might sing in the grey light of dawn, but always to an empty theatre. The freshness of the air, the haze of summer, the dew on the leaves of the lilac trees, and all the other magical devices conjured by Mother Nature were, without exception, lost on James Sedley, who, in common with everyone else, was bent on the successful completion of routine. Only for this reason, fog, rain or snow would seldom go unnoticed; such natural phenomena would bring down upon their own mischievous heads all the venom that is capable of expression, simply because they made it all the more difficult to pay due homage to routine. They were inconvenient; after all, trains and buses may be delayed and, office workers may be late for the office – a crime for which Mother Nature herself would be summarily beheaded could she ever be brought to the block.

And so, the Great Spirit, for whom there is no room in filing cabinets – available space there being occupied by spirits of a very different order – wanders un-thanked in the gutters of the city, while ingrates who would be on time at the office stride with confidence through the murky puddles of routine, mindless of the endless vistas of clean dry grass beyond the horizon where the sun shines fierce but wise.

But we digress.

~ ~

The black ebony clock chimed majestically in the living room of Mr and Mrs Sedley's tastefully modernised, compact, highly desirable semi-detached, which was located in the much sought-after southerly aspect of suburbia.

On the second chime, James Sedley checked his wristwatch and grunted approvingly. Clock and watch were perfectly synchronised, as usual. Harmony abounded. God was in his Heaven and the day would go well. He then passed from the living room into the hallway en route to the breakfast room, pausing only to check his appearance in the long mirror and flick his cuffs with customary dexterity. He marched into the breakfast room with a grunt of disapproval, having noticed a smudge on the mirror, and sat down at the table. Perhaps it would not be such a good day after all.

He was right. At least, it would not be such a good start, and, as it turned out, he would spend the day in a state of irascible recovery. On the other hand, he would be presented with an opportunity to do the decent thing and to assert his own authority into the bargain. First, a familiar ritual was about to begin.

A ritual prompted by *the letter.*

As he sat down at the breakfast table he glanced at Judith Sedley who, customarily clad in dressing gown and slippers, sat opposite him buttering her toast. Their eyes didn't meet, which was normal these days. Communication was restricted to the occasional utterance of banalities and the even less frequent remembrance of trivial pursuits.

He glanced at her over the rim of his cup. What he saw contrasted sharply with what she had once been. If she would only bother to dress properly, it would be something! Oh, yes, she'd been attractive – once. After all, if she hadn't been, he wouldn't have married her. He counted himself an above-average judge of everything worth judging, and now he felt he was married to a long-term investment which hadn't paid off. It wasn't simply that his returns were diminishing marginally, but that they had ceased to be at all discernible. What was all that stuff about growing old gracefully? He was still in the prime of life, and she ... well, anyway, he deserved better – he felt badly let down. He had worked so hard, and was still working hard, only to be served cereal and toast by someone he could hardly recognise, let alone talk to. It was all very disconcerting. Now had circumstances been different, and had he been less than the man he undoubtedly was, he might have been able to enjoy himself, to let his hair down a bit. There was that new girl in the office, for example – unquestionably desirable. Now what was her name? Oh, yes, Marcia. Marcia! Marcia, who insisted on turning up at the office in revealing blouses and short skirts. Marcia, who wore her hair so loose and her skirts so tight – most irritating, annoying, off-putting, distracting and, above all, *beautiful.* But no, not at all the thing for the respectable conduct of serious business. He had even thought of mentioning it to Benson, who'd be sure to agree. She should really be taken aside and given a little talking to about decorum. Still, she was young, very young – maybe the matter should be left where it is. No, he would not mention it to Benson; not yet, at any rate. He might speak to Benson at some point – but not today; no, he would let the matter rest. So young – in her late teens – a firm body, long legs, long brown hair ...

No, the point is that if James Sedley had been less than the decent, upright man he was ... but he could not help being the man he was – a man of uncommon decency, of unbending moral principle, of unshakable conviction when it came to doing the right thing or not doing the wrong thing, and that was that! Yes, that was that. Nothing more to be said. All the same, Marcia would dress even more immodestly today on the pretext that spring has sprung, so that the distraction would be more intense than ever, torturing the souls of the good. The trouble with people like Marcia was that they seemed to invite good souls like James Sedley to question the very validity of their first principles – never a healthy thing. Even now, he had, momentarily over his cornflakes, almost caught himself lamenting his sense of moral obligation, as though he should question whether his morality was really very good for him, with the potential corollary that his first principles should perhaps be abandoned, or at least be temporarily suspended! Almost, but not quite. No, there's no putting a good man down; the Dark Lord must look elsewhere for sport. No, he finally determined to raise the whole matter with Benson – if, that is, a good opportunity presented itself, which, of course, it might not.

Such were the silent, fleeting and half-formed cerebral meanderings of James Sedley as he skipped through his breakfast routine when, half-way through his cornflakes, he turned to the more sober and edifying financial columns of his daily newspaper, in particular to an article reporting an upward pressure on mortgage rates, for if anything would bring him back to moral sobriety that certainly would, like a lighthouse to those lost and tossed at sea.

There he sat, by turns shifting spoonsful of cornflakes to his mouth and sifting the news that might improve his financial armoury for the day ahead. Shifting and sifting. It was what he always did, every morning, in the same place, at the same time, as regular as the chimes of his ebony clock.

Thus engaged, he managed, by dint of practice in the art of automatic verbal reflex, to emit some sound, as though flexing his vocal chords for more advanced forms of communication later that day.

'Going to get dressed? Never see you dressed at breakfast these days. Don't want to let yourself go. Not over the hill yet.' As forms of communication, such remarks were like repeatedly unsuccessful stabs at a solitary pea on an empty plate. He raised his cup to his lips without taking his eyes from his newspaper – an accomplishment which no doubt owed much to his many years in insurance brokerage; conversation with a client was, of course, largely a matter of routine: he would ask questions pertaining to financial status while at the same time scanning the proposal form, eyes down and muttering as though addressing himself, much as many general practitioners treat their patients, and with much the same effect, thereby lending to both professions a mystique of expertise that neither clients nor patients deem it proper to question. In any case, it was not without cause that Judith Sedley often thought of herself as one of her husband's clients – and one that was not particularly favoured at that.

'It's there if you want to read it,' she said, feigning indifference as to whether he wanted to or not. He remained unmoved.

'Hmm? What's that?' He was now scanning an article of the extended role of the IMF.

'Adam's letter. There, by your plate.'

'Oh, yes ... really,' he said, absent-mindedly.

'Oh, James, we *are* going, aren't we? I mean, it's his first sermon in his very own parish. After all, we have a duty ...'

'*Duty* did you say? Well, that's a word and no mistake!'

'It's what he's always wanted ...' she went on.

There was no doubt about it, the peace of the morning, which is to say the routine of James Sedley's eminently civilised world, was cracking loudly at the seams. The rot had already set in and he had little option but to address it. Peace was for the office, not the home – not *his* home, anyway. Life might mellow a little by lunchtime, but right now confrontation was inevitable. If only people were as reliable as that black ebony clock sitting gracefully on the mantelpiece! But it was not to be.

In a mood of reluctant resignation, he abandoned his newspaper and entered the fray, sighing heavily as he did so.

'Has he *ever* known what he wants?' he asked rhetorically, giving his left cuff a flick as if for emphasis.

'That's unfair,' she said. 'Besides, we're lucky to be invited at all after ...' Another spark was thrown into the powder-keg.

'What?' he exploded. 'You mean, *I'm* lucky, don't you? You should say what you mean, my dear!' He spoke quickly and was obviously prepared for combat.

'If you're going to make a scene …' she said, getting up from the table.

Realising that the explosion had had the desired effect of placing him in a strategically advantageous position and that victory was already in sight, his tone mellowed.

'I've no intention of starting anything,' he said, in a tone somewhere between a sigh and a grunt. Judith felt sufficiently reassured to sit down again.

'So you want to go?'

'I want *us* to go – together,' she said, quietly.

'I'll think about it,' he said, reaching once again for his newspaper.

'If only you'd show more …' she started, after a pause.

'*Interest*! Is that it?' He put his newspaper down again. His voice dropped, as though he was about to enter a sad soliloquy. 'After all I've done for him. All the sacrifices I've made. *Interest*! I'm supposed to show more interest!'

'He didn't mean it!' she pleaded.

'Didn't he now!'

'He was only trying to defend me … to explain.' She spoke in tones of total familiarity with the ritual she had set in motion. She knew what was coming, almost word for word. She was resigned to it. You buy a ticket, and you sit out the journey.

James Sedley cleared his throat. It was time to restate the obvious. He was one who believed that a good tune is worth playing more than once, and he grasped this opportunity with both hands. He breathed deeply, and the first few words floated on a sigh. He was a man of style, and would probably have achieved great eminence in the Senate of ancient Rome when the empire was in graceless decline.

'I'll tell you what he wanted. He wanted a university education. Alright. I provided it. A degree in finance and accounting would have given him a good start – not that he needed a damned degree – I mean look at me! I worked my way up, my *own* way up, and *I* had no degree – depended on my own resources – well it's true! Alright, but then what does he do? After taking all the handouts I could give him, he doesn't even complete his degree – he jacks it all in and goes off to a theological college! And he didn't even consult me about it – all behind my back! In fact, I was the last to know. I didn't want to complain even then – but I had to tell him what I thought about it, and in no uncertain terms, and with no help from you, either, as I recall. But he got what he wanted, I'll grant you that. He changed horses in mid-stream – a horse for a donkey more like. And what can he look forward to now? – preaching half-baked sermons to half-baked congregations in half-empty churches. These churches – they'll be phased out, mark my words! Phased out! He'll end up in Hyde Park Corner preaching to the pigeons. Bah!'

Yes, Judith had heard it all before. It was like sales patter from the mouth of a professional. If there was any uncertainty, it was only the marginal uncertainty as to the precise order in which the patter would be delivered. She drew small circles on the tablecloth with the tip of his fingers, waiting for the patter to subside.

'He could've done so much better for himself. That's the galling part! When I think of all the chances he might've had – chances that were denied to me at his age. And I could've put him right, with or without a damned degree. Yes, that's where I got *my* degree!' He pointed at the window with his long index-finger. 'Out there, in the *real* world! Contacts, connections! That's what counts. The *university of life* – that's what matters in the end. I could've introduced him to the right people – set him up! But no. He's content to scrape a living instead. Y'know what? I think he's been brainwashed, and now he wants to brainwash others. Humph!' He gave his cuff a further flick, sighed deeply and nodded sagely to himself.

'You don't believe in God anymore, then?'

'I didn't say that. It's got nothing to do with that. That's a separate matter. That's a ... well, it's a *personal* thing. No, I'm talking about the real world – how to survive in the real world! Can't you see that? It's all a question of survival, that's all. Good God, that should be plain enough!'

'Well, anyway, it's *his* life, isn't it? I thought we'd settled that long ago,' ventured Judith. No doubt about it, she was careless with matches. But again, the ritual was well served.

'*His* life, yes. But he's got no business interfering in *mine*!' Judith resisted the temptation to respond to this.

'The nerve!' he went on. 'The sheer nerve to speak to me like that! And how d'think I felt, having to order my own son out of the house? But I wouldn't stand for it – no, no way!'

'He was trying to defend me, that's all,' she said. 'Trying to make you understand.'

40

'And you're defending *him*?' he blared. 'Everybody defends everybody round here. Except *me*, of course. No, I'm not worth defending. I'm just the guy who earns the money to keep everybody else in business. Take me for granted, why don't you? Don't mind me! And what's all that stuff about *understanding*, anyway? No one ever listens to me! What about understanding *me*? No one ever listens to me. No, that would be too much to ask. Well, I've done more than my fair share of listening.' He flicked his cuff once again, glanced at his wristwatch and sipped his tea.

'He wanted you to understand that I didn't do it for want of money,' she said demurely. But this time there was no explosion. The artillery was temporarily unmanned.

'I know that,' he said with a long sigh. His tone was suddenly calmer and more reasonable – for which she was most grateful. 'Yes, I know that. I know that very well. That's what makes the whole thing so incomprehensible. Have I ever given you the slightest cause ...?'

'No,' she interrupted softly. 'No, you haven't.' She spoke quietly and sighed – which irritated him noticeably; the gunners had returned and with a vengeance. After all, the ritual had not yet burned out; there was more to come; the actors had not yet played out their parts.

'No, you're damned right I haven't! I've worked too hard for that. And everybody knows it, too – so they naturally conclude you're in need of some kind of psychiatric treatment – and *he* has the gall to blame *me*, my own son! The injustice of it all! What I've had to endure! Oh, they pretended to understand, of course. Full of sympathetic phrases – but I could read them like a book; it was just giving them a chance to have a dig. 'Read about your wife, James. Sad. Very sad. Very embarrassing for you, too. It' probably just the change of life, you know. Besides, it's not as if it's a *real* crime – more a cry for help, so to speak.'

'Did they really say all that?'

'Yes. No! ... No, but they thought it. I saw it in their faces. Because that's the real world for you. I told you, it's a question of survival. I have to protect everything I've built up, built up from scratch on my own initiative – and no university degree, either! I just can't afford to be made the subject of cheap gossip. Yes, that's the real world for you.

'I didn't mean to embarrass you,' she said, again with a provocative sigh of resignation, having been this way before and wanting to play the game in the way he expected her to play it, just so the whole silly ritual could be played out with no loose ends. She stared up at the ceiling, her chin cupped in her left hand, as though some benign spirit were offering her solace, or perhaps a benediction.

'Yes, well, I know all that!' He glanced quickly at his wristwatch, now at his executive case which stood beside him like an obsequious adjutant, now at his teacup, which was empty again. 'And he had the nerve to tell me it was all my fault.'

'He didn't say that,' she put in, looking down at the tablecloth as though her kindly spirit had descended out of sight.

'Oh, it's what he meant. Are you forgetting? – he's a vicar of Christ – he's seen the light! Yes, and now he's content to pray to God and leave all the real work to others. The rest of us can slave away in the real world. Little does he care. But, to stand here in my own house and tell me – alright *imply* that my whole life's been some kind of *waste*, no it won't do. It won't do for *her*, either. No, he's bitten off more than he can chew there. She'll put him in his place alright, and before very much longer.'

'They love each other. That must count for something.' Judith spoke with rare emotion, looking hard at her husband as she did so. Yet it merely prepared her way for the next move in the game. She expected his set-piece, and she was not disappointed.

'It counts as long as there's a good bank balance to back it up,' he replied contemptuously. 'Oh, you think she's arty and doesn't care about such things?'

'No, she's a social climber – she's got untapped ambitions – mark my words. I can read people. I know what makes them tick. I ought to be good at it, I've had enough practice, yes, out there! In the real world! She'll soon tire of him. Just you wait and see.'

'I can't believe that!' Judith snapped.

'*Won't believe*, you mean!' he snapped back. 'Well, just you see how long it lasts. She won't put up with poverty for long. All that talk about art! She relied on her father all her life, as Adam relied on me. But things'll be different from now on. They're out in the real world now, not loafing about and sponging off their parents. Well, they won't get a penny from me. Not a penny. I've done all I'm prepared to do. They can't expect anything, especially after that … that *performance* in my own house! He's made his bed and he'll jolly well have to lie in it – and it won't be a bed of roses, either.'

The ritual was nearing its close. The mention of roses reminded Judith of his obsession with his, while it reminded James that he'd better be making tracks down the garden path. He was thankful that not every morning was like this. The chariots of hell might hinder the saintly before the very gates of heaven, but they could not make James Sedley late for the office.

He picked up his executive case and put into it his folded newspaper. Thus armed, he strode into the hallway, followed by Judith who, sensing almost beyond all hope a change of heart, let loose her parting shot.

'There's such a lot to make up. Please say we'll go.'

'I said I'd think about it,' he replied emphatically.

The ritual was finally at an end – an end which was, as usual, uncomfortably inconclusive.

He opened the door and, with a last sidelong glance in the mirror, marched down the garden path like a sergeant-major on parade, his black leather brogues squeaking and tapping along as predictably as their wearer and as tunefully as a regimental fixing of bayonets. When he reached the garden gate and closed it behind him, he glanced at the garden wall, giving it a slight nod, as though he and it enjoyed some kind of secret rapport, which indeed they did, before tapping and squeaking his way down the road towards the railway station for the train which would carry him into the corridors of free enterprise.

And as he tapped and squeaked along, his confidence in the day ahead was somewhat reaffirmed, which was merely an illustration and confirmation of the faith he had in himself. For everything else in the world, from socialists and busy-body do-gooders and lefty intellectuals and dithery clergymen to unsympathetic spouses were simply temporary aberrations to which he was sadly subjected from time to time. Indeed, the thought had struck him, not altogether unpleasantly, that he was living much before his time and that were he to be frozen, held in cold storage and finally resurrected, he would be readmitted into a finer world where such aberrations had long ceased to torment the wise, a world peopled entirely by James Sedleys; a world of clones, the only drawback of which was a deficiency in that variety which is so often claimed to be the very spice of life. He was in the main convinced that he himself could well do without that kind of variety – but then, a world without Marcias, for example, would be rather drab and possibly over-regimented; no, the young must have their fling; and, he reminded himself, he would say nothing to Benson – not today, at any rate.

Judith Sedley closed the door behind him. She was glad he had gone. She would dress, drink tea, look at some old photographs and just do as she pleased, and, more importantly, think what she wanted to think. These days, a single thought could occupy her for hours, a blessing since it shortened the day; indeed, the day often seemed too short to do justice to the pictures that popped into her mind without apparent provocation, all of their own accord. She had enough to do pottering round the house, but a mental picture, having appeared once, would return at decent intervals to be turned this way and that like some strange and fascinating object, and it would finally dissolve into the ether, to be reconstituted someday, perhaps.

Her thoughts would frequently feed, naturally enough, on her own perceptions of contrast.

For instance, there was James, immaculately dressed, tapping and squeaking his way to the office, his thoughts as measured and as precise, and therefore as restricted, as his attention to dress and to detail. Here was a man who knew his business, who revelled in what he knew, who was certain of himself and of his world, content with the forms of life he had inherited, not merely content with them but intensely jealous of them. Anything, even the merest speck of dust was intolerable if it was not consistent with the framework of unassailable assumptions in which he lived and breathed. And if it was a framework that he himself found unassailable, it seemed natural that he would wish to recommend it universally; what is sauce for the goose is sauce for the gander: good enough for James Sedley, good enough for everyone else. Here, then, was a man of enormous confidence and internal consistency, a creature of monumental common sense, the kind of stuff of which great men are made.

Into Judith Sedley's mind would pop a black and white photograph of Abraham Lincoln, from a dusty biography given to her by Adam. Here was a creature awkward in dress, speech and gait; yet a man who had questioned much that had passed for unquestionable; a man uncertain of many things, his only certainty being that what was should not be. It seemed that though he was human, and therefore imperfect, the profound uncertainty of men like Lincoln, and there were not so many men like Lincoln, was somehow preferable to the characteristic complacency of tappers and squeakers. She tried to imagine James and Lincoln together, James flicking the dust off his shirt cuffs as he marched well ahead of Lincoln; and Lincoln so far behind, ambling and fumbling in the rear. She found the contrast amusing.

And then into her head would pop the image of an even greater man, so great that many would deny he was really human at all. She tried to think of him ascending the Mount, his Sermon tucked away neatly in an executive briefcase like James's, with gold-plated clasps and locks and a velveteen interior, flicking the dust from his robes as he marched ahead in measured steps, sandals squeaking and not a hair out of place. The thought was self-contradictory. She smiled again, with a curious mixture of amusement and guilt. That man on his cross was full of uncertainty, poured out in the dying moments of his crucifixion.

No doubt her husband would also have regarded such images as contrasting. What may be doubted is whether he would have thought them in any way instructive, or whether he would have considered them suggestive of censure upon the smooth, deep ruts of conventional wisdom. The Socratic idea that an unexamined life is not worth living did not easily commend itself to James Sedley, if only because he was not at all clear what form the recommended examination should take. Such an aura of respectability and competence issued from James Sedley, both underpinned by such a monumental degree of conviction and certainty, that his wife, or indeed anyone else, felt, if anything, rather guilty of challenging him upon the fundamentals of religion or politics or anything 'deep'. He was as impenetrable as his thorny rose bushes and as impeccable as their blooms.

No, such reflection was, for James Sedley, time-wasting introspection with little relevance to the here-and-now. It all belonged to the meaninglessness of speculation for its own sake. It was a line of thinking to be engaged upon, if at all, in one's youth, and thereafter happily abandoned; for such stuff did not sit at all well with maturity. It was something to be grown out of, like diapers or a belief in Santa Claus. He had heard it said that idealism was respectable in one's youth but insupportable afterwards – he liked that and committed it to memory, to be aired in appropriate circumstances. 'Idealism' was, for him, simply a word that summed up every aberration he could imagine in the conduct of human affairs. The quest for the ideal in human life was just a wild goose chase; wild geese should be left in the wild, out of harm's way. In short: the ideal had no place in the real world.

~ ~

James Sedley managed to satisfy himself that it had been a good morning after all. He had asserted his authority and left no doubt in the mind of Judith Sedley that he was every bit a man in his own right, a *real* man who lived in the *real* world, a man with a good memory for personal hurt and injustice, and a determination to see things through.

He had, of course, made up his mind to attend his son's inaugural sermon, an invitation to which was the main thrust in the letter that morning. He admitted, at least to himself, that it was indeed somewhere on the scale of parental duties. Not that he retracted anything he had said to Judith. On the contrary. It was just that his compliance had to be purchased with an unequivocal act of self-assertion. He had made up his mind to go, because he was an inveterate believer in form, which he called 'doing the decent thing'. If anyone was to be caught out doing the indecent thing, it was not to be him. It was simply that compliance, like everything else, was purchasable. Everything has a price, and the price should be pushed as far as the market will allow.

Chapter Four

A Cry in the Wilderness

Skylarks abound in the green hills, where their plaintive notes are welcomed by those who sojourn there; while down below, their doleful tunes, lost in the discords counted fair, are twisted shapeless in the stale, polluted air.

~ ~

The rain fell in threadbare shrouds.

Thunder rumbled through the heavens, streaks of lightning flashed across the darkened skies, and when at last Thor's hammer was laid to rest, it continued to rain relentlessly, enshrouding a Sunday afternoon in spring that might otherwise have gone unremarked.

The church stood sombre with the sorrows of the world, its steeple pointing skyward, supposedly to better places, to better times, to better men. As the rain-drenched guttering overflowed, it might have seemed, to anyone lingering there with a sombre caste of mind, that the building wept inconsolably for the countless extravagant vices of mankind or for innocence lost and irredeemable, while gargoyles vomited forth the sins of God's sinful and unrepentant children, owing their own grotesqueness to the unspeakable failings of humanity.

It *might* have seemed so. But it did not. For the august members of the congregation were not at all disposed to linger in torrential rain. On the contrary, they were rain-swept into the dank and musty interior of that great edifice, shaking their umbrellas and their heads in unison, having been brought closer together by the indifferent turbulence of nature and the threat of influenza, in much the same way that people are said to be brought closer together by the threat of war. Yes, the grey, cold and stony place was dank and musty, like some vast, dark burial vault in a forgotten, unweeded garden of early Victorian aristocracy, unkempt, uncared for, as relevant as the dodo and as distant as Stonehenge.

The cold slabs that formed the flooring were a sounding board to the taps and squeaks of James Sedley, as he, together with Judith Sedley and Julia Sedley, made his way to the front pews, glancing from side to side at members of that venerable gathering of souls, as if to ensure that his entrance had not gone unnoticed. For he had not come to be instructed in the mysteries of Scripture.

He had come, not to hear the glory of God extolled, but to keep his side of the bargain: compliance in return for self-assertion. Moreover, he would be seen to be doing the decent thing, and he would be achieving some more workable degree of marital harmony into the bargain. While others might see through a glass darkly, all was crystal clear to him. He had little need of instruction in the ways of mankind and was studiously indifferent to the ways of God.

There was, of course, nothing remarkable in this. For some hundreds of years past, the stone floors of this edifice had rung to the taps and squeaks of the thousands upon thousands who had graced the place with their presence for no clearly discernible spiritual reason. These floors had rung to the taps and squeaks of all those who had acquired the habit of, as distinct from the taste for, religion; those who, as it were, wished to do the decent thing, particularly when the urge towards decency was prompted by a birth, a marriage or a death. Indeed, the vast majority of those who regularly tap and squeak their way down the aisles of these grey, sombre, lonely, stony places have much in common with all those tappers and squeakers who stay at home. The difference, one might suppose, is that those who stay at home do so because they cannot bring themselves to believe in the promise of a Life Hereafter – not that they would refuse more of the same, or preferably better, were it demonstrably offered, only that they cannot believe that it is truly on offer.f From time immemorial the tappers and squeakers had filled the pews as regularly as the black ebony clock chimed in the living room of the Sedleys. Such regularity might be taken as evidence that they were themselves only too aware of their spiritual shortcomings. No matter. They could at least console themselves with the very words of Scripture, in which it is written that Christ addressed himself only to sinners, as a physician attends only to those in need of his ministrations, with the corollary that to be imperfect is perfectly respectable. And many are those who are imperfect! Indeed, the circle of imperfect brethren is comfortingly wide, for who could say, in public, that he has no need of the Sermon on the Mount? What is more, each member of the brethren might avail himself of the thought, unspoken of course, that, imperfect as he might be, he is at least less imperfect than his fellows.

The graveyard of this great, grey monument to spiritual rectitude contained its fair share of imposing stony structure, the largest, the grandest and the most expensive of which seemed as much a projection from beyond the grave of the egos of their dusty inmates as expressions of the grief of those who had outlived them and laid them to rest, whilst the poorest and smallest amongst them were almost lost to sight amongst the unkempt foliage that entwined them. Tappers and squeakers perhaps fail to understand the levelling nature of death, this graveyard being a further instance of the wrongs of division between men, men who even in death are ranked one above the other, some clothed in their stony robes of distinction, whilst the least amongst them are barely discernible, like unsung heroes. For, while tappers and squeakers know the meaning of private grief, they seem not to know the universal truth that a man is no better dead than he is alive, that death can neither sanctify nor cleanse; such is the lesson which death teaches and which falls on deaf ears.

As though reluctant to give up on his stubborn pupils, Death calls upon Nature to drive his lesson home. And so it was that the oldest and grandest of these tombstones were washed by wind and rain so that no names were now upon them legible, their very shapes lost, their rich carvings brought low to surface and near to naught. Perhaps Nature had, in disgust, decided to wipe the slate clean.

And the corollary to the lesson of death, that those who grieve, while grieving still, should think as much of those that live, and grieve as much for those who fare ill, seems as lifeless as that place of the dead on that wet, dark, late afternoon on the verge of summer.

Church and graveyard resembled a staging house, a place of preparation for the journey to the dark underworld beneath the dank earth – at least that it how it might have seemed to the older members of the brigade of tappers and squeakers as they made their way past the gravestones on either side of the long, narrow path that led to the heavy wooden doors of that monumental piece of stonework. Perhaps the grave was a place of cleansing and of blessing, after all. A place of blessing – for the dank earth would not hold them if Heaven had its way. And it would surely have its way; for had it not been said that death shall have no dominion?

Such reflections were lost on the choirboys, who took every opportunity to make playful sport of this sombre place, who climbed atop of gravestones grand and lofty, and jumped around them like chimps at play, who scrambled astride the wooden pews like young gorillas on heat – all this when the choirmaster was late for practice; who would, at length, rush upon them, speeding through the gateway on his oil-starved bicycle, to reproach them for showing insufficient respect for the dead and the sanctity of the venue. Pews and graveyard were to the choirboys places for fun and games and laughter – an extension of life, not an insight into eternity. They could not be expected to know what awaited them in the years of maturity, or how they too, like their fathers before them, would scorn their offspring for laughing overmuch in the sleeping-places of the dead. Meanwhile, these boys would run and jump and blaspheme between sermons, making light of the reproaches of those who believed themselves to be decidedly more than children and only somewhat less than God.

~ ~

James Sedley sat flicking his cuffs and clearing his throat; the choirboys were in their places, the choirmaster ready to pounce upon the slightest indiscretion, his eyes cold as steel.

Had James Sedley looked to his left, he might have seen the Reverend John Burgess, former vicar of that parish, a small, clean-shaven man with an aristocratic stoop and small spectacles perched with some reluctance on the tip of his nose. Burgess was all smiles and ready for Bournemouth, to which he was about to retire to oblivion. Now a member of the congregation he had once served for so long, he had come partly to bid a final farewell to his old hunting-ground, partly as a gesture of goodwill towards the new incumbent, Adam Sedley, who had extended this rather unusual invitation. Burgess sat there wondering whether it would have been more proper to have declined it, whether the new incumbent felt as he had done when he gave his first sermon in what now seemed the dim and distant past, and whether he would like it in Bournemouth as much as people said he would, whether the reality of retirement was as pleasant in reality as it was in prospect, whether it was a far better thing to travel than to arrive – one thing life had taught him seemed incontrovertible, that the anticipation of a thing almost invariably exceeds its realisation. Just for a moment, he had the strange feeling that he was about to see and hear himself speak his thoughts out loud, as though he would exist outside himself; it was this kind of experience that had prompted him to think seriously of retirement, the feeling that he was somewhere outside himself, watching and listening to himself speak as he addressed his congregation – yes, he had sensed that this was the end of the line, that pastures new beckoned, even if they were pastures only to graze in before the end. He thought of the new incumbent and sensed a sad continuity; Adam Sedley would become like him: old, tired and on the verge of Bournemouth, his pilgrimage through life ending on the promenade of a seaside resort amid Coca-Cola and hot-dog stands and little children drowning in ice-cream. If there was a moral to be drawn from such reflections, he was simply too weary and perhaps too apprehensive to work it out.

In any case, there was nothing left for Burgess in the commuter land of leafy suburbia. His wife had died, and his daughter was busily, and precariously, married to a stockbroker. He hadn't seen her for some time – he couldn't remember when, and she seldom went out of her way to answer his simple texts. Indeed, were it not for a routine exchange of Christmas cards, he might have imagined himself childless. But he thought of her often; intensively, when he remembered her childhood and the special, cosy affinity that seemed to exist between them then that had somehow vanished with the passing of time. He had thought fondly of becoming a grandfather, almost as much as his wife longed to become a grandmother, and of bouncing small, soft, pretty, playful little things on his knee and telling them fantastic tales of fiery dragons and castles made of chocolate. He had thought of it; but perhaps such things didn't fit too snugly into the world of stockbrokerage. So he had at last surrendered, though not without recurrent difficulty, his self-image as a doting grandfather; and he hoped and prayed with all his heart that his daughter was happy and would continue to be so as the years rolled by. Now, he had Bournemouth to look forward to. And as for all those sermons he had written, they were all nicely tied up in large brown envelopes, and he intended to read through them again at leisure, perhaps when the weather was inclement, or in the evenings, or during the long, dark nights of winter. Why, he might even have them published! In any case, who was to say that there might not one day be a grandchild to read them and ponder their author? What vanity! But then, who can live happily without it? Meanwhile, he would think of Bournemouth, of the sea, of the sky, of pleasant walks, of restful solitude ... and not a little of loneliness. And what better place to reflect on loneliness than the very church which he served and in which he now sat waiting for the new incumbent to say his piece? This church, like every church in the land, was indeed a lonely place, in its dark, declining days.

Had James Sedley looked to his right, his officious gaze might have alighted on Charles Baxter, a *real* man if ever there was one; in his early 40s, he sported an impeccable moustache and an expensive three-piece suit. He was known to most people thereabouts as 'someone in the City', a title which pleased him on account of its vagueness and its aura of prestige. Lately separated from his wife, and not unattracted to the prospect of experimentation in matters sexual as well as commercial, he was a man of much initiative, and a zealous adherent of free enterprise, though it is unlikely that he countenanced the concept of freedom beyond its application to amorous and commercial undertakings; in affairs of the heart, discretion was his byword; in the pursuit of profit, one might be as indiscreet as one liked. Hardly yet middle-aged, the world was still an oyster from which he sought to extract the pearl. He was a member of that venerable band of aspirants known as commuters, respectably commuting from home to work and back again, a human shuttle designed to move the movers on in the world, albeit the motion is merely horizontal and over the same ground.

Charles Baxter did look about him – now to the left, now to the right, front and behind, up and down. And with the supreme efficiency that was the mark of all his doings, this human periscope soon located the form of Julia Sedley, who sat with her mother-in-law, anxiously awaiting her husband's ascent to the pulpit. In a single glance, he had committed every relevant feature of that lovely form to memory. Not for Charles Baxter the lure of the great stained windows that rose like frozen paintings to the heights above the alter; not for him the faded and fragmented murals pregnant with the ancestry of modern man and reminiscent of the puritan fanaticism that sought to destroy every single vestige of them during the Republic. A greater prize than these entranced him and held his gaze, gripping him tight, while all history and conscience hung limp and irrelevant.

It must be admitted that Baxter cut an entirely respectable figure in that closely-knit community. He was massively polite, especially to the elderly and the relatively underprivileged. There is no doubt about that, and it is widely acknowledged that politeness is a sure indication of respectability. He was admired, above all, for the organisational skills he could bring to bear on church fetes, church raffles, and similar charitable functions. He had been commended to Adam Sedley by none other than John Burgess, the outgoing incumbent, who regarded Baxter as a pillar of the local, not to say global, economy, to be cherished in his capacity as reliable helper, advisor and organiser. Moreover, and as an asset to crown all others, he was a regional councillor, and there was no telling to what great heights he might one day succeed if, as he himself was often pleased to intimate, he finally obeyed his inner voice and ran for Parliament. If he ran, it would be in a safe seat, and there was no safer seat known to political man than this. Meanwhile, he was content to play the role of benefactor in a community grateful to be the recipient of his skills though blissfully ignorant of his talent to turn every act of kindness into a self-advertisement.

Seeing but darkly beyond the rims of his spectacles, Burgess had nothing but praise for Charles Baxter. Indeed, when knowledge of Baxter's domestic troubles became sufficiently common to be brought to his attention, the good Reverend actually prayed for the salvation of Baxter's marriage by divine intervention. Little comprehending that these martial stresses and strains had as little to do with the Christian God as the stability of the stock exchange or the world price of copper, he attributed God's persistent inaction in this matter to the infinite depths of divine wisdom, such wisdom being immeasurably greater than man's and so, in a word, incomprehensible, though at the same time utterly reliable.

For his part, Baxter found Burgess's divinely inspired solicitude at turns amusing and irritating, and Burgess himself more than slightly dotty, which is essentially how he regarded all vicars of Christ of whatever creed or denomination. This is not to say that Baxter refused to call himself a Christian, not to say a Christian straight and true − or as straight and true as any Christian can be expected to be who enjoyed his earthly sojourn in the commuter land of leafy suburbia. On the contrary, he was firmly of the opinion that God is squarely on the side of all human industry and endeavour; all human industry and endeavour, that is to say, that he, Baxter, found unobjectionable. God therefore heaped His blessings on the creation of *wealth*, both personal and impersonal. The terms of the distinction between personal wealth and that of the public good could not in general be mutually inimical, since the pursuit of the former was the only effective incentive to the creation of the latter; and, in his view, all good Christians with even just a smattering of economic good sense would affirm that personal wealth is the basis and the foundation, if not the very essence, of all things bright and beautiful. Lefties and so-called intellectuals, while their hearts may, and only just *may*, be in the right place, were persistently and perversely apt to forget that while the heart of the Good Samaritan was also in the right place, he could not have helped that wretched fellow without a purse of gold; and what is gold if it is not wealth? In all this, Baxter was in very good company, for it was a philosophy that was commended by alternative faiths. Judaism and Islam, for example, found no difficulty ascribing primacy to the accumulation of wealth; indeed Islamists even commended hypocrisy, insincerity and downright falsehood in dealings with infidels provided that profit or gain was the likely outcome, though Baxter himself would have resisted this recommendation tooth and nail, and in all sincerity.

The philosophy commended itself to Baxter in terms of its very simplicity: the creation of personal wealth is a precondition of virtuous conduct; therefore, the pursuit and creation of personal wealth are virtuous. The very possibility that they are neither a necessary nor a sufficient condition of virtuous conduct never occurred to him for an instant, much less that they might actually inhibit such conduct. No, the beauty of the argument for the pursuit and creation of personal wealth lay in what he considered to be its immediate appeal to 'common sense', and he could not entertain the idea that it might be much less than perspicuous to those who knew better, if only because there could not possibly be anyone who knew better. Common sense cannot be bettered, because it is *sense* and that is why it is held in *common*. No, the argument was overwhelmingly clear, proven and watertight; so, in attending church, and helping out with charitable events, he was, as it were, giving a little back in return for the wealth he was amassing for himself, thus proving, by the sheer weight of practical example, that the wealth he amassed for himself was, at the same time, in the interests of all and was *consequently* deserving of the blessing of the Almighty. It was all deliciously rounded, simple and correct.

It was therefore quite in keeping with Baxter's view of the world that he should appear regularly in church and exhibit the proper spirit at all the relevant functions. It might be thought that he would have stopped short of prayer or that there was nothing like a personal relationship between Baxter and his God. Yet even this cannot be discounted since it was nicely accommodated by his *Weltanschauung*. God was no doubt grateful for his initiative, his innate business-sense and his perfect attention to detail. What Baxter would have made of Christ's admonishment of the money-lenders in the temple, we shall never know, and it is likely that the event was never an item in Baxter's thinking. He might have said that church fetes were a 'good cause' and that money-lending was not. But it is to be doubted that he would have attempted to make any such distinction. And he would have had exceptional difficulty entertaining the idea that Christ considered lending at a profit to be wicked. Though not a Semite, he had learned to emulate The Chosen, marry the Rate of Interest with Self Interest and assume that the pursuit of the latter is in the interests of everyone. And was not Christ himself a Jew? Indeed, the rate of interest was the very corner stone of respectable economic policy. No, Baxter would never have questioned the practice of lending at interest. And the idea that the market place is a place of business and the temple a place of worship and never the twain shall meet, is not likely to have been even remotely comprehensible. No, the fact is that had it been possible for Baxter to have been present during Christ's admonishment of the money-lenders, he would have probably walked over to the Son of God with a, 'Now, look here my good man!' or a 'You've got it all wrong, you know!' and left Jesus cold and staring. True, there is a time and place for all things, and Baxter would no doubt have agreed with the sentiment, when generally applied. But as for the creation of wealth – well, there was always time and place for that! No, as Baxter saw it, he and God got on well together. As for prayer, well, it followed that there could be nothing wrong in making wealth the subject of one's communication with the Almighty. And this is a conviction he shared with old Burgess.

Burgess believed that if you prayed hard enough, with sufficient faith, you'd get what you prayed for, unless, of course, what you prayed for was vetoed by God, and why He would apply his veto was seldom comprehensible; but then it had to be remembered that God was incomprehensible anyway. Burgess's God seemed to be an autocratic monarch, who harkens to the wishes of his suppliants with no obligation whatsoever to fulfil them. Even so, it was good to pray for anything that was lawful; if so, it followed that it was alright to pray that you won't be found wanting on your mortgage repayments, or for an early and happy retirement, or for some addition to one's stock of wealth. It was well-documented that the poor incessantly pray for riches and that Jesus had some sort of soft spot for the poor and the deprived. So, if it was alright to pray for wealth, how can any prayer for material enrichment be misguided, or frowned upon by God? The fact that you might not get what you prayed for might mean that you didn't deserve it – anyway, that was God's business, and He wasn't letting on. But to pray for wealth? Well, that was alright. If during lean or risky times, Charles Baxter had a word or two for the ear of God, in this he was one with old Burgess himself.

Burgess had prayed often enough for sufficient funds to fix the leaky church roof. Baxter knew that, and he would have regarded such supplications as living proof that God, if He exists, considers wealth a worthy subject of prayer. What's more, because Baxter organised things and helped create the wealth required, he might have regarded himself as an instrument of God, divinely appointed to answer the prayers of divine supplication. No wonder Burgess commended him to the new incumbent; to have omitted to do so would have bordered on the sinful. Or, to put the matter in terms with which Baxter himself might have been more familiar: If Burgess was the front man, Baxter was one of the backroom boys. Whatever the terms employed, Baxter saw himself as a pillar of the twin establishments of Church and State, which complemented each other and served to keep him in high standing. It has to be said that time and change are in the unfortunate habit of knocking things down more easily than they build them up. Both Burgess and Baxter entertained the chilling thought that the Christian God may one day be usurped by some other less accommodating deity and that their worlds may be shaken in consequence; mosques were beginning to dot the suburban landscapes as they had already done so in the cities, and Lord only knows where that might end. The thought was entertained, but not yet given voice. Threadbare vestments, empty pews and leaking roofs were quite enough to occupy one's thoughts without venturing into the darker recesses of the mind.

Charles Baxter didn't talk about such dark matters; he was not called upon to confront them; it was not his business. He would simply plod on and continue to regard himself as a Pillar of the Establishment; this was comforting, for he saw that the Establishment was good, and loved it. Profound criticism, profound *anything*, was not his business. He simply attended to the proper business of life, enjoying the unarticulated conviction that, if God is sensible, or anything like the good and powerful being He's cracked up to be, things would turn out alright in the end. As for the good works for which Baxter was himself responsible, his attentions would not go unnoticed and unrewarded, either here or, if it was there to be had, in the life hereafter.

Meanwhile, God was not the only one to notice Baxter's attentions. Julia Sedley felt them, as surely as if she had held a live wire in one of her bare and lovely hands. She sensed his attentions and glanced behind to ascertain their source while pretending to be looking elsewhere. But Charles Baxter was not a man to be fooled by such tricks; he congratulated himself on the successful completion of Stage One.

James Sedley was oblivious to all this. He sat flicking his cuffs, praying, so to speak, for an early start to the whole proceedings. The earlier the start, the sooner the finish, which was a truism he applied to all things irksome. The irksomeness of this occasion was, however, highlighted by the fact that he had already received a sermon good and proper, in advance, and in his own home, too! It was painfully ironic that he should be on the receiving end once again. But this time there was little excuse to walk out, and he could hardly expel his son from the house of God. He was stuck with it; and it was just sickening to think of all the belittling sacrifices one was called upon to make, and all in the name of 'doing the decent thing'.

He was not alone in his impatience. The congregation was composed chiefly of those who had neither much of virtue nor of vice and were generally oblivious to everything that did not demand immediate and undivided attention, such as movements in the mortgage rate, or the departure of the Royal Family on continental tours. They had, in the main, all been brought up on a strict diet of mediocrity, believing in the soundness of tradition, the infallibility of convention and the unreasonableness of dissent.

A small boy misbehaved, bringing down upon his little head the stony stares of the godly and the wise. Yes, it was clearly time for instruction through the vicarious workings of the Almighty, after which tea, biscuits and sherry would be available to all and sundry in the small vicarage nearby, at the warm invitation of Adam and Julia Sedley – but first, the lesson.

~ ~

The Reverend Sedley had chosen 'Fight the Good Fight' as a fitting hymn to anticipate his lesson on the Beatitudes:

Faint not nor fear, his arms are near,
He changeth not, and thou art dear;
Only believe, and thou shalt see
That Christ is all in all to thee.

Believing was the problem. More precisely, understanding exactly what it was that had to be believed, and this perplexity was doubtless reflected in the rendering of the hymn; for this familiar exhortation to praise and faith, strength and hope, was delivered with an enthusiasm infinitely less than its good author had surely intended, causing his dry bones to rattle in despair and righteous indignation. Faith was hard at the best of times, but what hope for faith now, when faith was in decline and disrepute, when Christianity itself was being usurped by an unfamiliar, or all too familiar, God, whose disposition was anything but amiable and all-embracing?

The words were sung, albeit feebly enough. After making all the customary gestures of welcome, and speaking at first with the hesitation, not to say monotony, that one might expect from a new incumbent, he began by referencing the Sermon on the Mount:

'In Matthew, Chapter 5, verses 1 - 11, we read:

'"And seeing the multitudes, he went up into a mountain; and when he was set, his disciples came unto him" …'

Just then, the huge door to the rear of the church creaked noisily on its rusted hinges, and in shuffled an old man, in his mid-70s, bearded and tramp-like; his raincoat, or what was left of it, was saturated with rain and secured round his waist with a length of thick string. He removed his sodden hat, beat it against his thigh, and, muttering incomprehensibly to himself, ambled gracelessly into the pews nearest the door and sat down. The old fellow was welcomed with various expressions of disapproval, discreetly vented of course. But, blissfully oblivious to the stir he had occasioned, he settled into place as comfortably as he could. The steely glances thrown his way failed to reach their mark. He searched nonchalantly through the pockets of his tattered raincoat and, failing to find what he was looking for, wiped his nose in his sleeve, smiling benignly at those around him, who returned the salutation with accusatory stares. But the small congregation was not prepared to be inconvenienced further. Apart from the occasional sniff and sneeze, the old man blended well enough into the scene and became acutely absorbed in the proceedings, as Adam Sedley quickly resumed his text with a curious vigour and fervour, almost as though the old man were a guest of honour, long-awaited and without whom the occasion would lack all justification.

Reverend Sedley went on to quote the Beatitudes; during which the old man warmly nodded his assent, giving an occasional *'humph'* in agreement, to the irritation, not to say disgust, of the good folk in the immediate vicinity.

'And later, he tells his disciples:

"Be therefore perfect, even as you Father which is in heaven is perfect".'

A further expression of approval from the old man caused further stares and a sea of silent condemnation from all those who had seen and heard, with the exception of the good Reverend, who had now begun to speak with a self-confidence that was not lost on Judith and James Sedley, nor on Julia, who wondered then and ever after what its source could possibly have been. For, soon enough, Adam Sedley would suddenly cease to be a run-of-the-mill clergyman from whom only the ordinary could be expected; he would reveal himself to all and sundry, and the seeds of that revelation were just about to be planted; yes, right there and then.

'I must apologise for taking The Sermon on the Mount as my text, because you must know it very well, and there's nothing more off-putting than the same old-hat over and over again – what's the point repeating the Beatitudes and the ten commandments when they are as familiar as the alphabet? Yes, but there are two things I should like to stress: first, that The Sermon on the Mount is all we really have; and, second, The Sermon on the Mount is all we ever really need ...'

It was once memorably remarked that the aristocracy of England would have snored through the Sermon on the Mount; but the aristocracy are in good company, for very few in that small congregation were following the Reverend's drift or cared whether his text was The Sermon on the Mount or yesterday's news. True, Judith Sedley was impressed by the earnestness of her son's delivery. But it had quite a different effect on James Sedley, who now wished more than ever that he had stayed at home. Doing the decent thing could be just too damned pricey! It might still be possible to make a respectable exit – he looked around – no, it was not quite possible and, after all, it was not the words that offended him so much as the tone of authority that went with them – the enthusiasm of youth could be so irritating!

'And let our sensibilities not be offended if a clearer analysis of The Sermon on the Mount affords us a better, though not necessarily pleasant, understanding both of ourselves and the society in which we now live, because the message it contains may help us to preserve what is good in both, against the twin onslaughts of decline and despair which are destroying Christianity itself and allowing superstition and false gods to reign in its stead ...'

The good Reverend need not have been concerned about offending the sensibilities of Charles Baxter, who would not have been disturbed at anything short of a catastrophe in the city. Besides, Baxter was deeply engrossed in an analysis of his own and of a very different character, namely Julia Sedley. Having impressed her image indelibly on his cerebral filofax, he was now engaged in the all-absorbing study of feminine geometry, with a dedication to accuracy and detail that would doubtless have impressed Euclid himself. It was not that the authoritative manner of the sermon had gone entirely unnoticed, only that Baxter had not come expecting to be impressed by mere words, or indeed by anything spiritual at all; he was predisposed to resist any impression that might possibly conflict with his own settled view of the world and his role in it. Simply, he was not programmed to be disturbed.

'... *If the Sermon on the Mount has any meaning at all, it must be capable of translation into our everyday lives. After all, Christ was not addressing superbeings, but ordinary people, just like us. It was precisely because of their ordinariness that Christ spoke to them in the way he did. He thought it was possible to bring about a change in the lives of ordinary people, and what he told them, and is telling us now, was then and is now intended as a guide as to what is possible. He is not telling us that we must cease to be human to be perfect; that's not what perfection means at all; no, it doesn't mean infallibility, as though we can never make mistakes. If we follow what he prescribes then we can be perfect, perfect as God is perfect, because that's what perfection means!*

'He was not interested in abstract philosophy. Here we are reminded of the Buddha, who, when asked to explain a metaphysical idea concerning the immortality of the soul, replied that whatever worth such an idea may have, it had nothing whatsoever to do with the explanation he was concerned to give; he wanted to explain some of the chief causes of human misery and how to go about righting them. He reproached his questioner for raising questions that simply got in the way of the message he was trying to convey to mankind – he would have no more to do with abstract speculation and had nothing to say on the subject. Doesn't his reaction remind us of what Christ said, when he said that the kingdom of heaven is within us? And that the dead should bury the dead? And that God is God of the living, not of the dead? No, Christ was concerned with human life, not life beyond the grave. You see, life beyond the grave is a fitting subject only for the movie industry and, far worse, false prophets, who profit from the ignorant and the vulnerable; they nurture in us a fear of the dark, while in fact by far the greatest atrocities are committed in the simple light of day; fear is their greatest weapon, wielded for power or for money; they use it to detract us from the proper business of life, and that business is living and those who live. Superstition is not simply a harmless diversion, it is as rife as ever it was and is used by

all faiths to justify monstrous atrocities. The so-called Life Hereafter has nothing whatever to do with the mission and the message of Christ ...'

With these last few utterances, the Reverend Burgess was brought back to the reality of the moment from his mental sojourn on the promenade in Bournemouth. It struck him that the new incumbent was treading on some mighty thin ice. To say that the Message of Christ had no connection whatsoever with the promise of the Life Hereafter seemed rather more than disappointing. After all, one had to have some sort of incentive, and a denial of an afterlife seemed to be a glaring elimination of all incentive, let alone earthly comfort; the elimination, indeed, of an entire system of belief, an entire framework, and one needed some kind of framework, some kind of system, some sort of incentive, otherwise it was all asking just too much – too much altogether! Why, even he, John Burgess, found it more than difficult to contemplate total extinction at the end of his days here on earth. Bournemouth may well turn out to be more than he had ever hoped for, but to suggest that there was to be nothing after Bournemouth – well, that was just asking too much. No, that couldn't be right. Yes, the young incumbent was certainly treading on thin ice. After all, hadn't Christ promised the thief on the Cross a place at his right hand in heaven? Yes, *promised*! On the other hand, the young incumbent hadn't actually gone so far as to say that the very idea of the Life Hereafter is a *nonsense*, only that it had nothing to do with Christ's message; so Burgess took some consolation from the fact that he hadn't gone even further. And the fact that he hadn't actually, explicitly, denied the very possibility of the Life Hereafter would probably save him from the possible reproaches of some members of his good flock. Should he raise the matter with young Sedley afterwards? No, no that wouldn't do at all. Besides, the congregation had in all probability failed to notice anything untoward at all, so the whole thing would attract no comment. Even so, young Sedley would need to temper his ideas with good sense and sound judgement if he was to remain at all credible. He could not possibly go round saying that the notion, nay the promise, nay the fact, of the Life Hereafter had no fundamental place in the Christian message; Christianity was perhaps suffering a decline, but if Christians were deprived of the promise of an afterlife, the decline would soon reach its lowest depths, and Christianity would indeed be totally usurped by religions that did promise an afterlife. No, no. And in any case, was not hope and the joy of hope part and parcel of the Christian message? Of course it was!

Young Sedley had been careless, that was all, being quite naturally overwhelmed by the occasion and temporarily bedevilled by an unguarded zeal; yes, time and sense would cure all. With such calming and incisive conclusions, the thoughts of John Burgess returned in a spirit of hope to Bournemouth and endless cups of tea on an endless promenade on endless days in summer. But, unfortunately, there was more disquietude to come.

'Yes, I say again, Christ was, like Buddha ...'

Burgess was not at all impressed by all this talk of Buddha; he felt mildly perturbed by the comparison with Christ for reasons that were at best vague and would remain so, since thoughts of Bournemouth had too great a hold over his imagination now to permit him to wander off into the foggy realms of the metaphysical and the theological. Foggy days at Bournemouth may cause havoc at sea, but this was naught in comparison with attempts at self-examination, which were at best indeterminate, and at worst upsetting. But there was more ...

'... Christ was, like Buddha, a realist who knew very well that he was addressing human, not super-human, beings. And also, like Buddha, he was not interested in philosophising on matters that he considered irrelevant. They were both eminently practical men. But Christ says, "Be perfect, even as your father in heaven is perfect". But this doesn't mean that we can't make mistakes, that we can be infallible ...'

Burgess also found this talk of perfection to be dangerous; to say that human beings, who are imperfect, can nevertheless be perfect, and as perfect as God himself, smacked of blasphemy of the highest order. So it occurred to Burgess, during a momentary return from his seaside reverie, that the ice on which young Sedley was skating on was getting even thinner.

'No, perfection or imperfection has nothing to do with mistakes. It is very human to make mistakes, and there can never be a time when human beings cease to be capable of making them. So, then, what does it mean to say that we can be perfect? Christ answers this question when he says, "Blessed are they that are poor in spirit." He didn't say, "Blessed are the poor," but, "Blessed are the poor in spirit" ...'

Charles Baxter, momentarily aroused from his reflections on the female form, was almost tempted to shout 'Hear! Hear!' at the implication that there was nothing particularly commendable about the poor; nothing, that is to say, that brought them any closer to God than he was himself. This was hopeful news – a confirmation, indeed, of the moral propriety of the path he had already set himself upon, an endorsement (had he seriously felt the need of one) of his conviction that in becoming more affluent he was doing nothing to incur the wrath of the Almighty. Yes, this new chap Sedley was doing a good job. Baxter sat smiling at his own joke, and returned to the pleasant occupation of speculating on what lay beneath the folds of Julia Sedley's Sunday Best, on whether the contours suggested were accurate representations of fact.

'... "Blessed are the poor in spirit. For theirs is the kingdom of heaven," and this is the key to understanding what is meant by perfection. Because to be poor in spirit means to be aware of one's moral shortcomings and to genuinely strive to put them right; and this means putting others first and ourselves in the background, a kind of self-negation. Perfection is not the elimination of error, but the desire that error be eliminated; it is a selfless love of mankind, and therefore of God, because one cannot love God without loving mankind. Perfection is attributed to God simply because God is love, the word "God" means "love". Christ is speaking of love when he speaks of perfection, when he tells his disciples that they can be perfect. And this appeal to love is the very heart and soul of the Sermon on the Mount. Of course, we make mistakes, but they are forgivable if they are founded in love; and when we forgive others their trespasses against us, we are like God, because forgiveness flows from love. The command "Be perfect" is not like saying, "Watch your step, or else!" It is a moral prescription as to how we should treat our fellow men. The fear of God is not the fear of what some kind of Almighty Superbeing might do against you if you fail to follow orders; no, it is the fear of offending the innocent, of hurting another, and of failing to grasp the opportunity to lend a helping hand. This is what it means to be "poor in spirit", for this kind of poverty means the absence of arrogance and selfishness, of greed, of moral indifference. This kind of poverty cannot exist if people worship the wrong gods; for there is only one God worth worshipping, and that is the God of love, as distinct from the gods of anger and reprobation, of self-seeking and of hate.

'I must stress this: God is not a super-being, because he is not a being at all. He is not some kind of creature, because he is no creature at all. If I say that God is Love, I mean precisely that. God is a concept, the concept of Love. Those who seek to deprecate and reprimand God for allowing inhumanity to flourish and for the death of innocent little children are greatly mistaken, for Love is incapable of such things, and it is precisely Love that makes such criticism at all possible. To blame God for allowing the atrocities of the world and man's inhumanity to man is a complete nonsense — for it is like blaming Love, and this is absurd. It is precisely Love that makes the condemnation of man's inhumanity to man at all possible! Those who reprimand God for the atrocities of the world are in fact making gigantic and unanswerable objections against a bogus conception of God — the *conception of God as an all-powerful super-being. Their invective entirely misses the point that the true God is not guilty as charged.*

'I must also stress that the Sermon on the Mount tells us everything we need to know and everything we need to do. There is nothing else. Everything else that passes for religion is nothing but pomp and illusion, hypocrisy and cant.'

By now, Burgess, Baxter, James and Judith Sedley, and even Julia Sedley, were, together with the rest of the congregation, so far advanced in their somnolence that had the good Reverend asserted that God was a Martian technocrat, the announcement would have been greeted without further ado. But as the sermon reached its close, the old man, who had listened patiently and attentively throughout, now stood up, doffed his hat to the Reverend, shuffled to the door, and left. If Adam Sedley had planned on making an explosive debut, it really seemed as though it had fallen on deaf ears, his words like seeds on stony ground. And so, no one felt capable of challenging the idea that God was simply a concept, an abstract idea; had they done so, there is little doubt that they would have taken this as an assertion of God's non-existence, and then gone on to accuse the Reverend of Satanism or the greatest heresy known to man, and therefore unforgiveable, even by God.

Chapter Five

A Parishioner par excellence

Hailstones that fall on hills, for longer sojourn there, while those that fall below on peopled plains will melt apace, and, having only just arrived, will vanish without a single trace.

~ ~

The shadows cast by the tallest gravestones had lengthened to infinity and the rain had ceased to fall before the reception got under way. The vicarage consisted of a small grey-stone house surrounded by an uncommonly spacious, well-kept garden consisting of lawn and flower-beds, with a trio of Lawson Cypresses at the far end that looked out onto school playing fields. House and garden were encompassed by a thick, high wall of grey stone, on the top of which fragments of glass had been embedded in concrete, presumably to discourage vandals, wayward youths, stray cats and acrobatic dogs; such methods of protection belonged to bygone days and were no longer lawful, but the authorities had not yet got round to removing them from the vicarage walls.

Compared with the rest of the house, the living-room was surprisingly long and roomy, and the guests stood around in small groups, chatting away in clichés on themes suggested by decorum and decency, the topics of conversation moving outward in scope, like a flower blossom, though not half as pretty: oneself, the vicarage, the weather, the property market, the international economic climate; and having exhausted these subject-areas in one huddled group, it was time to move on to another in which these same conversational pieces would be repeated, not necessarily in the same order but with an ever greater degree of fluency.

Julia Sedley, occasionally and ditheringly aided by Judith Sedley, busied herself distributing cakes and sherry, refreshments which most guests pretended at first to refuse emphatically. It was not long before the sherry began to breech the meagre defences of these good souls. Mild laughter and scraps of genuine conversation could be heard breaking out here and there like an embarrassing rash.

Adam Sedley, taking the aging Reverend John Burgess lightly by the arm, escorted him over to Judith Sedley, who seemed now to be alone and lost in thought as she stared at some unremarkable portrait that seemed to hang precariously over a large, stone fireplace. Having been introduced, Burgess smiled benignly.

'Yes, I'm on the way out, you might say,' he chuckled. 'To make way for your son, Mrs Sedley.' There was a pathetic plea for sympathy underlying his apparent light-heartedness, which Judith Sedley was good-natured enough to recognise. 'I must say,' he went on, 'I'm glad, *most* glad, I accepted your son's kind invitation to come along this evening – though it was unorthodox, you know – yes, *most* unorthodox.'

'Really?' she asked, amused by Burgess's dithery, even eccentric, earnestness.

'Oh, yes, well, you see, retiring vicars are an odd breed; yes, they're supposed to fade away into the background without a trace, you know. Yes, like a bubble of air. Fade away, and fade out,' he said with another chuckle.

'Oh dear,' she said, sympathetically.

'Yes, there it is. I'm expected to retire gracefully into advanced old age – "Keeping a low profile" I think they call it. But do you know, this parish could certainly do with some new blood. And this house – you may think it's quite modest, *quite* modest, but it's far too large for one old man – *far* too large. No, it needs to ring with laughter, Mrs Sedley; not to say the patter of tiny feet, hey Adam?'

'You really must stop putting ideas into my head,' said Adam, and all three laughed together, despite the fact that there was nothing in this the slightest bit amusing.

'Yes, too large for me – well, since my dear wife passed away, that is,' Burgess went on.

'I'm so sorry,' said Judith Sedley, and she really meant it.

'I still miss her terribly, I must confess,' he muttered musingly.

'It must be ...' Judith Sedley began.

'When I received your son's letter, I was intrigued,' said Burgess, cutting her short. 'Yes, *most* intrigued. To tell you the truth, I couldn't resist the temptation to take one last look at the place, a lingering farewell as it were – for old time's sake. Memories, you see. And ... and I must say,' he went on, as though eager to change the subject, 'I was impressed by your sermon. *Most* impressed. Mind you,

I wouldn't have chosen the Sermon on the Mount all in one go like that – a bit too ambitious for me, I'm afraid,' he said, smiling his benign smile, leaving the new incumbent wondering whether this was a compliment or a veiled reproach or something in between.

'Well, *I* enjoyed it, for one!' Charles Baxter had sidled up unobserved, his third glass of sweet sherry in one hand and a slice of Dundee cake in the other.

'Ah! Now you've met Adam, of course,' said Burgess with a hitherto unknown joviality, 'But I don't think you've been introduced to Mrs Sedley, Adam's mother ...'

'Very pleased, I'm sure, Mr Baxter,' said Judith Sedley, introductions having been made.

'Charles. Call me Charles. I'm delighted.'

'Yes, Charles is an outstanding member of this parish. *Quite* outstanding,' said Burgess. 'Just the man to know – caring, considerate, utterly selfless, modest, and, above all, indispensable. *Most* indispensable. If anything needs to be organised, you can depend on Charles, implicitly, to organise it down to the very last detail. Oh, and by the way he's a man of political aspirations. Destined for high places, I'm sure. *Quite* sure.'

'No, no, come along now! I've helped out with one or two fetes, that's all,' said Baxter, with feigned indifference, for he considered his organisational skills vastly underrated.

'There! What did I tell you? Modest to a fault!' said Burgess.

'I don't think you've met my wife,' said Adam, glancing at Julia who'd just joined them. Julia, meet Charles. Charles, Julia.' And with the simplicity, innocence and naturalness of social convention, a story within a story would begin to unfold; large things can indeed arrive in small packages.

'Well, hello,' said Baxter, looking deeply into her eyes and for as long as he dared, and touching her hand as though he expected it to melt into his with the sheer heat of passionate intent.

'I've heard a lot about you,' she said, with a smile so fetching that it could do nothing to diminish his intense appreciation of her physical assets.

'An outstanding member of this parish!' old Burgess repeated, like a budgerigar conditioned to respond to a given stimulus, or a clockwork toy which still had enough energy inside it for one last gasp of activity. Burgess's appreciation of Baxter was unreciprocated. As far as Baxter was concerned, it was just as well if Burgess was dead, cremated and forgotten. Burgess's compliments were all very well, but Baxter felt that they tended to cheapen him in front of Julia, on whom he wished to exercise a far more subtle yet at the same time primeval form of influence, with an equally primordial result.

Julia apologetically slipped away to resume her duties as hostess, obliging Baxter to waste yet more time with the Reverends Burgess and Sedley.

'Anyway, as I was saying, I enjoyed your sermon. Plenty of punch. Just what we need. Sorry about that little lapse, though — I mean the old fellow who stumbled in on us. Can't say you didn't notice him! Yes? Well, it was better to let the thing slide, I suppose — not to make a scene. No doubt just a one-off. But if people like that want a bit of comfort, they can toddle off to a hostel or something. It's not as if there aren't places they can go to. Now I'm not being callous, but a church is a place of worship, after all. It's not a glorified bus-shelter or shop doorway.' Baxter spoke with a zeal which he might have hoped would outmatch that of Sedley's sermon. He was not a man to be outdone, even when his time could be much better spent.

'I quite agree,' said James Sedley, emphatically and affably, as he joined the group.

Charles Baxter was introduced to James Sedley, once again as a pillar of the local establishment, an asset to the parish, and a man of political aspirations. But the introduction this time was made by Adam Sedley, and with a degree of nonchalance which contrasted with Burgess's appraisal.

'Politics!' exclaimed James Sedley. 'Well, I do my level best to keep out of it — leave it to the politicians, I always say. But what this country needs is men of ambition and drive. Ambition is sorely lacking these days, you know. Yes, ambition and drive, that's what the country needs. If you ask me, we've had too much of the softies and the do-gooders spoiling it for the rest of us. Discipline, that's what we need. Self-discipline and self-respect! Make people responsible for their own actions: they'll get credit if they get it right; they'll pay the price if they get it wrong. And I'm glad to see we're moving more in that direction far more these days. But there's a long way to go yet!' Momentarily placing his glass on a nearby coffee table, he flicked and straightened his cuffs, regaining his composure as he did so. 'Yes, we've been much too soft. No wonder we're in danger of losing our most treasured values.'

'You've the makings of a politician, yourself. I can see that!' said Baxter.

'Well, just armchair, you know, just armchair. Of course, time was when I might have made a go of it. Still, no use crying over spilt milk — or lost opportunities,' said James Sedley, as an image of Judith Sedley flashed through his head – as though she had been an obstacle to past, present and future glory. 'Yes, it's far too late for all that,' he said, picking up his glass and looking round for a refill.

'It's never too late to make a profound and lasting contribution to the improvement of mankind,' said Baxter, refilling James Sedley's glass. He enjoyed giving the impression that he was quoting from some unimpeachable source; had he been asked to identify his source in this instance, he would have had the unspeakable pleasure of claiming sole authorship of that remarkable insight. Much to his regret, he was not on this occasion empowered to claim it.

'Well said, well said,' muttered James Sedley, between sips of sherry.

'You speak a lot of good sense,' Baxter went on, clearly relishing the effect he was having on a man on whose friendship he was now eternally assured.

'Common sense, that's all. Just plain common sense,' returned James Sedley, who was now beginning to feel that he had already gone some way towards making a profound and lasting contribution to the improvement of mankind.

'Well, I can only wish that more people were endowed with it, that's all *I* can say!' said Baxter.

'Which party?' asked James Sedley, draining his glass.

'Hmm?'

'Which party? Where do your loyalties lie, young man?' asked James Sedley, smacking his lips. He felt instinctively that his question had already been answered, which is perhaps why he felt sufficiently confident to ask it at all; but asking the question gave him an opportunity to make another deft contribution to political wisdom, thus consolidating the positive impression he had already made; for all he had to do was to say that the question was out of place, and to say why.

'No, don't tell me. Never mind, shouldn't've asked. A cardinal principle of politics: let information be given on a need-to-know basis, eh? Very sound. Very sound, indeed.' Baxter was amused, and simply nodded in agreement.

Considerable affinity had now been discovered between James Sedley and Charles Baxter, who both cherished the thought that a secret shared was a secret doubled, no matter if the secret was only alleged. The very language of secrecy was an expression of mutual admiration. After all, a secret shared between men of like minds is a delightful thing. It is only a secret in the hands of an enemy that is loathsome, unsettling and insufferable. But these were two men who only believed in open Government only by and for like-minded people. They presented no ideological challenge to one another, and so there was really nothing to discuss. In lieu of discussion, there was merely an exchange of compliments. The absence of *ideological* challenge does not of course imply the absence of challenge of other kinds. Between such men, there is always the race to what they perceive to be The Top, in which all is counted fair – as it is in false love and very real war.

But right now all was peace and harmony between James Sedley and Charles Baxter, and, as they continued to exchange compliments, Adam Sedley left them to join John Burgess, who had at some stage earlier made his way over to the large bay-window overlooking the extensive garden beyond. Burgess looked through it into the creeping darkness, though clouds were still discernible and the tall silhouettes of unmoving cypresses could be made out against the vault of heaven.

'Peaceful out there, isn't it?' remarked Adam Sedley.

'Hmm? Oh, yes, yes. Quite peaceful.' Burgess seemed further away than Bournemouth.

'Care for a stroll? It's dry and the air seems ...'

'Oh, yes. By all means.' Burgess seemed very grateful.

~ ~

It was indeed peaceful. The rain had stopped and the vegetation gave off a pleasing aroma. Adam Sedley breathed deeply.

'It's a beautiful garden, and so well-kept. I must thank you for that – oh, and I was impressed too by the graveyard – graves so well tended and the grass nicely trimmed.'

'The graves? Oh, yes, well, we have someone to do that – although the older graves in the bottom end look fairly poorly,' Burgess remarked.

'Even so, they fare much better than many – I mean the cemeteries left in the care of private landlords – so neglected, the stones barely visible amongst the weeds ...'

'Awful. Yes, awful,' sighed Burgess.

'The darkness of our times,' said Adam Sedley. 'The darkness of our times,' he repeated, in a barely audible mumble.

'Quite so. Quite so,' said Burgess, whose mind was clearly elsewhere. 'You know, it's strange, most strange, being here in this garden, as though I'm noticing it for the first time. Well Olive, my wife, took much more interest in it than I ever did, and we had a gardener in to keep it up a bit. But I never seemed to notice it. Not as I do now, at this moment. It's almost like a person you've always taken for granted and never really known – and then, suddenly, that person is revealed to you – new qualities, new depths.' He paused and sighed. 'I often think how little I knew Olive. She was taken too much for granted, my Olive – like this garden. Perhaps it's inevitable, do you think? – taking for granted those people and things you love. Sad.'

'Well, so much is taken for granted and in so many ways, by most of us. Seems to be a human trait, and maybe very little good comes of it.'

'Quite so. Quite so. Well!' said Burgess, as though snapping himself out of a trance. 'I had thought I'd be able to manage to slip away from it all without much thought or feeling; dissolve into the ether, with all my thoughts, feelings, memories, past misgivings all wrapped up neatly in a suitcase – to be opened in Bournemouth at leisure, if at all.'

At that moment, Adam Sedley thought he knew far more about Burgess then before. It's as though the few words he had uttered had revealed another man, far less bumbling and dithery, far more pathetic and feeling, than he had reckoned. Burgess's initial assessment of Adam Sedley hadn't changed, but only confirmed: he was intelligent, of that there was no doubt, and impulsive – perhaps too impulsive for his own good; but time would tell, as it tells all things.

'It was thoughtless of me to invite you here. I never realised ...'

'What? Nonsense!' said Burgess, good-heartedly. 'I wanted to come. After all, I wasn't obliged to. It's not easy to leave a congregation you know as well as your own face – especially a diminishing one!'

'Nor *vice-versa*, it seems. They're all reluctant to let you go. I thought it might be fitting if you were to appear to make your final farewell as a member of your own flock, so to speak. But I'm truly sorry if ...'

'As I said, I wanted to come. In fact, wild horses couldn't have prevented it, and I'm glad, *most* glad!' returned Burgess, smiling affably. The new incumbent smiled in return.

'I ... I have something of a confession to make,' Burgess went on. 'I was not quite sincere – I mean when I said I enjoyed your sermon. I'm afraid I was far away most of the time. Lost in thought. Day dreaming. I hope you're not offended.'

'Not at all. Perhaps I should feel flattered if anyone managed to listen at all – we'll have to see about that,' said Sedley, with a chuckle.

'In fact,' said Burgess, unwilling or unable to share the joke, 'There were one or two things about it that er ... well, worried me a bit; but perhaps I shouldn't say that.'

'No, not at all. I value your opinion.'

'Well, as I said, my mind was elsewhere most of the time, and maybe I've got it all wrong. But when you said the Christian Message has nothing to do with the Life Hereafter, at least I think that's what you said, I er ...'

'No, that's right. That's what I said.'

Burgess had hoped for a different response, to be put right, to be told that what it might have sounded like was not at all what was intended. But Burgess knew better, and a succinct, definitive, unambiguous response is all he got out of him.

'Yes, well, it's a bit misleading, isn't it?' The word 'misleading' was not the right one, and Burgess knew it; but if it passed muster, it might suggest a flicker of hope that the notion of the Life Hereafter was not entirely thrown out of court.

'It's like what you said earlier about things being taken for granted – that goes for meanings as well. People take it for granted that words mean what they want them to mean. If the Life Hereafter is taken as a continuation of life somewhere, it's bunkum, and no amount of wanting it to mean something can change that.'

'But you're robbing people of incentive,' said Burgess, meekly.

'No, I'm robbing them of nothing that actually means anything. The Christian Message is one of love, and love has no incentive beyond itself. Can you persuade someone to love music even? Virtue is its own reward, and the love of one for another doesn't hang on anything outside it.'

'But the Resurrection ...?'

'But do we really understand what that means? Christ is surely not referring to longevity! Whatever Christ was saying, it wasn't a contribution to science. Love is eternal because there is nothing outside it on which it depends. It's unconditional. It's eternal, because it's undefilable, untouchable, pure, indestructible; and so then is a life lived with love; death can't touch it, can't defile it or undo it – but that doesn't mean that a person who lives such a life cannot live; human beings aren't indestructible, as well we all know; to think that they are is sheer superstition, and one that can get in the way of things that really matter, because it puts a condition on love, which must be unconditional. It just makes no sense to attach incentives to love, because then you make it what it is not – *conditional*. This is what I'm trying to get across – but I ...'

'But you agree this is purely a matter of interpretation,' put in Burgess quickly, while at the same time nodding slowly at the ground, as though he were thinking desperately aloud.

'Interpretation? Oh, yes, yes. Yes, of course,' said Sedley, after a pause and in a tone of sad resignation, as though he had reached an impasse which indicated that nothing more should be said on the subject, and as though he had said enough, perhaps even too much. The last thing he wanted to do was to make a sad man sadder than he was already.

'Well,' said Burgess, 'you would have some difficulty convincing your congregation of your interpretation. They come to receive hope. You deny them all hope.'

'Hope of a life after death, yes. Of a better life for them and their children, no; because we should focus on the living, love one another and never cease to show it. Superstition muddies the waters, in some religions more than others. Christianity is in decline; it's threatened by other religions riddled with superstition. It's time to wake up from our dreams and bring Christianity back to where it belongs, from the starry heavens to the market place of life; perhaps one day religions will stop vying with one another and people will stop killing one another in the name of some impossible and deplorable God, or what they *call* God. We really must stop dreaming the wrong dreams. I've made it my mission – at least to do what little I can.'

Adam Sedley was in his stride, speaking intelligently, eloquently and in a tone of some authority. Burgess was in no mood to contest matters further. 'Some dreams are a measure of our grief,' he found himself saying out loud – with no response.

They had walked slowly round the garden, as though in imitation of their conversation, which was equally circular. The huge cypresses began to sway perceptibly in a strengthening breeze. After an awkward pause, which seemed an age, Burgess began again.

'I remember, when I was young, I remember, I wanted so much to see God in everything I did. But that's hard. It's hard to see God in everything you do, even in everything you *have* to do. You need to, well ... how shall I put it ...?'

'Compromise?'

'I suppose so. Yes, compromise.'

'We can do too much of that. We've *already* done too much of that – people like us. It's a bad habit – gets hard to break.'

'Yes, I begin to think I might have enjoyed this garden much better,' remarked Burgess, after another long pause, and having encircled for a second time.

'No doubt you'll find far better in Bournemouth.'

'I really do hope I haven't offended you – I mean, what I said about your sermon.'

'No. That's perfectly alright. Wasn't there something else? You said there were one or two things ...'

'Did I? Oh, no, no. That was all.' It was not all. But Burgess had heard enough to know that this tack could not be either appropriately or successfully pursued. In fact, he wished now that he'd said nothing at all, as he had earlier resolved to do. A critical guest does not expect to win the affections of his host, and he genuinely liked Adam Sedley; he found his enthusiasm refreshing, and Adam Sedley, he decided, was a man of considerable moral mettle, one who would not take umbrage without great cause, who had about him a maturity of mind and feeling that was hard to confuse with any known vice; he was just starting out; his ideas were, to say the least, unorthodox, but there was no limit to the miracles that time could work on the hearts and minds of men, both the ungodly and the godly alike.

'It's getting chilly. We'd best go inside,' suggested the new incumbent. They turned towards the door. 'Oh, by the way, there's one thing I've been meaning to ask you. That old man ...'

'Old man?'

'He turned up during the service and sat in the back pews. Do you know him at all?'

'Ah, no. I don't. At least, I don't think so. You see, there are a few homeless people like that around here. They think there's rich pickings to be found, poor souls – trying their luck away from the more urban areas. Hard to tell them apart. They look for shelter when the weather's against them.'

'Not to worry,' Burgess added, casually.

'Worry?' Sedley smiled.

'Yes, well, it's a bit disturbing, isn't it? Shall we go inside?' said Burgess, somewhat embarrassed.

'Lead the way,' said Sedley, smiling enigmatically. He might have challenged Burgess as to what exactly he was supposed to find *disturbing* about the old man. But it was just a word and had no doubt been used carelessly. Besides, to have questioned him might have meant disturbing Burgess, and Burgess had been sufficiently disturbed for one day. In fact, Burgess had been disturbed most of his life, and there was a limit to the degree of disquietude he could handle at any one sitting.

So, Burgess led the way, and the breeze that had gently rocked the tall cypresses had begun to grow in strength – which caused the branches to hiss, dreading the prospect of worse to come.

~ ~

'Pleased, I'm sure,' said James Sedley, extending his hand after being quickly introduced by Adam Sedley, who then walked off in search of his mother. James handed Burgess a glass and filled it with warm sherry. 'Yes, I'm the father of the new incumbent, if that's the right expression.'

'Quite so. Well, I'm sure your son will enjoy his work here. It's challenging enough, of course – but I'm sure he'll do splendidly,' said Burgess.

'Challenging? Well, it's not the kind of career I'd have chosen for him, myself.'

'Oh, really?' Burgess sounded genuinely surprised.

'No. No, it certainly isn't. Still, it's *his* life, or so I'm constantly reminded. But with a little hard work, he might rise to the top of his chosen profession. We Sedleys are known for our grit and determination. You never know, he might turn out to be a chip off the old block yet.' James flicked imaginary specks of dust off each of his cuffs in turn, as he delivered this inappropriate monologue, as if to lend dignity to the hopes he still entertained, hopes of surrogate achievement which clearly extended to the very portals of heaven itself. If his son was not to receive the honours of the City Merchants, which was infinitely to be preferred, then at the very least he should straddle this world and the next when the honours were conferred by the Almighty on the most worthy of his earthly delegates.

'Yes, a little application and he may go far, don't you think?'

'Well, ... er, quite so, quite so,' poor Burgess agreed, finding himself at a loss to respond in any other way. He then hurriedly took a large silver pocket-watch, which hung on a large silver chain, from his waistcoat pocket. This simple procedure had, on innumerable occasions in the past, saved him from prolonged discomfort in the company of those he could not either understand or take to. On the pretext of missing an unmissable train, he took his leave of James Sedley, and quit the entire scene as quickly as decorum and decency would allow, leaving his sherry untouched behind him.

He took his leave. And no one in that worthy assembly of souls was ever to see him again. He was for many years to come to be found in Bournemouth, sipping tea from plastic cups on the promenade, oblivious to the pretty girls in their flimsy beachwear or the seasonal and vile-tongued banter of youths as they marched past, until time played the same trick on him as it had already played on Judith Sedley's mother: old age and senility forced him into the loving arms of a secluded geriatric hospice. There he remained until the end of his days, slowly but surely degenerating; he would simply sit and stare, cushioned in a tailor-made chair bought for him by his daughter, who regularly posted cheques to the hospice in lieu of visits, which could not be made as often as she would have liked due to the pressure of domestic and professional circumstances. From that throne of distinction he would sit and stare, apparently incapable of memory or reasoned thought, although he was known on occasion to cup his old head in his withered hands and exclaim, 'Oh, dear! Oh, dear!' as though in anguish at the momentarily clear and paralysing recollection of something either done and forever done, or something undone and forever undone. In all fairness, it should be said that his daughter had at first visited him conscientiously once every few weeks, but eventually she gave up these visits altogether, presumably because they were not considered to be worth the inconvenience, for he sat and stared blankly even at her. The poor girl, for so she properly regarded herself, could not bring herself to bear the absence of paternal recognition and thought it best all round to stay away, a decision which she managed to implement with considerable moral strength and singleness of purpose. From a pathetic state of vegetable incontinence, the poor Reverend John Burgess passed over the River Jordan. It is to be doubted whether, in these sad years of steady decline and living extinction, the dear fellow was ever capable of seeing God in anything he did or in anything that was done to him. Finally, one night, not unlike the peaceful, rain-soaked night on which he had stood with Adam Sedley in the garden of the vicarage for the last time, the possibility of seeing God in anything at all was forever lost to the good little man who, in his younger days, had striven, largely in vain, to see his maker everywhere.

But this was all to come. As he took his leave at the vicarage that night in spring, he was, fortunately, blissfully ignorant of the fate that awaited him in a chair geared to the needs of departing souls. He was, indeed, as ignorant of what awaited him as he was of the purposeful stares that Charles Baxter was at that very moment giving Julia Sedley, stares made all the more frequent and intense by the sherry, which still flowed, and the promising pregnancy of spring.

Baxter had engineered his way over to Julia Sedley, where she stood arranging clean glasses on an octagonal table in a corner of the living room.

'Well, I hope you'll enjoy living here,' he said, clearing his throat.

'Oh, hi!' she said, taken off guard by the suggestive look in his eyes, which she could hardly have failed to notice. 'You know, this was meant to be a simple get-together – but you'd never believe it, judging by all these empty glasses and bottles. I don't think we're creating quite the right impression, do you?'

'And what exactly is "the right impression"?' Baxter was determined to miss no opportunity, however circuitous, of starting out on a journey that, with any luck at all, would enable him to arrive at his desired destination. 'Sitting around with long faces, waiting on the Day of Judgement? I hardly think so! Life's meant to be enjoyed, don't you think – the very point you're good husband was making earlier! No, you're creating just the right impression. And not before time, either.' His voice dropped to a near whisper as he took half a step further towards his prey. 'Between you and me, old Burgess has been living on borrowed time here. Oh, he's well intentioned and all that. But we've needed a younger man – you know, with more drive and enthusiasm. And judging by events so far, that's just what we've got. And he's brought with him a beautiful wife, too – and that's a perk I for one did *not* expect!' Baxter was pushing it a little, thanks to an overdose of sweet sherry, mixed with one or two single malts which he had imbibed before leaving home earlier. Even so, he felt confident he was pressing the right buttons, and, in any case, if he was going too far, the sherry would let him off the hook.

'You certainly know how to flatter newcomers,' she said, pretending not to enjoy it, and failing.

'Not at all! You see,' said Baxter, in a mock whisper, 'Burgess, bless his heart, well, he's been lagging behind the times, and that's a fact. To tell you the truth,

I've had to take on quite a bit, what with the committee work and taking the lead when it comes to organising this or that, you know the sort of thing – and, more recently, getting the roof repaired ...'

'You mean, if you hadn't taken the initiative, we'd've all been soaked to the skin today!' They laughed together, which was a welcome indication for Baxter that he had already made quite substantial progress.

'Now who's flattering who?' he said, pleased as punch. 'But seriously, we must get together soon. I make excellent pizzas.'

'Nothing I like better than homemade pizzas – but do you mind if I bring my husband?' joked Julia.

'If you really must.' They both laughed. 'But seriously, you and Adam must come round. We'll arrange it. I'll invite a friend or two. It'll be fun. You'll be doing me a good turn, too. Life can get a bit monotonous around here, to say the very least – especially if you're unattached!'

'You're still single? Oh, but I thought ...'

'Not exactly. Separated. Divorce pending, as they say.'

'Oh, I'm sorry,' said Julia, in a kind of verbal reflex.

'It just didn't work out, that's all. I know it's a cliché, but she, Susan, just didn't understand me at all. She just couldn't understand *ambition*. I mean, it's all very well having the usual stuff that's supposed to make up a happy marriage – but it's not enough. No, there must be something else, some kind of ambition. She thought there was something wrong with that, and I didn't. Simple as that. "Incompatible" is the word, cut and dried. Happens all the time. Luckily no children are involved. A few years have been wasted, that's all. But I'm determined to make up for lost time, believe me. I may be many things, but a stick-in-the-mud is not one of them. We're really coming back to the same thing again: life is short and we must make the most of it – just what your husband was driving at today. Anyway, what about you?'

'Me?'

'I've been frank with you. You can return the favour,' he said, smiling most affably.

'Well, there's nothing ...'

'But you don't strike me as the typical vicar's wife, if you don't mind me saying so.'

'Is that supposed to be a compliment?'

'It's a compliment. No, I can prove it. For example, do you enjoy knitting?'

'No.'

'Do you play bridge?'

'No, I don't.'

'Do you enjoy cooking?'

'Not particularly.'

'Are you famed for your elderberry wine and your blackberry jam?'

'No!' she laughed.

'Have you taken out a subscription to *Church Magazine*, reading every issue with undying enthusiasm on Sunday afternoons without fail?'

'What?' she laughed again.

'See what I mean?'

'You're just having me on,' she said between chuckles.

There was no doubt that Baxter had hit a soft spot. He could make her laugh, and that was a hopeful indication of the road ahead.

'Well, there you are! A typical vicar's wife wouldn't react like that. Now, seriously, do you know where I got my idea of a typical vicar's wife? From old Burgess!' Julia laughed again. 'No, I don't mean the old fellow himself – whatever else he may be, he's definitely of the male gender. No, he used to invite me here to this very room on the pretext of discussing some church business or other. Then he'd sit me down and tell me all about his wife, God rest her soul. Now, what was her name? Oh, yes, Olive. Olive Burgess. What a name! – it sounds like a coastal town.' Julia couldn't help laughing. 'Anyway, he used to go on and on in great detail, as though I was her official biographer. Believe me, the only knowledge I don't have of her is carnal – thank the Lord for that.'

'The poor fellow must have missed her dreadfully,' Julia managed to say between laughs.

'Well, since then I haven't been able to imagine anyone in the role of a vicar's wife without thinking of her as an Olive Burgess – wine-maker, jam-maker, bridge-player and avid reader of *Church Magazine* – a perfect example of spiritual domesticity!'

'That's certainly not me!' said Julia, shaking her head and much amused.

'Point proved, then.'

'You win.'

'Okay, so if you're not into *Church Magazine*, how do you spend your time?'

'I paint.'

'Pictures?'

'Of course!'

'Had any exhibitions?' he asked with great interest.

'Exhibitions! You must be joking. I'm not *that* good. That's one of mine.' She pointed to a portrait over the fireplace. Baxter had received a further cue, and he was about to make the very most of it. His behaviour over the next few moments can best be compared to the display-antics of some strange, exotic and idiosyncratic bird. He walked towards the fireplace, slowly picking his way through the guests; having arrived, he looked up at the portrait, with his head now on one side, now on the other; he then took a backward step from the masterpiece, followed by another; then, taking a step to one side, he craned his neck upward and backward, as though attempting to remove a temporary spinal cramp; he then advanced once again toward the portrait and stood stock still in front of it for a moment or two, and then, shaking his head gravely from side to side, finally threaded his way back to Julia Sedley, carefully sustaining a gravity of demeanour and facial expression as he did so.

'You don't like it,' she said, in a tone which suggested that this was her natural expectation.

'Nonsense! That ... that is *talent*!' he said, wagging the index finger of his left hand for amiable emphasis. 'And if you have any more like that ...'

'Are you serious?' she asked.

'Completely!'

'You know something about art, then?'

'I know you could *sell* pictures like that. I have a *feeling* for such things. A feeling for what's good. Oh, I can't talk to you about art – you know, academically, so to speak. But I trust my feeling, my feeling for what's good, and *that* ...' he said with a backward glance, 'is good! And that means it can *sell*.'

'Flattery, again.'

'No. No, it isn't!' he said emphatically. 'Do you have others? Other paintings?'

'Yes, of course.' Julia had begun to find him irresistibly serious.

'Well, I hope you continue to nurture that talent of yours. Come to think of it, talent is just like ambition, you know. It has to be fed – it grows with encouragement and perseverance. Doesn't it?'

'I suppose so. I spend most of my spare time painting. Adam doesn't mind. He doesn't interfere.'

'Ah, yes. But does he *encourage*? Positively *encourage*?'

'Well, yes. Yes, I think he does.' This sounded more like a denial and was not lost on Baxter.

'I sincerely hope so,' said Baxter, with a knowing nod and in a tone of immeasurable gravity.

'And what do you sincerely hope, Mr Baxter?' Adam Sedley had joined them unexpectedly and, for Baxter, too prematurely.

'Charles, please.'

'*Charles*, then.'

'I was saying that I hope you and er … Julia will join me for dinner one evening for a spot of home cooking.'

'Why not? Delighted! Thanks!'

'Good. We'll arrange something – soon,' said Baxter, glancing at his wristwatch. 'Well, I must be off – be in touch with you soon.'

The Sedleys walked Baxter into the hallway. 'As I said earlier,' he said, 'that er … little incident earlier. We'll keep an eye on that sort of thing.'

'Hmm? Oh, the old fellow, you mean? He didn't do anything wrong, did he?' said Sedley, with something that might have been mistaken for a sigh.

'In a manner of speaking, no. But it's the kind of thing we can do without – rather upsetting.'

'Well, I can assure you, it didn't upset me in the least.'

'Oh, come on, Adam,' Julia put in, 'I'm sure Mr … er … *Charles* didn't mean anything unchristian by that.'

'No, of course not,' returned Baxter in a mildly offended tone. If he was offended, he was also elated. Julia Sedley had not only defended him, but had done so against her own husband. What might have been regarded by anyone else as an innocent desire to appease a guest, struck Charles Baxter as a clear indication of victory over the forces of marital obligation. He had won at least one friend that evening; the future was promising – which is how he saw it; he had, as it were, successfully completed Stage Two of Operation Amorous.

'Do you know him – or *of* him?' Adam Sedley asked.

'No, nothing. But, you see, what I meant was that although we're duty bound to help people like that, the trouble is, they don't seem to want it. They reject any real help – they bite the hand that feeds them, so to speak. But they have no right to be a positive nuisance, I mean bursting in like that without so much as a by-your-leave ...'

'It's our bounden duty to keep that hand extended, bitten or not,' Adam Sedley interrupted.

'Well, yes. Quite,' said Baxter, thrown somewhat off-guard.

'Er ... I do believe some of the others are about to leave. Please excuse me,' and with that the new incumbent walked hurriedly back into the living room and out of earshot, leaving Baxter and Julia alone once again. 'We'll arrange that dinner, then!' Baxter called out after him, but without response.

'He's very sensitive, your husband, isn't he?'

'It's his job to be, isn't it? I thought that's part of what you meant by *being typical*.' She smiled, and her smile took the edge off what otherwise might have been interpreted as an awkward realignment of allegiances and a reaffirmation of marital obligations, and hence a hindrance to the successful completion of Stage Two of Operation Amorous. Baxter was inwardly grateful.

'Well, I'll say one thing for old Burgess: he had a sense of humour, and that's worth a lot,' he said.

'You speak of him as though he's no longer in the land of the living!'

'Well, whether he is or not is largely a matter of opinion,' said Baxter, with mock seriousness. They both laughed, and Baxter felt as though she was back in his pocket again, safe and sound. With his confidence renewed, he felt able to leave, and did so.

Meanwhile, Adam Sedley was saying his farewells to his mother; his father had already left without a word of goodbye and on the pretext of bringing the car round to the door. Adam Sedley and his mother stood in the doorway, while James Sedley sat in the car, flicking at his cuffs.

'I know he wouldn't have come unless you had forced the issue.'

'No, he *wanted* to come,' said Judith.

'Under protest, I daresay. Anyway, we haven't had much chance to talk, you and me. How are you – *really*, I mean?'

'I'm fine. We both are.' She paused. 'It was a good sermon, what I could understand of it. It was strange to see you there, listening to you. I felt, well, for the first time, I felt you'd really made the right choice. I was proud. Honestly. And that poor old fellow, the one who came in from the rain – what a state to be in, and at his age, too.'

'You saw him, then?'

'I'm sure he slept through the whole thing.'

'Didn't they all?'

His mother laughed. 'That's the first time I've laughed since ...' She was interrupted by a quick, impatient blast from the horn. He made to escort her to the car, but she pecked her son on the cheek where they stood, and left him standing there, looking out into the gathering darkness, as the cypresses began to sway noisily and the car moved off.

Chapter Six

The Shadow People

Are there shadows on the hills? Yes, on sunlit mounds, from passing clouds, or when the moon is full and harmless silhouettes abound. Yet, on highways and byways far below, with shadows taking human form and resisting power of light, the bravest of the brave are there dejected, devoid of might.

~ ~

The few remaining guests had left when Adam Sedley closed and bolted the door against the wind that now howled through the cypresses whose long shadows had by now melted into the surrounding darkness. He found Julia sprawled on the sofa in the living-room in a state of comfortable collapse, staring at the portrait over the fireplace. He threw off his jacket, loosened his collar, and yawned.

'Well, that's that!' he sighed, slumping into a large armchair opposite Julia.

'What do you think of it?' she asked, still staring at the portrait. 'I mean, what do you *really* think of it?'

'Think of what?' he said, bemused.

'My portrait, of course. What do you honestly think of it?'

'It's good. I like it. Why?'

'Charles – Charles Baxter – thinks it's really good, very good, in fact. I just mentioned that I paint and he seemed ...'

'Does he dabble, then?' he asked, nonchalantly, as if half asleep already.

'No, but he seems to know what he's talking about.' Julia found herself helplessly poised to tell what she herself regarded as untruths, or half-truths at best – and this is not an uncommon phenomenon in the commuter land of leafy suburbia, or indeed elsewhere, the oddity of which seems all the greater in view of the zeal with which such falsehoods are expressed. 'Oh, yes. He seems to know a lot about art. Quite an expert, really. I was surprised,' she said, despite the fact that, being a woman, she could smell a predator a mile off. 'Mind you, I can't believe what he said about *my* poor efforts.'

'Well, I find him rather tasteless', said Adam, languidly. 'And I seriously doubt whether he's more discriminating in art than he is elsewhere,' he added, little expecting Julia to rise to the man's defence.

'Oh, come on, that's unfair. Burgess doesn't have a bad word to say about him – everything he's done has been in the best possible cause. Everyone I spoke to thinks very highly of him. He strikes me as a bit pathetic really – I mean, as though he's a big man doing small jobs. I feel a bit sorry for him. I suppose you know he's got his sights on higher things?'

'Oh, yes, I know that,' he said, ironically.

'Anyway, I'm glad you invited him.'

'That sort do a pretty good job of inviting themselves.'

'Sort? Oh, come on, Adam! He's harmless enough – just likes to enjoy himself, that's all. Where's the harm in that? He's got a marvellous sense of humour, too. Just the sort of chap you need to jolly things up a bit.'

'The way he went on about that old fellow ...' Adam mumbled.

'I'm sure he was only trying to be helpful and friendly.'

'Helpful and friendly?'

'Yes – it's probably just the way he has of putting things, that's all. Besides, he's bound to have a serious, sensitive side – otherwise he wouldn't be interested in politics, would he? And you above all people, Adam, should try to find the best in people – anyway, that's what you keep telling me!'

Julia continued to speak, but her husband's thoughts were spinning round in his tired head as he lay on the sofa either too exhausted or too despairing to give them vent. Was she assuming, for example, that political ambition is in itself sufficient evidence of *seriousness*, and that seriousness is, in turn, a sufficient condition of moral validity? Didn't it occur to her that someone might be serious and at the same time seriously mistaken, or that he might be sincere and at the same time sincerely stupid, or self-assertive and at the same time morally vacuous? The equation that political ambition equals seriousness equals occupancy of the moral high-ground, would have staggered Plato for one, since he withdrew from political life in the firm conviction that God was not to be found there. No, the equation could not withstand the scrutiny either of logic or of well-documented experience – after all, the sincerity of the Nazi commandant who, each morning smartly after a good breakfast, signed away the lives of the daily quota of helpless human beings, is beyond all question, and his dedication to his conception of progress is a monumental contribution to man's inhumanity to man.

But articulating such thoughts, if they were worth articulating at all, was for another day, another time, another audience. Adam Sedley was tired, and it showed.

'Well, Julia, yes, perhaps he *was* being serious! That's the most worrying thing! "They bite the hand that feeds them" indeed! Well, little wonder if it's a hand in an iron glove – and there's very little chance of your Charles Baxter understanding that!'

'*My* Charles Baxter?' she said, smiling from ear to ear and catching only the last phrase.

'Well, his interest in you was pretty obvious,' he said, trying hard to sound nonchalant.

If there was an answer to this, Julia decided not to give it. She decided to gaze once again at the portrait instead.

'Oh, by the way, I've seen a great colour-scheme for the bathroom!' she said, suddenly breaking silent communion with her masterpiece.

His thoughts raced again. Was she changing the subject because she had a reciprocal interest in Baxter and clearly couldn't let on? Or was it simply that the colour scheme for the bathroom was a vastly more important topic of deliberation? He was only too happy to opt for the latter. In any case, it was totally absurd to suspect his wife of even the slightest indiscretion. This was Julia, after all, and not some casual acquaintance. He was the newly appointed vicar of that parish, and Julia was the vicar's wife – anything else was sheer nonsense. What's more, he had been roundly and justly put in his place. Yes, it was undeniably true – he must try harder and at all times to see the best in everyone, and it was not at all to his credit that he had failed to do so in this instance. He had been properly chastised for his failings; and he would try his best to be glad of it. Meanwhile, it had been a full day, and it was time to draw down the curtain – on Baxter, Burgess, the old man, James and Judith Sedley, Julia and even ...

Leaving Julia to lounge a little longer on the sofa finishing her drink, he began climbing the stairs to bed, and, as he did so, the wind could be heard tearing through the cypresses. In the darkness of the bedroom, he drew back the curtains a little on the window which overlooked the garden below and stared at the motion of those tall, black, shadowy beings that were bent but not yet broken by the repeated and indifferent assaults of nature.

~ ~

He was enveloped in the deep folds of sleep as soon as his head hit the pillow. But it wasn't a dreamless sleep; not the kind of sleep that he had read about in the pages of Plato's *Apology*, where Socrates hypothesises of death as an eternally dreamless sleep and hails it as a great boon. Oh, no. It was a dream that was to haunt him in his waking hours, that would dog his steps, and even define them from that day to his last. Many would have considered it a nightmare, the sooner forgotten the better; but Adam Sedley was fated to remember it, albeit in much embellished form; for it was a catalyst and a beacon, for good or ill.

And in his dream the wind blew fierce. It was a grey-black and stormy night in which the dreamer struggled in unequal contest against the violence of nature, up through the graveyard and towards the heavy doors of the church that was barely silhouetted against the sky, the collar and lapels of his overcoat upturned, his hands buried deep in his pockets, his hair unkempt and blown across his face while the trees and bushes thereabouts hissed in anger like venomous snakes poised to strike. Some force within him contended with the elements and drove him on, in search perhaps of something he had lost or was yet to lose, something he could not, on pain of eternal damnation, afford to let slip away. He moved on, but as though his feet were made of solid lead, each urgent step slower still than the last, and, when it seemed he had made some ground, the rising wind stifled progress afresh and reduced his movements to those of a praying mantis.

Gravestone and sarcophagus were almost lost to sight under the weeds and shrubs that ran wild and covered every square inch of ground in a Sargasso of thorn and bramble, as though the whole place had been unattended for centuries and sacrificed to the whims of the elements. And as he made his slow and painful way towards the church doors, the Reverend Sedley was blown off course, this way and that, by the ever-increasing ferocity of the dark winds, as he fell into the undergrowth, cutting his face and hands in the process, stumbling and falling, feeling now and again some flattened headstone under the shivering grass and shaken bushes, and finding at last his own, with his name emblazoned in letters that seemed lettered in luminous paint: *The Reverend Adam Sedley – In*

Loving Memory. Upward and onward, upward and onward he staggered, until he reached those doors which creaked slowly and dolefully apart on their rusted hinges, as the wind blew him unceremoniously into the sanctum in which lay, perhaps, sanctuary at last – some temporary resting place, or else his mausoleum, he knew not what or which.

Once inside what he had once thought to be the house of the living God, there seemed little to console or soothe him. In the grey light he found there, everywhere and everything was covered by the dust of time and thickly enshrouded with cobwebs, which he began to tear down furiously; but where one was brought down, another replaced it, larger and stronger than the preceding. Covered in dust and webs and sweat, he finally collapsed into the pews, and, burying his head in his hands, sat there motionless, in puzzlement and despair, his face and hands still bloody from the uneven contest with thorn and bramble.

He was suddenly shaken out of this posture by a man in the pulpit above him clearing his throat as if to command attention. He looked up and saw the old man who had earlier that day been the subject of congregational derision. There the old fellow stood in his shabby raincoat, his head bare, his hair and beard snowy white, his eyes dark and deep set, his features sharp, his stare intense – altogether like some white wizard or demon from the realm of fantasy or folklore.

What passed between Adam Sedley and this fantastic figure was equally bizarre, as is the case in dreams; it was sufficiently disquieting and unsettling to wake Sedley in the early hours of the morning, in a bath of sweat, and to prompt him to make for his study and write down what he could remember; he wanted to join the dots, even at the risk of embellishment, to make sense of it all, to capture its essence, come what may. He would get up, carefully so as not to wake Julia, make for the study, sit down at his desk and write it all down, before it all melted away in the routine of the morning. He would recover what he could of his dream, and perhaps discover more about himself.

~ ~

At first his hand shook as he put pen to paper, like one half demented, or like one set on a course irrevocable, but riddled with self-doubt. His dialogue with the old man suffered from an embellishment the extent of which he was unaware and of which he became quite careless. He thought he remembered the old man's accent, but he found it impossible to determine; it fluctuated in his mind from erudite and refined to that of a country yokel emanating deep from the agricultural contours of a countryside of which he knew practically nothing at all; he gave up on the accent, it didn't seem to matter anyway. It was early morning, still dark, and he would do what he could. After completing the dialogue, he pinned the sheets together carefully, put them into a large brown envelope in a drawer of his desk, to be consulted at a time indeterminate. This is where the dialogue was found much later, presumably intact, and was read as represented in full here.

'Why? Why?' I asked, looking up into the old man's face.

'Why *what*?' The old's man's voice was ... well, rich and professorial – erudite, I thought, having about it a ring of confidence and profound benignity.

'Empty! This House of God. Why?'

'Oh, that! Well, it's always empty. Never been otherwise, young fellow – at least, ever since the shadow people inherited the earth.'

'Not true! It wasn't empty earlier. I can vouch for that myself. I was here, y'know.'

'Were you? Well, that's the shadow people for you,' the old man shook his head. You see, however full of them a place is, it's still empty! Like air in a glass. The more there is, the less you have, so to speak.'

'You a preacher? You sound like one.'

'Me? Oh, dear, no.' His voice seemed to change. Now he was a simple farm-hand from the West Country. 'Bless you, sir, no. *You* are a preacher, young man. I am a *Watcher*.'

'A what?'

'No matter. No matter.'

'Well, what are you doing up there, anyway?' I must say, I was beginning to get hot under the collar.

'Now that is no way a man of the cloth should ask a question!' Now his accent had changed again – back to the professorial tone with which he had begun. 'Anyway, *I'll* ask the questions, if you don't mind!'

'You're quite right – I'm sorry,' I said, 'But what right have you ...' I had been sitting, and tried to stand.

'Oh, every right, and well you know it. No! No, don't get up. There, that's right. Y'know, I think we'll get on very well together. Yes, very well indeed.'

I sat back down again and found I couldn't move – quite paralysed.

'But this is unorthodox – *most* unorthodox,' I think I said, sounding more like Burgess than myself.

'Yes, quite. Quite. But not on that account pointless, I very much hope.'

'What on earth are you talking about?'

'Patience! Patience, if you please!' He raised his hand slightly, a hand adorned with a glove, fingerless with the ravages of time and wear.

'If you're going to give me a sermon, you'd better get on with it – I've a home to go to, you know.'

'Now what's the hurry? Afraid of losing something, are you? Or *someone*?'

'Nonsense!'

'Nonsense, yes! Oh, nonsense, indeed! I quite agree. Utter nonsense. No one leaves anyone, you know – if only because no one really *has* anyone. How can you possibly lose what you can never possess? Illogical! Even *you* can see that! It's just that – well, even wise men can be plagued by utter nonsense. I myself was afflicted in just the same way, y'know.'

'Afflicted?'

'Oh, I could tell a story, alright. No matter. It's so much water under the bridge now. All over and done with. All put to rest. Buried and forgotten. Bigger battles to fight, and all that!' The old man sighed, rubbing the palms of his hands together.

'If you like giving sermons, you should enter the ministry!' I thought I whispered this, but the words seemed to echo loudly round the walls.

'Oh, I hardly think so. No, no, they wouldn't have that. No, they wouldn't listen to the likes of me. I wouldn't go down at all well.' Now he sounded like the country yokel again, and much more so than before. 'No, no my dear, my angel, my love, my beauty, my *treasure*!' This last word was uttered in a much deeper voice; I wanted to laugh, but could not. 'No, I wouldn't go down at all well. Y'see, I'd have to conform first, and I'm loathe to do it, yes I am. That's why I am as I am and not ... well, not as *they* are. I am what I am – that's what I am! Yes, my dear, my angel, my love, my beauty, my *treasure*! I am not as *they* are.' Cupping his hands, he said in a loud whisper: 'Not like the shadow people!'

'And now for my first question,' he went on, the professor having returned. 'What did you think of your sermon today?'

'Think of it?'

'I said I'd ask the questions. Yes, how did you rate it? Was it any good? Was it a job well done? Did it get through?' the old fellow reiterated, nodding his head slowly as if to facilitate an answer.

'I don't know.'

'Oh yes you do. You *do* know. Come on. Open up. Be frank. Don't be afraid – though I suppose that's a big ask!'

'It was a first beginning. A start! We all have to start somewhere. What are you insinuating, anyway?'

'Insinuating? Who? Me?'

'You have something to say against it.'

'I didn't say that!'

'You implied it.'

'Oh, now *that's* a word! *Implied*! Better be careful with that one, young man. Anyway, whatever I implied, I implied. After all, it's only a dream, isn't it? I say, it's only a dream!'

'Please come to the point. I take it you *do* have one.'

'Well, you see, that's precisely the difficulty!' sighed the old man.

'I haven't the faintest idea ...'

'Well, that's just it! That's the whole problem – not having the faintest idea what one is talking about. You see, if you're going to talk to people who haven't the faintest idea what you're talking about, and, what's worse, couldn't give a fig about it either, well ... well, it's all rather pointless then, isn't it? Take that fellow Baxter, for instance. Now there's goes a man who hasn't the faintest idea what you're driving at, though he professes to know, and he couldn't give a tinker's curse about it anyway. No, he wouldn't lose a moment's sleep over it. Now you stand a much better chance with Burgess – but, really, they're all much of a muchness. And you know the worst question they can possibly ask you after they've heard everything you can possibly say on the matter? It's the question, *"What is it that I'm supposed not to understand?"* Oh, dear, that question goes right down to the quick, doesn't it? And take Julia, for example ...'

'Now wait a moment! I haven't heard so much rubbish in all my life!' I was livid.

'Yes, yes, yes. I know. I know all about it. But it won't do y'know, my dear, my angel, my love, my beauty, my *treasure*!' said the yokel. 'No, it won't do at all. Y'have to face up to it!'

'But ...'

'No "buts" about it!' the professor put in. 'No, we must pursue this matter honestly and with all the moral, spiritual and logical vigour we possess. With Socrates, we must follow the *logos* wherever it may lead!'

'*Must* we?'

'Yes. Yes, we must,' the professor said, in a tone exceptionally gentle and sympathetic. 'We are, one might say, *doomed* to plumb the very depths of our being.' The earnestness in his voice seemed to affect me like some kind of soothing balm, as though the mechanism had been removed from an emotional grenade, defusing it; but the calm lasted only for an instant.

'But you speak in riddles!' I wiped away the sweat which had formed in beads on my forehead.

The old professor smiled and nodded. 'Well now, where was I? Ah, yes, all rather pointless and disquieting. And they're all much of a muchness. You noticed how they looked at me, how they despised me? I was an embarrassment to them. They didn't know how to cope with me. In fact, I don't think I could have done a better job of putting them out had I been a leper. Had I worn pin-stripes and a carnation in my lapel, they might have tolerated me better – even if I had brought ruin and destruction into their midst.' There was no hint of bitterness in his voice, only sadness. 'Yes, it's all very disquieting,' he went on. '*Most* disquieting. Indeed, I'm bound to ask myself why they bothered to turn up at all. Aren't you?'

'That's offensive.'

'Of course it is. It's meant to be. It wouldn't have any application, otherwise. More to the point, there wouldn't be much good in it, either. But there's good in it. Oh, yes, there's good in it, alright. Why! Christianity itself is offensive, and inevitably so! It's precisely when people try to make it *in*offensive that the trouble begins, when it becomes quite *pointless*, don't you know! Because then it loses all sense, all virtue. Now do you think that's a *riddle*?'

'Well, they did come, didn't they? Here, to the House of God. Surely that's in their favour. I suppose *you'd* advocate an empty church!' Once again, I was losing it.

The professor laughed heartily. 'But, my dear fellow, I've already told you – the church *was* empty!'

'Oh, for goodness' sake!'

'No, truly! Listen!' the old fellow started, in great earnest. 'Truly, it *was* empty! Poor fellow! You addressed a congregation of shadow people. Do you not know where you live? Which planet? Which part of the great cosmos? Do you not know that this, all this, is the land of shadows?' he said, his arms outstretched. 'Yes. Yes, you spoke to the shadow people, and with inevitable results. Yes, the shadow people, who are as much at home inside the house of God as they are outside it. Good fellow! You must understand that these sad creatures have inherited the earth and all that surrounds it. Until you do, you can never understand the difficulty of your task, and if you don't understand the difficulty of your task, how can you ever understand its importance? The task of a good man is impossible. A good teacher can teach the rules of musical composition and he can teach the teachable to play an instrument with competence. But there is one thing he cannot teach. He cannot teach *a love of music*. Do you understand that? But of course you do! I mean, look at you! Exhausted, bloodstained, quite beside yourself with fatigue and desperation. What a state! What a state to be in! Poor fellow.'

'So, I'm wasting my time. That's what you're saying, isn't it?'

'*All* time is wasted. But the question is only how best to waste it!'

'That makes no sense to me!'

'It's simple! Yes, you're wasting your time, but you are doing the very best you can. I find that commendable. *Most* commendable. Nothing more can possibly be asked of you or of any man: you are attempting the gloriously impossible, and that requires courage and, above all, love.'

I could not understand. His words were a puzzle. I sat with my head in my hands. But he continued.

'You want the words of Christ to make a real difference to people's lives, even those who are professedly, even aggressively, not of that faith. But first they must understand them. No, they must *feel* them, deep down and in their heart of hearts – oh yes, they have hearts! And if they feel them, they would make the kind of difference you want them to make. Is that not so?'

'Yes, yes!' I replied, feeling a mixture of anger and impatience.

'Well, let us say so. But now the question is: Can you give feeling where there is not even a *desire* to feel? Where there is desire, the ground is ready to receive the seed. But sow seed on barren ground, and seed it will remain.'

'They pray, don't they? – these shadow people?'

'Yes. The shadow people pray. But you must judge them by their prayers. Did not Plato say that we must pray to have the right desires before we pray that they may be fulfilled? But they pray their mortgages may be paid in full, or for a win on the lottery, or for some kind of self-advancement, for a continuation of their soul-less lives. No matter. It's all the same – their prayers are either self-congratulatory, thanking their God for things they've already got, or else they are supplications, asking their God for things they haven't yet got, as though the Christian God were a mail-order deity dealing always in *things*. Yes, the shadow people pray, but to whom? Who or what is their God. These poor creatures shy away from the light, with no desire to know its source and are doomed to live in the shadows they themselves create.'

'Well,' the professor went on after a pause, '... what does it matter what we say? Words are merely words. Love is what you wish to teach, young fellow, not words. And love cannot be taught. It can only be recommended. Oh, the shadow people have tried to love God through inducement, believing that God is some kind of delivery service – as though *love of Love*, which is what love of God really must be, is not enough, as though there must be something on offer: a promise of immortality, of heavenly gifts, if not here, then in some kind of hereafter, promises of eternal wine, and bevies of beautiful maidens to quench their carnal appetites with divine and everlasting licence, of a paradise they know not where – as if this really were a paradise and not simply an extension of their earthly and selfish desires. The shadow people teach their children the language and therefore the power of inducement, if they teach them anything; and these children never grow out of it but are stuck with it for life – shadows they become, like those who bore them. Shadows!'

'I know all this! Do I not know it? Did you bring me here to tell me what I already know, and know only too well?'

'I didn't bring you. You came of your own accord!'

'But I know all this!'

'You do indeed! Humpf! You are fated either to preach to the converted or to the impossible. The shadow people are impossible, Reverend Sedley, and it is they who have inherited the earth.'

'My task is not to preach to the converted.'

'Then tell me this. How do you teach the beauty of love? Those who know the beauty of love are reduced to a state of inarticulation by their perception of ugliness, by their knowledge of man's inhumanity to man, by man's pursuit of self-interest at the expense of all else and all others, by his unaffordable and unforgiveable mistakes, his blunders, his rank stupidity. Those who know the beauty of love cannot speak but in riddles to the shadow people of what the shadow people know not and can never know. Riddles! And what is more, those who know the beauty of love are *censured* by the shadow people for speaking in riddles! What irony! What intolerable irony! Tell me, Reverend Sedley, do *you* know the beauty of love? If you do, how do you propose to teach it? By example? Are you perfect, then, Reverend Sedley? Hmm? Tell me that – if you dare. But what hope is there in example if the seed must fall on barren ground? And besides example, what is there? There is no argument, for no man can be *argued* into knowing the beauty of love. Then irony is unbearable, because it is impenetrable. Those who know the beauty of love speak the very same words as those who do not, yet what both hold sacred are incommensurate and incommensurable. Yes, true prophets must bleat like sheep in the ears of the shadow people, and die like sheep, unheeded and unknown. You would be better employed attempting to square the circle. Can you teach the blind to see? If not, what are you doing here? What exactly is your mission, Reverend Sedley? And how on earth do you propose to fulfil it – to fulfil a mission that cannot be fulfilled? Tell me that!'

'Have you finished?'

'How many Gods are there?' the old man spoke sharply, as a teacher might test a wayward or intransigent pupil.

'This is nonsensical.'

'How many?'

'One!'

'Splendid! But you must mean only that there is one for you, and another for the next man, and so on ...'

'I mean, there is only one God worthy of Christ!'

'And how do you know that the God of another is the very same as yours?'

'A single tear in the eye of a good man can tell me that! By their fruit are good men known. If the fruit is good, so is the man, and if the man is good, so is his God, and if his god is love, his God is mine.'

'Splendid again! I knew from the start we'd get on very well together. But tell me, if a single tear can say so much, *who* does it tell? Yes, it tells *you*! And all those whose God is the same as yours. But who else? Who else does it tell? Does it tell the shadow people, too? How can it tell *them* anything other than its being a tear? No, no, no. It's clear to me that you just don't know the wilderness through which you have chosen to tread. Here you are, trying to teach the shadow people to love your God! Pathetic! My dear fellow, you dream such dreams as are born in heaven, to which place they must return, still in their infancy.'

'No, I shall not despair! I shall not betray my God!'

'The shadow people will teach you insanity, given less than half a chance,' said the old man. 'Perhaps you are right not to despair. Listen to me: if you merely watch and wait for a better world, the world is already the better for it. Indeed, one can achieve much in this dark wilderness, if one lives but a single day refusing to sanctify the evil thereof!'

'Only by watching, and waiting?'

'What else? Would you shake the shadow people into submission, thereby becoming one of them yourself? By what *means* would you shake them? Would you do violence to them, or threaten them with violence? No, then what, if words fail as words must? Yes, watching, waiting! What else can you do but simply watch and wait, doing the best you can all the while?'

'Speak out! We must speak out!' I cried. 'There are more shadows now than ever before. No, we must speak out!'

'What's that you say? Speak out? Oh, you may *say* what you like. But everything you say must be contained within limits, for you are forever under the watchful eyes of the shadow people – the very people you would wish most to bring to your God. You see, you must play the part that they allow you to play, and that part is clearly circumscribed by such delightful devices as political correctness. Such restraints are hardly new. You are permitted to give to the poor and to advocate giving; do such things and you will be considered a virtuous priest. But this is the trick of it; for while you are permitted to advocate the mitigation of poverty, you may not query its *cause*! You are suffered to declare the equality of all men in the sight of God, but not the equality of all men in the sight of men. You may praise your God, the name you give to love, but you are not permitted to declare him different from and superior to all others, to declare that all others are imposters and monsters of superstition. And all this in the sacred name of political correctness and social cohesion. I say again, the shadow people have inherited the earth, and they will never surrender their inheritance willingly. Still, I daresay, you will strive to achieve the impossible, the conversion of the shadow people. I know you have no choice, being doomed to make the attempt. I know that those who have seen the face of your God can see no other. No, there is no choice for a man such as you but to follow the path of heaven, the heaven that is within him, and bid others follow, too – that, God help him, is his fate.'

'Fate? No, *destiny*! Surely you mean destiny!'

'Doomed I say you are! Doomed to speak to those who will turn their backs on you and your words and make of them what they will against you to bring you down!'

'And let me tell you this,' the old country yokel had returned once more. 'What they did to Jesus – what an act civilised and gentle, compared with what they've done since to all those kind folk who've threatened them with the prospect of heaven on earth – and they'll do it all again and again if need be. Damn me if the crucifixion wasn't a tea party compared with what they've done since, yes and done in the very name of Christ himself, or some God we'd do well without. Oh, heaven's alright if it's on the other side of life – but they won't suffer you to bring heaven down to earth. Oh, no, my dear, my angel, my love, my beauty, my *treasure*!'

'And as for teaching love by example, I suppose you would cite the life of Christ, as the shadow people would expect you to do,' the professor said. But my dear Reverend Sedley, what example are you? What example do you think you set, that like a Pied Piper you will bring the shadow people trotting after you, all thirsting for transformation? Suppose you ask them to give their surplus to the poor and needy – what inducement will you offer when you have deprived them of all the inducements they have come to expect? Will you ask of them what you yourself have not done and cannot do? Your wardrobe is full, Reverend, but what will you give? Who are you to show what love is? What shining, guiding star are you? You, who are yourself ruled by fear! Yes, *fear*, Reverend Sedley! *Fear*! Do you not share the fears of your parishioners, all those who fear the loss of loved ones, in death or in betrayal? Have you a soul to show, or have you lost it already?'

These words were like arrows, aimed well and driven deep. The old man stood there, silent now, and the wind that had swept me inside the church seemed to gain in strength, and a horrendous gust blew through the stained-glass windows above the pulpit, bringing the glass down like a shower of rain in slow motion, yes, like coloured rain. The old man just stood there, unmoved.

'My soul is mine!' I cried in torment. 'I have not lost my soul, and I give it gladly to my God intact! I say my soul is yet mine to give!' I seemed to fall face down.

The wind that had blown out the glass subsided. Everywhere was silent. When I looked up, the glass had been restored, quite intact.

'I should like to believe you,' said the old man, as composed as ever. But consider what you must overcome. Fear, in particular. Remember these lines written of the Buddhist monk who aspires to a life blessed of God:

Son, wife and father, mother wealth,
The things wealth brings, the ties of kin:
Leaving these pleasures one and all,
Fare lonely as rhinoceros.
And rid of passion, error, hate,
The fetters having snapped in twain,
Fearless when life ebbs away,
Fare lonely as rhinoceros.

'Blessed of God? Some God, eh Reverend Sedley? Still, these lines make a point, do they not? Can you live like the rhinoceros, young fellow? Yes, but can you even get close? Can you at least overcome fear of consequence? It's fear of consequence that takes pride of place in the armoury of the shadow people, a weapon that keeps everyone in his place – as it will keep you, Reverend Sedley. Even those who ascend to the pulpit dare not speak too much or too loudly. Ruled by fear, if not by ignorance – oh, what sins are counted wise! For the shadow people believe that no caution should be blown to the winds of heaven; and for the sake of security, paralysis is given a good name and called prudence. Family, reputation, respectability, are things the shadow people hold onto as the shark holds to its prey and are thought mightily wise for so doing. Fear of consequence. Are you free of it, young Sedley? You! You who would aspire to teach by example? Or are you like the man and his luggage? Oh, yes. I can tell you a parable. The parable of the man and his luggage.

'There was once a man who, tired and dissatisfied with his life, decided to change it. He would come home on a Friday evening and prepare his suitcases for departure on the following day. Then, lying awake at night, he would plan what things he needed to take with him. But the following morning he would simply put his suitcases away again and return to his normal routine, only to repeat the same operation the following Friday. Are you like that man, Reverend Sedley? You might yet teach by example if you are a worthy example to follow. A child may fear the dark, and it is you who would tell him to put away his childish fears – for a wise man knows there is more to be feared in the light of day. But you – you yourself are still afraid of the dark, is that not so? And it is true that the world could hardly be a darker place than it is fast becoming. Go, then. Go! Go, go to your wife, who waits for nothing save what man can give.' With that, the old man waved his hand – dismissively, I thought. And disappeared! I found myself climbing into the pulpit myself, shouting after him, 'Wait, wait! In God's name, wait!'

Then I found myself in the cemetery, outside in the cold darkness, scouring amongst the gravestones for some sign that the old man had not deserted me and left me alone in that empty place, devoid of man and God. The wind made its exit, too, and the terrible silence of the grave was lord and master now, a dreadful kingship in a kingdom lost, the watcher having vanished into the magical ether of dreams.

~ ~

Thus ended Adam Sedley's fabricated account of a dream, a dream that was no more than a catalyst of self-examination and an attempted rebuttal of self-doubt, a scribbled catharsis to which, rightly or wrongly, he continued to attach enormous importance.

Chapter Seven

A Troublesome Priest

Shadow people kick and bite and scream against the chastening notes of wisdom's sense of right; they rant and rave, these poor demons of the night, never ceasing 'til their course is run.

~ ~

Scarcely a week had passed since Adam Sedley's remarkable dialogue with himself when he and Julia received an invitation to dinner from the Baxters, which Julia accepted with an alacrity inwardly resented by her spouse. Adam Sedley had convinced himself that Charles Baxter was a man to be avoided; but it was hard to argue the case with anything that was proof positive – or sufficiently compelling to satisfy Julia. There seemed to be no alternative but to go through the motions, and perhaps, with any luck, the liaison between the Sedleys and the Baxters would end with a whimper as innocuously as it had apparently begun. Besides, Adam Sedley might feel that Charles Baxter was something of an undesirable alien, but then undesirable aliens are by no means an uncommon phenomenon, and if you were to shake the dust off your feet at every objectionable encounter, you might as well give up walking altogether; moreover, it was the bounden duty of Godly men, insofar as they are indeed Godly, at least in theory, to seek the company, if not the intercourse, of all those who were not yet whole in spirit. Had not Christ come to heal the sick? Was it not misguided, though admittedly infinitely easier, to preach to the converted? Besides, it was difficult to counter Julia's insistence on the complexity of human nature and the well-documented unreliability of appearances and first impressions. Might it not be the case that Charles Baxter was a truly *feeling* creature, one whose hypersensitivities were rendered a trifle more bearable by a certain brashness, not to say callousness, of outward demeanour, as though he were employing a shield of insensitivity in self defence against the arrows of an outrageous surfeit of sensitivity, in much the same way as trench-humour is said to function as a survival tool when the Grim Reaper stalks so successfully abroad and threatens you with dark eternity every painful second of the day and night, with every rifle crack and mortar salvo? Could it not be that Baxter's brashness was, when the inner curtain of the man was drawn aside, simply more apparent than real?

In any case, there was one mitigating factor.

The arrangement had been made by phone between Charles Baxter and Julia Sedley, but he had distinctly extended it from himself and his wife, Susan! Yet this was inconsistent with what was claimed to be common knowledge, namely that the Baxters were separated pending divorce proceedings. Surely, they wouldn't dream of reuniting simply to keep up appearances for the space of a few hours! What's more, Baxter had himself expressly reported their estrangement to Julia. No, there could be no question of a temporary dissemblance. Sedley convinced himself that there could be only one feasible explanation: the Baxters must be mutually reconciled, and an invitation from a couple reunited in marital bliss could hardly be turned down on a whim or a gut-feeling concerning Baxter's predatory nature – a fear that was anyway doubtless quite mythical. Baxter's brash and objectionable sentiments might also be put down to the stresses and strains of domestic upheaval; now that his vessel was once again on a more even keel, a far better Baxter might be expected, one who would confound all Sedley's fears; and – who knows? – they might even become the best of friends, given a proper chance.

Or so Julia was quick to argue, leaving her spouse to grunt his approval. Adam Sedley was left to secretly ruminate on the possibility that a Charles Baxter civilised, even moderately, by a woman, was infinitely preferable to a Charles Baxter unchained, ravenously on the prowl and boringly self-assertive.

~ ~

The reconciliation theory was eloquently confirmed over an aperitif.

'This is,' explained Charles, his smile belied by his eyes, which seemed to lack all lustre, 'something of a special occasion.' He nodded towards Susan, whose smile and eyes had not made up their minds to act in unison, either. 'Yes, well, Susan and I have decided to make a fresh start.' Susan nodded. 'Mind you, I say this with some embarrassment – I mean, our little domestic problems have become sort of, well, common knowledge in these parts – bad news travels fast. But it's true, we've had some issues – no good saying otherwise. Yes, but we've managed to iron things out – we've come to a new understanding, as they say. I'm sorry if this is a bit embarrassing for you, too – but I thought, we *both* thought, it'd be best to put you in the picture, as it were – I mean, just in case you were wondering, er ... anyway, our all being here like this, as I said – it's really a celebration – well, a *double* celebration, really: welcome to the parish!' He raised his glass, which was not the first.

Baxter spoke with a rapid and unfaltering fluency that seemed strangely inconsistent with sincerity, and with a mock solemnity of style more suited to the party political rostrums of a time most people old enough to remember had by now relegated to the dim and distant past. Had he burst out laughing at himself, it would have seemed quite natural and appropriate and everyone might have shared the joke which traded upon an intentional pomposity of style. As it was, Adam Sedley was left pondering the relative advantages of declared and all-out war, on the one hand, and 'a new understanding' on the other, so insincere had Baxter's announcement seemed to him, and so unlikely its author as a candidate for re-election to the seat of domestic harmony. Julia, however, was content to remain on the surface of calm waters, so convinced was she that in human nature all things are possible. Besides, she of course noted that Charles smiled at Susan and Susan smiled at Charles, and she was content to assume without question, at least *pro tem*, that an exchange of smiles is more than enough to counter a dossier of incriminating evidence. Adam Sedley, on the other hand, was all too ready to give cynicism a head start, and remained unconvinced, preferring, despite his collar and vocation, that in this case it was a question of guilty 'til proven otherwise.

During the main course, Susan and Julia spoke chiefly of cooking and clothes and holidays abroad, these topics persistently vying for first place, while Charles eventually managed to get a word in edgeways by extolling the virtues of life in the city as distinct from life in the countryside, the former being more vibrant, the latter too slow and apt to cause atrophy. Adam Sedley smiled and nodded his way through it all, until, that is, the reference to the countryside eventually led on to childhood reminiscences, a theme to which he felt sufficiently inspired to contribute; so relaxed did he become that he was moved to temporarily abandon his predisposition to remain mildly aloof and quietly in the background.

'Oh, yes,' mused Sedley, after dinner, relaxing in a cosy armchair while Baxter poured him a light sherry. 'I called it Zulu Hollow.'

'Julia?' said Baxter, pouring her a sherry, too. 'No need to ask you, my lovely!' he chuckled, as he filled Susan's glass. 'I'm sorry, you were saying ...'

'I was saying, I called it Zulu Hollow. Yes, I must've been about twelve or thirteen or thereabouts. I used to roam about on the hills – not far from where we used to live at the time. It was a lonely place, I can tell you. No life at all, except for the skylarks and a few sheep – wide expanse of fern and short grass, gently rolling hills – seemed never-ending. Anyway, there was ... I'm not boring you, am I?' Sedley had noticed Baxter smiling at Julia.

'What? Oh, no. Not at all,' said Baxter, then mumbling, 'Didn't know they have ferns and sheep in Zululand!' as he turned quickly to Julia and back again.

'There was,' Sedley went on, doubtless not having heard Baxter's sarcastic quip, or perhaps hearing it and not caring a jot, 'There was, well a sort of circular hollow where the grass was relatively short. I suppose it couldn't've been more than about twenty-five feet in diameter ...'

'Not twenty-five feet high?' quipped Baxter with a grin, again turning swiftly to Julia, to Susan, then back again. But the barb failed to stick where it had been aimed. Sedley was being transported back in time, as though he were sitting inside a time machine and everything outside the machine was indistinct to eye and ear as the years rapidly rolled back.

'... and there were no ferns at all inside the hollow, but they grew round the edges, making the place look as though it'd been designed, man-made, and not just an accident of nature, y'know? Well, anyway, as it began to grow dusk, I would stand right in the middle of that hollow, and I'd be scared to move or make the slightest sound. I'd imagine a sudden, frenzied attack by a horde of painted warriors, beating their spears on their shields and yelling like mad – no, not yelling – chanting, like a death chant. And there was no escape. The fact is, I'd scare myself to my wits end – I'd even get to the point where I could actually hear and see them bearing down upon me out of the growing darkness. Then, I'd rush home, running all the way without stopping, almost feeling the points of their spears in my back as I ran. But it's funny, y'know – because not long after reaching the safety of home, I'd long to be back there, back in the hollow. The place was magic to me – white magic or black magic, who knows? But it was magic – just magic. And do you know, a couple of years ago, I revisited that place, that same hollow, and nothing had changed at all – even after twenty-odd years. Strange, isn't it?'

'Yes, yes it is,' said Susan, who had been listening intently.

'First time I've heard about it!' said Julia, smiling round at the others.

'Strange, you say? I don't know. It's a good thing we're not psychiatrists! I wonder what they'd make of it!' Baxter put it. Sedley had said his piece, and Baxter was not prepared to stand backstage much longer. 'Truth is, it's probably not strange at all – just a memory, that's all – we all have them y'know!'

Baxter's dismissiveness made a more than usually unfavourable impression on Sedley, because he was in fact for the first time giving a public airing to a memory that had stuck to him burr-like since those childhood wanderings in the hills – those very hills that had been revealed to him by Uncle Alan. Dear Uncle Alan, who had spoken to him about the Roman legionaries patrolling the hills and byways of this green and pleasant land, dressed in their gleaming armour and holding their Eagles aloft. It was Uncle Alan who had first stirred his imagination, until at last he was able to do the job himself on his own lonely wanderings, substituting Zulu impis for Roman soldiers. To be so dismissive of imagination seemed unintelligent, and also an affront to Uncle Alan, and to all those like him, and lord knows, their number is hardly legion. No, the memory of Zulu Hollow was like a ghost which would not lie still; and had he been told that it was to Baxter, of all people, and not simply in Baxter's presence, that he would rattle the chains of his beloved spectre, he would have found it easier to believe in autumnal fairies. For he knew that such secrets were treasures, rarely, if ever, to be revealed, and only then to like minds.

The fact is that during Sedley's narrative Baxter's attention had been drawn magnetically to the immaculate form of Julia's long legs, which were deftly unhidden by a loosely fitting black gown with a slit down one side which tantalisingly terminated at the knee; the admixture of feminine charms and, by then, half a bottle of sherry had put to a most gruelling test all his powers of dissemblance, as he endeavoured to nod, unconvincingly and momentarily, in Sedley's direction: Baxter's eyes would sweep round the room, like a panoramic lens, as if he were trying the get his head round the profound and veiled insights contained in a deeply mystical narrative, when in fact the movement was much more purposeful than reflective, resembling an arm of radar which would bleep whenever it encountered a solid object, to wit, Julia's irresistible architecture.

'Anyway, after all this time – I mean, I thought it would have changed by now – grown over or something. But it was just as I remembered it – or *think*

I remembered it – memories, how far can you trust them? They can be such tyrants.' Sedley knew his memory was accurate – he was as certain of the details as he was of his own name, but he just said it, anyway.

'There you are! Maybe it's not a memory at all! Maybe it's just ...' Baxter had grasped at some kind of straw.

'But I'm glad it hadn't changed' Sedley quickly put in. 'I mean, the place might've been swallowed up by property developers or ...'

'Oh dear! You don't think much of them, do you? They provide housing, don't they? That can't be a bad thing, can it?' Baxter's blood was not up, but he had smelled blood and was ready to probe. His words were carried on the mitigating wings of laughter, which was just as well.

'You know, I actually began to feel threatened as I stood in that hollow again – yes, I began to feel afraid – after all these years – in broad daylight – and me a grown man! Still, I was glad to get away. Odd, isn't it?' Sedley wasn't addressing Baxter or indeed anyone in particular. But Baxter responded in a perfunctory sort of way.

'Odd? Oh, quite! Yes, I suppose so!' Baxter's eyes were restless again.

'I suppose you never had that kind of experience, then?' his spouse inquired.

'Me? At that age I was safely packed away at boarding school. Didn't have much time for running about the hills. Good experience, though – boarding school. Yes, they certainly knew what they we doing when they packed me off there. That investment paid off, and no mistake. Tough life, but I've never regretted it. It brings you out – fast. Stands you in good stead.' Baxter took a large sip of sherry, as if in memory of his coming of age.

If the implication was that running round hills and feeling threatened by imaginary Zulu warriors on the hills of England had precious little to do with the growth of maturity in masculine youth, and that Baxter himself had been rescued from such idle imaginings by his beloved and selfless parents, who were now in consequence revered as shining examples of parental wisdom and foresight, the point was not lost on Adam Sedley. It was perhaps a blessing that Sedley had begun to feel rather amused by the pomposity and arrogance of the fellow who now appeared rather ridiculous, almost like someone who had suggested that someone of literary talent would have been better employed in the shoe trade than in the embellishment of myth and fable. Baxter was beginning to appear as a kind of Alice-in-Wonderland character who, when asked the time, gives a completely irrelevant answer. After all, how on earth could the free exercise of imagination be deemed inferior to incarceration inside the walls of an academic institution? Or again, how on earth were they mutually exclusive? What on earth was the connection? Sedley was almost visibly amused by the thought that if boarding school had brought Baxter out, it would have done far better to have left him *in*. Naturally, he kept the joke to himself. He began the reflection that such institutions might at last begin to justify their existence if they were to leave certain people *in* and thereby earn for themselves the eternal gratitude of right-thinking men and women. This amusing and entirely improbable idea sprouted wings and flew, never to return, as Baxter got up and offered to refill glasses all round, an offer that was declined, except by Susan and Baxter himself.

Julia and Susan had lent only half an ear to this latest masculine banter. They had, for the most part, exchanged the usual banalities, ranging from the decor in the immediate vicinity, which Susan repeatedly argued had to be 'seen to', to the cost of living in general and rising property prices in particular; it only remained for some appropriate references to be made to the weather for that time of year. Yes, conversation was definitely sagging, despite the sherry, and a large troop of cavalry was called for from over yon proverbial hills. On they came, sabres flashing and bugle blaring, and Colonel Baxter in the van.

'Now what's all this?!' he exclaimed, almost shouting, but with a smile, and with a sparkle in his Cambridge-blue eyes. 'This won't do at all, you know! No, not one little bit! Since when have we all converted to Islam? Men in the men's corner, women in theirs! I know we're all going that way, God help us! – but for goodness sake, I thought you ladies were all against gender apartheid these days! Yet you practise it on your own home ground!' He laughed, as good-naturedly as he could. 'Tell me, is this what equality for women is all about? The suffragettes must be rolling in their graves at a rate of knots!' he said, turning his chair to face Julia and Susan squarely, with Sedley following suit. 'There, that's better,' said the colonel, fully in control of the field once more.

They had scarcely managed to compose themselves when Baxter and Julia were talking animatedly together, while Sedley and Susan, rather than vie for second and third fiddle, seemed content to listen, politely nodding or shaking their heads when appropriate. The subject of their gripping dialogue was Julia's artistic talents and how best to make them known to the world at large, and, in particular, that portion of it that had, like Charles Baxter, a nose for extraordinary artistic merit. And all Baxter had to do to secure Julia's attention, to say nothing of her affections, was to pepper his dreary suggestions with a few big names. Oh, yes, Baxter had done his little bit of research. 'Now take Van Gogh, for instance, or Rembrandt for that matter...' Julia was only too pleased to take them. Pretty soon, even her own name, Julia Sedley, began to take on a lustre hitherto lacking, with such a roll-call of august personages. In all this, the twin concepts of ambition and drive, persistence and endeavour, self-belief and undying hope, figured large, and, judging by the occasional swift glance Baxter was giving at Adam Sedley, which punctuated the advice he was giving to Julia, it seemed that exhortations in their favour were aimed as much at Sedley as his better half, as though he were a creature from another planet and was being taught for the first time the importance intelligent humans attached to such stimuli to success. 'Indeed,' said Baxter at one point, 'a life without ambition isn't worth living; wasted; a candle unlit, so to speak.' (This prompted Sedley to remember the dictum attributed to Socrates, that an unexamined life is not worth living – but Baxter had already moved on, and Sedley said nothing.)

During Baxter's profound analysis of the meaning of life, Sedley stared at a point marginally above Baxter's head, unable to bring himself to observe the sage's facial expressions, which seemed to become more extravagant as time and sherry flowed past in delightful unison. Sedley's eyes focused on the magnolia wall; he wondered whether the small spot he saw there was a hole, a mark, a shadow, or an insect; insects brought flowers to mind, flowers roses, roses his father, James Sedley – then he thought how his father would lap up all this stuff about ambition, drive and getting places, and ... but if the spot were a hole, he wished he were an insect or a fly, that he might crawl through it and escape all this banter, all this posturing.

After what he judged to be a respectable lapse of time, Sedley glanced demonstrably at his watch and smiled at Julia, in a bid to bring this torture to a well-deserved conclusion. The prospect of losing Julia to Sedley's bed, and the bed of a mere vicar at that, proved too much for Baxter, who was now obliged to focus his attention on Sedley in a bid to prolong the evening as far as discretion might possibly allow. It was an opportunity, therefore, to offer coffee and tea, which at least signalled that the end was at last in sight and could not be too long in coming.

'Do you work in the city all the time, then?' asked Julia, as Susan poured the coffee from an expensive ceramic jug. The fact is that the Sedleys had not yet succeeded in discovering just what it was that Baxter did for a living, despite making the occasional enquiry amongst parishioners who had managed to bring his name into the conversation. He was one of those people who managed to keep their livelihoods a secret by creating an aura in which it seems indecorous, or at any rate irrelevant, to satisfy one's curiosity.

'I commute daily to and from The Big World. It's a relief to come home after a hard day's work, despite all the virtues of city life. Weekends are, in particular, well, shall we say *restful?*' he said, stressing the last word with a sigh and putting his hands behind his head, assuming a laid-back posture.

'When you're actually here to enjoy them, you mean,' said Susan. Sedley expected to see her smiling, but her face was expressionless, if not sour.

'Does you work take up your weekends, too?' Julia asked.

'No. Well, yes, sometimes I find it convenient to stay up in the city. Friday evenings especially. Commitments of the job, y'see.'

'That's what you call it, my dear!' said Susan, trying to sound quite casual, but again with no trace of a smile on her expressionless face.

'It's called dedication and industry, my lovely!' retorted Baxter, with an attempt at an amiable smile.

'Of course,' said Susan, dryly again.

'My dear wife is sometimes suspicious of my doings, which naturally I take to be an *overt expression of excess affection,*' returned Baxter, using a phrase he'd read in a magazine article.

'Very impressive, I'm sure. My husband has an answer for everything. But it pays to be alert, don't you think, Julia?' she said, turning to her guest.

'John Burgess sang your praises the other day, saying you had great organisational abilities,' Sedley found himself saying something he would never otherwise have said, in an effort to turn the flank of an awkward, embarrassing and ridiculous exchange. ('If this is reconciliation, I'm Whistler's aunt,' he thought.) It almost succeeded, too, but not quite.

'Charles is very good at raising money, you know,' said Susan, so dryly that it sounded like a reproach. She seemed determined to bring something to a head and that she had chosen, with or without premeditation, this delightful occasion to expose a charlatan – no doubt due to the growing influence of sherry over the wisdom of discretion.

'For which you are eternally grateful, my lovely!' he retorted, for the first time raising his voice as if to say enough was enough. Susan simply raised her eyebrows and fell silent; the message had been received.

'Oh, by the way,' said Baxter. 'Have you read that bit in last night's standard – about the old man? The chap who ...'

'Yes, that's right – you remember, that poor old fellow who came into the back of the church!' explained Susan.

'Anyway, they found him in the river,' said Baxter.

'Dead?' Sedley asked.

'Dead, yes. As the proverbial ...'

'You can't say that,' said Susan.

'What? Doornail?'

'You can't say it was definitely him!'

'Well, he fitted the description!'

'What happened to him?' For the first time that evening, Sedley seemed interested in something.

'Well, nobody knows. They're asking for witnesses. Probably had one too many and fell in. It wouldn't be the first time ...' said Baxter.

'Nor the last,' Sedley mumbled, as if thinking out loud.

'You look as though you could do with a stiff drink. Wasn't a relative of yours, was he?' Baxter joked. 'Sorry, that just came out,' he added. Susan looked at him as though he were something the refuse collectors had forgotten to take away. It was a look he had failed to notice as he got up, picked up the newspaper and walked back to his chair.

'Ah, here it is. "He had a photograph in one of his pockets," it says – family group by the look of it, wife and child – maybe. Years old though. And, as you say, Watson, it may not be him after all! But I think it is. What d'you think?' He handed the newspaper to Sedley.

'I don't know.' Sedley spoke quietly and seemed far away as he strained his eyes over the photograph. 'Doesn't look much like him, but then ... it must be years old, as you say. Yes, hard to say.'

'I suppose they printed it hoping someone can identify him,' said Susan.

'Brilliantly deduced, Watson!' said Baxter. No one was amused. 'Oh, it wasn't the only thing they found in his pockets, either. I was talking to Tom Lawton, *Inspector* Lawton – good friend of mine – in The Green Baron. Anyway, he happened to mention the thing. He described the old fellow and asked whether I'd ever seen him around. Well, from what he said I guessed he was the same chap who bounced in on your sermon. Of course, I said I hadn't seen him before in my life – hadn't a clue sort of thing ...'

'Why?' asked Sedley.

'Why what?'

'Well, why didn't you say anything about your suspicions? – that he might be the man who ...?' asked Susan.

'Why? Well, because I might be wrong, as you say my lovely. And in any case, it's best not to get involved in this sort of thing – never does any good, and it sure as hell wouldn't do the old fellow any good! ... Anyway, being in the river like that the old boy was in a bit of a state. But they found his overcoat, Tom was saying, high and dry on the embankment where he'd left it – his body was found not far off, wedged in some branches a little way down river.'

'Well, it's all very sad,' said Julia.

'Yes, we won't be graced with his presence ever again,' said Baxter.

'Why do you talk like that?' Sedley had by now sufficiently recovered from his musings regarding the photograph to be cognisant of his immediate surroundings.

'What? Well, I just meant ...'

'Yes, that's right. Do say what you meant, because quite frankly I find it offensive.' Sedley spoke calmly and inquiringly, which was all the more disarming.

'Well, look ...' Baxter stammered.

'Charles didn't mean anything, Adam,' Julia said, coming to his aid. 'You shouldn't take everything so seriously. Honestly!' she added, turning to Susan with an awkward smile. But Susan was simply looking down at the floor, apparently willing to let things go, come what might; they were on a raft on rough waters and bound for a waterfall ahead; she had given up, thrown in the towel and was simply awaiting consequences.

'I mean, it was Charles who brought up the subject in the first place,' Julia went on.

'*Quite!*' Sedley said, nodding ironically, as though perplexed, for his tone seemed to suggest a question. After all, who had brought up the subject and when it seemed to have no bearing whatsoever on the matter in hand.

'Now it's my turn to ask you what you meant by *that*?' said Baxter, with an apparent show of good humour. He smiled at Julia, who smiled back. 'No, look, honestly, I just meant that he was dead, that's all,' he added, as if in an attempt to placate some newly awoken god which only a few moments ago had seemed perfectly tractable.

'You mean you wished to tell us what we knew already!' said Sedley. Clearly, tractability was hard to purchase at a reasonable price.

'Oh, come on! I'm sorry but you seem determined to ...' Baxter started.

'This is all a bit silly. Anyway, it's time we were making tracks,' Julia interrupted.

'No, hold on a minute, he's accusing me of something, and I'd like to get to the bottom of it.'

'Fine by me.' Sedley was as cool as an iced cucumber.

'Right! Look, people die every minute of the day and night. If we took everything *that* seriously, we'd ... well, we'd all go crazy. In any case, why am I telling *you* this? You're a man of the cloth. You should know about these things better than anybody. Do you propose to get involved in the personal affairs of each of your parishioners? Of course not! A good doctor can't afford to get emotionally involved with his patients – well, if he did, he'd have to give up medicine! We just can't afford to get involved with every Tom, Dick and Harry that just happens to come along. If we did, we'd *all* end up in the river! Yes, but that doesn't mean I don't care! Well, does it?'

'But isn't that *precisely* what you meant?' said Sedley, calm and poker-faced.

'What!' said Baxter in a tone of disbelief. 'Of course it isn't!' He felt as if he was talking to a schoolboy who persistently, perhaps wilfully, misunderstood – but he stopped short of saying so, thinking better of it.

'Then I'm afraid I'm at a loss to understand what you *did* mean. Julia is right. It really is time we left,' said Sedley, getting up. But there was more to come.

'Damn it! If you're sitting in judgement on me, I have a right to know why,' demanded Baxter. Sedley sat down again, this time on the edge of the chair, as if to spring if necessary.

'Look, just what do you think my job is if it isn't to get personally involved with other people? Do you think it all begins and ends with a bit of ritual, or just wearing the cloth, as you might put it? Just what do you think the Christian message is if it isn't about *getting involved*? You were embarrassed by that old man, weren't you? That's why you said we wouldn't, you meant *you wouldn't*, be graced by his presence again. Because he reminded you of what you can't feel able to do – to get involved!' Sedley's soft-spoken delivery was all the more galling – just like another sermon, this time with a barb which stings.

'Adam!' Julia herself was taken aback.

'No, let him get it off his chest,' said Baxter. The words found their way out; he didn't know what else to say; he was not in control.

'When he "bounced in", as you once put it, heads turned, including yours. By the way, I seem to recall that he shuffled, not bounced, as befitted his age and no doubt his indisposition. Afterwards, you made a point of saying it "wasn't the thing". You even told me not to worry about it. Now why should you think I had anything to worry about? Unless, that is, it was a simple case of self-projection: it worried you, and so you thought it worried me, too. And it was not the old man who worried you, I mean not his being destitute or being homeless. What worried you is that he, "the likes of him", should trespass on your territory and invade your space, that he should have the effrontery to enter your home ground without so much as a by-your-leave, without so much as a knock on the door. But, of course, had he knocked, he wouldn't've been admitted. You felt you had to apologise for him, because he was either unable or unwilling to apologise for himself – and an apology was due because he had offended your sense of propriety. You were ashamed of him, because he was not ashamed of himself. You know, I rather think it's a bit like a man who's been found guilty but who refuses to acknowledge his own guilt, and so you acknowledged it for him. Oh, I admit, you're not alone in any of this, and it's left to the priests of this world to show the compassion that others are afraid or unwilling to show. But even priests fall far, far short of the mark – and I include myself in this judgement, I'm ashamed to say. Yes, I'm ashamed to have to recognise my own shortcomings, my own hypocrisy – but at least I have enough decency to know this, enough courage to say this. I *think*. I *hope*. I don't *know*!'

If there was any merit at all in any of this, and perhaps more than a hint of genuine pathos, it escaped Baxter, who had not, of course, listened to a word of it, devoting the time instead to the preparation of his retort.

'Patronising nonsense!' he blustered, and the torrent of words seem to emerge with the rapidity and thud of a machine gun. 'I'm sorry, but that's what it is. And I expected far more, I must confess. I'm as good a Christian as any man, and, no, I'm not ashamed to say it, better than many who *call* themselves Christians, better even than some men of the cloth, let me add!' With this last remark, he was thinking of John Burgess, but his sense of self-preservation stopped him short of naming names; after all, he was not about to genuinely impugn the very source of the praises heaped upon him; he was prepared to risk much, but not his own reputation, the very thing upon which his definition of himself depended.

'I'm very much afraid you may be right,' Sedley muttered, clearly enough to be heard.

'Now that *is* offensive! I don't like your tone, not one little bit. It's grossly unfair! Grossly unfair! If I don't care for people, and it's *doing* that matters, you know, yes, *doing* – not just *talk* and the odd sermon! – well, if I don't care about people, why should I bother to raise money for church roofs, and why, indeed, did I invite you here this evening?'

'I suspect you know best the answers to your own questions,' said Sedley, as he walked briskly into the hallway in the manner of a man who was determined to shake the dust off his feet, come what might.

Julia followed him, of course. But not without pausing *en route* to apologise for her husband's behaviour: 'Charles, Susan, I'm so dreadfully sorry. He's been under a lot of pressure recently, you know – a new place, and having to adjust ...'

'Think nothing of it,' said Baxter, 'I can assure you, *I* won't!'

'Are you coming Julia?' Sedley was standing in the doorway.

Charles Baxter nodded to Julia Sedley, and Julia Sedley nodded back, as though an invisible string attached them, a pull at one end causing a commensurate reaction at the other.

~ ~

'Well, well, well! And what do you make of that!' said Baxter, appealing to the air, arms raised, as he heard Susan closing the door behind their guests. 'I just don't know what to say!' he went on, as Susan entered the room. 'Childish nonsense! Wet behind the ears! We've got a boy scout for a parish priest. Oh, I'm not saying he's wrong. It's just ... well, it's all too simple. Well, he'll learn. Then again, maybe he won't. Maybe he's just one of those people destined to plod through life in rose-coloured spectacles, come what may. Just like a schoolboy – no practical appreciation of the facts of life at all. "*Involved*" indeed! Well, I'll say this for old Burgess, half-soaked though he was, he knew his job, knew its limitations – yes, at least he was content to live and let live. Yes, come to think of it, he was a good man, Burgess. Can't imagine him getting into a tantrum like that – and all for nothing, that's the best part of it, all for nothing!'

'Tantrum?' said Susan, sleepily.

'Going off the deep end like that, just because I happened to say ... well, it makes no sense, no sense at all. And to think I went out of my way to make him feel at home – part of the community. He thinks he can look after himself – well he'll damn well have to. Under pressure? The only thing he's under is an almighty illusion, and the sooner he divests himself of it, the better – the better for all of us. The last thing we need around here is a troublesome priest, interfering all over the place, a do-gooder, patronising and ...'

'You asked for it. You deserved it!' said Susan, languishing in an armchair. She sounded completely laid-back, as if she felt she might as well have said nothing as something.

'Oh, really? Well, I wouldn't expect much support from you. And so much for our *arrangement*, I think?'

'You *made* it!'

'You *agreed* to it, remember? – and you might at least have kept your personal digs for more private consumption. If we must have them, and I suppose we *must*, you should keep them in the *family* – so to speak.' The reference to family was painful, as intended.

On that note, Susan went to bed – alone, desperate to avoid a resurrection of matters best left where they had been deposited, under the carpet and hidden from view.

The fact is, the Baxters had agreed to attempt a reconciliation, though one proving to be progressively devoid of emotional commitment, in view of Baxter's reluctance to stir the muddy waters of marital discord at a time when his political aspirations were best served by a veneer of marital stability. The fact that Susan's pregnancy was about to become visible, that he felt that he had only a reasonable expectation of having been involved, and that she was unwilling to entertain a termination, were not unimportant considerations in Baxter's own assessment of his chances in what he was to term The Big World. For her part, Susan Baxter was mindful of her spouse's ability to turn base metals into gold, and of the opportunities which such a talent offered for both herself and her offspring. Such were the factors that prompted the Baxters towards a, for the want of a better word, *open arrangement*, in which appearances might be kept up while, at the same time, they might acknowledge, at least between themselves, their mutual incompatibilities; such an arrangement had been agreed upon, with the proviso, spelt out with uncompromising clarity by Charles Baxter in particular, that in the going-of-separate-ways the utmost discretion should be observed, which is why he was put out, to say the very least, by his partner's verbal indiscretions earlier that very evening; quite simply, she had let him down by not playing the part on set as previously scripted.

Certainly, confrontation with Adam Sedley was the very last thing he had expected, and it was poor consolation to say that at least he now knew where he stood with the new incumbent. The problem, of course, was that it made future dealings with the Sedleys more difficult than had been anticipated; the very object of the invitation to dinner had been unambiguously defeated. No, it was important to appear on speaking terms, at least, with the new incumbent. The prospect of now building bridges over troubled waters did not at all appeal to him, for it might make it seem as though he was in the wrong, and he was entirely confident that he was not. On the other hand, he was aware that sacrifices, not excluding an occasional loss of face, were frequently necessary in the theatre of political ambition. Besides, it was worth a slight loss of face, if only to appear a champion of peace and reconciliation. *It takes a strong man ...* and all that. What's more, he was stuck on Julia, whose deliciousness had been slowly consuming him despite his own lecture on freedom-with-discretion. No, it had not been the kind of evening expected. On the other hand, it might yet be turned to his advantage.

After all, it was a question of cultivating the right sort of image, and Baxter knew all about that – none better. If one wishes to achieve maximum sales, product image is not to be ignored. It was elementary, really – too elementary for words: a favourable image has to be devised, projected and sustained; and in selling oneself is it not exactly the same? Yes, despite all appearances, he could perhaps take advantage of uncomfortable and unforeseen circumstances and emerge a man of compassion and understanding, the kind of man which of course truly he was. A stable marriage, with at least all the appearances of stability, was a fundamental step in the right direction – even Susan had understood that.

It was really a question of making the right kind of investment decision. Such decisions can at times be quite painful. He might therefore need to make some conciliating overtures in the direction of Adam Sedley which would, at length, turn up trumps of one kind or another. Who knows? Perhaps one day he and Sedley would laugh together over the whole thing; and he, Baxter, though denied by ambition and consequent discretion, any delightfully carnal knowledge of Julia Sedley, might still manage to reduce the distance from her somewhat and ... well, a man can at least dream, provided he does so with a modicum of discretion.

Moreover, it had to be remembered, reasoned Baxter, that vicars were invariably amiable by nature, content to busy themselves with matters parochial and essentially irrelevant. They were, as a *genre*, uncomplicated, forgiving creatures who made it their very business to cultivate a spirit of simplicity and forgiveness, as they shepherded their imperfect flocks towards the gates of a better life beyond the trials and tribulations of their present lot. Surely, Adam Sedley could hardly be very different from the common run. And so, no doubt it was true that Sedley had indeed been under considerable pressure, just as Julia said; after all, vicars are not known for their resilience and strength of character, what strength they appear to possess no doubt being the effect of a limited imagination and an inability to recognise, much less to handle, the more perplexing and practical difficulties thrown up by the necessities of life, the larger questions of governance, of economic organisation and commercial endeavour; which is why their role is to support, and not question, the political *status quo*. Yes, no doubt Sedley would come to his senses and was probably, at this very minute, bitterly regretting his behaviour earlier that evening, as any reasonable man, and particularly a man of God, most certainly would.

It was with such salutary and comforting reflections that Charles Baxter blissfully fell asleep later that night; not, alas, in the arms of his spouse, but wrapped in the warm embraces of wishful thinking; which felt just as good – well, almost.

~ ~

The short drive home for the Sedleys was more than usually reflective. Julia drove, as usual, while Adam stared out of the window into the darkness beyond. The only bright spot of the whole evening for him was that Zulu Hollow had been brought to mind. As he looked out into the shadowy darkness, he tried to picture a young boy standing stock still, facing an impi army. But he was sitting in a car and married now, and that young boy who thought he held the world in his hands was gone, and gone forever; and those lights he saw outside were not the torches of an advancing enemy, but the street lamps of suburbia. Mundane, perhaps. But he was still a man with a mission, and that evening he had been reminded of it. When Baxter mentioned Islam, it was like a trigger pulled, a button pressed. Sedley had read the Koran and tried hard to find it salutary; instead he found too much that was disquieting, not at all consoling. And then there was Christianity, which suffered from the same common denominator – too full of superstition and overdressed in ritual and irrelevance – it just gave people like Baxter a completely false credence, opportunities to be insincere and boot-licking. Both religions were in need of purification; it was time to defuse the one and revive the other, and bring out the best in both; they needed to be pruned, until the bare essentials were visible for all to see, for all to live by – for the universal message was simple: Be Good! If only everyone could say 'God is Love' and be content with that, the world would be a better place, almost by magic. Religions must not be allowed to pander to the worst in us; they must be divested of all their superstitious superstructures, their pomp, their arrogance, their false promises, their hypocrisy, their sham – all the rubbish would fall away, leaving Beauty glimmering in her robes of simplicity and truth and …

These turgid reflections had to be left unfinished, punctuated as they were by a mundane reality: the journey had ended and the Sedleys needed to fumble about to fit the key into the lock of the vicarage door.

'It was wrong to go off like that, Adam – wasn't it?' Julia said, softly, as they eventually found themselves in the living room.

'Was it? I thought I was wonderfully restrained the whole evening.'

'Well, I think it was childish to make so much of it.'

'Do you? Do you, really?'

'You *know* it was. It's just his manner – his turn of phrase. I'm sure he cared about that old man. Anyway, we haven't been here five minutes and you've offended a pillar of the parish …'

'A man of *consequence*?'

'Sarcasm doesn't suit you, Adam.' There was an awkward pause. 'All I'm saying is that a man like Charles Baxter is …'

'Useful?'

'There you go again. But, yes, of course he's useful. He extends the hand of friendship, and you bite it off. Yes, I know he's a bit … well, in any case, people are different, and thank goodness they are. In any case, this parish had a life before we came on the scene, you know.'

'No doubt,' in a tone of rebuke.

'Okay, so a new broom sweeps clean, and you're the new broom, is that it?'

'What's wrong with a clean sweep?'

'Well, for one thing, new brooms are not generally liked – and you're supposed to be a man of peace, remember? You're supposed to set the right sort of example – you're not supposed to make enemies – especially when we're trying to settle in and get ourselves accepted. We need all the help we can get.'

'Help? I wasn't aware we needed any help. Even if we do, we can do without that sort of help, thank you very much.'

'Maybe *you* can,' she said.

'What?'

'Look, we just need to establish ourselves here, that's all I'm saying. I mean, this is just the first step.'

'First step to what?'

'Getting established, gaining respect, support,' she said, with some irritation and difficulty. 'And you heard what he said – he might be able to introduce me to one or two people who …'

'Ah!'

'Well, don't I count? Can't I have just a few plans of my own. If … when we decide to start a family, I'll be more tied. I mean, I need to do what I can now to … to help me later on. Have you thought of that – or doesn't it matter what I want out of life?' She sounded persuasive, and looked even more persuasive than she sounded. She didn't raise her voice; she spoke gently and gave him the kind of smile that had won his affections when they first met – a piece of magic that Adam Sedley had not experienced either before or since and that had curiously seemed to evaporate over time. But, now, she was suddenly the girl he had first met. The word 'family' was also relevant. If Sedley was the sort of man who feared losing his wife to a more able competitor, though he hoped to God he was not, the mere mention of family seemed to indicate a firm commitment on her part to continue the relationship into their dotage, which was most reassuring. It was almost as good, if not better, than actually saying that she loved him, and the wordless thought that she really did flashed through his consciousness like an arrow of Eros through hot butter. Did she count?! What a question! How could he possibly allow her to doubt it? His was an unmistakeably loving smile as he gave her his warmest assurances.

'Your expectations are a bit too high, though.' She couldn't resist giving him a piece of advice, or what sounded like advice. He nodded, and smiled, and said nothing.

'That old man ...' he began.

'He's really got to you, hasn't he?'

'Strangely, yes. Something about him! You know, the other night ...' He began to tell her about his dream and about all the things he'd written down. But she interrupted him.

'And it isn't just me. I'm thinking of you, too! I want what's best for you, for us!' She sat up straight, held his hand in hers and spoke with a renewed confidence. 'When I met you, I knew straightaway you had something in you, something special, that you weren't content with a drab sort of existence. I felt you were, well a restless spirit – I mean, behind all that quiet reserve – I knew you wouldn't be content just watching the world go by. I'm right, aren't I?'

'Julia, you married a parish priest – a simple parish priest. Surely ...'

'Yes, I know the man I married – and I'm only saying you can make a name for yourself here. Life is what you make it, and you can make it something – I know you can! And it's such a nice place, though a bit on the quiet side for my liking – I mean, if I'm honest – but that suits me in some ways. And there are some very nice people here – Charles, for example – I mean when you get to know him, know him *properly*; and Susan – she's very nice, too. But if you're going to jump at people for the slightest reason and ... and find offence in the smallest thing, well, I mean, it's obvious, just common sense really.' She ran her fingers lovingly through his hair, like a Delilah on slow heat, and Sedley, like a Samson bewitched, was in no mood to contest her conception of common sense. It was late, and somehow too late: you might argue down a point, but you'd be hard put to contest a whole world of difference.

Feelings. He merely had feelings, feelings that were slipping through him, feelings that would not pause for analysis, for he would not dare subject them to analysis; his thoughts would not be articulated, for he wished above all to resist giving them closer inspection. They came again, more slowly this time and in more ordered rank, after they had made love. Oh, yes, they made love alright.

But for him it was an overrated thing which he just managed to execute with some show of enjoyment; he hoped it'd been better for her. No, desirable though she was, his mind was more than half elsewhere. When it was over, he was glad; he was relieved, not as one who loves is relieved to have given and received, but because he wanted time to think things through, all by himself in the silence of that dark bedroom. Never had he felt more alone than he did that night.

Chapter Eight

Of Sheep and Goats

Shadows, like weeds, come creeping; like water, they come seeping; 'til what was once light is shade looming, and what was once shade is now darkness dooming.

~ ~

Sedley's priority over the following days was to prepare the text for his next sermon. He sat in his study looking through the window at the cypresses as their forms began to melt into the greys of gathering darkness. Pleasant though idle postponement was, it was inconsistent with his mission. He switched on the light and closed the curtains, leaving the cypresses to the dead of night. He sat down at his desk.

But concentration was unusually hard that evening. His eyes wandered over to an empty bookshelf, empty save for the framed photograph of himself and Julia, taken just before their wedding. He walked over to the bookshelf, picked up the photograph and stared hard at it, almost as though he was trying to recognise the people pictured there, to form an intelligible link between those days and now, between the happy young man in the picture and the moody, questioning fellow he had become – after all, only a few years stood between them, yet they seemed worlds apart. As for Julia, she had changed, too; at least, she seemed somehow less 'innocent', more outward, and more argumentative, though every bit as guileless in matters affecting their own relationship. No, he preferred just to muse rather than put names to anything – dissection and analysis could be discomforting, gratuitously so. No, things were different, that was all; the difference could be felt, but not entirely understood, and that was perfectly fine. People change, and no one had promised that change would be painless. But Julia had called him 'a restless spirit', and it occurred to him that he should have asked her how she meant it. He certainly felt restless, dissatisfied, discontent, irritable even – and impatient, with himself and with others, and he was far too young to be losing patience at a rate of knots. He felt guilty as charged, whatever Julia had meant by it.

He remembered what he had told Baxter about Zulu Hollow. Yes, there was something about the boy who had stood in Zulu Hollow – something wonderful, beautiful, hopeful, powerful in its innocence, something that was in danger of extinction, if it had not died already. What could it be? Was it not simply the adult longing for the lost and irretrievable years of childhood, for a lost world of innocent dreams – the adult intensely aware of the inexorable passing of time? Yes, but there was one occasion in particular, when he had stood in the middle of Zulu Hollow in the gathering darkness, feeling more than usually afraid, when he promised God that he would never betray him if only he could be delivered out of that place safely and into the fond embraces of his mother inside the warm womb of home and all things friendly and familiar; after his prayer, he bolted home – and then all was forgotten.

Forgotten until now. Sedley smiled at the recollection. Had he kept his promise? Well, he had become a priest. But that was little more than simply acquiring a name or a suit of clothes. Had he not betrayed his God? The smile melted away and was replaced by a frown. He tried to console himself with the thought that it was quite impossible, even for saints, to live so much as one day without betraying the very God they purported to love.

And it was not simply God. There was that young boy in Zulu Hollow. Had he not been betrayed, too? – that boy who was powerful in his very innocence? That boy was gone; dead, one might say; but had he lived in vain? All that power of innocence gone? What had happened between then and now to make Sedley feel less of a man than he was then? For he felt that in childhood he had been a man, and that since then it was all chiefly downhill. Uncle Alan had taken him to the seaside, and he stood on one of those 'I Speak Your Weight' machines, which also spat out a piece of paper on which was written, *You have the courage of your convictions.* He hardly knew what it meant then; but he knew now, and he wondered about it; wondered if it was still at all true. How could you become less of a man the older you grew?

The sermon had to be written. Yes, enough was enough; he would make a start – in a moment or two. He replaced the photograph on the bookshelf, sank back in an armchair next to the bookcase, stretched out an arm behind him and turned on an old radio just above his head. Burgess had left it behind, and the thing sometimes worked and sometimes didn't; it cracked and crackled and condescended to emit a series of more or less intelligible sounds, though not without irritating lapses. It was the news, with its daily diet of calamities:

' … which then gave rise to disturbances involving the police. Petitioners were protesting at …. described as "intolerable cutbacks in health and social welfare services which …" Scuffles broke out when police … The Reverend Richard Lambert, accompanying the marchers … to our reporter John Cunningham … This state of affairs just can't go unchallenged … only last week one of my parishioners took his own life … it's high time the Government was …. understand the terrible social costs entailed by their own policies … the Church has a duty to … Certainly not! The Church can't condone acts of violence but …. atmosphere highly charged. If we are a Christian society … and if people in dire need can't look to the Church for support …'

The radio cracked and crackled, and Sedley was left to ponder the completion of the last sentence. A further crack and crackle, the radio produced this enlightening conclusion in almost pristine condition:

'A spokesman for the Government later commented that while the views of the petitioners and their representatives were respectfully received, it was not to be assumed that the Government was unaware of the unfortunate side-effects of policies which there nevertheless designed and guaranteed to be in the national interest. Moreover, the views of the Church needed to be viewed with a considerable degree of circumspection, since it was commenting on matters on which it could claim little or no expertise …'

And then:

'The Mayor, the Right Honour … attended the opening of a large new mosque just outside the city centre at … hailed as … major step forward and as … in a more tolerant society … and welcomed the …'

Sedley turned off the radio. He pondered the uncompleted sentence, 'If people in dire need can't look to the Church for support …' Sedley took this as a reminder about where he himself stood and the stand he should take. What was the Church, or what had it become that it had no voice, not even for those oppressed and unable to help themselves; what was the Church that it was not permitted to reproach those who, according to its own doctrine, were bending its basic principles out of all shape? And how could it possibly be that the Church was itself reproached while under threat from an alien religion that, to all appearances, and in the minds of so many of its own adherents, was a blueprint for totalitarian horrors and the total subversion of democracy? How could it possibly be that the Church was in decline while a religion that is a hotbed of intolerance and contempt was allowed to flourish?

Of course, he had asked himself such questions before – but never as pointedly as now. He began to do the mathematics. There was the dream which he had set down on paper; even if he had embellished it, there was too much in it to be ignored; then there was the recounting of Zulu Hollow to a man who was incapable of making head or tail of it; and now the radio announcements. Yes, things were coming together. Everything seemed topsy-turvy, upside-down, inside-out. Clearly, the Church, indeed every religion known to man, the whole world for that matter, was oh-so liberally populated with shadow people – creatures devoid of real understanding, with no real desire to understand anything outside the narrow boxes of their consciousness, particularly anything that threatened their own version of the *status quo* and their own self-interest and security. And it really did seem that the shadow people now had the upper hand, both inside and outside the Church; the Church itself was a Church in name only, as competing religions were religions in name only; they might call themselves Islam or Judaism or Buddhism or Hinduism – but they were all tarred with the same brush and populated with the same unreflective, unfeeling, box-ticking limpets; hangers-on of such low degree that they had become wraith-like; either these religions were morally irreproachable but demanded far too much of their adherents, and were therefore useless, or else they were no better than their adherents, and on *that* account useless. If the Christian Church were no better than those who composed it, it was falling far short of the principles it purported to espouse. Of course, a handful of individuals had, from time to time, stuck their necks out, even literally, for the Christian God. Trouble was, such individuals were rare and never seemed to act in concert; it was almost as though they represented not the Church but themselves, individually! Where the Church itself stood was more questionable, painfully so; especially now, when even politicians of note felt the need to apologise for being of the Christian faith and might even need to resign from public office on account of it, while if they were either orthodox Jews or orthodox Muslims their confessions were accounted creditable.

Everything that had happened over the last few days became a pertinent reminder of what Sedley had known for some time. Christianity needed to reassert itself, not by ceremony or ritual or the usual set of clichés which amounted to nothing. It had to return to basics and be stripped back to the Sermon on the Mount; this would be a wake-up call and at the same time a rallying call; this was the only way to save it, and he, Sedley, had now to do his bit. Well, if it were possible for an individual to stand as a rock in the midst of a stormy sea, he would be that rock; though all those about him were shadows, they could do him no real harm. The Church itself might not act aright or in concert; but perhaps it had been up to individuals all along to assert what the Church would not or could not assert – because, after all, what had to be asserted had to be asserted by real example, not simply by word of mouth. Christ himself had stumbled to the cross with only a few stragglers to accompany him and with shouts and curses ringing in his ears – had he waited for the collective wisdom of those in the synagogues to instigate a change of heart, people of his own kind, many of whom had known him since his early childhood, he would have waited for ever; but of course it was precisely the collective wisdom of that Church that had pronounced against him. So be it. If the shadow people had inherited the earth, it was at least some consolation that they had not contaminated each and every soul beyond redemption. And if there is only one soul to cry out, well better one voice that sings in tune than a thousand in discord. The Establishment might hold the Church by the scruff of its neck while competing religions rocked with the laughter of malicious satisfaction, but brave individuals, though few and far between, were the thin cracks through which the light of truth would eventually shine, as from a distant black hole, from another and better universe of ideas.

Armed with such thoughts, Sedley believed himself to have been 'called'. He was infused with courage, the kind of courage Sedley the boy had felt in Zulu Hollow, even in the darkest moments. Certainly he had been deeply afraid, but it is well known that courage is not the absence of fear but the determination to persist in spite of it. The child had finally spawned the man, and there was no stopping him now. Much had been lost in the intervening years since Zulu Hollow, and merely going through the motions of becoming a priest had compensated for nothing; it was now time for action, a time he had long known was to come. Sedley had come to see that being a priest was not like being a something else. His was a defiance of a kind of compartmentalism. One man is a baker, another a doctor, another a policeman, another a banker, another a politician, another a teacher, and so on. But a priest! That was something ultra-special. A priest didn't occupy a compartment. He was everywhere and had every right to be so. He could not pronounce upon the skills of a physician or a teacher or a banker, but he had every qualification to say what was morally right or morally wrong. It was the duty of a priest to spread himself around – and for this he could never be subject to legitimate reproach. If you chose to be a priest, you chose a posture of questioning and of criticism, and the questioning and the criticism had to be fearless, ubiquitous and outspoken. It was no less than a mission, and because it was a divine mission, it was fragile and so easy to betray. The overpowering desire to speak for God was mysteriously implanted somewhere, sometime, like a seed dropped by who-knows-who, who-knows-why, who-knows-how; but if it took root inside you, well it showed you the way you had to go – it was as involuntary as genuine grief. And that feeling, a feeling of uncompromising commitment, had somehow been understood by that boy in Zulu Hollow – and it was a feeling that was ultimately to dominate all others. The seed had been planted right there, in Zulu Hollow.

Whether Sedley was right to think in this way is impossible to determine. All he knew now was that commitment to Christ was incumbent upon him, totally and uncompromisingly. Either the God of Christ was paramount or he was nothing at all. And the trouble, as Sedley saw it, was that for most priests the God of Christ, and therefore Christ himself, and therefore all that Christ taught, was not paramount. Since Sedley defined God as Love, and nothing more or less than Love, commitment to God meant a commitment to Love. The trouble with competing religions is that for them God was not Love but some kind of super-cruel vengeful beast that would kick you into hell if you failed to do his bidding; it was therefore most alarming and profoundly disconcerting when peaceful adherents of competing religions were criticised by their spiritual leaders for being hypocritical, as though they were reproaching them for being insufficiently warlike and murderous. The God of Love, of nothing more or less than Love, was not paramount to the shadow people.

Sedley was sufficiently clear about that. It was courage that counted now, courage over intellectual conviction. And courage was elusive; here one moment, gone the next. Uncle Alan had told him about his great grandfather who'd fought in the battle of the Somme. Uncle Alan was in his late teens when his grandfather would relate the battle to him, almost as a staunch Roman Catholic might confess to a priest. In a way, uncle Alan told him, it had been a kind of confession. The old man would sit one side of the hearth, the fire glowing in the grate, while Alan sat on the other. The narrative was anything but exciting. The old man would simply be stating things as coolly as though he had himself been a mere observer at a boring football match – but there was a sad undertone, as though the events described were tragically irrecoverable. A confession, indeed. He told Uncle Alan how he'd come to win the Military Cross entirely by default. He said he was running away from the battle and was mistakenly believed by his officers to be running towards it, rifle in one hand and Mills bomb in the other; a misconception that was helped by the fact that a pair of enemy machine-gunners abandoned their foxhole in fright at the sight of him, having been caught by surprise and thinking they had insufficient time to gun him down; the result was the capture of the machine-gun post and the surrender of its occupants, and the Military Cross for Adam Sedley's great grandfather! Uncle Alan wanted to see the medal, but his grandfather refused. 'It's upstairs somewhere. What d'you want to see that thing for? I'd thrown it out years ago, but your grandmother wouldn't hear of it. I only hang onto it for her sake, God rest her soul!' He spoke as though his holding the Military Cross was an act of continuing and unforgiveable blasphemy, or that such things should only be worn in hell and discarded in heaven.

Courage. Yes, courage could be praised where it did not exist. But then, there was also the courage of confession. His great grandfather had had the courage to confess that his Military Cross had been awarded by default, when he could so easily have said otherwise and earned for himself the undying admiration of all and sundry. He had loved his grandson too much to tell him such a lie. His headstone did not bear the initials *MC*, and never would.

He had told Uncle Alan that the very air he breathed was peopled by the ghosts of men, women and children who had somehow to be appeased, consoled or calmed with a solemn and lasting promise that the insanities of war would never happen again; they would never happen again, because Christ would at last come into his kingdom; the promise had to be made, even if it could never be kept, because some promises can be permitted amongst those that are made and can never be kept. Yes, it was, uncle Alan said, a mighty powerful image – all those sad-faced spectres walking silently along through the shadows of history, one vast, endless, protest march of the dead.

Adam Sedley now knew, even if he did not know as he listened to Uncle Alan, that the insanities of war are eminently repeatable, and he could quote Plato that only the dead know the end of war. But he had at least dedicated himself to this principle: that one who stands for what he believes is right must stand for it to the extent that he is prepared, without fear or favour, to actually say, and say clearly, repeatedly and wholeheartedly what it is he stands for, come what may. If what he says goes with the grain, all very well and good. If it does not, then so be it. In terms with which James Sedley and Charles Baxter were familiar, such a principle is non-transferable and non-refundable. It was not something he felt he could share with Julia, as recent events had indicated; no, this principle and the whole background to it was something he had to keep secret, or share only with his God and those who shared his God; he would not discuss it; he would simply *live* it. True, this principle had been softened and laid low since Zulu Hollow. But now it was time for the Grand Resurrection.

Having satisfied himself that the framework was firm enough to withstand the weight he was about to impose upon it, Sedley still had to write the text of his sermon, which in the event and perhaps unsurprisingly, wrote itself.

~ ~

The church was unusually well-attended; perhaps word had got around that the new incumbent had some fire in his belly and had something worth saying. Julia Sedley was there. So were the Baxters, who had walked in arm in arm for the sake of appearances. There was also a selection of local tradesmen, some minor dignitaries and a Justice of the Peace, all of whom would normally have attended only for weddings and funerals of relatives or close friends, and grudgingly at that. Still, the pews were filling up; there was no doubt that at least Sedley had his audience. Charles Baxter sat behind Julia Sedley, a position which he could hardly have bettered; he tapped her shoulder lightly as he sat down and then put everything he had into the smile he gave her when she turned round.

Charles was in attendance for a specific purpose and one entirely unrelated either to the possible receipt of spiritual edification and comfort, or to the immediate appreciation of Julia Sedley's physical charms. His objective was to seek a fresh start with Adam Sedley. Having decided firmly against the simple expedient of phoning the vicarage, much less paying it a visit, since he considered such approaches far too direct, condescending and lacking in the degree of dignity he had come to expect, and which he firmly hoped others expected, from himself, he had decided to attend the next available sermon with the object of speaking to Sedley afterwards, and in a manner suggesting that all had been forgotten, that all was water under the bridge. It would have suited his dignity far better if Sedley had made the first move instead; but, on reflection, he decided that if Sedley had taken the initiative, it would have deprived him of the very advantage he sought, namely the moral high ground; no, Baxter was anxious to appear the good-natured fellow that everyone claimed he was, and if that necessitated a small sacrifice of personal dignity, it was an investment worth undertaking; he was determined to play the role of the great conciliator and peacemaker, and, like justice, it not only had to be done, it had to be *seen* to be done. And amongst those who would see it done was, above all others, Julia Sedley. If the good Reverend refused to take the olive branch when handed to him so readily, it would hardly be to his credit. Either way, Baxter would emerge a knight in shining armour; he just couldn't lose. So, there he sat, hoping to catch Sedley's relenting eye, and later the man himself at the church door as he shook hands with his homeward-bound flock.

First, of course, the sermon had to be endured. And although their eyes met once or twice before things got under way, there was no indication from the Reverend that time and reflection had brought reconciliation any nearer, because Sedley seemed to look through him rather than at him, which Baxter found disconcerting. But appearances can be most deceiving, as everyone knows. No doubt things would turn out well; after all, a man of the cloth makes it his business to build bridges, advocate goodwill to all and sundry and make fresh starts. And so, all Baxter needed to do was to hang around sufficiently long, go through the usual time-honoured motions, endure the unendurable, and all would come out in the wash.

Sedley began in fine voice and was from the start endowed again with that peculiar tone of self-confidence that some had found slightly worrying in his inaugural sermon. He started with an apology for quoting from *Matthew*, Chapter 25, verses 31-40, since, he said, it was boringly familiar to everyone. This in itself was an uncomfortable start, if only because no one in the congregation had the faintest idea precisely what he was about to quote, and some either didn't know, or could not quite remember, who or what Matthew was, let alone exactly what was written; perhaps there was more than a hint of sarcasm in this apology. Sedley began to read, using the King James version, and the reference to *sheep* and *goats* seemed to go over everyone's head – but, regardless, Sedley read on about those who would inherit the kingdom of heaven and those who would not:

'"*I was hungry and you gave me food; I was thirsty and you gave me drink; I was a stranger and you took me in. Naked, and you clothed me. I was sick, and you visited me. I was in prison, and you came to me.*

Then shall the righteous answer him: Lord, when did we see thee hungry and feed thee? Or thirsty and give thee drink? When did we see thee a stranger, and take thee in? Or naked and clothed thee? Or when did we see thee sick, or in prison, and come to thee?

And the Lord shall answer and say to them: Verily I say unto you: inasmuch as you have done it to one of these the least of my brethren, you have done it to me." I shall spare you the full text, which I am sure you know very well already.'

Those who at last recognised the text were glad, like Baxter, to be spared the whole thing. They had heard it all before; it was a tired text and contained little of interest. Indeed, it was hard to see how Sedley could feel justified in making so much of it, as though it was something original he'd found yesterday lying under a stone on a forgotten hill somewhere outside Jerusalem and was now airing to the world at large, hailing each word as some kind of new and startling revelation. No, it was like an old, battered hat; high time it was discarded for something – well, something new and better, more stylish, with a bit of shape to it. Baxter himself knew the words well enough – perhaps too well. He had to learn them all by heart, as a schoolboy. He had been chosen to recite stuff like this in assemblies, and even on parents' days. The trick had been to learn it off by heart and then recite it with one's head buried deep in the text, so there was no danger of losing your place. He'd been pretty good at it, too, and he might have made Head Boy on the strength of that sort of thing had it not been for that silly incident when he was caught by the Head and caned, all for trying to grow a moustache, and hiding it with a handkerchief on the pretext that he was suffering from an everlasting cold. His face had never fitted with the Head, anyway, but this incident had spoilt his chances completely. Yes, such recitations had all been good schoolboy stuff. But that's where they belonged – to school and to growing up and the smell of polished wooden floors and the rattle of paper and the banging shut of books at the end of lessons, and the pranks, and all that.

But here it was again. And it was hard to justify it; hard, at any rate, to have much of a liking for it. It was like an old tune vastly played out, and he couldn't get his teeth into such stuff; not in the old days, and not now, either. In any case, the essence of the thing had been grasped long ago. It was merely a prescription to be good, with a bit of poetry slung in for good measure; it was too sloppy, and too obvious for words. He was tempted to say, though never in public, that the promise of Heaven and the threat of Hell was alright for those who felt the need for it, because, for them, there was no Heaven, no reward, otherwise; nothing at all after a life of hardship and routine, after paying your taxes, paying off your mortgage, nothing after all the trials and tribulations that made up the process of living. But he, Baxter, knew that there could be nothing, and that no promise and no threat could make it any different. The difference was that he was sensible enough, intelligent enough, wise enough, and sufficiently knowledgeable to get along without such promises and threats. If there was nothing after all these trials and tribulations, then you just had to get as much out of life as you could, and that was that. Simple, really.

Baxter suddenly looked up, realising that Sedley was speaking his very own thoughts. Sedley had paused and was scrutinising the congregation as though looking for someone in particular; his expression was intense:

'I have quoted a little from Scripture, as you no doubt expected. But you might think these words lack a certain, shall we say, lustre? Well, I couldn't agree more. They are so well known that you would hardly expect them to be reported in the press or discussed on television with any degree of enthusiasm at all. It's seems very much a case of familiarity breeding contempt. What's more, I quoted them in the English of the 17th century, and no doubt some of you would say that that is an indication of precisely where they should belong, in the childlike nursery of the past. But I am not afraid to quote them again and again, as many times as it takes. I make no apology. In fact, if any apologies should be made, they should not be made by me. Quite the contrary!'

It was the fluency and, in particular, the tone in which he spoke that struck everyone as unusual in what was considered to be a traditional treatment of a tired piece of Scripture. The congregation was all ears, and even Baxter began to hang on every word, which was totally unexpected. Julia Sedley began to perk up and glance uneasily around. The atmosphere, though not yet electric, was not quite conducive to the usual passivity.

'Let me tell you what you may already know, but not yet understand clearly. The Christian Church is in serious decline, and the only way in which to arrest this decline is to cleanse it of the hypocrisy and the superstition that surrounds it and infests it; the consequence of all this hypocrisy and superstition is that people have become indifferent to its teachings as expressed in the Sermon on the Mount; therefore, they have thrown

the baby out with the bathwater. And the Church will leave in its wake a vacuum that is already in the process of being filled by alien systems of belief, equally hypocritical and superstitious, but yet far stronger because their adherents fail to understand the true nature and extent of the hypocrisy and superstition that infests them; systems which cannot hold a candle to the moral validity of the Christian virtue of tolerance.

'As for hypocrisy, we fail badly as a purportedly Christian nation. To speak, as in Matthew, of feeding, clothing, and generally ministering to the needs of the poor and the oppressed is as relevant now as ever it was. The poor and the needy have hardly ceased to exist! Quite the contrary! And I do not speak simply of the so-called Third World Countries, but of our very own. And surely ...'

Suddenly, Sedley looked up and stopped in his tracks; his attention was attracted to some commotion at the back of the church, the heavy doors having creaked on their hinges, followed by the shuffling of feet and some confusion in the back pews. He turned pale with astonishment. For there, now taking his seat, was the old man who had been presumed dead – the very same. This most unlikely spectre slowly and unassumingly took his seat and folded his arms. He looked up at Sedley and nodded, as if to suggest that he'd better get on with it. There he sat, bearded and unkempt, certainly, but not the ghost Baxter might have taken him for at first sight; divested of his old raincoat, he wore a tweed jacket that had seen better times.

Sedley cleared his throat:

'If ... if we feed the hungry, they will no longer be hungry; if we give drink to the thirsty, they will no longer be thirsty; if we give shelter to the homeless, they will no longer be homeless. Oh yes, the words I quoted have very practical relevance to the here and now. Those tired words of Scripture should inform Government policy. Instead, hypocrisy at every level, from individuals to collective Government, reigns supreme. It is bad enough to encounter hypocrisy in a single individual; how much worse, then, when a whole society claims to be based upon the Christian ethic, but is manifestly organised and governed by those who consistently fly in the face of that very same ethic!

'I have recently heard a very stark statistic, that more than 25 percent of the people who sleep rough on our streets are patients from psychiatric hospitals who can no longer receive hospital accommodation because of the cutbacks ...'

Baxter was brought to life, one might almost say galvanised, by the word 'statistic', as though it were an electrical charge, which explains why he began to smoulder with irritation. Sedley had hit a raw nerve. Baxter himself was a master of statistics. He frequently used them himself to show that, despite the undisciplined protests of misguided minorities, all was well with Government policy. While the ignorant and the unrefined raged against the Government austerity programme, calling it inhuman and penny-pinching, using in the process the most pious language they could muster to denounce the pundits of Government strategy, Baxter was ready and willing, with the irrefutable evidence of statistics, to reduce their arguments to absurdity and to demonstrate beyond all reasonable doubt that the error lay with the critics and not with Government policy. It was natural enough, therefore, that he should take it as a personal affront to be presented with something that pretended to be statistical evidence in support of the unquestionably absurd claim that the Government of the day, to whose policies he fully subscribed heart and soul, was in any way in error. More specifically, the charge (allegedly based on statistics, mind you!) that the Government was not a paragon of Christian virtue was pernicious and damaging, not least to his own political ambitions.

What's more, it was one thing to hear statistics dubiously quoted by Her Majesty's Opposition, statistics which were of course invariably incorrect, but quite another to hear them paraded from the pulpit. Men who earned their living by spreading the word of Christ were seriously risking their credibility by dabbling in matters far beyond their job description. For one thing, those who believe that thousands might achieve full stomachs with five loaves and seven fishes were making a plain mockery of statistical probability. No, men who preached the word of Christ should confine themselves to that, and leave statistics to statisticians, and to politicians who understood them. Dabbling vicars were not, may the Lord be praised, common phenomena, but those who stepped out of line were abusing the freedoms made possible by a free society, the guardians of which were the very politicians who were at the receiving end of their polemics. The irony was intolerable!

Yes, Baxter's feathers were certainly ruffled. The more he thought about it, the more problematic the whole thing became. One might laugh off the statistical ineptitude of a frustrated member of the Opposition as a lame attempt to gain public attention, but when vicars dabbled in the same coin, there was a chance, slight though it may be, that they would be taken seriously. Of course, no one with more than an iota of intelligence could take these pious dabblers seriously, but, truth to say, parish congregations were not normally composed of citizens of proved intellectual ability. In short, this kind of dabbling was at best negative canvassing for the Government, and at worst a positive asset to Opposition candidates.

Baxter was articulate, unlike most members of the congregation. But they shared with him the kind of compartmentalism to which he undoubtedly subscribed; and on that score he need not have worried unduly over their political allegiances: they cherished the belief that Government is Government and Church is Church and never the twain shall meet. And there went with this a tall assumption about expertise: if you wish to know how people should be governed, consult a politician; if you wish to know about God, go see a priest. It seemed to follow from this that it was an error to consult a politician about God, or a priest about politics; so the best you could expect by mixing areas of expertise was a mere approximation of the truth. It was the kind of compartmentalism that would have delighted Adam Smith, that mentor and saviour of the free world who was never at a loss for words when recommending the perceived wisdom of specialisation and the division of labour.

After this blatant and brazen reference to statistics in a context of political criticism, Baxter found himself articulating the thought that the good Reverend was undeserving of his attempts to make amends. The price of appeasement was beginning to look unaffordable. Moreover, Susan Baxter's attention seemed far too intense, and he began to wonder whether her fascination was intellectually or physically motivated; either way, Baxter had to live with her, and he was determined to hear no kind words on Sedley's behalf should his attempts at reconciliation backfire or be withdrawn. And there was now every likelihood that Baxter's policy of appeasement would come to nothing; Sedley was digging his own grave with every new sentence he formed.

'If it is the duty of the Church to attend to the souls of men. It also has the duty to attend to the souls of Governments when Government policies leave it in no doubt that compassion has been sacrificed on the altar of greed and moral ignorance. The Church cannot allow Greed to become a Creed. If the Church is the guardian of Christian principles, principles without which the needy and the oppressed would doubtless be even worse off than they are already, then it is clearly failing in its Christian duty if it does not choose to guide and warn and reproach, but remains silent when these cherished principles are flouted – and there is no doubt whatsoever that they are being gravely flouted. The time can remain silent no more; it must speak out. It is precisely because it has so far failed

to do so that it has lost favour and is in a state of decline, a decline that must be halted if alien and unsavoury systems of belief are not to occupy the vacuum that it will leave behind.

'The wealth of the Good Samaritan without the soul of the Good Samaritan does not in the least impress the Christian God. Our society and its leaders lack soul. They lack moral purpose. Greed and hypocrisy reign supreme. Because there is no moral purpose, policies are pursued which are detrimental to the poorest, and the Christian ethic is turned on its head. Any society which allows the old and the infirm and the mentally sick to eke out their miserable existence in cardboard boxes under bridges cannot possibly claim to be founded upon the teachings of Jesus Christ. Governments are more interested in appeasing extraneous elements and imported faiths than they are in looking after the most deprived of their own people; they are, in fact, aiding and abetting the decline of the established Church in this country, thereby setting the stage for its disappearance altogether. We are in fact uprooting our cherished values and witnessing our own demise. Churches like this one will become mosques and synagogues, or gambling dens and disco venues.'

As Sedley brought his peroration to an end, Baxter's worse fears were very amply confirmed. This was indeed a troublesome priest, one who mixed religion with politics, which is to say oil with water – in fact, not unlike the tendency amongst what Sedley himself had called 'imported faiths'. No, if anyone was aiding and abetting the decline of Christianity, it was Sedley himself – simply by turning it into an alternative political party, and a party with decidedly Marxist overtones at that!

Even so, there was yet one more straw that would break the back of the camel beyond all hope of recovery.

As the concluding hymn was drearily sung and sleepily ending, then old man began to make his exit. At that very moment, Sedley descended unceremoniously from the pulpit and made his way hurriedly up the aisle, determined not to miss the old man a second time. The chase was on. For it was as if his dream, or at least his fabricated account of it, had come to life again, and what he had lost there he was not prepared to lose again. Besides, the old man had been thought dead, and it was only right and proper that he should be welcomed back to the land of the living. But there was only one thought truly uppermost in Sedley's mind: he must meet this fellow, exorcise the ghost of him and discover the man in him.

Sedley could hardly have moved faster had he possessed wings. Julia was amazed at the speed and manner of his exit, since the closing words of the hymn had hardly been sounded. There were times when Julia tended to revere the unorthodox; but this kind of exit was stretching things too far; a modicum of decorum is a salutary thing, but there was very little reserve in Sedley's ungainly departure.

Her misgivings were intensified when he failed to position himself at the church doors, as custom and decorum demanded; each member of the congregation had to make his way out without the customary handshake or nod of appreciation. The good Reverend was nowhere to be found.

The camel had thus laid upon its poor back that straw that laid it low. Julia was joined by the Baxters, and all three wondered what had become of him. Charles Baxter was in no mood to wait around. He had made up his mind that Sedley was quite beyond redemption. He might have tolerated his sermonising on matters beyond his competence, but not to have made himself available for Baxter's good-natured, even sacrificial, attempts at reconciliation was quite unforgiveable; not of course that Baxter himself had had any real intention of making such attempts – but that was not the point! If Baxter had been the kind of man to put any store by signs and omens, Sedley's absence at the doors of the church would have been a sign writ large that he and Sedley had never been destined to achieve common understanding and mutual trust. After all, it must be remembered that he had been fully prepared to acknowledge any weaknesses in himself (though he could not at that moment guess what they might be) in the interests of goodwill and fellowship. He, Baxter, had played his part, fully and on his very own initiative, and he had been under no real obligation to do so – and certainly he was under no obligation now to try any harder. Perhaps Sedley was now, at that very moment, attempting to practie what he preached, ministering to the spiritual needs of the old man, the very least of his flock.

Seated comfortably on a high cloud of righteous indignation, Baxter whisked Susan away to a place of safety and purity, namely anywhere that would not expose her to the perverse influence of Adam Sedley; in the very act of doing so, he thought of how he would very much like to be the means of Julia's rescue, too; for she was clearly too good for Sedley, who was patently outclassed all round. Baxter wondered how Julia could possibly be attracted to the likes of Sedley; it was a mystery, one which was harder by the minute to live with, almost like a personal affront.

Chapter Nine

Eccentrics and Martyrs

When the wise from their hills at times descend, and when shadows then encroach, themselves they must defend, from the wrath of lesser gods and the bile of turbulent men.

~ ~

Baxter poured himself a whiskey and downed it in one, as Susan emerged from the hallway in a calmer, perhaps even slightly amused, mood.

'Feel better?' she asked, tongue very much in cheek.

'Who the hell does he think he is, anyway?' he said, quickly pouring himself another.

'It's his job to give sermons, you know. He's actually paid to do it.'

'Sermons, yes, not political speeches! He should stick to what he knows – if he knows anything at all. And very close to the bone, too. "Unsavoury systems of belief", "extraneous elements and imported beliefs"! We all know what he means. He sounds like a far right pamphleteer. What's he trying to do? Sow as much social discord as possible? Hardly the Christian thing, I'd say. Then again, with all that stuff about the poor, he sounds like a Marxist propagandist. No, he just doesn't know what he's talking about. Totally confused. Meddling, meddling!'

'Oh, come on Charlie!'

'Well, I wouldn't expect you to see it! And don't call me that.'

'See what?' she smiled innocuously. 'No, really, see what, exactly? What is it I'm supposed to see? You know the trouble with you – you're developing a persecution complex, and pretty unsightly it is, too,' she said, pretending to take things seriously.

'He looked straight at me,' he said, as though turning things over in his mind. 'Seemed to make a point of it. Didn't you …? No, no you wouldn't've noticed, would you? Too wrapped up in other things. And I bet you didn't understand a word he was saying, either.'

'Oh, he really has got to you, hasn't he? In any case, if you really think it's something personal, why don't you speak to him about it and get it all out in the open? But you won't do that, will you? – because you're not sure, are you? And you wouldn't be able to tolerate being shown up and shown to be wrong, would you?' Her sarcasm was adroitly intoned – that much can be said for it.

'Oh, I'm sure alright. Talking to him? Haven't I tried that already? I sat through that crazy sermon with the express intention of … oh, what's the use? He obviously preferred the company of some down-and-out to that of his own hard-working parishioners – and I suppose you'd have the gall to say he was ministering to the needs of his flock!'

'Good God, it's simple enough! He probably just wanted to meet the old guy. After all, we told him … I mean it was quite a shock to see him after what we read in the paper! Well, it couldn't have been the same man, could it? Yet another of your wonderful theories in tatters!' She mumbled the last sentence, but it was heard. 'But look,' she went on, 'If you really want to make your peace with him …'

'No. Not after that so-called sermon of his.'

'Do you honestly think he sat down and planned out his entire sermon as a personal attack on you? Oh really, I need a drink myself!' She picked up a whisky decanter.

'No,' he said, taking the decanter from her. He filled his glass and replaced the decanter on the side table. 'No, the whole point is, he's poking his nose into matters that don't concern him in the slightest. All that stuff about greed and hypocrisy, and in the same breath as Government policy. Oh, I'm prepared to be reasonable. The fellow has a perfect right to his opinions, but he has to learn to keep them to himself. Do I go about the place quoting Scripture on street corners? No, I confine myself to what I know best, and all I'm saying is that he and others like him should do the same. If he has any political ambitions, he should give up the Church and run for Parliament. On the other hand, with his opinions, I certainly hope he never does – the man has no diplomacy, no discretion. All those thinly veiled references to Islam and synagogues, and whatever – well, the man has no respect for political correctness – and I'm not sure what he wants, anyway. He'd be good on a soap box in Hyde Park Corner spouting Marxist claptrap. No, I hope and pray he leaves politics well alone. Burgess had better sense, and what was good for Burgess is good enough for his successors.' Baxter cleared his throat to round off the point.

Susan had filled her glass and, while he was holding forth, could hardly resist the temptation to laugh out loud; instead, she hid her smiles with her glass and was grateful for the reference to Burgess.

'Burgess, bless him!' she laughed. 'He was a lovely, dithering old idiot!'

'Yes, perfect for the job,' said Baxter under his breath.

'He was perfectly innocent and kind hearted,' she said, shaking her head benignly.

'You mean you didn't fancy him. A bit too old for your liking. Yes, but you do, don't you? You actually fancy our brand new vicar!' Baxter enjoyed teasing her. He had nothing to lose in her affections, and he had none left for her.

'I *like* him, yes. He speaks his mind, and I like *that*.'

'Speaks his mind? You're assuming he has a mind to speak. That's reckless! Wishful thinking, I'd say.'

'Oh, that was below the belt,' she said, speaking with a firm but reflective calmness, irritating Charles all the more since it sounded like the kind of rebuke a wise and patient parent or teacher might deliver to an unreasonable and unreasoning adolescent.

'Oh, *was* it? Now don't tell me you're developing socialist tendencies. You'll be voting for the Opposition next.' His laugh was contrived. He was not at all amused by his own joke.

'And that would never do, would it?'

'Damned right it wouldn't! Not for as long as you're associated with me. And as for you Reverend Sedley – if this is the way he intends to carry on, he can't depend on *my* support. The church roof can develop more holes than a colander before I'll do anything about it. It's so typical! Scornful of money, until there's a leak in the roof, which prayers to the Almighty are incapable of fixing! Well, I've done more than my share in the past, but I'm washing my hands of everything from this very minute! Strange thing is, I felt it in my bones from the very start – knew it would go from bad to worse. You just have a feeling about people, and you know how it's going to be. I've never felt comfortable with the fellow – from the moment I first set eyes on him. I meet a lot of people, and I've developed a keen sense of what's on and what isn't – I've learned to trust it and it hasn't failed me yet. But I never thought we'd be saddled with a lefty vicar. I must say. No, that's one disease I thought we were pretty well immune to in these parts!'

'You're dramatising everything, as usual,' sighed Susan.

'No, no no. This sort of thing has to be nipped in the bud. It's up to respectable and intelligent people to come together and do something about it. No, it just won't do. We can't have vicars dabbling in politics.'

'Charles, it was a sermon, that's all. A bit out of the ordinary, yes, and certainly not Burgess's style – but, even so, and in any case nobody bothered to listen ...'

'There's no "even so" about it. And they did listen. I saw their faces. No, whatever you say, it's a lame defence. And it wasn't so much out of the ordinary, either. There's too much of this kind of dabbling going on these days – getting to be quite fashionable, and I don't like it, not one little bit. It's high time these dabblers were taught a lesson. The Church has to be put in its place – you see, I'm not denying that it *has* a place. But it has to *know* its place, and if it's forgotten its place, it has to be reminded – clearly and unambiguously, by people with courage and integrity. After all, here he is, some know-it-all, accusing the Government of the day of downright hypocrisy! – a democratically elected Government, mind you, consisting of the brains of the country, people more familiar with the practical problems of Government than that intellectual ragamuffin could ever hope to be. Admittedly, if we were all living in a fascist state ...'

'You'd praise him instead of criticising him,' Susan interrupted.

'Exactly! Because a fascist state deserves criticism from every possible quarter. Yes, but *we're* living in a demonstrably *free* country! – and, I might add, one that enjoys a greater degree of freedom now than ever before! You need only look at the strides we've made in improving consumer choice, for one thing. Good God! The fellow lacks all judgement! He's obviously got his wires crossed, and the sooner they're uncrossed the better.'

'Look!' said Susan, fast running out of patience, 'the more fuss you make, the worse it will get. These things can get out of all proportion. The best thing is to ignore the whole thing. Everybody probably regards him as a bit of an eccentric, anyway, especially after the way he ran out of the church today – a bit of comic relief, if anything.'

'You obviously haven't understood a word I've been saying. Of course he's eccentric! But it's the principle of the thing that matters. The Church has its place, and when it steps out of line, something ought to be said. After all, the time may come when total idiots might take the eccentrics seriously – have you thought of that?'

'You know what? I think you're afraid of him!'

'What!' boomed Baxter, obviously shocked and offended.

'Afraid of him.'

'Ridiculous!'

'So why have you got it in for him? He's very persuasive, isn't he?'

'Persuasive! Oh God, we're just going round in circles. Do you think anyone in his right mind would be persuaded by that claptrap? No one around here is even mildly interested in *his* politics. Couldn't you sense that? No, it's just that eccentrics attract idiots, like magnets. That's the only worrying thing. He's using the Church as a soapbox – and that's just not on.'

'Alright,' said Susan in a tone of tired resignation, 'so what do you intend to do, then?'

Without replying, Baxter marched off to the bathroom to wash his hands literally, having already done so figuratively, while Susan sat in an armchair sipping her whisky and shaking her head slowly between sips, her sense of humour temporarily suspended.

Charles Baxter had spoken in the calculating tones of a bully working out a master plan to achieve his ends, a fact not lost on Susan, but she had bigger battles to fight, not the least of which was to continue the 'arrangement' with as little boat-rocking as possible. In disposition, Baxter had made little progress since his schooldays. True, he no longer stuffed the heads of rivals down lavatory basins, taking delight in their muffled screams as he pulled the flush, nor did he order weaker souls to obeisance on all fours while he stood heavily on their fingers, watching them grimace, squeal and squirm. Of course not! Things had come on apace since those immature and mindless days of youth when, as a senior schoolboy, he was undisputed master of all he surveyed, managing even to keep the Head Boy in his place. The techniques of hegemony now employed were far more sophisticated, and they were satisfactorily justified in terms of the glorious dictum that all is fair in love, war and business. Quite irrespective of what he might have learned in school, the Nature of Things, in one of her innumerable lapses, had equipped him with all the accompaniments, not to say prerequisites, of success. He was what marketing men might call a 'front man', and endowed by Mother Nature for the very task, being tall, large-framed and masculine; and when to these qualities were added an educated middle-class accent, an authoritative tone and tasteful tailoring, success seemed a foregone conclusion, or, as some of his more unfortunate associates might have put it, a *fait accompli*.

So it was that the most powerful weapon in Baxter's armoury was an inclination to intimidate, almost without trying; a power nourished by an aura of superiority that others tended to confer on him at first glance, an aura which he did his best to maintain in public, though he would drop his guard in private, sometimes to the consternation of the secretaries he employed, who, when permitted a vision of the man within, tended to bend their thoughts to alternative forms of employment, if not alternative climes. Baxter was therefore a natural bully, aided and abetted, unwittingly, it is hoped, by the hand of Nature herself. It is little wonder that he was wedded to the view that the best form of education was 'a practical preparation for life' and that 'experience is the best teacher'. For he carried from school into adult life the conviction that bullying, when required, almost invariably paid off, a conviction so firmly rooted that he was perfectly incapable of seeing it for what it really was. Faith in the efficacy and propriety of bullying was now as inseparable from the man as grain is from wood: often hidden, but never eradicated.

It is therefore little wonder that Baxter's deceased father, Maurice, was uppermost in Baxter's thoughts as he washed his hands in the bathroom, for nature's gifts had been more than amply channelled by that illustrious figure.

The simple and wonderful fact is that Maurice Baxter (*Bishop* Maurice Baxter, no less!) had been a great admirer of George Armstrong Custer. Maurice had bestowed all his own physical accomplishments on his son, and, according to whispers that circulated through the corridors of ecclesiastical patronage, had achieved clerical status less through spiritual competence and devotion and more through the subtle aura of superiority he had managed to cultivate and the air of authority that had thereby been engendered. The memory of this great man was extremely dear to Charles Baxter and affected him enormously, and a picture of him would be brought to mind in times of urgent reflection, in much the same way that the Bishop would recall a painting of Custer's Last Stand when the need for courage had assumed an almost intolerable degree of urgency.

Charles Baxter's mother, Grace, was still in the land of the living – very much so. In her late seventies she was as spritely as ever, still adored her late husband and would not have heard a word against him; in fact, she found him as faultless as Libbie Custer is said to have regarded her knight exemplar. It was more that Maurice had achieved status at all, as distinct from his having achieved it in the Church, that had set him, in Grace's eyes, apart from and above all other men. Charles got on well with his mother, largely because they both revered the same man and for much the same reasons. She would sit in a large, dark but otherwise opulent room surrounded by photographs of her late husband dressed in his clerical finery, while one large portrait dominated, you might even say intimidated, the entire room. With strangers she would often begin, 'My husband is ...' and then correct herself by supplying the correct past tense, not, it must be said, on purpose, but because her thoughts were genuinely more in the past than in the present. She was not, or not quite yet, senile, but while true senility was pending, she was simply doting in dotage on one to whom dotage had been denied by the indifferent hand of fate.

Fate had no doubt decreed that dotage and Maurice Baxter could never walk hand in hand. For Maurice Baxter had been no Burgess. Far from it! Not for him the timidity of the country mouse. Not for him, either, the temerity of the town rat! Neither a Burgess nor a Sedley, he would give loud sermons on classic themes, and always well within the framework that was customarily expected from the Church and its hierarchy. Endowed with a booming voice to complement the natural majesty of his frame, it has to be said that he boomed much and said little – which was, by some accounts, a characteristic he shared with his hero General Custer, a personage whom he thought had been much maligned and little understood. The parallel might be pursued further. For Bishop Baxter's minions might have said of him what the General's rank and file certainly did say of that fine fellow, namely that they were divided like chalk and cheese in their opinions of him, that they either loved him or detested him, but that no one was ever undecided. Divided but never undecided were Maurice Baxter's minions. And the good Bishop would know how to handle those of rebellious nature who dared step out of line. Much like the Sioux and Cheyenne that Custer hotly pursued over the expansive plains and undulating hills of Montana and Kansas, clerical rebels would be pursued and brought to acquiesce by the vicarious and corporeal hand of God Himself, namely the shepherding hand of the good Bishop, who might, if necessary, speak in thunderous tones, suffering neither slight nor doubt, until the field was won. The Bishop was feared, even revered, for his very bearing, and for his ability to charge into a piece of Scriptural text with almost military fervour, due no doubt to an unshakeable belief, or at least hope, that God was on no one's side more than his own, he conviction he may have shared with the General, whose spirit survived the battle of the Little Big Horn far better than it might have done had he lived to tell the tale.

As for the Bishop's 'last stand', ironically he suffered a stroke in the pulpit before he got anywhere near his peroration and had to be carried down the aisle in a rough and ready manner, rather as a window dummy might be removed for a rapid change of clothing during a fashion publicity stunt; all to no avail, for he died peacefully in a hospital bed without ever having regained the use of his voice or his mental faculties. Generals may be denied their final victories, but it was the Bishop's lot to be denied his last word on a theme he had meticulously prepared and was keenly anxious to expound with characteristic booming intensity.

For her part, Grace Baxter was equally keen to minimise this momentous loss to mankind. Like her son, who had no doubt inherited it, she had developed a remarkable facility to refashion unfortunate and even tragic events so that the final product had about it all the redeeming features of an acknowledged work of art. So, she spent subsequent years tirelessly extolling the mystery of the Almighty's Movements, they being known to Him alone and to no other save those who, like Maurice Baxter, had a closer affinity to the creator than most ordinary mortals. 'He moves in mysterious ways' became her set text with friends, relatives and strangers alike, and those who knew of her loss might have been forgiven for thinking that the phrase 'He moves in mysterious ways' was in fact a heartfelt reference to the immortal and restless spirit of the dearly departed himself.

When Charles Baxter and his mother met, which they did quite regularly, they would sit and remember old times. She would hold a silver-framed photograph of Maurice in her hands and, gently stroking the glass with her index-finger, announce how proud his father would be of his only son and how happy he would be to know that he and Susan now enjoyed a state of marital bliss and were looking forward to starting a family of their own together, how wonderful it would be if Maurice had been able to picture a little grandchild, and how proud he would be of Charles himself, the very picture of a well-rounded son. For Grace knew that her son was doing every bit as well in the service of business as her husband had done in the service of God.

144

Maurice Baxter was very much in his son's mind, like a genii called forth in time of need. If a man has a job, and if he does what is expected of him and more, he can expect to make strides, like Maurice Baxter, like Charles Baxter. Charles Baxter regarded Sedley's ministry as a job for which he was paid, and in which he might make strides provided he did what was expected of him. Being a vicar was a job whose perimeters were well-defined. It was a job, and, though perhaps not nearly as important as banking, it was arguably more important than digging holes for lamp-posts. A company manager would be likely to receive short shrift from his bank manager if he ventured to instruct the latter in the principles of sound banking. How much shorter the shrift if the digger of holes for lamp-posts should dare to inform his employers that they had got it all wrong! In any case, there was getting it wrong and there was getting it wrong. After all, a digger of holes might show the way forward to larger profits or to improvements in cost efficiency, and this advice, though from a totally unexpected source, might yet be welcomed for the kind of advice it was. But should the digger inform his employers that the profit motive was itself suspect ... well, it was not only unwelcome advice, but totally absurd, because it tore the foundations from under their feet. Not only was Sedley interfering in matters in which he could claim no expertise, but he was also refusing to be a priest! Priests are fellows who are paid to hold forth to all and sundry in time-honoured fashion; they are employed in the service of God, for which they receive salaried recognition. Far from being rebellious and recalcitrant, priests should be forever grateful for the place allotted to them by the collective wisdom of civilised men. If God was good, so were the values enjoyed and upheld by pillars of the Establishment like Maurice Baxter, the very Establishment that Sedley was appearing to challenge.

Maurice Baxter had been no man's fool. He had carefully prepared his texts, which always accorded with Scripture; minded his flock, who were eternally grateful; abided by the canons of his trade; done what was expected of him, with gusto and deliberation; and achieved the highest ranks of his chosen profession, which some called 'vocation'. He had been of strong character, yet never stepped out of line; never questioned things which, if ever seriously questioned at all, should only be questioned by those with the requisite expertise. The whole point was that Maurice Baxter had done well, and what was good enough for Maurice Baxter was unquestionably good enough for the Reverend Sedley. Maurice Baxter had allowed his son to choose his own profession provided two conditions were met: first, it had to be respectable, and, second, it had to be one to which the young Baxter was sufficiently committed so as to achieve the top rungs. Let it be business, let it be politics, let it be the law – anything respectable, provided he achieved a status commensurate with his dedication. From which it may be deduced that Maurice Baxter was not a middle-of-the-road man. Like his hero, Custer, who had hotly pursued the laurels of military victory, Maurice Baxter had pursued his God with a zest for distinction.

For Charles, as for his father, the service of God was a respectable pursuit. A club might unwittingly, and much to its detriment, admit as a member someone who was not of the right sort of calibre. When this happened, the club had to tighten up its rules, and the individual concerned ought to be given an ultimatum: acknowledge the preconditions of admittance or else leave. As a respectable club, the Church had to ensure that its members and officers were of the right calibre, if, that is, it wished to remain respectable; and it could not possibly remain respectable by challenging, or even seeming to challenge, the very Establishment that nourished it.

As Baxter dried his hands, he lamented, as much as ever he did, the fact that his father was no longer in the land of the living. There is no doubt that he would have sought his father's advice. Since this was not an option, he would need to consult others on the best course to be pursued. And it was on this that his mind was now set as he emerged from the bathroom.

~ ~

That same evening, as Baxter was contemplating strategy, Adam and Julia Sedley were relaxing in the cosy fire-lit living room of the vicarage, Julia flicking through a glossy magazine on home decor, Adam re-reading a text with which he was already very familiar; he was so engrossed that his responses to Julia were little more than guttural. She was sprawled on a sofa, clad in a light-blue velveteen dressing-gown that bared her shapely knees and lower legs, while her pert upturned breasts heaved gently beneath this seductive garment with all the pouting seductiveness popularly, perhaps mistakenly, attributed to Cleopatra of Egypt – a sight that would have driven Charles Baxter, like most men, to distraction, but which seemed to make no impression on her spouse, who seemingly found the text far more engaging.

'Ah, yes,' he said suddenly, 'Here's something that might interest you. It's about James Naylor, a Quaker in Cromwell's time – 17th century. Listen to this:

"James Naylor denied that the resurrection of Christ was to be understood physically, and placed upon it a spiritual interpretation. It was this that provided a suitable pretext for his arrest, an excuse for which the authorities had been eagerly waiting. His criticisms of Cromwell and other leaders of the young Republic could not be challenged on apparently religious grounds, thus depriving them of overtly political content ..."'

'Well, you couldn't be arrested for that these days, could you?' she said, turning a page in her magazine.

He read on:

"He was first arrested in Exeter, and imprisoned as a disturber of the peace and agitator. But this only increased his authority amongst his admirers. Women fell down before him and kissed his feet, and miracles were attributed to him. He was sent to London to be finally heard by the House of Commons. And here he was found guilty of 'abominable blasphemy' and only just escaped the death sentence. But he suffered severe punishments: he was exposed in the pillory for two hours, whipped through the streets of London by the hangman, and pilloried again; his tongue was then perforated with a hot iron, and the letter 'B' (Blasphemer) was branded on his forehead. He was then taken to Bristol, conducted through the town seated backwards on a horse, and whipped back through the town. Finally, he was sent to the penitentiary and kept in strict solitary confinement. His punishments were so severe that they had to be interrupted. He nevertheless faced them all with stoic bravery. During his interrogations he asserted that he possessed the 'inner light' and said that the homage paid to him by his followers was not meant to apply to himself, but to God speaking through him. But the political threat which he now represented was illustrated by the devotion of his followers. During the perforation and branding, one of these followers stood beside him, holding a placard over his head which read, 'This is the King of the Jews', which was quickly torn up by the hangman's assistant; and during his torture, his followers pressed forward to kiss his hands and feet ..."'

'Remarkable, yes?'

'Sounds like a bit of an eccentric to me,' said Julia.

'Exactly – and that's how they'd deal with him now, you see. I mean, the powers-that-be would rely on people regarding him as eccentric,' said Sedley, with some animation at last, as though he was keen to make her understand the significance of some new revelation.

'Well, they don't brand people nowadays!'

'They don't have to. They'd find other ways.'

Julia continued to flick her way through her magazine, though a little faster now.

'Anyway,' he went on, 'Many thought Naylor must be insane, and they tried to make out that he was. There doesn't seem to be much evidence of insanity, though. Apparently, he was a great debater, rational and very persuasive – and, therefore, of course, all the more a political threat ...'

'But all that stuff about miracles, "King of the Jews" and so on. I mean it's all very weird,' said Julia, who had momentarily stopped flicking.

'Yes, but they weren't things he said himself – that's the point. His high-spirited followers supplied all that, and it didn't do him much good, obviously. It only fuelled the charge of blasphemy. No, it seems he was doing his best to disown all that – during his interrogation. And it could be that all that stuff was just trumped up against him. I mean, Cromwell's Government was a school for spies – it would've been easy to frame him from any angle they chose. Anyway, it only provided the edge against him. What the authorities were really worried about was the political threat. Well, they'd just fought a civil war at great cost in lives and property. It wasn't easy to arrest a man just for criticising the Republic, much less find him guilty of treason. No, they had to find a pretext – and blasphemy fitted the bill quite nicely – just what they needed. Very effective, too – it carried the death sentence in those days.'

'But you said a *political* threat.'

'Well, he accused Cromwell and the rest of betraying the people, the masses of very ordinary people who'd fought for freedom and justice and landed up with tyranny and oppression instead. Naylor's message has a very modern ring about it, don't you think? He could've been talking about the kind of society we're living in now!'

'What? Oh, come on, you must be joking! There's no tyranny or oppression – not in this country, anyway.' As if to prove the point, she flicked several pages in one go.

'Really? They can take many forms. Anyway, the thing is, Naylor said you couldn't rely on individuals alone to bring about a better society, because that depended on the cultivation of a proper spirit, the spirit we call the Christian Ethic – that's what I think is so modern about Naylor. Simple, really.'

'Tyranny and oppression – that's rich,' mumbled Julia, who hadn't been listening, as she rapidly flicked several more pages.

'Well,' Sedley went on, as if talking to himself, which he was, 'He spoke well enough to worry the authorities. They just couldn't tolerate the claim that they were no better than Judas – so they broke him. If someone today accused the Government of being a Judas, either nobody would understand it, or they wouldn't give a damn anyway. But his whole point was that the needs of the poor and the deprived weren't being addressed because the Christian spirit wasn't cultivated amongst men and that the Government of the day should set an example and do its level best to cultivate that spirit. Oh, the *form* exists, alright – but what's the use of form without substance!'

'All I can say is he must've seemed odd and eccentric to many even then. Can't say I blame them, either,' she said, bringing flicking to a momentary halt. 'Perhaps you should enter politics!' she added, as the flicking resumed.

'But I did! When I decided to serve God!'

'Can we please change the subject,' she said, in the tone of the long-suffering. 'And please put that book down for a minute.'

'I'm all ears.'

'Well, about what happened today ...' she started, finally putting her magazine aside.

'Oh, not again!'

'But he wanted to talk to you today. He told me. He didn't say what it was about, but I think he wanted to make his peace with you – a kind of goodwill gesture, after that silly business the other evening.'

'May the Lord spare us!' he said, with raised eyebrows, as he contemplated the ceiling.

'The Lord preached forgiveness, too – if there's anything to forgive. You agree with that guy Nay ...'

'Naylor. James Naylor.'

'Yes, about cultivating the right sort of spirit – well, here's your chance to do some cultivating.'

He laughed. She smiled. The argument was won.

'Anyway,' she went on more confidently, 'I think it's time we invited them over. It's our turn anyway – and I think you ought to give him another chance. Not that it was all *his* fault! It's time to bury the hatchet, don't you think?'

'Invite them then!' He could say nothing else, having been hoist by his own petard.

'Right. Good. I'll give them a ring, sometime tomorrow,' she said, picking up her magazine and giving the pages a more studious flick. 'By the way, you haven't said much about the old man you ran after. You were with him long enough.'

'Oh, there's nothing much to say. His name's Jack, or so he says. Interesting sort of fellow, though. Now suppose we invite *him* to dinner, too?'

'What?! You haven't, have you?'

'No. He wouldn't come anyway.'

'He'd be too embarrassed for one thing.'

'You mean, it'd be taking the cultivation of the Christian spirit a bit too far?'

'What were you talking about?'

'Well, he seemed reticent at first – a bit unsure of me, I suppose. He relaxed a bit when I told him we thought he'd been found in the river. I told him about the raincoat. He said he'd given his overcoat to someone else. Anyway, he didn't seem to want to talk about it, and I dropped the subject. So, there we are – mystery solved!'

Julia seemed satisfied with this peremptory explanation, and much relieved that the idea of inviting the old fellow round to dinner had been no more than a joke.

She lay awake that night, pretending to be asleep. There was all that stuff about – what was his name again? Mayler, no, *Naylor*? Yes, Naylor. And tyranny and oppression, as though there was a great conspiracy and Adam was waging a war against it, some sort of personal crusade, as though he wanted to become some kind of martyr – at least, that's how it was beginning to seem. If Adam was a restless spirit, this kind of kicking against the traces, this rebelliousness, this talent for rubbing people up the wrong way – well, this subversiveness was not the way to get on in the Church – or anywhere else, for that matter! It was hard to see how they could even settle down to a sensible existence if this was the attitude he adopted. Now if only he could be restless in another way, if only he could channel his energies towards something positive and constructive, the sky might be the limit – that kind of restlessness she could not only tolerate but actively encourage. But she felt helpless as things were. After all, he might rock the boat so much that he would be swept overboard into very stormy waters, taking her with him. Had that thought occurred to him? Did he love her sufficiently to think of that? But he was quite prepared to make enemies, important enemies at that if the fancy took him, and that was not a recipe for a peaceful life, let alone a successful one. But then, on the other hand, perhaps he would settle down. After all, age and idealism seldom sit well together. Trouble was, neither he nor she could wait that long. He was in danger of destroying all his chances, and perhaps hers into the bargain. It was all very ironic. She had found him attractive at the outset precisely because he was a restless spirit, and yet it wasn't meant to turn out like this. And it was all very well to say that a woman should stand by her husband, but what if she felt he was on the wrong track entirely, so much so that he threatened the wellbeing of his own marriage, and even of his family should they decide to start one in the near future? For the very first time in their relationship, Julia began to experience an uneasiness that she had little idea how to cope with. It also went to show how little you knew about the person you married before the deed was done – almost like buying your dream house only to find it uninhabitable. Could it really be that everything might change in what seemed an instant, so that you felt you were married to someone else, as though a stranger suddenly inhabited the body you slept with? It was all very confusing and disquieting.

But, then again, things might turn out alright in the end. Things always seem better in the light of day. And at least he had agreed to have the Baxters round to dinner, and that was progress, already. It was his almost schoolboy idealism that concerned Julia most; but she felt there was no telling argument she could use against it; anyway, there was no arguing with Adam; he seemed to have an answer for everything. She consoled herself with the thought that there are some waves you simply have to ride out; Adam's restlessness and her consequent disquietude were probably amongst them. Nevertheless, it was not until the twilight hours that she finally managed to catch what little sleep she could.

Chapter Ten

All Stuff and Nonsense

The histories of the wise are fables to unfold; but, when all is said that can be said, so much remains untold.

~ ~

For his part, he felt he had done the right thing to keep his account of the exchanges with the old man as skeletal as possible. Julia had given James Naylor short shrift, and there was every likelihood that she would have treated Jack in much the same way. She must have guessed that there was far more to it; but as long as she didn't probe, Sedley was content to leave things alone, for a marriage of minds should not be forced. In fact, the conversation was surprising and unforgettable, and it would haunt him for the rest of his life.

After catching up with the old fellow and reassuring him that he was not for any reason under suspicion, Sedley managed to whisk him off to the remotest corner of the vicarage garden where the cypresses were in full view. Bereft of his overcoat, the old man wore a green tweed jacket that had seen better days, grey baggy trousers, shoes of faded and be-spotted brown suede, and, upon his head, an old and almost shapeless fedora, owing so much to the ravages of time that the debt was beyond all hope of recovery; his beard was unkempt and greyish-white, and his hands, though deeply wrinkled, had perhaps once been resonant of those of a classical pianist. His accent was neutral, and he spoke like one erudite – which indeed he proved to be. Remarkable, too, was the speed at which he spoke – at least at first, though after a while he spoke in calmer tones. His opening remarks came like a torrent, like someone who has not spoken form a long time, or like one who had finally met a like spirit after years of solitary confinement, as if the vents had opened on a dam fit to burst.

'Just look at those!' he said, pointing at the cypresses. 'Straight and steadfast, just like men of the cloth. Wouldn't you say,' he said. Sedley smiled.

'You know something about trees?'

'Not a thing! But I'm very fond of them. Lifeblood of the earth!'

'You didn't tell me your name.'

'What's in a name?' he said, still looking up at the cypresses. Sedley smiled with a little embarrassment.

'Alright, you can call me Jack. My name's Jack – least it was when I was human.'

'When you were ...?'

'*Human*, yes. But I stopped being human – or at least I've done my best. Opted out of the human race, you might say. So my name doesn't matter anymore – not that it did before, when I was human, I mean.'

Sedley's first thought was that the fellow was demented; he was definitely not inebriated; Sedley was momentarily at a loss for words – which didn't matter, because the old man was beginning to get into his stride, like a machine that was difficult to start but unstoppable once started.

'No, no. I haven't lost it, if that's what you're thinking – you *were* thinking that, weren't you? Mind you, I've heard it said that insanity is a sane response to an insane world. But, no, I'm quite sane. On the other hand, you might say I've lost *something* – lock, stock and barrel. Well, I came to the conclusion long ago that, apart from a handful of exceptions, too rare to be bearable – I mean those few who manage against all the odds to transcend their human natures, well, apart from these, the great mass of mankind are far less than what they might at first seem – way below expectations, you know, yes, very disappointing. And then the horrible thought struck me that I was one of them! Well, I struggled alone for as long as I could bear it – but in the end I decided the best thing to do was to opt out altogether, and to do that I had to swim against the tide, so to speak. I remember, when I was human I used to pray to God, I should say *my* God, because, as far as I could see, my God couldn't possibly have been the same God as everybody else's. Anyway, I remember I used to say to my God, "Father, protect us from those who appear to be human but who rend the flesh and spill the blood of the innocent and the good" – and then I realised what this meant – it meant that we should be protected from the mass of mankind, because the mass of mankind were really no better than those who only appeared to be human and weren't. So, then the idea came to me that even the mass of mankind only appeared to be human. Well, so there we are – I decided the best course was to opt out and not call myself a human being anymore. You see? And then, if anyone asked me whether I believed in God, I replied that I believed in the

Devil, and they thought I was a Devil-worshipper dipping into the black arts. Can you believe it! But, you see my point? It's really very simple: if human beings worship God and continue to act as they do, continue to be what they are – well, I would prefer to call my God by another name, not to sully my God by using the same word as everyone else. My God and their God are totally opposite, so it seemed fitting to call my God the Devil instead.

'So, why have you come to the church?' asked Sedley, bemused and intrigued.

'Down from the hills, do you mean?' he said. But Sedley looked blank; there were no hills thereabouts. 'Well, I suppose, from time to time I need to remind myself why I opted out. And so far, the rightness of that decision has been confirmed time and again. Sad but true. Sad but true. Now who was it that said that if he had to choose between the average human being and the average cat, he'd choose the average cat every time? Whoever it was, he's taken the words out of my mouth.'

'Look, that's a very glum outlook on life, isn't it?' Sedley ventured.

'Realistic! – You see, it depends on your worldview. If you've somehow convinced yourself that one fine day all will be well, that war will be a thing of the unthinkable past, man's inhumanity to man forever banished from this globe, life on earth finally a paradise – well, if you think like this, yes, I agree, I do hold a glum view. But you see, I don't think such a paradise will ever be possible – and my only hope is that there will always be someone, somewhere, who will somehow and to some extent at least resist the worst in man – some spark, some glimmer, some glow in a very dark room! Always some Christ, some Socrates, some Ghandi, some Mandela – to hold the torch, you know?'

'To hold the torch?'

'To hold the torch.'

'So, the world is no better than it was in the past?'

'You should know better than to ask,' said Jack, nodding slowly.

Sedley said nothing, but he believed that he certainly did know better. Listening to Jack was like listening to himself in another body. This was precisely the torch he himself wanted to hold, and hold aloft, burning more brightly than ever.

There was a pause as a gentle breeze rustled the leaves on the cypresses. Then Sedley ventured another question.

'Before, well, before you, er … *opted out*, what was it like? What did you do – I mean, did you have a job, a family …'

'Both. A job and a wife and a son.'

'Your wife and son, did they pass ...?'

'Hell, no. I left them – or maybe they left me – the jury's forever out on that one!'

'I was a teacher, you know,' Jack went on. 'What, surprised?'

'What ...?'

'History! I taught history, well at first. And then I taught it in my own way, and that's what they couldn't abide – tried to throw me out, said I was incompetent – irresponsible in my duties towards the young, that sort of thing.'

'How's that?'

'Well, think about it! History! There's a feast of error for you! Yes, what impressed me most about the history of the human race was all the error in it – I mean, compared with all that, the so-called achievements pale into insignificance, don't you think? Anyway, I had the idea that if you could learn anything at all from the study of history it would be about the value we should attach to human life. So I tried to put that across to the kids who were already on the threshold of manhood – so that they could understand all the waste that fills the pages of history books – waste of life and human potential for good ... well, it was all about values and how to get those across, you see? And to do that I had to teach something they could relate to – *feelings* – feelings of *pain*. I had some authority for it, too – from the Romans – someone had said that the world couldn't be made better until you could imagine the pain of others. Something like that. Anyway ...'

'No, go on.'

'I wanted to explain feelings, not events – people, not names – because I wanted to *condemn*, like an angry god – condemn man's inhumanity to man, and events without feelings seemed irrelevant. Wasn't enough to say Nelson was killed on the quarterdeck of the *Victory* – I'd tell them how the musket ball burned into his left shoulder and lodged in his spine, paralysing him from the waist down, how he said he felt a sensation like a gush of blood in his chest every few seconds, how he said he couldn't feel his legs, how he said his breathing was getting harder by the minute until near the end he said he felt he was suffocating. And it was essential to tell them that it wasn't just Nelson who felt pain and anguish. So I'd tell them about Thomas Jenkins of Merthyr Tydfil whose arm was blasted out of his socket, how he lay there in a pool of his own blood, still conscious, while a mate tried to comfort him, and how he saw his arm lying just a few feet away still in its shirt sleeve, a pale anaemic thing, and how the sight of it struck him as odd – to be looking at his own arm detached from the rest of him like that, while the blood gushed out of his arm socket with every heartbeat, staining the decks red, how he lay there straining to tell his friend what to say to his mother, his wife and his kids back there in Merthyr, where the hills were green and tranquil, far from the sound of men blasting each other to pieces, there where the only sounds were of skylarks and the occasional bleat of sheep; how he died there on the deck not managing to say what he wanted to say. And then I'd ask the kids, those adults of the future, how they'd feel if their fathers were lying there like that. You follow me? I wanted to teach them how to feel, so they could draw their own conclusions about the mindless waste of it all. Yes, yes, I know it was gory stuff – but I wanted to take the glory out of it!

'Not that it happened to anyone called Thomas Jenkins – though there were legions like him. But I found myself inventing names sometimes. But I wanted to say how people felt, because they were people – *human beings*! – human beings with a right to life. Anyway, that was more important than explaining how the Battle of Trafalgar was won – winning or losing didn't make much sense, and I didn't want it to make sense to those men and women of the future, because if it did, if it *did* make sense, it would happen all over again and there could be no end to it. No, I'd be abdicating my responsibility. It would be like, well like some monstrous lie, and I could never live with myself, never look myself in the mirror – I wanted to tell them that the glory of God is preferable to the glory of war – a different morality – so at least they would ask themselves questions about the sense, or nonsense, of it all, and if they came to despise war, well, they might come to despise other things too – cruelty, poverty, slavery in all its forms, debasements of human dignity. Trouble was, none of this was included in the curriculum! Ah!'

As if to add further weight to the point, Jack rose tall from the bench, turned and looked at the cypresses, and sat down again heavily, presumably in a state of moral exhaustion.

'Inventing things the way you did – I don't suppose they considered that history,' said Sedley, resorting to the obvious and not knowing what else to say, having been shocked into silence by Jack's narrative.

'Well, some well-meaning people said it was all about facts and conformity *versus* imagination and personality, but that was only the tip of the iceberg – they couldn't understand the rest. Anyway, they gave me an ultimatum. Told me to stick to the curriculum – said the kids went home talking politics, and parents complained, calling me incompetent. They thought I'd lost it. They really did. I tried to explain – I mean, what's the good telling kids about battle strategies when what you really want to do is stop them going to war? But they wouldn't have it. No, they wanted me to talk about kings and queens, and I wanted to talk about ordinary people, because it's the ordinary folk who suffer most. History's about facts? Right, well, pain is a fact, and I taught them about pain – so I taught history, didn't I? But no, they wouldn't swallow that. *Of course* they wouldn't! They wanted me to resign, and I refused. So, they said they'd give me another chance – which meant of course that from now on they'd be lying in wait to catch me out, and then that would be that – I'd be given the final push. You see, they couldn't get rid of me just like that – I was an amiable sort of fellow and, if anything, over qualified, and the kids took to me, too – so they were obliged to follow protocol. They said they wanted the exam results to prove I was a changed man. They wanted, as they put it, the kids to stop moralising and get good grades. I guess they didn't expect the kids to do well, and then they could get rid of me. Well, I accepted their ultimatum, thinking I could manage to keep my job and serve my conscience at the same time. Anyway, I got them good exam results and, whenever I could, I encouraged the kids to ask searching questions. Jesus Christ, it was hard! I kept up this charade for about 20 years! 20 long years! Oh, I know what you're thinking. You're thinking I could've resigned there and then with "To hell with the lot of you" on my lips. Well, I thought of it, day in and day out, and went on thinking of it every day for 20 years, and it plagued me to death – but, and here's the horrible irony of it, such thoughts were a luxury I thought I couldn't afford. Why? Because I had a wife and child to think of, and jobs were hard to come by; it was a betrayal to leave them in the lurch with a mortgage and responsibilities to take care of. I saw it then as a choice between a betrayal of them and a betrayal of myself – and I decided to betray *myself*. So, I tried to compromise. I played their game most of the time, and I played my own whenever I could. But Christ! It was hard, and, in my heart of hearts, I knew I couldn't keep it up forever.

'So, there it is. I spent those years trudging into work, doffing my hat to the Head, who deserved no more respect than the rest of us and perhaps a good deal less; and I talked rubbish in the staff room to people whose lives were defined and confined by a small framework of routine, all living for the weekends, their better selves stifled and strangled by the necessity of keeping themselves afloat, though I myself felt I was drowning, deeper and deeper into a weir of despair. By God! – what we do to keep a ship afloat whose destination we dare not question! And then, I guess, I expected something from my family – as a kind of compensation for my willingness to compromise, for my loss of principle. A vain hope! Lose yourself, and nothing and no one will find you. But I loved my family. Love carries a price-tag, and the question is whether it's affordable – I thought it was.

'I thought many times during those long years that one day I might go to the hills and be free – free of them all, no, not free of my family, just free of those *others*. I hoped one day I'd be able to follow my conscience as far as it could carry me, follow what I knew deep down to be right – to get to my hill in the end, but the fear was, I'd have to abandon everything, I wouldn't be able to pick and choose, it was all or nothing at all. You see?

'But do you know, I waited all those years for something that proved in the end to be as easy and as ordinary as going to bed. It was a cold morning in February, rain coming down in a fine spray, traffic hardly stirring. I remember, the rough cord that bound my suitcase round the middle wouldn't stay tight. Funny what you remember, isn't it? I wrapped myself up in my best overcoat, put on my hat and gloves, picked up my suitcase, closed the door gently behind me and set out for the train station on the first leg of my journey to goodness knows where – but, I imagined, to my hill, somewhere away from it all. Just think of it, all those years I'd walked or cycled down those streets and in all weathers, seeing the same faces and places every day of the working week – the shy red-faced man with his plastic briefcase who would nod shyly at me as though it was forbidden to greet a fellow creature on the way to the treadmill ... and here I was at last, walking as cool as you like down those same streets on that cold, wet morning. At the station, I paused to fumble in my pockets for money – not for house keys, no, not anymore, no, I'd have no need of house keys on my hill. I had done my bit – much more than my bit, and now I was free! I could just live for myself, by myself. Yes, here I was – and I just couldn't believe the ordinariness of it.'

'Yes, strange,' said Sedley.

'Finally it happened in such an ordinary way. After all those years of missed chances to leave. I stayed with my wife and children all those years, but what kind of example did I set them? All I did was teach them acceptance of all those things I knew deep down to be wrong – I should've taught them to question, not to acquiesce. You know, it's like a man who believes that war is mass murder and then goes on to teach his children to do more of the same!'

'Nonsense! You weren't a murderer!'

'Worse! I tried to murder the voice within me! I didn't *condemn*! Not as I should've done – not as often as I should've done. I should've told those school governors to stuff it, and I should've taken my son aside and taught him to condemn – war, cruelty, injustice ... and I didn't do that because I was too weak to condemn these things myself – at least openly.'

'It was the weakness of love, not of self-interest – you chose to ...' said Sedley. If Jack drew any comfort from that, he did not show it, for Sedley was not allowed to finish his sentence.

'Courage! – yes, that's the thing. For a long time I was afraid to live, I guess because I was afraid of death – but when I saw that death was inevitable, inescapable, I learned to embrace it; you see, it was all about learning to *believe* what I, what we *all*, know to be true – and then I began to learn how to *live*. How many of us die without ever having lived? Yes. I had to wait all that time to follow my conscience, to follow what the spiral of consciousness dictated to me long ago! Ah, yes – *the spiral of consciousness.*'

'What's that?'

'No matter. No matter,' said Jack, getting up from the bench. 'I must go.'

Together they walked out of the vicarage garden without exchanging another word. They stopped at the side gate and Jack turned to take one last look at the cypresses, which could still be seen in the distance. Sedley noticed that despite his advancing years, the old fellow walked erratically, now striding quickly ahead, now slowing or stopping unexpectedly, then striding again. They stopped altogether a little way down the road away from the church. They shook hands. 'It's all nonsense, you know – everything I said back there. All stuff and nonsense!' With that, he walked off and was soon out of sight. Sedley watched him go and stood looking in that direction for several moments, even after the old fellow had dissolved away.

~ ~

The things the old man had said passed through his mind in a torrent of words, much in the way they had been spoken. 'All stuff and nonsense,' he had said. Sedley thought long and hard. He thought he understood the old man's bitterness as well as anyone could — his anger and his resolve. But there were things that remained obscure and unexplained. What was 'the spiral of consciousness'? — if it meant anything at all! But why had he said 'All stuff and nonsense'?

Yes, Jack had gone, but his ghost lingered on. Only a corporeal visit from the Lord of Hosts himself could have had a deeper influence on the Reverend Sedley. But second best was pretty good. His dream had, in essential respects, come to life. He had, in a sense, been visited by the dead. No, there was nothing for it but to give his own conscience the fullest possible rein. Unlike the old man of Sedley's dream, Jack seemed to mingle hope and confidence with despair. But Sedley regarded all this as a clarion call to arms. And once in the fray, who knows from what quarters help might come?

Hope indeed there was. Jack had had a family to consider. Sedley had no children. On the other hand, he had God's children to minister to. Yes, Sedley had a family commitment infinitely greater than that of the old man's. And luckily there was no conflict between that and the voice of his own conscience. Here, on the contrary, was the best possible marriage of earthly and spiritual obligations. How fortunate he began to consider himself. Fortunate to be paid to do what he knew to be right. He ought that night to have slept the sleep of the hopeful and the determined — like a general before a battle, fully confident of the rightness of the campaign, and vaguely confident of the outcome against vastly inferior forces.

But, truth to tell, he did not know what to make of Jack; the picture he had painted was like a puzzle with some pieces missing. If Jack had fabricated history, perhaps he had fabricated his own as well. Jack said he had 'opted out' — but had he really? Was it at all possible to opt out — to opt out of something without at the same time opting into something else? Something else equally problematic? If you jumped out of a frying pan, you might succeed in avoiding the fire, but only by jumping into another pan. Jack said he was free. But what kind of freedom was that, if it was freedom at all? A bird might fly too high and die from lack of oxygen; a bird that leaves the nest may be ill-advised to fly too far. He didn't know quite what to make of Jack's decision, if it really was a decision and not something that had been imposed upon him. Jack had wanted to ask him how he managed to live at all, since there could be precious little assistance from Government or social sources, and whether he really wanted to call this *freedom*; but it hadn't seemed at all appropriate to ask; Jack would have remained silent on such matters or dismissed them with a wave of his hand. No, there was much too much that remained unsaid, unexplained. Sedley was left with the skeletal notion that, whatever else may be fabricated, he should himself do what was spiritually required of him; he should have the courage to follow his conscience or quit his job — and the latter was out of the question, being nothing more or less than an admission of defeat.

Chapter Eleven

A Marriage of Minds

With no kindred spirit to share the load, life's a tortuous, perilous road; and marriage, though a fine and wondrous thing, must be insufficient if in depth it is deficient.

~ ~

The essential upshot of Sedley's encounter with Jack was that the latter had now evolved in Sedley's mind as an heroic and tragic figure that he had been somehow destined to meet, albeit a figure more to be pitied than Socrates; after all, Socrates had lived the good life until his incarceration and even then had been treated well by friends and sympathetic jailers; he had also been remembered, and fondly, whereas Jack and his like, though a rare and wonderful species, were, far from being revered in memory, fated to be entirely unknown and therefore unremarked upon. Jack was alone and destitute, and even the river had refused to give him passage to eternal sanctuary. Despite the puzzle still and for evermore incomplete, and despite, perhaps because of, the bitterness underlying Jack's narrative, Sedley was convinced that there was a marriage of minds between them, an understanding that was profound and indissoluble. Sedley was more than content to believe that his meeting with the old man was a confirmation of the rightness of his own mission to rescue Christianity from the doldrums of superstition and elevate the Christian ethic to the heights where it belonged, infinitely far above its competitors, like a moral giant without peer, compelling and unassailable.

The meeting with Jack, since it was seen as a confirmation of his mission, was something that Sedley felt he had to protect; the whole episode had become iconic and symbolically as valuable as a perfect Ming dynasty vase to an avid collector of Chinese ceramics. Sedley could not suffer it to be questioned, let alone dismissed. So when, the following morning, the subject was lightly alluded to at the breakfast table, Sedley was only too happy to give the matter as little attention as possible.

'So what on earth do you find to talk about?' asked Julia, nonchalantly, while spooning her cereal.

'Oh, this and that – nothing much really. In fact, I think he was the worse for wear, so I just had to humour the poor fellow.' Sedley found himself telling a lie to protect the integrity of his mission, and inwardly regarded it as the whitest of all possible white lies.

There was of course more to it than a mere feeling that Jack's story, fabricated or not, was hardly a fitting subject for casual and sleepy exchange over a bowl of cereals. The fact was that the quality of marital confidence was rather less than he would have wished it. The problem had to do with appearances and expectations and the way in which they could be so easily deceptive and unreliable. After all, the expectation was that two people who were bonded together so as to have become one person must share a super-affinity and a mutual understanding and should enjoy an attachment to the same ideals and values. Naturally, there may be all sorts of ways in which the Sedleys might disagree one with the other, yet they had at least to share the same lens through which the world was viewed; perceptions may at times diverge, but only because the lens was temporarily clouded and vision superficially clouded. Two people joined together in holy matrimony may, to the casual observer, appear, particularly in public, as one might expect them to appear: a harmonious duo sharing the same conception of what life had to offer and of what they had to offer life; some rough edges may appear here and there but are allowable and in no way insoluble. Reality may of course differ from the ideal, as a real engine may differ from a diagram in a manual, and, in the case of engines, differences are to be expected, and the diagram is taken for no more than it's worth. But when it comes to romantic ideals, ideal notions tend to be taken more seriously, and departures from the ideal are more apt to cause a more than inordinate degree of disquietude.

Expectations and appearances might, then, prove painfully unreliable in this particular case. The Sedleys had sat down to breakfast quite naturally and amiably. They talked casually and sensibly. They would have appeared to any rational observer a picture of marital bliss. True, their conversation may have appeared somewhat terse, but it is seldom reasonable to expect much more at that time of day and eminently reasonable to expect even less or nothing at all. But as Sedley added a second spoonful of sugar to his cereal, he found himself reflecting that the tips of icebergs can present a pleasant and innocuous aspect at sea, especially as the bright light of the early morning sun renders the ice a glistening, not to say inviting, prospect, but that such an aspect is at the same time insidious since the dangers are hidden from view and are falsely represented. Human icebergs were, well … in essentials quite similar.

It was a short step from here to the question, which seemed so obvious that it posed itself, whether there were icebergs in his own marriage. He felt obliged to ask whether there was really a marriage of minds, and the answer that had already begun to trickle through a mass of natural resistance was anything but palatable. In particular, he felt that were he to relate Jack's story as the old fellow had related it to him, there was too strong a chance that Julia would dismiss it before he'd taken a few preliminary steps; she would either get it all wrong or she would fail to get the best out of it. There was every chance that she would condemn it as all stuff and nonsense though not, of course, in so many words. Now it was one thing to hear Jack use such words, one thing to hear him dismiss his own account as all stuff and nonsense; he could talk disparagingly about himself; but it was quite another thing to hear such derogatory sentiments from a person like ….well, like Charles Baxter, for example. In fact, it might not be too much to suggest that Jack's dismissal was an invitation to take it all seriously – the very opposite of what the words themselves conveyed; yes, he might simply have intended an expression of self-defacement, as when someone who has achieved something remarkable dismisses it all with a quite genuine 'It was nothing, really'. Well, whatever Jack may or may not have meant by the phrase 'all stuff and nonsense', it was one thing coming from him, but quite another coming from someone else – especially from the likes of a Charles Baxter!

But if it would be irritating to hear that sort of disparagement from Baxter, to hear it from Julia would be excruciatingly painful. There had to be a marriage of minds between Jack and a listener if the old fellow was not to be regarded as a dotty eccentric with nothing coherent to say, because, despite appearances, there was a strong chance that he did have something to say worth listening to; but the question was whether Julia was capable of disregarding appearances, whether she had the patience, whether she had the disposition; and if she was not capable, it would seem to suggest something unpalatable. Sedley felt in no doubt that there was a marriage of minds between Jack and himself; even though Jack had thrown in the towel while Sedley was bracing himself to fulfil his mission, they had in common the premise that all was not well with the world and that something should be done about it; Sedley had decided that something *could* be done about it, and Jack might have conceded that Sedley was a fitting candidate for torch-bearer albeit lacking the stature of a Jesus Christ or a Socrates, or a Ghandi or a Mandela; he might at least have conceded that Sedley had the right sort of idea, though he might well have entertained doubts as to whether he could actually bring off anything significant.

Sedley might be a minor torch-bearer in Jack's estimation, and (who knows?) his efforts might be doomed to failure; but at least there was a marriage of minds between them; but it was better not to say too much to Julia, otherwise it would be like exposing Jack naked on a rock for the vultures to pick at. Vultures? Surely, Julia was anything but a vulture! Well, perhaps not a vulture – but it was best not to take any unnecessary risks. The conclusion Sedley did his level best to resist was that there was no marriage of minds in his marriage. Surely, Julia was not one of the shadow people; surely not, because Julia was Julia, the woman he had married. Sedley resisted such thoughts because he was convinced there in the absence of a marriage of minds, there was really no marriage at all worthy of the name. If it was not worthy of the name, then it was not worth holding on to. And if it was not worth holding on to ... Well, these were silly, dangerously intrusive thoughts against which the doors of the mind must be barred and bolted.

'Well, anyway, what happened?' she asked, as she was collecting the dishes after breakfast.

'Happened? Well, I told you. I had to humour him and ...'

'No, I mean when did he leave? Where did he go?'

'Oh, I walked with him out of the garden, and away he went – I don't know where.' Sedley thought of saying 'to his hill', but this would have invited trouble. 'I tried to advise him where he might, er... but, no, he wasn't interested, So er ...'

'Right. Just passing through I suppose. Er, pass me those, will you?'

Sedley passed her two mugs which she then put into the dishwasher, and so the subject was interred as easily as it had been given life. On the one hand, Sedley was glad. But, curiously, he was also disappointed that Julia hadn't pressed him further; he was keenly aware of his ambivalence, and he was annoyed about that, too. He felt like a spoilt child refusing an ice-cream and blaming the refusal on the one who'd made the offer in the first place. The fact is, Sedley would have loved to have confided in Julia the whole encounter point for point, detail for detail – Julia who was, after all, his wife; and he felt he could not.

The absence of a true marriage of minds is like a wall. But it must be remembered that every wall has two sides. Julia was on the other side and was well aware of its solidity, brick by brick.

'Oh, I meant to tell you, I had a chat with the Baxters yesterday – before the service, and er ... well she said she'd contact us to let us know.'

'They'll phone *us*? But I thought we were inviting *them*?'

'Well, yes, but she said they'll be busy for a while, and they'll let us know when they get a chance to come over – and then we can arrange it properly.'

'Oh, I see,' he said, with a noticeable lack of enthusiasm.

'Well, you know, they're very busy – especially Charles. His only chance is on the weekends, and even then ...'

'Right, right ... I'll leave it to you,' he said brusquely. And then, after a pause, 'So you had a good little chat, did you?'

'About this and that. Nothing much. Usual stuff.'

This brief exchange ended right there, omitting the most important element. Charles Baxter, who now had little time for the Reverend, had all the time in the world for his spouse. During their little chat, Baxter said that he could drop Julia's name to a few friends of his who were the kind of people whose judgement could be trusted in the world of art, people who were capable of recognising unpublished talent, people who might give Julia some guidance if not some patronage of sorts. He asked Julia if she would mind a little name dropping. Of course, she minded not at all. She was delighted and most appreciative. There was hardly time to go into much detail, but Baxter had said enough to ensure that something would take root and flourish in Julia's ambitious psyche. He had even mentioned the possibility of her meeting some of his influential friends, and he would, he said, be delighted to be instrumental in bringing these introductions about. From that moment on, and during the entire length of her husband's sermon that morning, she was absorbed in the most fanciful speculations concerning her future as a professional and distinguished artist. After all, she mused, it is perfectly true that the biggest things can grow from the smallest beginnings; there was no certainty about things; but, all the same, big oaks have been known to grow from little acorns; and if that happened, it would all be due to the trigger of fate in the hands of Charles Baxter. Imaginings of success were delicious and irresistible; before the morning was over, she was already being feted worldwide as the artist of the century.

This, infinitely more than the prospect of entertaining the Baxters, was the priceless essence of her brief conversation with them. And yet, she felt she could not share it with Adam. It was clear that Adam and Charles didn't see eye to eye, so had she related these matters to Adam, the best she could have expected was a lukewarm response and the last thing she wanted was a dampener – in fact, it was not beyond the bounds of possibility that he would have flown off the handle. To err is human, to forgive divine; but Julia doubted whether Adam had about him sufficient divinity to overlook his dislikes. But even more important, she knew that Adam had little sympathy for ambition in general, and for Julia's artistic future in particular; it wasn't that he was completely unsympathetic or that he didn't wish her well, only that he was not as keen as she was to give her talents a public airing; and to enlist the help of Charles Baxter in the process was just asking too much. Adam, she thought, seemed to be quite blind to the fact that it was sometimes necessary to seek the help of those one neither admired nor respected for the purpose of achieving something admirable and respectable; provided one's objectives were not themselves morally questionable, such a recourse was quite unobjectionable; Julia regarded Baxter's intervention as an instance in which the Machiavellian principle of 'the end justifies the means' was not only morally neutral but positively desirable. Nevertheless, it was better to say nothing about this to Adam, at least for the time being. She considered duplicity to be quite foreign to her nature – but, well, this was not really a case of duplicity; more a matter of withholding information on a need-to-know basis; it was a question of tact and correct timing; after all, it was all too simple for words, and all perfectly above board. Things had to be taken step by step. And as for Baxters being physically instrumental in bringing about personal introductions – well, that had to await the building of bridges and the burying of hatchets; all in good time. Perhaps there would be no time better than when the Baxters came to dinner, when all these things could be brought up during, say, an after-dinner chat – all very natural and amiable, when all her present misgivings and frustrations would be silly things of the past.

But for now, there was no telling how Adam might take the idea of Baxter's kindly intervention – he might begin to imagine all sorts of things. No, the least said the better – for the moment, at any rate. Just a temporary expedient. Nothing more. Yes, but at the same time, she was frustrated and irritated by the fact that the whole thing had to be hidden away at all, as though it were nothing more than a future possibility. She expected far more – a comfortable openness, for one thing, between husband and wife.

She stood on other side of the wall and could do nothing more than peak occasionally over the top; no breach was possible, let alone an open door. And despite all her caution and reserve, despite the fact that what she omitted remained omitted, Adam did indeed begin to imagine all sorts of things, in a muddled sort of way; he needed no further catalyst than what he knew already.

~ ~

That same evening Sedley presided over a meeting of the church finance committee, commonly, even affectionately, referred to as the FC, which consisted of members for whom there was nothing but a marriage of minds, indeed an indissoluble bond which only death could break asunder.

More precisely, it consisted of three local businessmen and two ladies, one of enormous proportions, the other diminutive, but both stalwart members of the local women's guild and both now retired from the little corner shop they had run amicably together, and last, but by no means least, Charles Baxter. Meetings were formally chaired by John Burgess, who tended to go with the flow, and whose presence was hardly noticed. In fact, this grand alliance had been formed by Burgess himself, acting on the advice of Baxter; and Burgess had planned ahead and arranged dates and times when the committee should convene, all such dates and times having been mutually agreed and noted carefully in the diaries and on-screen filofaxes of the membership. (Indeed, the lady of enormous proportions had gone so far as to acquire a handsome, expensive, crocodile-leather filofax in polished brown for the very purpose, the diminutive lady immediately following suit, while Burgess, contrary to what was naturally expected of his standing, still wrote his memos on any slips of paper that came to hand, frequently losing them and having to phone round members for reminders and confirmations.) Burgess had loudly extolled the virtues of this grand alliance between Church, on the one hand, and commercial expertise and experience on the other, and had urged the new incumbent to keep it up and going at all costs. Sedley had agreed that it should continue, if only because he could see no compelling reason why it should not, or, rather, no reason that would appeal equally to the committee itself for its dissolution – once again, the ability to persuade others as to the rightness of your position would require at least sufficient common ground, and where a marriage of minds was lacking, the ability to convince was necessarily limited.

On this evening in particular, each member dutifully turned up in good time. All, that is, except Charles Baxter. Baxter's absence was noted and underlined in red in the crocodile filofaxes even before the meeting was scheduled to begin, since he was, everyone said, invariably the first to arrive, himself noting lateness amongst others – an assertion which Sedley had no trouble accepting at face value.

The minutes wore on, and still no sign of Baxter. Baxter's lateness, even his non-attendance, would not have struck Sedley in the least bit noteworthy had it not been for the others, who did nothing less than marvel at his continued absence, pointing at the empty chair as if to confirm it – indeed, it might not have seemed unreasonable had they approached the chair itself and waved their hands through the empty space simply to verify a proposition that they scarcely believed to be true, namely: *Charles Baxter is absent.*

The proposition having been confirmed, it was time for possible explanations. Had he known about the meeting? Without a doubt! Had he forgotten? Impossible! He was there when the schedule was made and had taken due note of each day and date, and days and dates had been arranged to avoid clashes with any other activity, business or social. Baxter was invariably meticulous about all dates and times. Well, then – was it possible that something had arisen to ... No, Baxter would have informed Sedley without delay – because that was the kind of man he was, thoughtful and considerate to a fault. He was a stickler for detail, especially details that mattered – and since a meeting of the FC was no mere matter of detail. It mattered enormously. Everyone agreed that it mattered enormously – so would Baxter, if he were here – so why wasn't he there? And so the questions and inadequate answers would do the rounds again, while Sedley sat there listening to what seemed so much inflated drivel, for all but Sedley agreed that the meeting could not continue in the absence of its most cherished member.

So distressed did everyone become that it was suggested that Sedley should call Baxter, at least to ascertain that he was still in the land of the living. It was not, of course, an idea that Sedley at all relished; but who was Sedley to question the mood of the committee? More to the point, how could he question the mood without at the same time breaking into a character assassination or, at the very least, betraying his feelings towards Baxter, which were anything but amicable, and – who knows? – he might even go on to question the continuance of the beloved FC itself. No, where there is no marriage of minds, it is best to tread carefully.

Susan Baxter answered his call, and, after what seemed to Sedley a most pregnant and suggestive pause, announced that Charles was well but indisposed, and she said that she would try to get him to phone back later. This response only added to the consternation of the finance committee, who were now at a loss to comprehend cause and effect. Needless to say, the dour expressions of wonder ad regret emanating from the members did little to impress Sedley favourably, nor did it endear himself to them when he dared to suggest that the meeting should proceed without the absentee; finally, the meeting was aborted; the two ladies had not even removed their coats, expecting to do so when Baxter arrived, and one of the three local businessmen had even remained standing, as though it were a mark of respect for absent friends. Everyone left, murmuring one to the other as they ambled down the vicarage path as daylight was fading and darkness was pressing. Sedley watched them as they gestured and frowned their way to their family hatchbacks gleaming in the streetlights.

Sedley was the first to admit, albeit to himself, that it was a peculiarity. Baxter was obviously pretending not to be at home; and Susan Baxter had sounded nervous, which was odd given that they had chatted to Julia a short time before. While he had little time for the respect afforded Baxter by the members of the finance committee, he had to agree that the object of their veneration, a man who took to money matters as the proverbial duck takes to water, had acted very much out of character, being most unlikely to miss any opportunity to shine like a star in the firmament to all who looked up to him. What Baxter enjoyed most was an audience, the more attentive the better; when he could address himself to large numbers he was in his seventh heaven and his natural element; the committee was an audience of sorts, but on this occasion it was chaired for the first time by Sedley, and Baxter had missed an opportunity to assert his superiority in matters touching finance and funding for church roofs. Nor was it to be forgotten that the august members of the FC were also voters whose opinions were highly respected in the locality and that word gets around. Votes counted in elections, and Baxter had set his sights on the governance of nations. A vote was a vote and, as Baxter well knew, it mattered little whether he was voted in by imbeciles or by the intelligentsia, by murderers or by saints; had he known that a deciding vote in his favour was attributable to lunatics, he would not have lost much sleep over it; lunacy, like beauty, was in the eye of the beholder, and it did not enter Baxter's head for one moment that an adoring electorate might, despite appearances, subsist on a diet of bigotry and complacency and a side-dish of ignorance and mediocrity. Appearances mattered. His own political future relied very much on appearances, as indeed does that of every other aspirant to political status. It was important therefore that appearances should be kept up. Every voter counted, for birds of a feather flock together.

Take, for example, the lady of enormous proportions.

A more tastefully dressed, a more sweetly spoken, a more cultured specimen of the human species you could not possibly hope to find. Nor could it be said that she lacked flexibility, for she could alter her disposition from that of the gentlewoman, slow to react and as pensive as the proverbial owl, to that of the aggressor as an arch defender of the faith. For God, as she defined him, was the supernatural dispenser of absolute justice. Illness, for instance, was one way in which the will of the Almighty might be discerned, and the greater the severity of the malady, the clearer the Divine Will. Woe-betide the AIDS sufferer, for she had a sermon or two up her sleeve for the likes of him; let no one attempt a compassionate brief for the stricken, for she would condemn his defence counsel with even greater zeal. (How she might have held forth on the subject of toothache is, it must be said, rather less certain; here, no doubt, the will of the Almighty had to be discerned through a much darker glass.) Let no one, in her presence, hold forth on the rights of the gay community; let them not subscribe to the view that the sexual leanings of a vicar of Christ are irrelevant to their ability to cite scripture meaningfully. Let no one, in her presence, so much as read their own horoscope, and much less hers, for she would read them a sermon on sorcery and witchcraft, on devilry and defilement, at the drop of a hat. The unhappy victim would, at first, laugh at the drama, and then, seeing that she actually meant every word of her hideous tirade, would fizzle to a crisp and wish himself elsewhere – what else could he possibly do in the obvious absence of anything that could, even at the furthest stretch, be called a marriage of minds? A marriage of minds is a bridge over which we might cross troubled waters – no bridge, no crossing.

Yes, the lady of enormous proportions felt herself at God's right hand and was not one to question whether God had a right hand, or indeed a leg, or for that matter any body at all. To have denied any kind of corporeality to her God would have been to commit a blasphemy compared to which all other blasphemies pale into insignificance. At the same time, this feminine monument to intellectual sagacity would have hit the roof if one had dared to speculate on the size of the gloves and shoes the Almighty wears. Her opinions on disease as an expression of divine will and her views on the satanic nature of homosexuality, were, and still are, shared by those of very different faiths, faiths which she herself would rule out of divine court, suggesting that questions should be asked with some immediacy about the moral integrity of such systems of belief and the common strands that hold them all together. But the lady of enormous proportions, in common with those of other faiths, was not one to question what for her was bedrock.

This gracious lady was, in short, a fundamentalist, who believed that her fundamentalism was as safe as houses in the capable hands of men like John Burgess and Charles Baxter. If Baxter was a no-nonsense man, she was a no-nonsense lady. They were made from the same mould, these two, though the castings looked different depending on the intensity of the light and the angle of vision. Baxter would poke fun at this lady's fundamentalism though he had no logical brief to offer against it, just a gut feeling that nothing north of the North Pole could possibly matter that much. But he would never ridicule her to her face, for, after all, a vote was a vote; he was not one to look a gift-horse in the mouth, even if the poor creature was doomed for the knacker's yard. If she thought of the Almighty as the just dispenser of punishment both here and in the hereafter, Baxter was not one to scrutinise the idea and espouse the virtues of an alternative and loving God, for one who is fevered with the discovery of gold is not one to question its source.

Sedley did his best to relegate Baxter's absence to the back of his mind. It was not easy to do. It retreated somewhat but did not dissolve away. No doubt Julia would be dismayed to know that he was beginning to imagine all sorts of things; or perhaps the thought would excite her. He didn't imagine them all at once; they came to him singly, like occasional drops of water from a leaky tap, but, in the dead of night, a single drip can sound like a clap of thunder to a susceptible imagination; added to which it is well to remember that parts of a puzzle may be more intriguing than the finished whole – after all, it is not what you see in the dark, but what you do not see that racks the imagination and frays the nerves.

~ ~

Sedley's sleep that night was far from the dreamless sleep that Socrates imagined death might be.

He dreamt that he entered the moon-lit bedroom late at night to find Julia and a man together. They paid him no attention as they tossed and turned in passionate embrace; he called out to Julia, but either she didn't hear him or she heard him and couldn't have cared less. As they writhed lustfully this way and that, Baxter's face was suddenly turned towards him and then in the next instant it turned away again, yet, though recognising Baxter, Sedley seemed to find nothing unnatural in all of this, let alone distressing, let alone agonising. Sedley didn't raise his voice in anger, for there was no anger. He made no attempt to stop them and question them, no attempt to demand an explanation. It was all so natural that Sedley might have offered them a cup of tea. In the next scene, the love-making had stopped and they both lay there asleep, the sheets barely covering them in the half-light. Sedley approached the bed and placed the sheets over them as if to protect them from the chill of early morning, and with all the solicitude that a father might show his small children in the dead of a winter's night.

If this was a nightmare, it had nothing about it suggestive of the rage or the distress of a cuckold. Or, perhaps that is how it is when the cuckold is also a fatalist. Sedley felt ashamed of his dream; where was the trust he ought to have placed in her? The whole thing was absurd! But his feelings were complicated by a sense of inexorability about the events in his own life and in the lives of those around him. He felt, above all, that he had to follow a certain path, and he was not at all sure whether he could take Julia with him. He wondered whether it really mattered that much if Julia couldn't make the distance that had to be travelled. The path he had to travel mattered less to her than to him; so she would have a choice. But he could not choose. It was his destiny, or his fate. There was no question of trying to appease Julia and living happily ever after; appeasement was out of the question; the more he attempted appeasement, the longer he delayed his crossing of the Rubicon, and the unhappier he would be, they both would be. What's more, that crossing had already begun, and its completion was as inevitable as sunset.

There was no doubt that Sedley was a fatalist of sorts. He could actually *feel* an inevitability about events. He remembered a story he had been told about a cyclist at a road junction. The cyclist turned left at that busy junction every day, left into a lane where drivers drove fast and careless; life had let him down, and he decided to end it all; but it was essential that a good job should be made of it, with no loose ends; he decided to cycle to that junction and wait for a large lorry to come down that road at speed; then he would cycle into the path of the lorry and ... But that lorry never seemed to come. Each morning he would hope to see that monstrous beast roaring towards that junction, but it never came. Then he gave up, gave up waiting for it. He even began to forget all about ending it all, thanks perhaps to the numbing effects of routine and because life began to offer brighter prospects and wear lighter hues. And then, one morning, with his mind far away, he accidentally took too wide a turn from the junction and was knocked down and killed by an oncoming lorry whose driver, perhaps also stultified by routine, failed to see him at all until it was too late.

Wherever he stood, Sedley felt he was not on safe ground. Even if he turned his back on his God ... But, no, he could not turn his back on his God. The course was set and he had to run it. It was as simple as that. And Julia? Well, he felt a curious detachment, as though it did not matter ultimately whether she stood with him or not; and sometimes it seemed to matter enormously. When he felt that it did not matter, how far could that feeling be trusted? He would not know until the course was run. There was still a lot of running to do, for the race had hardly begun. If there was a battle to be fought, it was not yet enjoined. There had merely been a preliminary alignment of opposing forces and a cursory reconnaissance of enemy entrenchments. He knew that the members of the Finance committee had already begun to distrust him; he could see it in their faces and in the faces of others in his congregation. But there was no help for it. He would not and could not deny his God. There was no doubt in his mind that the battle would need to take place.

It seemed to him that the devil himself had for a long time ridden upon a pearly white charger called Religion – the Devil himself dressed in the very finest and brightest apparel and was armed with a sword that was by all and sundry mistaken for the sword of Justice and Compassion. It was time for the Foul Fiend to be defrocked and shown for the wicked imposter he truly was. That was the rationale behind the battle to be enjoined, and who better than Sedley to be Commander-in-Chief of the Army of Divine Liberation?

Chapter Twelve

And so to War ...

Is he from Heaven, or is he from Hell? Oh, he can't be from Heaven, for we know him too well. And back to the hills? Yes, that's where he'll go, for madness is rife where the cold winds blow.

~ ~

Sedley's guns delivered a broadside the following Sunday during a service that was, it was plain to see, more than usually well-attended, with some new faces to puzzle the mind; Julia was conspicuous by her absence, but they had both decided that her initial support had been appropriate and that further attendances were at best optional.

Baxter was there, his right flank protected by a newcomer – a neat, clean-shaven, well-groomed gentleman in his mid- to late-30s, with heavy horn-rimmed spectacles, a bowtie in Oxford blue, a dark-grey suit with a red carnation in the lapel, and brown leather brogues that had had an encounter with a ferocious tin of shoe polish. This immaculately dressed, and therefore formidable, personage wore his hair short and combed back tight and flat, like a male cabaret dancer of the 1920s. Although this newcomer seemed much younger than he actually was, he looked as dour and single-minded as any young lieutenant in the field ought to look in the company of a Field Marshal.

The gentleman with the red carnation described himself to all and sundry as a journalist and carried business cards in his pocket to prove it; he was in the habit of producing one of these minor literary masterpieces each time he was introduced. Perhaps this practice was merely an example of the gentleman's dedication to efficiency, since it saved him the trouble of asking the other fellow what his profession was before declaring his own; in short, these cards enabled him to get to the heart of the matter, namely himself, at maximum speed and with as little dead wood as possible. Efficiency to the man with the red carnation was what following orders is to the dedicated career soldier, namely a thing to be accomplished in the total absence of any restraining doubt.

Like his great mentor, Baxter, the man with the red carnation had little time for any of those wishy-washy philosophical sort of people who seemed to raise questions endlessly and at every turn. In his view, the world should be peopled entirely with *doers*, not with thinkers. Thinkers, especially those whose reflections seemed to call into question the principles of a sane and settled existence, were little more than a hindrance to the dignified progress of mankind, a progress should plod and not jerk. No, the gentleman with the red carnation had fully addressed the matter, turned it over and over in his tortured mind and concluded, a few moments later, that in a world of computerised efficiency and accessibility and consequent momentous economic growth there really could be no satisfactory place for philosophers at all of any description. It had been all very well for the ancient Greeks to walk about all day in sandals, flirting, drinking wine and speculating about the nature of the heavens, but, nowadays, anyone with more than an iota of intelligence knew much better than to waste their time on such barbarous trifles as celestial speculation; which is not to say (quite the contrary!) that he set no store by flirting and drinking wine, such aspects of Greek leisure being, in any case, timeless human pursuits without which life would be devoid of any meaning at all; no, it was more the cerebral activities of the ancients and their modern-day counterparts that filled him with disdain. It has to be admitted that philosophy in general, and ancient Greek philosophy in particular, were not subjects in which he was even remotely well-read. He had 'tried' such things and had immediately found them wanting, as some people try Kalamarakia Tighanita and find the dish tasteless. In any case, people didn't walk about in sandals anymore, unless they were on a package holiday in Crete – and even then they had spent money on it, thereby making a real contribution to economic growth. The gentleman with the red carnation had sensibly concluded that philosophy, whatever it was, was as extinct as the dodo and as of much practical use as Egyptian hieroglyphics. It should come as no surprise therefore that although vehemently anti-Marxist, he had never read a page of Marx and therefore had at least this much in common with those who are avowedly Marxist yet equally ignorant of Marx's literary corpus.

Unsurprisingly, he did not regard questions as helpful unless the answers were immediate and unambiguous. He was not an unreasonable man. He was prepared to wait until tomorrow for an answer to a question posed today if a faster response was not immediately forthcoming. Thus far he would go. But when the answer came he expected nothing short of crystal clarity and mathematical precision. His love of facts may not, therefore, strike one as out of character. He doted on them. He regarded them as his stock-in-trade. 'Facts are sacred, comment is free' was his favourite slogan (especially the first part) dedication to which he cited as demonstrable evidence of a free press.

By calling himself a journalist he meant to imply that he was no mere reporter for some local rag, but a writer of no mean distinction. In fact, he was a reporter for a national rag, and one who was appropriately sparing in his commentaries. But it was not as though he allowed any old fact to parade itself without some assistance, for he was of the belief, which he held in common with his professional colleagues, that facts had to be selected before they could be allowed to speak for themselves, and that, once selected, they required a little prodding and shoving. There was no doubt that the gentleman with the red carnation was a born prodder and shover; indeed, he would not have got where he was without a good deal of prodding and shoving, for he was more than happy to toe the editorial line, and following the editorial line required a prodder and shover of the very highest calibre. For he and his editor considered that the best facts (and there were many facts that neither he nor his editor liked and many that they positively loathed) were opportunities and that opportunities were not to be missed; facts were openers, they were angles, they were pegs, they were, above all, the means to improvements in the circulation figures. Good newspapers were, by definition, good at exploiting the opportunities that the right kind of facts presented. Not that the gentleman with the red carnation wanted to be thought of as a mere newspaperman – a word that was somehow reminiscent of fish and chips and was curiously demeaning. No, a journalist he was, and he carried yet another card stating that he was a member of the National Union of Journalists, and that clinched it; for no one who belonged to that august body could be considered anything but incorruptible and a martyr to sober truth and a paragon of moral integrity.

The gentleman with the red carnation was a friend of Charles Baxter. Which is to say that he liked Baxter and Baxter liked him, which is another way of saying that between them there was a tried and tested marriage of minds. Exactly what this marriage of minds consisted in was hard to say and would require a separate volume or two to elucidate to its fullest extent, yet it had to do with the fact that each regarded the other as the very rock upon which the Faith of each was founded. What that Faith consisted in was also difficult to articulate with precision, yet there was little felt need for articulation. There was, one might simply say, an affinity between them, a feeling of brotherhood, a sense that they were birds of the same feather. Needless to say, Baxter would have fully subscribed to the editorial line of the newspaper for which the gentleman with the red carnation worked had that line been articulated and set in stone. Both they and the newspaper were spiritually as one in the art of telling the rest of mankind what it should and should not do, how it should and should not live; in other words, in the art of adopting a superior stance over all and sundry. The newspaper in question was one of only several that enjoyed the epithet *Quality Press*, and all that enjoyed it were engaged in the same enterprise of telling their readers the difference between right and wrong. Each publication in this category was engaged in the process of selecting, according to its own political perspective, the best facts, the *very* best facts, and after these facts had been selected, prodded and shoved into an acceptable perspective, they were then presented with an eye to the linguistic styles and aesthetics of the language commensurate with the expectations of the relevant readership. The newspaper which employed the gentleman with the red carnation was steeped in facts and was founded solidly upon them; had the newspaper been capable of taking human form, it would have sported the old school tie and reached for a decanter of reliable claret.

Baxter and the gentleman with the red carnation had attended the same school, though not at the same time; and this simple fact was enough to secure their partnership in this world and the next. Baxter had made such an impression during his schooldays that his reputation lingered long after his departure, like an afterimage in the wake of strong light. Baxter had been all too ready to bully the new arrivals until the butter that would not melt in their mouths began to curdle. He was nevertheless revered by the more senior boys as much as he was feared by the juniors, and some of the seniors naturally studied hard to emulate him, and not without success; indeed, Baxter actually took some of his would-be disciples under his wing and, like a conscientious Fagan, instructed them in the art of getting out of life with the minimum effort everything that others put in; all that was needed, he taught them, was the moral courage necessary for the task, and that is to say, a little bullying here and a little bullying there; and this kind of moral courage was the one dubious quality that both the gentleman with the red carnation and Baxter shared in abundance, Baxter's mere reputation alone serving as a template for future aspirants. In all fairness to both, the rough edges of this crude morality had been smoothed by adulthood and the better examples set by others; nevertheless, once a bully, always a bully, is a fair generalisation and might have been applied to these two worthy gentlemen with more than a smattering of truth.

Let it be remembered that since the gentleman with the red carnation was in the employ of a *quality* publication, not only was his moral courage in defence of the principle of the freedom of the press incomparable, but his brief and exhortation were presented in the very best style, syntax and lexis that the language is capable of producing, thanks no doubt to the well-founded allegation that his educational upbringing was the very best that the country could offer. Hear him speak and there could be no doubt that the aforementioned principle was perfectly absolute and binding, that it existed not simply as a mere abstraction but as a real and living thing, and no conceivable doubt that the country in which he was so proud to have been born led the world in the exemplification, nay the very creation, of the same. In speaking thus, the gentleman with the red carnation could produce a tearful response in his hearers, though in conjunction with several glasses of good burgundy the response could have been considerably wetter. Indeed, he could bring tears to his own eyes; and there is much to be said for an education that can induce emotion in a hypocrite in the very act of dissemblance, and the probability that for many of its beneficiaries it is *all* that can be said should not deter us from giving credit where credit is due.

Sitting on Baxter's right, and partly shielded from view by a large stone pillar, the gentleman with the red carnation fumbled in his pockets for his notepad and pencil, for he could write copiously in shorthand should the need arise, and he was quite determined that arise it would. He was capable of balancing the notepad on his knee and writing while at the same time looking straight ahead, a trick he had picked up at the many party conferences he had attended; he would perform this feat with a flair for espionage and in the frenzied manner of one who was working, against all odds, for the betterment of the human race – an attitude of mind which, like Baxter, he had no doubt contracted during his tender schooldays and which then, as now, was nurtured by an overwhelming self-confidence and a strong belief in his own material destiny.

There was no doubt that Baxter was on this occasion accompanied by the very best that sincere patronage could offer. For his left flank was protected, not to say over-protected, by no lesser personage than the lady of enormous proportions who, through no fault of her own, took up two places in the pews. Her large leather handbag was balanced on her knees yet still managed to look miniscule, amply demonstrating the relativity of space and time. She looked imposing, if not threatening; she too was fairly brimming over with self-confidence, as though her corporeal magnitude was outward proof of her intellectual prowess touching divinity and Government – two elements which she considered quite distinct and never-the-twain. Now and again she would clear her throat, as if about to drop a pearl of wisdom into the laps of those who could both hear and understand, while the gentleman with the red carnation repeatedly cleaned his spectacles with a piece of blue lint made for the very purpose.

Baxter, seated between these two stalwarts, felt as confident as ever a general was that his flanks could not be turned. His confidence was rewarded in the faces of these two lieutenants, whose intellects, razor sharp as ever, were poised to detect flaws in logic and departures from doctrine and to take due note of any irreverence that might occur.

From the very outset the lady of enormous proportions had found the Reverend Sedley a queer sort and strangely unapproachable – quite unlike the kind and affable Burgess, who would always defer to her superior grasp of divine essentials with a 'Quite right, dear lady, quite right!'; and she knew for a fact that she hadn't in the least been fobbed off or patronised when Burgess said that. No, she had known where she stood with Burgess, and she totally agreed with Baxter that it was important to know where one stood, especially where your vicar's concerned. Burgess had been an anchor in a troubled world, for she was thankfully far removed from the shores of her own land, in which the essence of her very real Christian Faith seemed to have been shaken to the very core, not to mention the fact that those socialists had a great deal to answer for and hadn't even begun to answer yet; no doubt they would be amply punished in the life hereafter; indeed, it was only by divine intervention that those morbid atheists hadn't established a serious foothold in her country – Ah, the very thought! No, Sedley had not created a good impression. If only one could make a start with him; but there seemed to be no inroad into the man. Sedley was young and a man of the cloth; but there again, wolves can appear in sheep's clothing, and perhaps that was what Sedley was – a wolf underneath it all. Yes, she had agreed entirely with Mr Charles Baxter that any doctrinal hanky-panky was to be nipped in the bud – and nipping wolves in the bud was one of her specialities. Perhaps Sedley was well-meaning. If so, one sometimes had to be cruel to be kind. Either way, the matter must be looked into, and Baxter had been quite right to approach her; in fact, she had felt honoured to be approached at all on such issues, but it had been an special honour to be approached by Mr Baxter, a solid citizen if ever there was one, a champion of right and a defender of undefiled tradition. She had attended both Sedley's sermons to date, as she had regularly attended those of the Reverend Burgess, bless his heart, and she had certainly not favoured the tone and direction of Sedley's exhortations. She had not found him particularly easy to understand, either. The Reverend Burgess, bless his heart again, had always gone out of his way to make things brief and clear. He had exercised as much refined judgement in his speaking as he had when properly deferring to her almost divine intuition in matters scriptural. Oh, what a man was Burgess! But, no, she had not been happy with Sedley's performances to date. Far from it. But she had kept silent about it, as befits a Christian woman who at all times prefers to give others the benefit of the doubt. But, when none other than Mr Charles Baxter had approached her and helped her to grasp the essence of Sedley's message ... well, she had been immediately persuaded that the matter required urgent attention. He had asked her to keep an eye and an ear open; and to prove how thoroughly she appreciated his confidence in her, she had come ready to devote both eyes and both ears to the matter in hand; had she had three pairs of eyes and four pairs of ears, she would have devoted them all to the service of the Almighty, but, as it was, she had to make do with the little with which nature had endowed her.

When Baxter had introduced the gentleman with the red carnation to the lady of enormous proportions, they took to each other immediately; he was such a nice young man: solid, respectable – not, it was true, overly knowledgeable in matters of Scripture, but a good and reliable Christian at heart nevertheless, who had come to do his duty as she was doing hers. The marriage of minds was immediate. Besides, he was a good friend of Mr Baxter's, and they'd even been to the same school; he was courteous, polite, spoke with an educated accent and worked for a quality newspaper; he was an avid supporter of the Government and a patron of the Church. What better credentials could a young man have? Yes, it was marriage of minds all round.

~ ~

The good Reverend Sedley, having taken mental note of how packed the congregation was on that Sunday evening, and relishing the dictum 'the more, the merrier', arranged his forward batteries and commenced to deliver his first salvo. He had worked out the bare bones of the message he planned to deliver, and to deliver come what might. He would say:

1. That the Christian ethic, as encapsulated in the Sermon on the Mount, was the only worthwhile ethic that any religion could possibly commend or had ever commended.

2. That the superstructure of Christianity, and of all other Faiths insofar as they were comparable, was mere superstitious baggage designed at best to coerce and at worst to frighten and exploit. Central to this superstructure was the belief in the Life Hereafter, the Resurrection and the working of miracles.

3. That since the essence of Christianity was its moral message, it was absurd to distinguish between it and politics as if to suggest that Christian political commentary was irrelevant. Politics without moral scrutiny was simply a form of barbarous dictatorship.

4. That given all the above, it was necessary to protect and preserve Christianity from the encroachment and domination of alternative Faiths which, at best, offered infinitely less and, at worst, preached intolerance and hatred. The abandonment of the Christian Ethic, and its substitution for an Islamic or competing Judaic mindset, would signal the eventual decline and fall of any civilisation worthy of the name.

Sedley had worked out his propositions, rather in the manner of a Martin Luther who had posted his 95 theses for debate to the castle church in Wittenberg. But Sedley's propositions were not up for debate; in Sedley's mind they were crystal clear and almost self-evident and, given the constraints of time and circumstance, he was determined to take the fullest possible advantage of a packed and captive audience.

Even his opening Scriptural reference managed to raise some eyebrows:
'I refer to Luke, Chapter 20, verses 19 – 26:
"And the chief priests and the scribes sought to lay hands on him;
and they feared the people.
And they watched him and sent forth spies" ...'

Baxter, the gentleman with the red carnation and the lady of enormous proportions might have exchanged meaningful glances had they been able to do so without drawing attention to themselves, for this reference to spies was ironically appropriate, and they immediately felt suspect. These three felt a twinge of discomfort at the time, though afterwards they merely joked about it. It was not of course that they doubted for one moment the propriety of what they were doing, only that they were unwilling at this very early stage to be found out in the prosecution of their moral and civic duty by the very subject of their observations; Sedley had to be given enough rope to hang himself with; patience was key, and good things come to those who wait. Had Sedley seen them? No doubt. Did he know they were there to monitor his sermon, to vet it for flaws? Surely not. At the same time, the thought seemed inescapable. The plain fact is, they were all thoroughly enjoying their conspiracy. It was a kind of game – serious enough, indeed, but nevertheless a cat-and-mouse affair that had about it the character of some wartime exploit behind enemy lines, or at any rate a good public schoolboy prank – like watching the Latin master to see if he would put a foot wrong with Matron. The whole thing had something about it reminiscent of jolly times at school – or so it certainly seemed to Baxter. The occasion might be intensely important, but it was exhilarating, too. We might remember, *en passant*, that Baxter's father, the good bishop Maurice Baxter, might well have had something to answer for here, for his intense admiration for general George Armstrong Custer had repeatedly led him to relate the fellow's exploits to his young son as soon as little Charles was old enough to comprehend sustained narrative. Charles would later recall, and with no small relish, the gleam in the bishop's eye as he recounted Custer's boyish exhilaration as he rode with his men down on the Washita encampment of the Cheyenne, killing everything that moved – even the camp dogs were too shocked to bark; for the Cheyenne it might have been a good day to die, if only because there was no alternative; but for the general it was a day to live, and to re-live in the officer's Mess. Of course, the bishop said it was all wrong, wrong to kill, and even worse to glory in killing, but, even so, the old boy would dwell far more on military tactics than on moral condemnation, and his relish, so thinly disguised, was conveyed to his young offspring, who subsequently failed to graduate much beyond it – so easy was it to fix the impression that killing can be a jolly sort of thing.

So while the scriptural reference in Luke to spies was purely coincidental, it was intriguing all the same – though there could not of course be any serious comparison between Sedley and Jesus, the son of God; any such thought, even if a demonstrably bad joke, would have been utterly dismissed as flagrant blasphemy by the lady of enormous proportions in particular. While she believed fervently in the Second Coming, such an event would require the support of an undisputed miracle or two. She was a most demanding and discriminating witness, and we must wonder whether anything short of miracles offered in evidence of divine origins would have sufficed to quell her doubts on the matter, and in this she was prepared to quote the authority of the Established Church itself. In short, the lady of enormous proportions had managed to elevate Jesus Christ so far above and beyond human kind that a man of simple faith would be hard put to discover any possible connection between the exhortations of Scripture and the lives of mere mortals. Such a degree of elevation had at least one salutary practical result. It obviated the idle conjecture that there might exist somewhere in the world of mortals a creature who could rightly claim to be much better than she. She was prepared, at a pinch, to consider equality, but to have expected much more than that would have been treading on thin ice, though she would never have admitted as much in public. It was just as well for Jesus that he had already completed his mission here on earth, for he might have had a hard time convincing here that he had very much to add to her own vast stock of morality – again, an authenticated miracle or two would have been necessary if his brief was to have had a decent hearing.

All this is so much idle speculation. The fact is that Sedley couldn't even get a look in. It was precisely his own fitness to espouse Christian doctrine that was in doubt, and had been ever since she'd heard his first sermon. That is why she was bequeathing both eyes and ears to the unimpeachable task in hand. The lady of enormous proportions and the gentleman with the red carnation had much in common, but in particular they both disliked questions whose answers were ambiguous or less than immediate. There is nothing so unambiguous and immediate than a miracle, and had Sedley worked a few of them … But since his powers did not extend in that direction, he was a marked man.

After his opening reference to Luke, Sedley looked about him, like a general surveying the terrain over which much blood is to be spilt. A commander who had come thus far could hardly call a halt in the face of opposing forces, even if he had wanted to. There could be no honourable retreat. It was all into the breach now, with guidons flying, sabres drawn and flashing. Some of the bloodiest battles known to man had been fought on and for a miserable piece of land. But worthless plots of land were not the stakes for Sedley.

His salvoes were delivered in relentless waves, and they were preceded by a defiant communiqué as he proceeded to quote from Luke:

' ... *But These words, "Render unto Caesar the things which be Caesar's and unto God the things which be God's" have not been correctly understood. They suggest a division between Christianity and politics and a licence for political oppression. Quite the opposite is true, because if you give to God what belongs to God there must be limit to what you can give to Caesar! These words are in fact an invitation to the moral criticism of Government, an invitation to the moral guidance of Government, not an abdication of political responsibility for Christians. As I have said before, God is not some super-being residing somewhere up in the stratosphere poised ready to exact vengeance on all those who oppose him – this is a cruel, barbaric and irrelevant superstition. This kind of God is bogus. No, God is the concept of Love, nothing more; so it follows that to love God is to love Love itself, to love what is right and decent, to do right by your fellow man, and it is absurd to suggest that politics excludes love! Politicians who tell the Church to keep out of politics are in fact serving the anti-Christ...*'

His tone was more authoritative than ever before. The gentleman with the red carnation was already scribbling frantically in his best shorthand, while Baxter's facial expression, already grim, was getting grimmer with every word; and the lady of enormous proportions was not prepared to be spoken down to like that, in a manner which explicitly questioned not only her understanding of Christ's answer to the chief priests and scribes, but of God's very omnipotence– 'a cruel, barbaric and irrelevant superstition' indeed! Her disquietude could hardly keep pace with Sedley's pronouncements:

'*It is absurdly ironic that so many of the Jews regarded Jesus as a supporter of the status quo, as though he were collaborating with the Romans who oppressed them. The truth is, he was the most radical and influential leader that a Jewish rebellion could have hoped for ... His words implied the most radical opposition to cruelty and inhumanity, short of a call to arms, which the Sermon on the Mount excluded. In this, he and Mahatma Gandhi and Nelson Mandela might have been at one, because the principle of passive resistance ...*'

The lady of enormous proportions breathed deeply at the very idea of including Jesus in this list of notables; after all, neither Gandhi nor Mandela was the son of God! And as for the idea that to love God was only to love Love itself, well she could make neither head nor tail of that; all she could say was that it sounded profoundly subversive; quite simply, she didn't like it one little bit. But there was worse, much worse, to come:

'*... The only God worthy of worship is Love, love of humanity, of human kind. And it is a love that we must all show while we live, because it cannot exist in death. The very idea of a Life Hereafter is a complete nonsense. Your death is not an event in your life – it is the end of all events in your life – because there is nothing for you but total extinction, except in the memories and legacies you leave behind. The idea of a life hereafter diverts our attention from the here and now and our responsibilities in the here and now; it might have been invented as a primitive incentive to do good; instead it has created all kinds of false expectations which we can well do without. It is part of the superstructure of many religions and is fit only for superstitious children. Some people want to say that if you believe in the right religion you can expect eternal paradise after death; all too often the 'right' religion is one that preaches intolerance and hatred. We must dispense with this fiction, which surely we have outgrown, and preserve the essence of the best kind of ethic. The Sermon on the Mount provides that ethic, and tells us quite simply, "Be Good!"* ...

'*I have no hesitation in declaring that we are now living in the age of the anti-Christ, an anti-Christ that is dressed up to look like competing religions, religions which do no more than herald the decline of civilisation as we know it. I implore you to rescue Christianity from the doldrums and to speak out for its resurrection as the source of a galvanised social ethic, an ethic which will challenge Government policy when it is perceived to be unjust and ...*'

~ ~

It is perhaps understandable that Charles Baxter, the gentleman with the red carnation, and the lady of enormous proportions, did not stay to sing the hymn 'O Gracious Spirit Dwell With Me'. They quickly made their way out of the church, a solemn and disgruntled trio. Nor did the remainder of that congregation render the hymn with any noticeable conviction, despite Sedley's appeal. There was all about such a degree of uneasiness that it seemed to many of those present that they ought, in all conscience, not to have come at all and that they ought now to be doing penance for having heard Sedley out. It is doubtful whether Luther's nailing of his proclamations on the church door at Wittenberg, or his burning of the Papal Bull, generated greater discomfort amongst the Doubting Thomases who may have been present. Hymn 165 was, therefore a mumble of indifference, and the Gracious Spirit, not having been extolled with much enthusiasm, no doubt sought hospitality elsewhere.

The gentleman with the red carnation had taken due and careful note of Sedley's principal declarations, pronouncements which all three spies considered distinctly heretical. It was quite clear that Sedley had at last revealed his true and hideous nature, refusing to regard the rule of law as paramount or the sovereignty of parliament hallowed. He had nailed his colours to the mast of a pirate vessel, for pirates flouted the law of the land, and here was Sedley inviting the Church to interfere in matters which parliament, a democratically elected assembly, had already pronounced lawful, legal and valid. Communists, pirates, troublesome priests and terrorists – into the same box with them all! Had there been a box big enough and close to hand, there is no doubt that these three worthies would have tumbled Sedley headfirst into it, blocking all possible exits with innumerable locks and bolts.

The lady of enormous proportions was obviously beside herself with rage. For anyone who knew anything about the subject knew that Jesus was drawing a clear and eternal line of demarcation between the mere earthly phenomenon of politics and the heavenly aspirations of Christianity, between the Here Below and the There Hereafter. But Sedley was committing the most horrendous blasphemy in denying the Hereafter altogether, something on which the dear lady, in common with many others of different Faiths, was pinning her hopes. And did he really have the temerity to accuse the Government of being anti-Christ? – well, she could hardly bring herself to repeat the accusation. It is to be remembered that she believed in miracles, and she believed that one of the most marvellous of miracles had only recently been performed by the Government of the day, namely the virtual silencing of trade union agitation and the rebirth of the principle that the interests of the lower paid sections of the community were best served by a general attitude of subservience towards their masters and betters, and towards the authority of Market Forces; indeed, so great was her confidence in the philosophy of the free market that she based upon it all her hopes for the eventual establishment of God's kingdom here on earth, in terms of material wealth. Since she believed the Government of the day to have performed miracles of sorts, her convictions seemed to beg questions as to the divine origins of the Prime Minister and the Apostolic nature of his cabinet. But on this she would not have been drawn. However, Sedley it was who was turning everything upside-down, and if anyone was anti-Christ, it was he!

Baxter had nothing but sympathy for her distress. But he was pleased that at last Sedley was nailed and that he had in effect nailed himself. Sedley had been given sufficient rope by the very width and breadth of all he had sought to discredit, tightening the rope round his own neck as he did so. It could not have been neater. How right he, Baxter, had been to solicit the help of the gentleman with the red carnation, who was as anxious as he was to make the very most out of the affair.

It was in such a mood that the trio marched almost arm in arm through the portals of the church and out into the fresh air of the graveyard.

They then repaired to Baxter's house where the immediate damage inflicted by Sedley's guns was mitigated by a glass or two of the finest French brandy.

There was nothing but sweet unanimity amongst them concerning the errors of Sedley's ways. As for Sedley's declaration that the distinction between Christianity and politics was either a confusion or a political lie, they agreed unanimously that he was accusing Jesus himself of incompetence or duplicity, and this they had no trouble in pronouncing blasphemous. They interpreted Sedley's tirade as an attack upon Christ himself, which they naturally went on to repudiate vehemently. It was really quite simple: Christ, being the son of God, could not have been wrong in what he meant to say, and what he meant to say was that political matters were no business of the Church; therefore, Sedley was not only wrong, but also wrong in the 'implication' that Christ must have erred, whether it was argued that he erred in good faith or erred on purpose. Sedley could therefore be accused of an arrogance that went far beyond the bounds of credibility, let alone Christian conscience. They were all delighted with this spurious piece of logic and were only too ready to take it further.

For example, was Sedley inviting people to refuse to pay their taxes merely on the basis of whim and personal decision, which he had had the effrontery to call moral integrity? He had suggested that the Established Church was the guardian of public virtue, a point they were willing to concede; but, more than this, he was suggesting that it was the *active* guardian of both public virtue *and* public affairs, in competition with the elected Government of the day! The Church was not a publicly elected body; he was advocating a select and unelected body to preside over one that had been popularly elected according to the due process of law and custom. What's more, he was suggesting that the Church should be a coterie of revolutionaries and a harbinger of revolutionary doctrine. That the

Church might discover grounds on which to pursue the popular subversion of the State was, therefore, not in Sedley's view an impossibility. Therefore, Sedley was morally and intellectually confused. Poor fellow! Yet it was hard to sympathise with the likes of one who denied the promise of the Life Hereafter. The trio likened him to the communists and the socialists (in fact to both at once, since there was no really discernible difference between them), and since they believed socialism and communism to be dead ducks, struggling in the final death throes of disgrace and abandonment in the wings of the world's stage, they also considered Sedley to be ill-informed and out of date. Sedley was therefore arrogant beyond belief, frightfully out of touch, and an idiot of monumental proportions who was busily fanning the flames of popular dissent and heresy, blind to the norms of political correctness that now pervaded social, political and religious life and ignorant of the plain necessity to foster social cohesion in a changing society and a changing world, for, far from uniting those of different Faiths, he was preaching religious ascendency over them all and inciting them to discontent, rebellion and the closing of ranks.

The arguments cited against him seemed only to multiply as the minutes rolled excitedly by, this delightful impression no doubt occasioned and strengthened by the relentless consumption of deluxe brandy. They concluded that Sedley was, in a phrase, demented and that a course of firm action had now to be decided upon.

Chapter Thirteen

Reluctant Persecutors

Cracks and fissures, flaws and lesions, encompass he who makes a stand, as if on ice he tests his weight, and sinks, never more to feel dry land.

~ ~

The Sedleys sat together in the living room. It was evening and the good Reverend sat in his favourite armchair, eyes closed, but not sleeping. Julia sat opposite him holding a copy of the local newspaper. She was infuriated by his immoveable passivity and was doing her utmost to preserve some semblance of feminine dignity and charm in a situation which was, she thought, quite critical. She had telephoned the Baxters earlier, while he was away from the vicarage, though she said that Susan Baxter had phoned them. On his return, she had insisted that they sit down together and talk seriously and sensibly about certain matters which had somehow or other got quite out of hand. So, here they were, facing each other over a gap considerably wider than the Grand Canyon, and infinitely more difficult to bridge.

'I just didn't know what to say! Adam, are you listening? She just said they wouldn't be coming after all. She made some lame excuse about being far too busy. But it was so obvious – and it wasn't as though we'd tied them down or anything. She sounded so stand-offish – cold, even. I didn't know how to react. I should've asked her what ...'

'Yes, why didn't you?' He was listening, his eyes no longer closed.

'She didn't give me much of a chance. She hung up! I felt really embarrassed. Something's up. No wonder we haven't heard from her. And then this morning – when I went out – I felt people staring at me, as though I had two heads or something – I thought I was just imagining it. But now I'm not so sure.'

'Really?' he remarked, indifferently.

Julia was understandably irritated. Her poise and charm were decidedly wearing thin. But she was doing remarkably well under the circumstances. 'They obviously had a bee in their bonnet. They didn't even acknowledge me – and everyone was so friendly when we first got here. But now it all begins to make sense!'

With that, she threw the newspaper onto the low octagonal coffee table that stood between them like an innocent bystander, and the force with which she did so served to underline the seriousness of the situation while also indicating her fears that the sensible talk on which she had pinned her hopes was likely to be much harder to conduct than she had anticipated.

But some explanation is called for as to why Julia's preamble to Adam was, once again, a selection of half-truths and suppressed facts, a selection, it goes without saying, she had made in Adam's best interests and in the interests of sustained marital bliss.

~ ~

Julia had impatiently phoned the Baxters with the simple intention of trying to tie them down to a definite dinner arrangement or of suggesting a few clear options. Her call had been answered by Susan Baxter who, after a few curt social preliminaries, passed her over to Charles Baxter, who seemed eager to explain the situation.

Baxter was anything but curt or distant. He was fairly brimming over with his customary charm. He appeared afflicted with a burning desire for reconciliation. He was, he said, delighted at the opportunity to speak to Julia, especially when told that the good Reverend was not at home. He wanted, he said, to explain matters fully, and he was sure that she could be taken completely into his confidence, respecting some delicate matters, and that she was capable of helping in a way that no one else could, that she was uniquely and ideally placed. And help was certainly needed – help to avert strong feeling and possibly disastrous consequences. He had, he assured her, their very best interests at heart and therefore it mattered very much to him what others said about them; it mattered to him that they should have a future there, and the very brightest future possible. It was imperative therefore to elicit her help. He knew he could count on her, and she said he certainly could.

Having set the appropriate tone of urgency, he went on to explain the basis of his fears. He had noticed that Julia had been conspicuously absent from Adam's last sermon. She could not therefore be expected to appreciate the significance of recent events. He would spare her the details — suffice to say that Adam had confused religion with politics and had consequently gone on, though perhaps unawares and in all innocence, to preach anarchy and disrespect for the rule of law; not only that, he had only brought into question some of the most basic tenets of Christian doctrine, confounding the hopes of his parishioners concerning the promise of a life hereafter, and sowing doubts about the very existence of the miracles attributed to Christ himself ... She would of course understand the difficulties at once. And she did. Or she *said* she did. And Baxter was delighted that she said she did, though it was, he said, nothing more than he had expected.

And while, he went on, anarchy from the pulpit could never be approved of, the last thing he wanted was to see Adam's career go down the chute as a result, and not least because it would also compromise Julia's own standing in the community and perhaps outside it and pose a potential threat to her own happiness, not to mention her own creative aspirations. Baxter repeated that in all probability Adam was himself unaware of the true implications of his stance and that his intentions had no doubt been laudable. Even so, the road to hell was paved with good intentions, and if he continued down this path he could not rely on the patience and goodwill that had so far been shown him; his parishioners were for the most part simple, hardworking people who looked to his guidance and protection, as lambs look to the shepherd.

Julia said she understood everything. Indeed, she was most grateful that Charles had trusted her sufficiently to confide in her so readily and so fully, and she was obviously more than willing to do her part to avert the disaffection and disaster to which he had so discreetly and diplomatically alluded. In fact, at no point was his friendship and confidence more esteemed than now. She offered her apologies on her husband's behalf for any offence caused, and she felt confident that any offence taken could not possibly have been intended. To which Baxter replied that apologies were all very well but that they had to emanate from the relevant source — the good Reverend himself. Indeed, said Baxter, feelings were running so high that nothing less than an outright apology from Adam himself could possibly put matters right, and, even then, a return to normality could not be expected overnight, for trust was far more easily lost than cultivated — but it was true that an apology was an obvious and immediate step in the right direction.

This was the gist of the conversation between them which concluded with Baxter's profound hope that all could be resolved to everyone's mutual satisfaction, and his intimation that he expected to be in a position fairly soon to introduce Julia to some influential contacts in the art world. It was all strong stuff, but Baxter came across less as an accuser and more as a solicitous advisor, as impartial as he was sincere. The effect was to win over the confidence of Julia and elicit her solemn promise to do all she could to iron things out and bring Adam to his senses. He had thoughtfully directed her attention to the local evening newspaper, saying that he, Baxter, had been told what to expect and that it was only right that she shouldn't be shocked by it, either – adding that should she encounter any coolness out and about, she ought, in all fairness, know something of the cause.

Baxter firmly believed, though one he was most anxious to keep to himself, that an apology from the offending quarter was as likely as the squaring of the circle; but he made it clear that should attempts to appeal to Adam's 'better sense' fail to produce the desired result, matters would undoubtedly be taken further to the severe detriment of Adam's career, for the Church itself would naturally look askance at one who preached anarchy in its name.

Julia herself believed, though she dared not say as much to Baxter, that a snowball in hell had more chance of survival than Adam's reputation in the wake of an appeal to his 'better sense'. But she felt she had little option but to try the impossible, since the alternative was unthinkable.

Julia had been wooed by Baxter's tone of sweet and deep solicitude. Pieces of a puzzle immediately began to make sense – not simply the cold shoulder she'd received from the locals earlier that day, not simply that the Baxters had made no attempt to follow up her invitation to dinner, but also the change she had felt in Adam, the 'stranger' she'd been living with recently, the disregard he'd shown for her own aspirations, the way he seemed to waive aside the pragmatic necessity of getting on and achieving great things in their new surroundings, the way he'd confronted Charles Baxter, even the appearance of the old man, who seemed to haunt them somehow in the background; yes, it was all beginning to fit together, and with a most disquieting symmetry, though the picture the puzzle depicted was hazy – like a real puzzle when the surfaces of the pieces are faded, flaky and scratched. It was as though Adam had become a rebel, and one without a clear cause. She felt bound to acknowledge, to herself at least, that things had changed for the worse. The prognosis was equally bleak. Which perhaps explained why her initial reaction to that conversation with Baxter was short-lived, why her initial ambivalence was not to be sustained.

Ambivalence? Well, the conversation had taken her completely by surprise. But then she actually began to wonder whether her reaction towards Baxter should have been quite different. Perhaps she should have been offended, because whatever Adam was up to, it was her business to support him. She actually thought, for a moment or two, that Baxter should have been put in his place, roundly and soundly. Was it not the role of a good wife to stick to her husband through thick and thin? To support him, come what might?

Thankfully, such ambivalence was of short duration and dissolved away. She decided she could do both – she could wholly accept Baxter's narrative and advice and at the same time play the role of the supportive wife. She could proceed as though Charles and Adam were both right and attempt to steer a course between the two. For a good wife must also be true to herself. If she thought Adam was taking a wrong turn, it was her wifely duty to set him on the straight and narrow; and she could not help but think that the turn he had taken could lead only to ruin, for *both* of them. What could Charles possibly hope to gain from such simple solicitude on her and Adam's behalf? This was no place for cynicism. And he was entirely consistent. Had he not from the very outset expressed a sincere interest in her creative aspirations? True, there had been that silly business about that old man who seemed to be dead and caused people no end of distress in consequence. But it was Charles himself who'd attempted reconciliation and Adam who'd snubbed him at the church – and even now Charles had just gone to all that trouble to explain the difficulties to her, reasonably and carefully, sensibly and warmly. No, it was Adam that was being unreasonable, if not downright unchristian; and when Charles had shown an interest in her artistic talents, it was Adam again who'd proved so unreasonable, so cynical. If you speak as you find, all the evidence suggested that Adam was the offending party and Charles the offended. Yet, here he was, Charles Baxter, still trying his level best to put things right, and with the utmost discretion and diplomacy – by soliciting the help of Julia herself, the person he said was best suited to the task. If she were honest with herself, and she *really* wanted to be honest with herself, she had to admit that she could find nothing whatsoever to complain about in Charles Baxter – no, nothing at all. Honesty is sometimes painful, it has to be said – and the honest truth was that there were issues in Adam that had to be addressed.

In this way Julia managed to reconcile her wifely duties with those of wider application. For conventional wisdom dictated that partners should not stagnate in a relationship but should grow together as *individuals*, and a couple rightly matched would help one another to do just that. Putting right whatever issues were to be addressed in Adam would also remove obstacles to the furtherance of her own ambitions; what is sauce for the goose is sauce also for the gander; a healthy partnership must allow growth for each partner, each allowing the possibility of growth in the other. So it was that Adam began to appear to Julia as a pupil, a difficult and wayward pupil admittedly, but a pupil of sorts all the same. She would do her bit, for herself, for Adam, for her conscience, for her marriage. It would be hard, but everything seemed to hang nicely together, all parts consistent, all desirable and right.

It was fitting therefore that she should fulfil her promise to Baxter. She would appeal to Adam's better sense, as she had attempted to do on previous occasions, though not altogether successfully; but on this occasion the chips were down and he had little option but to listen to good sense. It wouldn't be easy, but she remembered how adamant Adam's cynicism towards Baxter had been and how she had managed to soften it somewhat – and she took what courage she could from that.

She needed a strategy. She would not tell Adam that she'd spoken to Baxter; were she to tell him, it would be the end of all argument before any argument could get going; there was no *need* to tell him; she could play her part more astutely than that.

It should be explained here that, following Sedley's salvo, the gentleman with the red carnation and the lady of enormous proportions had duly deliberated and finally agreed that Sedley was in all probability a hardened creature for whom chatty, informal appeals to reason and common sense were most unlikely to bear fruit. Reluctant though they said they were to apply a thumbscrew, they felt bound to agree that the argument of force was likely to prove more effective than the force of argument.

Even so, force, they further agreed, was to be applied in easy stages, no stage following upon another unless judged by all parties concerned, namely Baxter, the gentleman with the red carnation and the lady of enormous proportions, to be strictly necessary. And so, instead of a frontal counter-attack with all guns blazing, which would include an article in the national press, they would attempt a flanking manoeuvre in the local rag, a preliminary move which was easy to effect due to the influence that all three worthies could bring to bear in that direction, not that they needed to do much more than exercise a mere fraction of their natural charm to bring about the desired result.

It was therefore to test the determination of the enemy to withstand the rumblings of the local press. And if the protest was made in sufficiently forcible terms it might have the desired effect of curbing the activities of the lawless and restoring to the local ministry the quiet dignity and repose that was expected of it and manifestly belonged to it by nature and by custom. Forming the basis of such a hope was the conviction that an appeal to matters touching personal career and familial security, and future prospects and standing within the Church itself, were mighty big medicine. What's more, in limiting their opening manoeuvre to the local press, they believed themselves to be demonstrating more than their fair quota of Christian virtue and moral restraint, proving themselves merciful as well as mighty. But the gentleman with the red carnation was fully prepared to exercise his own influence at national level should it prove necessary. They all hoped it would not prove necessary, that somehow the good Reverend could be brought to heel by some last remaining vestige of common sense. Besides, exposure in the national press might inadvertently give Sedley's position far more credibility than it deserved; such things had been known to happen before and should not be risked unless and until all else had failed; such, by analogy, were the hazards of litigation.

~ ~

'Since when have we been taking it?' asked Sedley, referring to the newspaper which lay askew on the octagonal coffee table.

'We haven't. I found it lying in the hallway.' Not true. She had bought a copy after her conversation with Baxter and had turned the pages frantically in search of the article in question, and, having found it, had read it as many times as the paragraphs it was composed of.

'Opened at the appropriate page, and the article circled in red,' said Adam, picking it up and giving it a quick scan. 'Very thoughtful. A well-wisher, no doubt. Hmm. Very flattering. Fame at last!' he added, as he replaced it on the coffee table.

'Flattering? Hardly that!' said Julia, as she picked it up, determined to read it out loud, word by painful word; for her stubborn pupil must be left in no doubt as to the seriousness of the situation. The article, presented on the Readers' Page in the form of a letter was signed anonymously 'Members of the Congregation, St Mary's Church':

Pulpit or Soapbox?

'It is most upsetting when the Church, the most respected institution in the land, renowned for its proper impartiality in all matters of State, and particularly matters of party politics, allows its clergy to engage freely, not only in political comment, but in comment that is divisive and seditious in spirit and in fact. And this in a country which rightly prides itself upon its democratic traditions, and indeed leads the world in the importance it attaches to parliamentary democracy, representative Government and the rule of law.

'The gospel according to the Reverend Adam Sedley would require all those of Christian conscience to conduct some kind of passive resistance to the lawfully constituted and duly elected Government, perhaps in the form of withholding the payment of taxes. If this is not an invitation to lawlessness and the flagrant breach of the rule of law, then nothing is! We should not expect to hear from any man of the Christian cloth that nothing is sacred, but this, apparently, is precisely what we are being told. If Christians were to follow the advice of the Reverend Sedley, the foundations of parliamentary democracy in this country would be shaken to the very core. If otherwise solid and law-abiding citizens are invited to flout the law of the land, this is tantamount to inciting them to violence, for violence invariably follows in the wake of a refusal to comply with the rule of law. And incitement to violence is surely the very antithesis of the Christian Message, which is essentially one of peace and harmony.

'A genuine democracy is committed to the free expression of opinion. But it is one thing to have to put up with the ravings of the Loony Left on the hustings, and quite another to tolerate the sheer perversion of sacred Christian Scripture from the very pulpit of the established Church itself. The Church should take steps to ensure that its clergy do not overstep the bounds of decency or exceed their remit in such a way as to threaten the existence of civilised society and, in so doing, commit blasphemy by basing this threat upon Holy Scripture. If the Church should fail to take appropriate action, it is abdicating its responsibilities; and parishioners may feel obliged to take matters into their own hands to ensure that their own voices are heard in such matters.

'*The Reverend Sedley should desist from the habit of confusing religion with politics. His congregation has no wish to be subjected to political speeches; people have every right to hear the unadulterated words of Scripture, with the promise of our Lord Jesus Christ of life eternal. This is what they expect and this is what they should receive. Words of harmony and unity are now more important than ever in our changed and changing society, not calls to arms and words of contention; there must be unity between peoples of different Faiths if we are to go forward together in a civilised world, yet the Reverend Sedley seems to be suggesting that one Faith is better than another, which is contentious and needlessly upsetting.*

'*Should any members of the clergy persist in misunderstanding their true role, they will no longer be able to rely on the continued support and goodwill of their parishioners. They may find that, like intelligent voters, their congregations will vote with their feet an absent themselves from the House of God for as long as this holy place is defiled by the dust of party politics. The Reverend Sedley is forgetting the advice given by Jesus Christ himself: Give to Caesar that which is Caesar's and to God that which is God's.*

'*It must be stressed again that the good people of this parish rightfully expect far more from a man of God, appointed under the wise auspices of the Church. It is the fervent hope of his congregation that he will take this appeal to heart and that he will not betray the trust placed in him by his congregation and the Church.*

'Well,' said Julia, barely having paused for breath, 'what are you going to do about it?'

'Do?'

'You'll have to write an apology or something.'

'Apology?' He sounded incredulous.

'Yes, an apology!' snapped Julia, whose patience was now threadbare. 'Or an explanation at the very least! I mean, you've got to do *something*!'

'*Have* I?'

'Adam!'

'I've really very little to add to what I've already said in my sermons. You know, I was

hoping it would be clear enough – but I'd be very happy to repeat it all – in fact, that's precisely what I intend to do. Yes, if anyone needs further explanation, they should attend my sermons regularly.'

Julia sighed deeply, like a teacher despairing over the progress of an obviously backward or recalcitrant pupil. How she managed to restrain her temper must be counted the eighth wonder of this world and the next. 'How can you talk like that ... I mean when your future, *our* future, is at stake?' She shook her head incredulously, directing her incredulity to the octagonal coffee table.

'I wasn't aware anything's *at stake*, as you put it,' responding on behalf of the octagonal coffee table. 'Oh, yes, I've offended the sensibilities of some people, I know that – I fully expected it – I'd have been disappointed if I hadn't. It's high time some sensibilities were offended. I noticed Charles Baxter and his cronies wincing more than once, but ...'

'Ah, there it is! I *knew* it. So, I'm right, you've really got it in for him, haven't you? I can't believe this!'

'Got it in for him, Julia? Well, come to think of it, maybe I have, in a way – though I can't say I favour your turn of phrase. No, I wouldn't put it like that – makes it sound like some sort of personal vendetta – and it's anything but that.'

'No, that's just what it is. You've never liked him – and you've liked him a lot less after he tried to give *me* some sound advice. Yes, it's true – you can't stand him, and mainly because he's shown some real interest in me. Yes, it all comes down to selfishness, jealousy, narrow-mindedness, in the end ...'

'Well now, that's something I *can* agree with. I suppose it does come down to selfishness, jealousy and narrow-mindedness, in the end – for a man like Baxter!'

'Oh, this is ridiculous!' she'd known it wasn't going to be easy, but this was just too much. He was being unusually intransigent and truculent. Walls of granite are no push-over. She might need to resort to the key weapon in her arsenal sooner than she had expected, and she'd hoped to avoid it altogether; but now it was clear that she might need to openly question the stability of their relationship, to question whether they were truly compatible – achieving by fear and sentiment what cooler reason had failed to achieve – and if *that* failed to produce the goods ... No wonder she was temporarily lost for words. She would try common sense reasoning once again.

'Adam, you haven't really understood what I'm driving at – and I thought we'd settled all this already – I mean about trying to establish ourselves, about needing to ...'

'"Compromise" is the word you're looking for, I think.'

'Is that such a dirty word, then? Is it wrong to be liked, to make friends?'

'It depends,' he said coolly, in a tone suggestive of someone about to consider a philosophical issue.

'On what?'

'On *who*, and *why*?'

'Oh really!' she said, exasperated. 'Look, we've really got to get to the bottom of this.'

'Well, the bottom line as far as I'm concerned is this: I don't like Baxter – what he stands for – what he believes – how he feels – what he values – what and how he thinks. Whatever it is that makes him tick just turns me *off*. Of course, it's not just him – the world is full of Baxters, and I can't live easily with that – it's just too much. I suppose that's why we have a Church at all – in any case, that's why I joined it. If what I say offends the Baxters of this world – well, that's too bad, because that's my job! If I'm saying something worthwhile, and if the cap fits, so be it – I'm doing what I'm paid to do – not because I'm paid to do it, but because it's the right thing to do! And if you don't see that ...'

Faced with this torrent of self-defence, Julia was so lost for words that she visibly shuddered with irritation, and the words she came out with were the very best she could do.

'What I can't see is what's so objectionable about Charles Baxter. Even if I understood you – and I don't pretend to – but even if I did, the only thing you're doing is alienating yourself, and me, from all decent, respectable people – no, that's right, they can't *all* be bad! Anyway, how do *you* know what he thinks and feels? For all you know he might have your very best interests at heart, and he's probably just as much a Christian as you are.' She wanted to say *more Christian*, but managed to resist the temptation. 'I mean, even if he *is* wrong about some things. I mean, *you're* wrong about people sometimes, aren't you? Unless you think Christians are infallible – that'd be a new one! Well, I think you're wrong about Charles. You see, you're whole view of things is so ... well, so *patronising*!'

Adam said nothing, resting his gaze on the octagonal coffee table – rather like a naughty schoolboy, she thought. She sensed a possible crack in that wall of granite through which she might manage to squeeze. 'Can't you see how unfair it all is? I mean, Christianity is a pretty broad church, isn't it? To hear you talk, you'd think it's an exclusive one – only the perfect need apply!'

'Christians are far from perfect,' he said, with a sigh.

'Well, that's a good start. I'm glad you're admitting it.'

'Julia, I don't feel obliged to *admit* anything! If making mistakes disqualifies us from being Christians, I'd be the first to go, and the circle of the brethren would soon come to nothing.'

'Right!' She was hopeful. But her hopes were now to be dashed, as though she'd awoken a sleeping giant.

'Right. But it's not a question of mistakes – it's a whole disposition, a mentality – it's all about moral perception, of basic values. Christians must be ruled by love – love must dictate what is and is not possible – and love isn't a sentimental thing. It's putting others first – that's what it is! Now, Christians don't always manage to do that, that's for sure – but at least they must know what it is they are failing to do – yes, they should know *that* at least! And that's something! Christianity just *is* this mentality, nothing else. This is what the word 'God' really means, don't you see? This is the *Christian* God, anyway. This is what believing in the Christian God *means* – putting other people first, counting them as equals, valuing them as you value yourself. Of course, Christians fail more often than not to do this – but being a Christian means that they *know* what they are failing to do. It's not about miracles and life-after-death – as though that made any sense at all. It's all about the here and now, because there is nothing else. We need to love one another, help one another, value one another. There's nothing else, nothing else at all. Do you see that? God is not a massive computer perched somewhere we know-not-where, no! God is not a super-being in charge of heaven. God is a mentality, and ...'

'Have you quite finished?' Julia broke in. 'I can do without a sermon, thank you very much!' It was clear that the crack in the wall of granite was narrowing.

'Can you?' Adam was fighting back! 'Can you, Julia? Can you really? Well, you're lucky. Because, you see, I *can't*. I need sermons. I need to give them, and I need to be on the receiving end, too – yes, even on the receiving end of my own sermons.' He was in a fighting mood, alright. 'I suppose they help keep me sane,' he added, quietly.

'Oh, this is crazy! Do you mean to tell me Charles isn't after what you're after? – a better world, or something like that?'

'They'd like you to believe that.'

'*They?*'

'Yes, **THEY**!' The phrase 'the shadow people' came to mind, but stayed there, safe and sound. 'They'd like you to believe that. We all want a better world, they tell you, and we just disagree about how to get it. But it's not true. Love judges the means as well as the end – some things are just ruled out, however laudable the end may seem – it's not just a better world, but how you achieve it that counts. Means and ends! Well, some means sanctify the end, and other means pervert it. The problem is not in the end or in the means to achieve it – it's in *us!*'

'What?'

'Yes, alright. I've said enough.'

'Well, the thing is, they'll listen to him – not to you. And people around here can make life very difficult for you – for us – impossible, even. What happens if you lose your entire congregation? – if your flock turns against you? You can't minister to the bare walls!'

'Oh, I don't know about that. Perhaps that's just what I've been doing all along – ministering to the bare walls.' He seemed to have an answer for everything.

'Okay, so what sort of life have we got to look forward to? What sort of future have we got?' Julia seemed to plead. Was this a last ditch attempt to widen the crack in the wall of granite, assuming that it was not after all illusory?

'And what would you have me tell people, Julia?' She was startled by his particularly abrupt tone. 'I suppose you think I should offer my profound apologies for having caused some grave offence. Perhaps I should say it was all a temporary aberration, promise to be a good boy in future and to be everything they expect of me. Maybe I should promise them a place in heaven if they contribute towards roof repairs, if they support the summer fete, if they turn up dutifully every Sunday to hear stuff from me that I don't believe in myself? Would that satisfy you, Julia? – make you happy? Well, it would make me profoundly sad. So, there it is! We have an issue, and a pretty insurmountable one, it seems – wouldn't you say?'

No, the crack in the wall of granite was decidedly and irrevocably illusory. His tone was undoubtedly all wrong – not at all what she had been hoping for – hoping for against all the odds. Perhaps his tone and his words were all put on; no, he really did seem to be taking matters far too lightly, or far too seriously, depending on which side of the wall you happened to be. She had one recourse left – to bring out the most powerful weapon she had and assert herself in one last desperate effort to turn the tide. The words she'd dreaded having to use limped out of her mouth on crutches, but they came out all the same.

'Perhaps ... perhaps we should think of splitting up, Adam.' She paused, almost reflexively, as though she expected him to protest, to ask her to repeat what she'd said because he found it unbelievable, to insist on an explanation. But since none of these things happened, and since the expression on his face was inscrutable and as placid as ever, she was obliged to continue and offer an explanation whether it was demanded or not. 'I mean, look at us! We just don't seem to see eye to eye at all. Somehow we've drifted apart. You have your view of things. I have mine. You have your ambitions. I have mine.'

Adam smiled. (How dare he!) 'Ambitions? I have my ambitions, maybe – of sorts. Yes, of sorts.'

Was that all? Was there to be no word of protest? No plea to make a go of things? No attempt at compromise? No attempt to fill the gap and bridge the gulf? It looked that way, and Julia didn't like it.

'So, you seem content just to let us drift further apart. It's amazing – when all it would take ...'

'Let me try to finish that one. All it would take to keep our marriage alive and well is for me to make a simple and sincere statement. All I have to say is that I didn't intend anything political to be read into what I've said, that life eternal awaits the god-fearing, that all can be put right in the life to come, that miracles are as natural as rain in spring. Yes, all I have to do is recant all my heresies, even though I believe for one moment that they are heresies.'

'I'm in no mood for sarcasm, Adam. But I'm shocked you want to compete with politicians.'

'I don't! I want politicians to compete with *me*.'

Julia shook her head, as if constrained at last to acknowledge his premature senility. 'Well, I'm glad you know what you want. And I'm glad *I* know what you want. Because I know it doesn't include me. I give up!' She didn't quite mean it, about giving up, but she tried to sound as though she did.

'It's not a question of what I want, Julia. It's a question of what I can and what I cannot do. You're expecting me to say what I cannot say. It's useless to demand of others what they simply can't give.'

'Alright, then. That works both ways. It's not right to expect others to want what *you* want, is it? It just goes to show how different we are, Adam. We each want what the other can't give. That's not exactly a recipe for happiness-ever-after, is it? But it's better to find out now before it's too late altogether!' Her blood was up.

'We've got different ideas about happiness, I suppose,' he said, too calmly to give Julia much comfort. 'A happy life isn't necessarily a pleasant one. For me, it's a question of doing what I can't do otherwise. What is it for you, Julia? – just one pleasant experience after another like some endless funny movie?'

'Don't be ridiculous. I want something out of life – and that's doing what I *want* to do, not just what I *have* to do! It's easy enough to understand – if you're *reasonable*.'

'Developing your artistic talents?'

'What's wrong with that?'

'Oh, nothing. Nothing at all. It's quite alright. Laudable, even. You want to be a *real* artist, right?'

'So?'

'Well, I just wonder what you think a real artist is? Is it someone who does what he wants to do, or someone who does what he has to do?'

'Oh, for goodness sake, don't practise your sermons on me!'

'I'm only asking what it is you want, or think you want. Do you want to make a contribution to art. Or do you want the limelight?'

'Both! Can't I want both? What's wrong with limelight? What's wrong with wanting it?'

'Nothing – and everything. Limelight is something you might get – but that's different from wanting it. If you begin by wanting it, it's liable to take over and get between you and real art. You can't be deep and at the same time make a big thing out of it. It's like trying to win a race, and looking over your shoulder every step you take – you lose something important that way – it gets between you and the finish – you're more likely to lose the race altogether.'

'Limelight! Real art! – it all comes to the same thing in the end – anyway, you don't seem to realise how damned patronising you sound! It's incredible. I didn't think I'd ever say this – but I don't think you know what you're talking about. You're confused. All messed up.'

'I'm sorry. No, really. I'm sorry if it comes out that way.' He really did sound apologetic.

'Not sorry enough, though. Not enough to make a difference!' she said.

He got up from his armchair and made for the door of the living room, and then turned towards her in the doorway.

'I tell you what,' he said, 'in my next sermon I'll be most careful to say nothing that should cause even the slightest offence to intelligent, decent people.' He paused. 'Oh, and just for the record, I don't *hate* Charles Baxter. Hating is not *my* problem.' Then he smiled that benign smile of his and left the room, closing the door gently behind him.

She was left alone in the living room with his last words ringing in her ears, words which she found hard to get hold of. Had the confrontation with Adam concerned some other more routine theme, she might have followed him and had it out further, or he himself might have left, only to return in the next instant. But it had not been a routine confrontation. She felt it was a compound fracture that crude splints and simple surgery couldn't put right. She desperately attempted to sort things out in her own mind.

To begin with, his parting words were the very words she wanted to hear, and were she to report them just as they stood to Charles, it would appear that she had emerged victorious from the confrontation; yes, taken at face value, they might even be understood to be an apology, or as near an apology as she could ever hope to get. So, there were some grounds for the expectation that Adam would go away and think things over – weigh things up in his own time, and later, a stronger more heartfelt apology might be expected. Things had to sink in, and that would take a little time. No, the situation was not entirely hopeless – not yet, anyway.

Such thoughts occurred to Julia as she sat alone in the living room, and she tried very hard to give them some credence despite the possible irony his last words contained, and despite some incontrovertible facts, notably the fact that the appeal to their marriage prospects had been a dead duck – shot down before it had really taken flight from the calm waters of Julia's complacency, and despite the fact that the compound fracture spelt gangrene and amputation in the absence of a complete change of heart and soul.

It was irrational to ignore what she knew deep down to be true. But she decided that irrationality was the best course. It was actually a conscious decision. It was either that or an unambiguous admission that their relationship was already at an end, because he, Adam, had said so, or so much as implied so. He had distinguished so firmly between what he wanted and what he had to do. That was not the talk of someone who was in two minds and therefore ready to be persuaded. But, no – she decided to be irrational. (She had even heard or read somewhere that being irrational was sometimes a key to success – that irrational people tended to be lucky!)

She decided to wait. To wait and see, yes, to wait and see, and hope that her diffident pupil would at last see sufficient light to justify the faith she was placing in him by the very fact that she had married him for better or worse. If he admitted the error of his ways, their marriage would be saved and her hopes for the future, for her future, could be kept afloat. It was not that she put too much store by her marriage, but she was not about to be rejected and put down by someone too hard-headed to admit that he was wrong. In any case, to have made a bad choice of partner and to have to admit it in public was to be avoided if at all possible – but not avoided at *any* cost! No, if push came to shove, she wouldn't be found wanting, for she was capable of shoving with all her might.

Yet, it was too early for such thoughts. Far too early. After all, Adam was quite like a schoolboy, really. He was afflicted with the notion that he could change the world for the better; and, of course, the very idea that one could possibly do that was entirely illusory. At the same time, such an illusion must surely have been born in a soul that was basically good and, therefore, reasonable and malleable, although somewhat misguided. She was determined to help him get over his malady, though doubtless it would take more time and more effort – yes, all is possible in the fullness of time.

Such were Julia's cerebral and circular meanderings as she sat alone, her mood fluctuating between hope and despair, depending on which turning she happened to take next.

Chapter Fourteen

The Cup that Doth not Pass Away

When Fear dissolves away, Caution is soon to follow, and the guns of the commuter land, until then still, begin to groan and bellow.

~ ~

An opportunity soon arrived to test whether the preliminary turn of the thumbscrew had had the desired effect.

Sedley stood stiff and erect in his pulpit before a particularly full house. Julia was there, too, seeking confirmation, though not of a spiritual character. As Sedley looked round he failed to recognise some of the faces there, not that they had come from far afield, but simply because they hadn't bothered to put in an appearance hitherto; there were people there who had never considered themselves particularly religious; some who felt let down by the Church, and some who were decidedly hostile to every religion under the sun. It was indeed a motley congregation. For instance, the presence of two brothers, Toby and Clifford Anderson, was particularly noteworthy and justifies a meaningful diversion.

In their late fifties, and destined not to see three score and ten, the Andersons were unidentical twins who lived together in a whitewashed farmhouse on the fringe of the commuter land; though it was known thereabouts as 'the farm', what had once been a farm had been allowed to run down so far that all appearance of order had long since disappeared, though some small outhouses remained, in a dilapidated state, and the foundations of a pig-sty were still visible in the long grass and the fern. The house itself was rundown; the white-wash had greyed and flaked, so that the house stood like some aged giant who had known better days far too distant to recall with clarity; the curtains on the windows had long since faded and looked even sorrier at night against a light within that seemed to shine grudgingly.

The place had been owned and worked by 'Old Anderson', as he had been known locally, and his wife; and their bones now lay at rest in the graveyard of Sedley's church. The land had been sold to land speculators on the death of Old Anderson, his wife having passed away before him, and when Toby and Clifford were in their mid-forties, with the proviso that the house itself, together with its immediate environs, be leased to the brothers for the following 35 years, or their deaths, whichever was the sooner. The land was passed on to property developers (in return for a tidy sum that somehow managed to escape fiscal obligations) who considered the lease an unfortunate obstacle, though not, obviously, one of infinite duration. The brothers would not forfeit their right to the lease, try as the developers might to convince them that it was in their best interests to do so. They would not be moved; the developers would have to wait – though not, as it turned out, for long. For some considerable time before the death of Toby Anderson, the brothers would sit together in their living-room lulled by the sweet and melodious effusions of bulldozers and cranes not too far away, across the fields over which the skylarks once played. They would sit like old soldiers before an advancing army, having nowhere to run and incapable of effective retaliation, too old to shake with fear, too wise in the ways of war and men to expect the cavalry over the hill, while each blast of machinery did nothing but wish them ill and bid them be gone. No wonder the brothers liked their Sundays best. For on Sundays the machines held their peace and gave them an unintended respite from eventual overrun, but no release from thoughts of death, which inevitably assail us all with the passing years. But the drums of war would beat relentlessly again on weekdays, and the long wait would continue, resistance getting weaker and memories stronger.

Everyone thought them an odd pair. They were men of very few words who would, each in turn, walk their dog in the surrounding fields, the scrawny mongrel barking as if in protest at the rumble of machinery in the distance. The brothers would give no more than a nod, and that reluctant enough, to the occasional passer-by. They seemed to do little else but walk that poor creature, leading it, or being led by it, like men bewitched, cursed to roam the world in the company of dumb beasts.

Since they were both unmarried, and were assumed always to have been so, stories, as wild as stories can be, circulated regarding their sexuality and, therefore, their personal integrity, their moral rectitude, even their sanity, and, in consequence, their suitability as company for the respectable and, certainly, the godly. Such questions hovered over them like vultures bent on picking the last remnants of flesh from an already emaciated carcass. They were known as The Brothers, a phrase which had come to instil fear and loathing, discomforting doubt and speculation, abhorrence and disgust in all those for whom knowledge and proof, compassion and understanding, take second place to ignorance and rumour.

But the fact is that Clifford Anderson had indeed been married with one child, until a road accident deprived him of his wife and small son – of everything save bitter-sweet memories, after which he went to live with Toby in the white-washed farmhouse – an unhappy refuge, but one which seemed to him fitting and inevitable. That large, grey, flaky building, with its eyes downcast and veiled at night, seemed a suitable place where penance might be done for all those wrongs we all believe we routinely do to those we love most, wrongs that stand out in hideous relief when we outlive those we love and are left to reflect at painful leisure on what we should and should not have said and done.

The decision to move in with Toby had been taken years ago. Thereafter, he and Toby roamed the fields around in all weathers, they, together with their mongrel, aging slowly, while their reputation for eccentricity and mystery grew apace. They lit the interior of the farmhouse with candles during the long dark winter nights, and they would sit facing each other before a log fire on cold winter days and nights, surrounded by faded photographs in dusty frames which stood in state on a cheap reproduction sideboard, like old soldiers in dishevelled formal dress. Clifford, cursed with the weight of memory, would sometimes sigh, prompting Toby to place a loving hand on his shoulder – but quickly, without ceremony, without sentimentality and without so much as a syllable being uttered; such was the thread that bonded them together that neither time nor circumstance could sever. And so, they grew older together, memories seeming to grow stronger and clearer with every heavy, dull tick of the old grandfather clock that had stood for years beyond count in the dark hallway between the cold, semi-darkness of the living room and the small kitchen which was lit by a minuscule window that looked out mistily over an unkempt landscape beyond. It was the silence that reigned between them that struck the saddest, or profoundest, or oddest note – depending on how it struck the observer; but, of course, there were no observers, and that silence remained hidden behind white-washed walls, in an interior unknown to all save Toby and Clifford. Since the data remained incomplete, the stories circulating about the brothers lacked any perception of depth that would have transformed them from absurd tittle–tattle into something infinitely more humane. As it was, the stories grew wilder in fits and starts, and few were prompted to reflect that here, as elsewhere, theories may come and go, while facts remain unchanged.

Toby Anderson had his memories, too. Widely travelled, he had tired of travelling and of the very sound of foreign tongues. He had been blown hither and thither on the high seas aboard cargo vessels, and he had climbed mountains and choked on rarefied air. He had, in particular, found himself in what those around him at the time called a 'revolution', and he had himself spoken zealously in favour of it, so much so that he had found himself repeating the foreign equivalents of such words as 'integrity', 'mercy', 'truth' and 'compassion'; but his insistence on such strange ideas had merely earned him a short stretch in a revolutionary gaol; once freed, he vowed never again to place trust in revolutions, which have a tendency, as the very word might suggest, to turn 360 degrees; but his temporary incarceration, effected with the assurance, very readily given, that he would never again attempt to darken the doors of the country in question, at least gave him a welcome, though painful, opportunity to reflect on the hopelessness of the human condition and the virtues of a quiet life.

The Andersons had done all the talking they wanted to do years ago and had heard more than enough of it themselves. Smiles passed between them now more frequently than words, and smiles were of infinitely greater comfort. It was as though the words they loved most had lost all credibility; after all, an axe that can't cut, or a hammer that can't drive nails, are tools that are best discarded if they are incapable of repair. Words were unnecessary; each of the brothers knew where the other stood, and, what is more, they each knew that they both stood in exactly the same place. But standing there, even together, was still hard, and a smile or two seemed to help. Words were blunt instruments, incapable somehow of cutting a straight line – not that they had always been like that, but that is how they came to seem to the brothers, who agreed that they had been brought with the illusion that words made an appreciable difference. Old Anderson had quoted from the Good Book whenever an opportunity presented itself, and he would do so in tones which suggested that the words uttered made a mighty difference. A death might prompt Old Anderson to say, 'The Lord giveth and the Lord taketh away', or reports of crimes or serious indiscretions might call forth the recitation of an appropriate Commandment; and the brothers in their younger years would vaguely reckon that their father's pronouncements made some vast difference, as though they corrected some huge fault, or as though the words had either sanctified or condemned a fact without question or without the necessity of further deliberation. But the brothers had come a long way since then, it's hard to say whether forwards or backwards, and both were singularly unimpressed by the vocal eruptions of their fellow creatures, which seemed to them merely one long and un distinguished trumpeting of hypocrisy compared to which the braying of an ass was good philosophy and music to the ears.

So they sat within the white-washed walls, or walked over the fields in their battered hats and overcoats and old and trusty walking sticks, like ancient mariners of the meadows. The Andersons have now ceased to exist, Toby succumbing to cancer, and Clifford following soon after. No one remembers either them or the wild stories that surrounded them; and this despite the fact that they had about them the makings of a ghostly legend; and all those burdens of memory and nostalgia that the walls of their unkempt white-washed mausoleum had once embraced are as ethereal as the brothers themselves. The cold silences of winter nights betray not the slightest hint that the brothers ever existed. The white-washed house is gone, bulldozed by a property developer anxious to make the most of the need for parking facilities for a supermarket which will adamantly remain open on Sundays to compensate for the unintended respite given to the brothers long ago.

Odd. Mysterious. Eccentric. And few of those who had thought them eccentric considered them harmless, which is why children were seldom allowed to roam un-chaperoned in the vicinity of the farmhouse, especially since that one occasion when Clifford Anderson was imprudent enough to be caught staring too long and hard from his bedroom window at a small child passing by in the company of his young parents; yes, from his bedroom window – like one haunted, some said – like one fevered with desire, said some others with an infinitely furtive imagination and zero generosity. From that moment in particular, he was a man to be watched, and, since few bothered to distinguish between the brothers, they were both immediately tarred with the same brush, neither one escaping the suspicions of decent, right-minded people.

In the farmhouse. In the fields. But never ever in church. The last time Clifford Anderson had seen the inside of a church had been for the christening of his baby son, and since the road accident it had been left to Toby Anderson to lay flowers on the graves of old Mr and Mrs Anderson, who had been buried side by side and were now as inseparable in death as they had been in life. Clifford would have nothing to do with the place, not even for the sake of his parents; his wife and child had been cremated and their ashes scattered elsewhere. After the loss of his family, Clifford would have nothing to do with the Church, any Church at all, even the Church itself. Yet, it was not as though he blamed God for the tragedy. It was just that he had become thoroughly indifferent, as though all religion had been knocked out of him. Toby understood him well enough; he felt pretty much the same; and while he would lay flowers on the graves of the old folk, he could never be prevailed upon to listen again to what seemed to him the cultivated gibberish of the pulpit or the pious but hollow utterances of a self-styled spiritual elite.

Yet there they were! There they were, after all that time and on the very day when Sedley stood stiff and erect in his pulpit. And all because some of their groceries had been wrapped in a copy of the newspaper containing Baxter's counter-blast; for it had certainly been written by Baxter. Well, it had to be something significant to stir the brothers to action, to get them into the place that they had studiously avoided for such a long time, to prompt them to don what they considered to be their Sunday Best and make their way to church, amongst people they cared for not a jot – amongst all those who held them in suspicion, if not in contempt.

Heads turned alright. But since the chief object of interest was Sedley himself, heads were not turned for long, and the presence of the brothers was noted only *en passant*. But there they were, dressed in old, dark suits that smelled of moth balls, and in stiff shirt collars which, though clean enough, were frayed and creased, and in farm boots which had been given an extra wipe with a dry cloth.

Sedley could not take much note of them, lost as they were amongst other unfamiliar faces. Had he done so, he would not have known them. Baxter was equally oblivious of the Andersons. His interest was very much elsewhere, and he did not quite know what to expect. Sedley was stubborn; he knew that; on the other hand, pragmatic considerations and a heart-to-heart from Julia might well have turned the tide, if she had delivered the goods. From his own experience, adequate applications of the thumbscrew had hardly ever failed to work. Baxter had been brought up on a diet of success in his handling of others, and, having grown fat on complacency, it never usually occurred to him to question the efficacy of pressure and intimidation. But in this instance he had decided to keep an open mind. Sedley would either impose self-discipline, or discipline would be imposed from without, and steps would be taken to lessen his credibility. Meanwhile, and flanked once again by the gentleman with the red carnation and the lady of enormous proportions, Baxter would await with interest the outcome of Sedley's deliberations.

Julia felt ill at ease and did her best to look inconspicuous, feeling that this was not an occasion to flaunt her connections with a troublesome priest. Baxter of course did not fail to notice her. He smiled and inclined his head towards her. He noted how striking she looked, despite her best efforts to look anonymous, and how irresistible she would have seemed even in sackcloth; he was a man of surprising imagination when it came to picturing amorous possibilities; despite his present surroundings, he had no trouble entertaining himself with sexual fantasies, and such mental pictures were infinitely more compelling and gratifying than the unmissable image of the crucifixion carved in wood which hung from the stone pillar to his right. Although God in his infinite understanding might have forgiven Baxter for the thoughts he entertained, the lady of enormous proportions would not; indeed, it was only his occasional sidelong glances at this great personage that served to sober his thoughts and remind him that he was in the house of God and not the red light district of Amsterdam – this latter being a venue of clear preference in Baxter's mind, a mind which, lucky for him, was closed to the lady of enormous proportions, who would never have forgiven such lapses into the baser instincts of mankind, especially from one who had already demonstrated his superior spirituality by his unfailing dedication to the upkeep of the church roof. It might therefore be said that this lady exercised over Baxter a moderating, not to say purifying, influence entirely unbeknown to her, helping him to return to the land of the mundane from the celestial realms of unlicensed imagination.

But Baxter was not there to fantasise about Julia. He was there to see if Sedley had accepted the ultimatum that, supposedly, Julia had conveyed to him. Julia was there to see whether her own ultimatum had been taken to heart; she was ready to regard Adam's behaviour as anything but an end in itself. Whatever he did or said now would be an indication of something else – either a sign that he was prepared to see sense, mend his ways, and give his marriage the importance that he should attach to it, or else a sign that he was prepared, come what may, to follow the rocky path he had already set himself upon. The atmosphere in the vicarage had been strained since the subject was first raised, and, despite all the routine exchanges between them since, it remained the most important item on the agenda. Julia was not prepared to take second place, not even to Sedley's God, unless it was on her own terms.

~ ~

Sedley was not put off by the packed pews and the unfamiliar faces or by a feeling that he was a man on trial. Far from it. He had come too far to be discouraged by such thoughts. He was free, for the moment; as free as a bird cleaving the air in a kind of new-found liberty, and he was determined to make the most of it. He had tasted from the cup that did not pass away, and there was no going back. If he was to be hanged, it was for the sake of the Lamb of God, and the sheep could either follow or go to blazes. And in this mood, he began:

'I am consoled to see so many of you assembled here this evening. I can see faces here that I cannot recollect having seen before. Well, the more, the merrier ...'

Baxter already felt uneasy – he felt that if he had come to hear words of repentance, he might just as well get up and leave. Here was Sedley once again holding forth in a tone that smacked of anything but contrition; no, he was far too relaxed and assertive. Even so, it was all valuable grist to the mill, and it was at least cheering to feel that with every sentence Sedley was digging a hole deeper than the one he was in already – so deep that a withdrawal would be more than Herculean. If Sedley was about to validate the judgement already made against him, that he was unfit to minister to the spiritual needs of a broad church, then so be it. Baxter actually managed to feel cheerful at the prospect, and not a little amused; his doubts, if any there were, about the outcome of Sedley's deliberations were all but removed – and the sermon had not even begun!

'However,' Sedley went on, 'I cannot help but think that this most welcome improvement in attendance is due in great part to the equally welcome publicity recently afforded my sermons by the local press. Allow me to read in full what was obviously intended to be a scathing attack upon me, for this article is in fact a scathing attack upon Christianity itself ...'

It must be said that Baxter, the gentleman with the red carnation and the lady of enormous proportions, might have expected a *grudging* retreat, a *proud* withdrawal, simply because Sedley had already, on former occasions, demonstrated an unacceptable degree of intransigence and un reasonableness; and, in any case, he would have to be allowed to save some face. But this! This was most unexpected! That he should actually have the gall not only to make explicit reference to the article in question, not only to quote the whole thing lock, stock and barrel, but to preface it with the statement that its author or authors were in fact attacking Christianity itself! Sedley was in fact seriously compounding a felony – could anything be further removed from repentance and contrition? This was nothing less than arrogance and obdurate wickedness. It was utterly brazen. It was an affront to fundamental decency and contrary to the principles of civilised confrontation and debate. That he should dig in his heels while at the same time holding up to ridicule, in full public view, the protests of the reasonable and reasoning majority, that he should show the basest contempt for those who had, with his best interests and the interests of the Church at heart, raised their voices in quiet and democratic protest – well, it was all just too much! But, at least, it was a most thorough vindication of the views and sentiments of that decent and respectable majority – a total justification of the very article which he now quoted at length and with obvious vindictiveness. Oh yes, he was not quoting the article in order to agree with it, at least in part, which would have been more than could have been expected. No, he was out for blood! His was not a tone of respect, but of stone-cold contempt.

The worthy trio were outraged. But it was important to grin and bear it, or at least to bear it. If Sedley was hell-bent on self-destruction, he should at least be given a free rein and an opportunity of doing a good and lasting job. Baxter therefore experienced a mixture of fury and exhilaration; he glanced sideways at his trusted companions, with the confident expectation of victory against the troublesome priest, who he now regarded as the most contemptible of adversaries. The expectation strengthened as the sermon proceeded.

' ... I believe the accusation of blasphemy,' Sedley went on, 'to be the worst of all possible accusations – if only because it suggests a contempt for the *essence* of the Christian Message, which is Love. I was hoping I had said enough to clear myself of such an idiotic accusation. But apparently not – it seems that when the Devil rides out, he knows no rein but his own. If the accusations levelled against me are no more than a request for clarification, I would be only too delighted to restate the case. The accusation is so absurd that I have wondered whether I should lend it any false dignity at all by defending myself against it. But I shall resist the temptation to remain silent – for silence now would be understood by some to be an abdication of my duty as vicar of this parish, and almost as bad as surrendering to the intimidations contained in the article I have quoted in full. For I regard this article as a challenge, and as an opportunity to preach no less than the Word of God ...'

All this was monstrously galling. Sedley sounded like some 17th-century martyr making the very most of the few minutes left to him before the flames did their work at the stake. Equally galling was that while to some he might seem an absurd, farcical character in a bad play, to others he might seem compelling; and Baxter was wise enough to know that there might be no telling which way opinion might eventually swing. After all, even a grotesque and farcical figure might at the same time sound convincing. But, no, Baxter wanted him to get on with it, so that the lever might be pulled, the rope might tighten and the dead weight hang limp. It was not so much getting the job done, for of this Baxter was reasonably confident, but of getting the job *well* done; it had to be complete, all or nothing at all – an order for execution that the hangman would find unambiguous and irreversible. A stay of execution, for example, was unthinkable. And so, it would not do to have Sedley sound too convincing. The chance, however slender, that he might appeal to the hearts and minds of a significant minority was understandingly unsettling. Baxter's mounting exhilaration was therefore tinged with a degree of apprehension – though, with the super-human strength of which he was capable, and which he had on many occasions demonstrated, his concern was beautifully controlled, or it was – as it might prefer to put it – gagged in infancy.

But, say what he will, Sedley was not likely to make much of an impression on anyone save those who were of like minds and already disposed towards him, and there were precious few of those on this or on any other occasion. Jesus himself had spoken of a generation of vipers; perhaps he had meant the shadow people, a generation that was persistently and eternally self-perpetuating; and Sedley had read a philosopher who was persuaded that human beings were mutating in a downward spiral. Sedley's expectations were therefore most modest. However, he had his pitch and was determined to exploit it for all his might. To Baxter and some others he might have seemed like a crazed prisoner in a cell, already found guilty by due process of law and serving a life sentence, yet still rehearsing his defence as though his trial had not passed but was to come tomorrow – always *tomorrow*: a prisoner pacing his cell, backwards and forwards, reciting his credentials to an imaginary jury, boring and irritating his jailers and fellow inmates, who had to endure the daily ritual over and over again ...

'I shall begin by asking you this: what should we count more important, the frame or the picture inside it? Because when I speak of the essence of the Christian Message, I am talking about the picture and not the frame. In comparison with the picture, the frame is useless. The idea of Life Eternal, of Life after Death, is a nonsense, a frame that can be discarded, and it is time now that we discarded it and focussed our whole attention on the picture inside it, the essence of the Christian Message – which is Love! We have for centuries been blinded by superstition, and religions other than Christianity have laboured under the same illusion and tragically still do. The essence of any religion worthy of the name should be Love, but because this message has been diluted or missed entirely in favour of a framework of superstition, religions are competing with one another and are hostile to one another, such that they become the very antithesis of Love; instead they breed mutual suspicion, contempt and hatred and are even regarded in some quarters as licences to kill opposition. Instead of unity, unity through Love, religions have become instruments of disunity and destruction. No wonder Christianity itself has declined in importance; many fail to see its relevance as an instrument for positive change; they see only the framework of superstition and they wish to discard it, but in doing so they throw the baby out with the bathwater – they discard the picture with the frame! Meanwhile, Judaism and Islam praise a vengeful God, so that those who believe in such a God believe also that the killing and destruction of unbelievers can be justified in his name, are indeed *called for* in his name! – and this simply turns any religion worthy of the name on its head!

'If Love is the essence of Christianity, there are implications for politics. The words of Jesus Christ have been quoted against me: Give to Caesar that which is Caesar's and to God that which is God's. But we must remember that not everything we give to Caesar is acceptable to God. The *conventional morality* of paying your taxes and your bills, of being honest in your dealings, and so on, is all very well. But Christian love is much more than this and provides us with a *target* we must strive to aim at, though I am the first to admit that we forever fall short of it. You will remember the parable of the young rich man in Matthew, Chapter 19, when he asks Jesus how he can achieve eternal life; Jesus tells him to keep the Commandments; the young man replies that he does so, and asks what more he can do, and Jesus tells him to give away his riches; the young man cannot do it and turns away sorrowfully, and Jesus tells his disciples that it is easier for a camel to pass through the eye of a needle than for a rich man to enter into the kingdom of God, and then he adds, "With God, all things are possible." We must remember that the phrase "kingdom of God" is not meant to refer to some place or state in the stratosphere, because the kingdom of God is *within* us. And if the young man thinks that "eternal life" actually means living forever he is victim of superstition. "Eternal life" means spiritual enlightenment; it is not a plea in favour of cryogenics.

'Jesus is telling us that with perfect love, all things are possible. Perfect love may be rare indeed. But what should alarm us is not so much the improbability of achieving perfect love, but the fact that we fall so incredibly short of it! The fact that a country like ours can still tolerate increasing numbers of the poor on our streets, can impose crippling taxes on those who are least able to pay them – this must raise questions in our minds as to how far this country is a Christian country. If it is not a Christian country, it is sheer hypocrisy to claim that it is, or ever was, or ever will be. Indeed, it seems at times that successive Governments worship the devil if they worship anything at all! Perhaps we should all come clean and admit that this is a Godless country! The fact is, we cannot claim to be Christian unless we strive to love others as ourselves, and this means acknowledging our imperfections and striving to be better than we are – but of this I see very little!

'I believe that in these days of a declining Church, we should do all we can to restate the Christian Message, but without the paraphernalia of an outdated and primitive superstructure, that we should rescue the picture from the flames before it is engulfed by a mixture of mediocrity, indifference and competing and morally inferior religions, some of which preach death instead of life, which is to say they savour of the Antichrist.'

And as a parting shot, Sedley had the gall to say, 'Now I hope, I *sincerely* hope, I have made myself sufficiently clear to all my detractors.'

This was the bare bones of Sedley's sermon, and certainly more than enough to tighten the noose around his own neck. He could be accused of advocating devil-worship, while he himself was accusing everybody else of serving the interests of the Antichrist – whoever or whatever *that* was. The gentleman with the red carnation had never stopped to question what 'Antichrist' might mean, but since it presumably meant anything and everything that Christ was not, and since Christ was everything bright and beautiful, then it must mean something despicable and grossly offensive. If so, Sedley's accusation would be eminently usable in the national press; it was hot stuff, hotter than a bolt out of Hell. The more turbulent Sedley grew, the more the noose tightened. Naturally, the lady of enormous proportions was almost in a state of seizure; but a gentle pat on the hand from Charles Baxter proved more than enough to restore her composure. Toby and Clifford Anderson exchanged glances more than once and regarded the whole thing as first-class entertainment or, as Toby later put it, 'a dignified blow for sanity, long overdue and all the more welcome for that.' But such a judgement was by no means the majority view.

There were rumblings and stirrings in the pews. Needless to say, Baxter and his associates had reached the end of their tethers and considered themselves deserving of the very highest honours the land could bestow for having sat the whole thing through from beginning to end. Julia Sedley left in the very wake of Baxter, and within seconds only a handful remained to sing, or mime, the closing hymn, and amongst these were Toby and Clifford Anderson who followed Sedley to the door of the church and were seen by several of the departing flock warmly shaking the hand of the offending priest, an act which some of his detractors considered to be a most fitting end to a most alarming fiasco. Sedley's parishioners were unsure on whose behalf the sermon was meant to be given – God or the Devil, but the highly questionable company in which Sedley had been seen at the church door seemed to clinch the matter in favour of the Dark Lord. It may be noted that the Andersons had done no more than shake the Reverend's hand; for they would not answer his earnest enquiry as to who they were or from where they came; they simply smiled and nodded and departed in haste, in the manner of men who had no wish to outstay their welcome.

As for Julia, she had by now decided that Adam had all but put an end to their marriage, that he had resolved, as it were, to relinquish all his worldly wealth and follow Jesus Christ – or least that part of his worldly wealth that included Julia. She was angered and disillusioned, but she was also determined that her life and her prospects should not be ruined. She caught up with Baxter who had sauntered ahead in the company of the faithful.

The gentleman with the red carnation had now accumulated more ammunition against the Reverend than Rothschild could have assembled against Karl Marx. With all the infinite skill of a first-rate journalist, he was able to contrive hypnotic headlines by culling words and phrases from Sedley's turbulent stock of lexis. Sedley might, in turn, be represented as an advocate of devil worship, an enemy of material possessions, and therefore a supporter of stark nudity since he would have the shirts off everyone's backs, a blasphemer since he denied the possibility of an afterlife and the existence of heaven, an arch troublemaker since he threw into disrepute the moral and intellectual legitimacy of Judaism and Islam, a disrupter of social cohesion and the harmony of different Faiths, and a major transgressor of political correctness, and since Jesus Christ himself had been brought to the stand as a witness in Sedley's own defence, Sedley was also guilty of supreme heresy. The word 'Antichrist' was particularly useful and could not possibly be left out, for Sedley was accusing just about everybody of serving the interests of the Antichrist – and as for what the word actually meant, readers could work it out for themselves, though it ought to be self-evident and would in any case no doubt be treated as such. And if Sedley was advocating the total abolition of private property, that, too, was not at all clear, but it would certainly arrest the attention of even the most casual reader and would sound as inviting as the prospect of Armageddon. Yes, the beauty of Sedley's position was that it was so easy to rebut; for example, property was as natural to human beings as petals to the daisy, and to talk of living according to one's needs was demonstrably feeble, for the needs of the rich were obviously more complex, *richer* one might say, than those of the poor; and as for blasphemy and heresy and transgressions against social harmony and political correctness – well, the case against him was just too obvious for words. Yes, in short, Sedley hadn't a leg to stand on; at best, his position on one or two issues might be described as pious but wildly impractical, at worst simply Satanic. So grateful was the gentleman with the red carnation for the juicy journalistic opportunities afforded him by Sedley, that he might have stopped to shake his hand; as it was, he was content to leave the church in a state of quiet elation.

The lady of enormous proportions was equally elated. It was pleasing, positively vindicating, to know that Sedley had no one but himself to blame. He had cast himself out of the society of the decent and the respectable. A marked man he had been; and now he had condemned himself thoroughly. As Baxter put it to her, Sedley had sewn up the case against himself seamlessly; his sermon had been crude, blunt, perverse and long-winded. All that was necessary now was to make formal arrangements for his 'execution'.

It was also of no small comfort for Baxter and Co. Ltd. To reflect that for the majority of the congregation the sermon had probably been either too boring for words, too repetitive, or simply too unintelligible to be swallowed whole or even in small pieces. Sedley might at first have sounded compelling to some, but the novelty was bound to have worn off, and to many his style of delivery had doubtless been more attractive than the nature and substance of his pronouncements. Eyebrows had indeed been raised here and there, but they largely belonged to those on whose support Baxter could rely.

As for the Andersons, they were content to go home to stay and never return. Like some good fellow after his first sexual experience, who had for too long done without, subsisting instead on a heavy diet of sheer speculation and consequent anticipation, they were quite content to sit in their armchairs and remember – at least for the foreseeable future, listening, as they were accustomed to do, to distant church bells on Sunday evenings before the sun went down.

Chapter Fifteen

Of Logical Men and Unreasonable Kittens

We stop at nothing, we shadowy forms; we twist and turn, cajole and rage, creating storms and wrecks of men who will never more with us engage nor raise a finger of disdain.

~ ~

Sedley's handshake with the Andersons was scarcely 48 hours old before the gentleman with the red carnation had, with the full blessing of his editor, published a lengthy, authoritative but fanciful rebuttal in his national newspaper; the article did not of course rank as first-page material, but was tucked inside under the heading, 'Incensed Parishioners to Boycott Church Services'. The gentleman with the red carnation had, in accordance with the irresistible demands of journalistic integrity, began by making a beeline for what Sedley had had the temerity to call 'conventional morality', a morality, it was claimed, he had attached only a secondary and grudging importance. With a determination to follow the Socratic 'logos' wherever it might lead, the article went on to deduce an illogical and despicable conclusion from a perfectly reasonable observation, namely that Sedley was tantamount to inviting people to tell lies with impunity, because as far as the Christian Message was concerned the conventional morality of truth-telling and honest-dealing was of minor importance, and perhaps of no importance at all! Sedley was therefore ignoring the dictates of integrity and starkly rejecting the bedrock values of art and civilisation, since both art and civilisation were devoted to Truth in its many forms and guises. What Sedley was advocating was an anarchy comparable to the lawlessness of the jungle. The minor importance he was said to be attaching to conventional morality was also interpreted as a licence to refuse to pay one's debts, such as taxes, and was therefore a challenge to the very framework of civilised society within which Christianity had both sense and substance: if loving one's neighbour did not imply a readiness to pay one's debts in full and on time, then what on earth could it possibly mean? Sedley had referred rather clumsily to frames and pictures and said that frames could be discarded, so presumably he would say the same regarding the framework of a civilised society, namely conventional morality and the rule of law. So wrote the gentleman with the red carnation, who prided himself on his painstaking ability to pursue to the kill any wilful fantasy with the sharpest tools logic could provide. It should be noted that this gentleman was never backward in coming forward whenever and wherever he considered the terms 'logic' and 'logical' and their derivatives applicable. He and Baxter were logical men who believed that the very utterance of such terms was sufficient to condemn any opposition to intellectual oblivion on this side of the grave and the other.

Sedley, they agreed, had posed a challenge to logic itself! Because he advocated, they said, the surrender and distribution of surplus wealth, he was removing all incentive for the creation of wealth in the first place, and had, 'therefore', removed the very possibility of wealth. (The gentleman with the red carnation was most unsparing in his use of the word 'therefore', one of the very few commodities with which he was known to display such generosity, very possibly because it seemed to preclude any counter-argument.) Sedley was 'therefore' posing a challenge to the very basis of civilised society, and a challenge which reduced his own position, given that it merited the appellation 'position', to absurdity, because to impugn civilisation was to render Christianity impossible. Sedley was 'therefore' proposing an anti-Christian solution to the very evils he purported to address. Sedley's position was likened to the removal of a man's head in an attempt to cure him of toothache. The gentleman with the red carnation was proud of himself for thinking of this analogy, and both Baxter and the lady of enormous proportions smiled wryly when their discriminating eyes lighted upon it. (Indeed, they smiled a great deal, each smile wryer than the last.)

But, truth to tell, the gentleman with the red carnation excelled himself on this occasion. Having delivered the main course he went on to serve a dessert of unparalleled quality. For not only had Sedley shaken the very foundations of decency and respectability to the core, removing in the process any real incentive for the accumulation of wealth, but he had also failed to provide an incentive for Christianity itself. He had set little store by the promise of eternal life, regarding it as a nonsense. This was not simply one weakness amongst others, because he was posing the most 'devastating challenge imaginable' to the Christian Faith, and not just to the Christian Faith but to Islam and Judaism as well. He had 'therefore' succeeded in challenging both the foundations of civilised human society and the basic rationale of the Christian Ethic. For what was the Ethic without the promise of the Life Hereafter. Why should anyone be good if there was nothing at all at the end of it? What's in it for him if there's no paradise to look forward to? Christ had promised otherwise – if you are good you will go to heaven, and heaven is in the hereafter; yes, he had been very clear on that point. What had Christ said to the man who was crucified with him? – he promised him a place with his Father in heaven. That much was clear, said the gentleman with the red carnation; he conceded that his readers were free to believe in such a thing or not, but it had to be admitted that Christ had promised it; 'therefore' if you believed in Christ, you would believe in the life hereafter also; the logic was really very simple; and yet, all Sedley could say was that the dead should bury their dead, and there was very little hope attached to that! – it was merely an instance of the truth that the devil himself could cite scripture for his own purpose. Sedley had spoken of 'superstition' and he had made reference to beliefs which Sedley believed turned Christianity on its head. But on the contrary, wrote the gentleman with the red carnation, it was Sedley himself who was turning Christianity inside-out and upside-down. It was not simply that he had somehow forgotten to mention the Life Hereafter, as though its existence is something he took very much for granted; on the contrary, he had dismissed it out of hand, as though it had no bearing on the Christian Message whatsoever. In view of this, the gentleman with the red carnation was ready with a crushing finale: if he had sought to furnish Christianity with an essential role, he had succeeded in depriving it of any role at all. Quite simply, if he dismissed belief in the Life Hereafter as a mere superstition, he was really admitting that Christianity was not a viable proposition, but instead a meaningless jumble or complexity of superstition and, 'therefore', something that could no longer be taken seriously by any intelligent, rational creature.

Of course, the gentleman with the red carnation was at pains to disassociate himself from such a depressing and nihilistic view, for there were things in Heaven and Hell that were not dreamt of in all our philosophies. No, he himself was pinning all his hopes on the Life Hereafter, since, whatever it was, it had to be better than the life Here and Now; which is why he was a Christian; and, he said, he could produce a long list of dignitaries who shared exactly the same hope – of a life somewhere in the mysterious ether of the universe, far beyond the comprehension of mere mortals. Far from believing that Christianity was a dead duck and a tissue of superstition, it was the bedrock of his spiritual life.

By giving primacy to Christianity while at the same time depriving it of its legs, Sedley was 'therefore' trapped in the snares of self-contradiction. And to the extent that he was implying that Christianity was no more than a childish mess, he was soiling the Cloth he purported to represent, and was 'therefore' a hypocrite; more than this, since he was discrediting the Church as a respected and respectable *institution,* he was also public enemy number ne and, 'therefore', the true antichrist. One obvious and restrained response would be to advise Sedley to find another job, but, the gentleman with the red carnation went on, it would be infinitely better if the Church itself took a firm hand in the matter and guided the errant priest back to the 'true Christian fold', and, failing this, boot him out altogether by unfrocking him.

The upshot was the belief that Sedley had nothing of value to offer. All talk of love and compassion, coming from him, was plainly hypocritical. The best that could be said of him was that he had a gift for stating the obvious, when it came to advocating love and compassion, and making it appear to be a newly discovered truth of enormous magnitude; anyone could utter truths about love and compassion, and frequently did. But, henceforward, all those who had read the article and weighed carefully the beautifully measured invective against the offending priest would be forewarned and forearmed against false prophets in the guise of over-zealous priests. The grand conclusion, argued with all the logical finesse of a St Thomas Aquinas, was that Sedley had made much of the obvious in the process of knocking Christianity squarely off its feet, and that his appeal to a morality allegedly superior to the conventional was comparable with the ravings of the 'Loony Left' and 'we all know how utterly discreditable and heretical *they* are!'

It was, of course, much to his credit that the gentleman with the red carnation was unwilling to rest content with the assertion that Sedley was merely a controversial eccentric. Eccentricity was all very well, but the danger, as the author of the article well knew, was that this kind of irreligious talk might possibly be taken seriously by many who were unaware of the power of illogic. Since Sedley was imputing superstitious nonsense to the very core of Christianity, he could not be let off on the mere charge of eccentricity. Eccentricity was one thing, and downright spiritual sedition was quite another.

The implication, of course, was that spiritual sedition should never be suffered to wear the Cloth of the Christian Church, and that if the Church allowed its ministers to preach doctrines that reduced Christianity to absurdity, it was pouring hot coals upon its own head and could not possibly expect to sustain the respect it customarily deserved and received. It was simply not on to attend church only to receive doctrines that were inconsistent with the very spirit and logic of the Christian Faith. It followed that Sedley were to find his own church ill-attended, or not attended at all, then those who refused to attend were in fact committing a truly Christian act. And suppose all churches were unattended for the same reason? Well, then, that would be the end of the institution of the Church, for no organisation could allow anyone in its ranks who were so clearly opposed to its own ethos!

What particularly worried many readers of the article in question was that the kind of misrepresentation of the Church exemplified by Sedley might not become an isolated case unless appropriate measures were taken to nip it firmly in the bud. The confusion of the secular with the spiritual, the political with the divine, was a dangerous perversion of the very essence of Christianity. Something had to be done, and it had to be seen to be done – and quickly, too.

Unsurprisingly, the article was well-received, both by those who despised the Church and by those who believed their best interests were served by it. For those who despised the Church, the article had succeeded in putting the institution in its rightful place, which is to say outside the arena of adverse political commentary. And for those, like the lady of enormous proportions, who believed their best interests were served by the Church, if not on earth then at least in the Life Hereafter, the article had restored, or at any rate confirmed, their faith in the doctrine of Life Eternal. In fact, this lady was heard to have said that she felt quite refreshed, even elevated, by the article, and that from now on 'til her dying day she would entertain only the highest respect for its author, who had sounded the clarion in the shrillest tones for decency and respectability – and for hope, which must spring eternal if it springs at all, and to the very primacy which he had given to the promise of things to come. She was indeed impressed with its author, whose impeccable logic had appealed to her most. It was his impeccable logic, indeed, that finally drew her attention to his penetrating blue eyes, though she kept this fact very much to herself. It may be noted here, though it is of little relevance, that the lady of enormous proportions was a spinster, who had once thought of marriage, as every girl does, but had managed to put such thoughts so far to the back of her mind that they began to wither there for lack of light and air and finally succumbed to the practical exigencies of life and the necessity of growing older if one is to grow at all. Yet now she began to wonder whether, had she met the gentleman with the red carnation in her youth, she might not have allowed herself ... But it was too late for such thoughts, even if such thoughts were allowed, which they were not, for one who had devoted herself to a life of spiritual integrity and tranquillity in the service of the Almighty.

All in all, the article made a most welcome appearance in the pages of the national press. It called forth congratulatory letters to the editor extolling its virtues; one from a bishop, no less, agreeing that men of the cloth should refrain from political comment and reaffirming the Church's 'obvious' endorsement of the promise of the Life Hereafter; another from a politician calling upon the Church to 'reassert its authority over its more recalcitrant brethren'; but, curiously, none from any clergyman on Sedley's side – a fact from which readers were perhaps invited to draw their own conclusions.

~ ~

The evening prior to Sedley's sermon, Julia had taken the dramatic step of discreetly packing a suitcase and hiding it at the back of her wardrobe. This might have turned out to be no more than an expression of exasperation than an indication of real intent because it all depended on the ultimatum she had given him – in a somewhat veiled but nevertheless unmistakable form. She had also written a note, which was ready and waiting to be placed on his desk should the need arise; it was very simple, the simpler the better, she'd thought; it merely told him that they should go their separate ways, that she couldn't share his religious commitment nor understand very clearly what that commitment was all about.

The suitcase was packed; the note was written. Now she would see whether the suitcase should be unpacked and the note destroyed. She had promised herself what the outcome would be if he failed to respond to the ultimatum, and this was a promise she was determined to keep. Now the outcome was crystal clear. His sermon was an unanswerable case for separation. Leaving him, if only temporarily, would be a final test of his loyalties. She would not tell him where she was going; there was no need, and her departure would be all the more dramatic for secrecy. He would assume she was heading for her sister's in the metropolis, because that was where she always went when she went away by herself.

As Baxter and his associates made their way to Field Headquarters (Baxter's house) after the offending sermon to assume battle stations, and while the Andersons wound their way home, Julia decided to open her own broadside by making off as quickly as possible before Sedley returned to the vicarage, which was not difficult to do, for minor matters always kept him in the vestry for about an hour after every service; her suitcase was already packed, the note already written, so it only remained to pick up the one and put down the other, and then make her way to the railway station.

The big and annoyingly persistent question was whether she should actually go ahead with it – a question she had asked and answered in the affirmative many times recently. Things were not at all as she wanted them; either a short, sharp shock would restore Adam's priorities, and she hoped that she was very much amongst them, or she would prove beyond doubt that theirs was not after all a match made in heaven and should never have been made in the first place. And if it proved right that they should separate permanently, she would thank her lucky stars that this was brought to light sooner rather than later – the very thought of bringing children into a less-than-perfect world in an infinitely less-than-perfect marriage, was naturally abhorrent. She managed to thank God for something, after all – that they hadn't yet started a family.

She had thought about children quite a lot, not so much about having them as the kind of life she would want them to have. What sort of children would Adam want them to be? If left to him, they would grow up deficient in that vital ingredient that made life worthwhile, that gave life its very rationale – ambition. No, she wouldn't rate their chances if they were brought up on Adam's philosophy; they would be chewed up and spat out. Besides, the competitive spirit belonged to man, to his very essence, and without it there could be no progress – everybody knew that. So what would he teach his children? He would no doubt teach them to stand on the roadside of life idly watching the traffic go by, criticising it whenever it jammed or congested, which was something anyone could do. No, it was possible to be just too wise, and if you were too wise, everything stopped for you, because you were asking too much of everybody, expecting them to be more than people, more than human, which was wrong. Or maybe you'd be asking the wrong things of them. If Adam was right about what Christ wanted of us, well it followed that Christ was wrong, too; that he was asking too much, like a dreamer with the best of intentions, but a dreamer all the same. Maybe there was a place for dreaming now and then. But Julia didn't want her children to be dreamers, for if they were dreamers, it followed that they were asleep, and the world, *this* world at any rate, was no place for sleepers. She did not want her children to go to sleep. And she herself was not prepared to spend the rest of her life standing on the roadside while Adam poured forth diatribes on the progress, or lack of it, of mankind. In fact, if she refused to have his children she was doing them and herself and Adam a big favour. The overwhelming odds were that they would not turn out saintly – and she thanked God for that, too. But if they fell short of sainthood, how would Adam take it? Either they would have failed him, or he them. No, the whole idea of having children with Adam was, given his mental state, beginning to seem increasingly unthinkable. Adam was much better off pontificating on his own and lecturing to himself. Unless, that is, he could be reined up now and brought to see the unreasonableness of his ways. And that possibility, however unlikely, brought her back again to the recommendation of the Short, Sharp, Shock.

Thoughts about children raised the spectre of sex. For all her physical charms, sufficient to bring Baxter to the threshold of indiscretion, she was not particularly libidinous. Even so, she expected more attention from Adam than she had become accustomed to receiving. Sex may not be a guarantee of affection or of love, but she had agreed with her mother, when that noble matron had attempted some years past to school her, quite unnecessarily, in the facts of life, that a healthy sex life was a prerequisite of a healthy marriage. 'A good marriage will stand up in bed,' her mother used to say, wagging her finger sagely, bringing forth a quizzical expression from Julia, who needed a moment or two to give it the sense intended. 'Oh, yes, you may smile, but a good marriage will stand up in bed,' she would repeat, as a prelude to referencing her own marriage, which by then was quite incapable of resuscitation, let alone of standing up, in bed or out of it. Nowadays, Adam tended to shut himself away night after night in his study, reading or writing, emerging late and falling into bed without so much as a goodnight kiss – proof positive, thought Julia, that his inclinations were otherwise directed, his energies otherwise channelled. And that was just not good enough. True, there had never been a time when Adam could have been described as over-sexed; but no there was nothing at all. Nor did she feel able to talk about it, even if she had really wanted to — with Adam the topic would've seemed incongruous, irrelevant, silly even. It was just as well that, for her, the subject wasn't that important — not itself, anyway; no, what was important is what it indicated. But it was part of a much larger and infinitely more depressing picture — part of the disillusionment she felt; she ought to be getting far more attention, if not in bed, then at least out of it.

The more she had thought about it in the days and nights prior to the last sermon, the more her mind was made up. She was fully prepared to use that sermon as a deciding factor, whether or not Adam himself was fully aware of it.

And so, she placed the note on the desk in the study, picked up her suitcase, and made a dash for the station. If Adam came after her like a knight in distress, imploring her to stay, pleading that it was all a misunderstanding, promising to revise his priorities, or at least endeavouring to prove that his religious convictions were entirely compatible with his marital loyalties ... well, then she would listen, certainly, but would make no promises; she might agree to return on a sort of probationary basis. She would do her very best to exercise discretion and restraint and not betray the slightest emotional twinge.

She had a much longer wait for the train than she had anticipated, having forgotten that Sunday services were more infrequent than on weekdays; she half expected to see Adam turn the corner, waving frantically and rushing up to her with a flurry of questions. But that did not happen. During the minutes that rolled by she even thought of calling the vicarage just to see if he was at home – but she managed to pull back the thought by the scruff of its neck. She even thought of missing this train and waiting for the next, but the next would be too late; no, it had to be this train or none at all. She examined her feelings. Was she really disappointed not to see Adam materialise on the spot, before her very eyes? The train was delayed one hour, and still Adam was nowhere to be seen. Yet he must be home by now, home from the church, from the vestry ...

She grew angrier by the minute, and ten minutes before her train actually arrived she had convinced herself that she was doing the right thing and that as far as she was concerned there could be no turning back, no even if he got on his knees and begged her; not at least until he had fully descended from his high horse promising never to remount. She could hardly contain herself as she paced slowly to and fro, with a feminine grace more contrived than usual, from one end of the short platform to the other. She did, however, contain herself sufficiently to call Charles Baxter, explaining that she was about to spend a few days in the metropolis and hoping that he might suggest a meeting to talk about making the contacts he had previously mentioned.

She was not planning an affair. She was not physically attracted to Baxter at all. She was thinking entirely of her career, to which she now felt completely dedicated, and of how it could possibly be furthered in the shortest space of time. If Adam knew that she had called Baxter, of all people! It was like a stab in the back, but one which she felt he thoroughly deserved, especially as the minutes rolled by with no sign of him. Yes, like a stab in the back, and no matter that it was one that would not be felt by the recipient; the joy of it was in the act of it, and the act was simply a gut reaction, much as children will respond to an attack, either with tears or with a retaliation in kind. After all, she herself had been stabbed in the back by Adam's refusal to meet her ultimatum, by his inattention to her unpublicised talent as an artist, by his persistent unreasonableness, by his apparent willingness to frustrate her own ambitions in his resentment towards Baxter, by his selfish commitment to Jesus Christ; and who could she possibly blame but Adam for her own acute apprehensiveness about starting a family? Having listed these thoughts one after another, they now all rushed upon her in a flood. The sun had gone down on her wrath – hence the speedy call to Baxter almost as her train turned into the station.

Baxter was understandably shocked to receive the call. His first instinct was to assume that it might be a plea for clemency on behalf of the miscreant. But the thought hardly had time to form when it was pushed out of sight. Julia simply said that she was in a hurry and that it might perhaps be possible to meet up in the metropolis. Baxter stammered an affirmative, followed by a promise to call her back. The conversation was brief, hurried and terse; but Baxter was delighted and bemused. He decided that it would not do for either the gentleman with the red carnation nor the lady of enormous proportions to be privy to the fact that he had just received a call from Sedley's wife wishing to meet up with him. He was quite right. He took the conversation into the hallway while his fellow conspirators took to his brandy in the lounge.

Julia's train journey was an angry one. She was to become angrier still when it became obvious, first after hours, then after days, that Adam was unlikely to attempt to contact her, let alone plead his case, let alone throw himself at her feet groaning in contrition. But anger gave way, as it so often does, to cool resolution and an iron will.

Not long after the article of rebuttal had been penned by the gentleman with the red carnation and rolled through the press, Baxter and Julia were sitting together at a small table in a quiet restaurant in a side-street in the metropolis – a scene far less romantic than it may sound to some. Far from making a plea for clemency, Julia poured forth some small talk followed by an apology for having failed to make the right kind of impression on Adam. There was no pleading his case. On the contrary, Adam, she said, had made a bed of nails for himself, and that was his look-out, she was sorry to have to say. No, she did not share his views, insofar as she understood what they actually were, and she was ashamed to have to admit that she could do nothing to save him from the kind of reproaches he was receiving, that she could not, well ... save him from himself. But she did not really want to talk about that. She had come to spend a few days with her sister and had wondered whether Baxter had made any headway in the little matter of establishing some contacts between her and certain people who might prove helpful to her. Baxter didn't want to talk about Adam either. He was very sorry for the way things had turned out, but he could not agree more that Adam had brought it all on himself and should be left to carry the can. But he was more than willing to talk about Julia, instead.

But when Julia refused to carry any brief, however short, however clumsily, Baxter knew full well what that meant. It meant that the way was clear for him to exercise his power of seduction, which, when utilised with discretion, was a priceless gift bestowed on him by the gods. Indeed, he could feel the power there and then, and all he had to do was invoke it and it would arise like some inexorable demon from the deep and misty realms of his being. He began to stare into Julia's eyes, speaking when appropriate, responding when necessary with all the clichés he could command, but all the time his words were like ethereal things, lacking substance; he was simply paying lip service to respectable convention, while his eyes did something else. His eyes penetrated to her very mind, or so it seemed to him, with words and thoughts of their very own, such that the words emanating from his mouth seemed quite hollow by comparison. While he spoke to her of art or of contacts that might be formed, his eyes requested her to disrobe and do his bidding. It was what he likened to an electricity over which the object of his designs had little or no defence. It had also occurred to him, of course, that such notions were nonsense; but if they were nonsense, they were delightful nonsense all the same and he relished the thought of them; he preferred to believe that such a power of attraction existed, that he possessed it and that he could exercise it at will.

To Julia, however, he merely came across rather sleepy, and suffering perhaps from overwork, which he certainly was, though not at all in the sense which she imagined. The lusty reciprocity which Baxter was convinced existed was simply not there. Not this time, at any rate. The bill for the light snack, respectfully placed under his nose, together with Julia's snappy insistence that she must now be making tracks, served to bring him to his senses, though he was smugly confident that his eyes had delivered their message and that it would only be a matter of time before he could savour her – always provided, of course, that the savouring was done discreetly, or as discreetly as circumstances would allow; after all, it was not the thing to be found having an affair with the vicar's wife, even one who had so obviously made such a bad choice, and even if the vicar in question was as contemptible as Adam Sedley. But, yes, given the right circumstances, he was prepared to take a moderate degree of risk.

The plain truth of the matter is that Baxter had, as they say, 'got it more than usually bad' or, as the Italians might humorously say, 'he had fallen like a stewed pear' for Julia Sedley. So much so that he dreamed about her, and dreams, or the dreams he could remember, were a rarity indeed. But this one topped all the others: they were naked on the floor of what appeared to be a church and were in the classical posture of penetration; that it had been merely the classical posture he found disappointing when he later recalled the dream, but then he considered himself fortunate to have remembered any of it at all; that it happened on the floor of a church he found curiously thrilling; more interesting still was that with every lustful push a nail was driven into the hands and feet of Adam Sedley, who was being prepared for crucifixion directly above them. The crucifixion was unpleasant and distressing; but all things considered, and one thing in particular, the dream was well worth having.

Yes, the crucifixion had tended to spoil things. It reminded him of the time he had bedded a brunette in her own apartment. His enjoyment of the occasion was spoiled by a kitten which she kept; the playful little thing insisted on clambering on top of the bed and clawing at Baxter's toes all through his love-making, the sheets having disappeared in the opening scene. Try as he might he could not kick the little beast away, not at least for long. He could hardly have complained about it – it would have been unseemly and ridiculous, and not a little unkind, and, besides, the apartment was a bedsitter and there was no place to put the offending monster, other than the bathroom; the bathroom was too risky; in his irritation he might have drowned it in a bath of ice-cold water, or flushed it down the loo to claw its way through Hades. There was nothing for it but to grin and bear it; which was very hard to do, since, as Baxter became more passionate, the furry gremlin would redouble its efforts, making to chew off Baxter's big toe, thus adding insult to injury. The little fiend almost spoiled things completely; all the same, it did not quite succeed, and so the experience was worth having, claws and all.

Baxter never read into his dreams. Such mumbo-jumbo was not for him. If dreams are letters we write to ourselves, his lay unread in the wastepaper basket where he had dropped them.

~ ~

Within days of the last offending sermon, the case against Adam Sedley gathered greater momentum. The main brief had already been presented in the national press, aided and abetted by some local television and radio coverage of protestors who had positioned themselves outside the church and the vicarage, carrying slogans like 'Restore our Church', 'Christianity, not Politics' and even 'Christ, not Marx'. All this, together with an effective boycott of regular church services, did a great deal to make Sedley's position uncomfortable, if not untenable; for a shepherd without a flock is effectively redundant.

A written petition to the bishop, amply signed, brought the matter squarely to the attention of the hierarchy. The appeal contained a statement to the effect that no 'personal criticism' of Adam Sedley was intended and that an amicable resolution of the situation was sincerely hoped for and expected. It was only in deference to 'Christian principles of Faith' that the petitioners had seen fit to approach the bishop at all. They merely wished that Christianity 'untainted by politics and other excesses' should be the true business of the Church, and that the bishop should do his utmost to clear away confusions which served only to 'cloud the true meaning of the Christian Gospels', 'to denigrate the Promise of

Life Eternal and to sow the seeds of dissension and conflict between different Faiths'. Since the lady of enormous proportions had had more than a mere hand in the wording of this pious document, and since she had performed the function of Chief Whip with consummate skill, it is not to be wondered at that her signature was the very first to grace it and was penned with a flourish pregnant with confidence and determination, rather like that of Cromwell's on the death warrant for Charles I.

Chapter Sixteen

Of Bishops and the Fuehrerprinzip

To call the shadow world the 'real' world is to stand the real on its head, as if black is white and white is black, and those who live are dead.

~ ~

Sedley found himself standing in the bishop's study, with the bishop seated in a heavy and imposing mahogany chair, at an even more imposing mahogany desk. He explained that he had invited him over to discuss certain matters in leisurely circumstances. The bishop endeavoured to sound a casual as possible, but managed it so well that there could be no doubt that what he alluded to in the phrase 'certain matters' was anything but casual.

The very grandeur of that study, indeed of the whole house, gardens included, mocked the very idea of equality between men, let alone men in the sight of God. But nothing outdid the study itself for quality to the square inch: the heavy lined curtains; the plush, dark red carpet; the mahogany desk and chair; the inspirational paintings of lesser-known artists, incarcerated in expensive frames; the fireplace surround, massive and constructed in black oak, with large winged armchairs, one on either side; the high ceiling; the tall windows which looked out over the expansive lawns where oaks and elms formed the perimeters; and not least the walls, lined with leather-bound volumes penned in ancient tongues. All this, and a silence broken only by the deep and clear tick (almost thud) of a valuable antique grandfather clock in a walnut case.

Were such surroundings intimidating? Grandiosity is a well-known instrument of intimidation. But it must be said that the bishop's study would not have compromised a man like Charles Baxter. He might well have compared it with his Headmaster's study, with which, as a pupil, he had had a closer acquaintance than many. But, as master of the art of intimidation himself, such places could never have charmed him into a compliance that he neither foresaw nor desired.

Baxter had a precise and comprehensive understanding of the psychological utility of interior design. It was not a subject he had read about, for little if anything has ever been written on the subject. Nor was it something he had learned about from anyone else. The psychology of ambience is something he understood intuitively and took very much for granted. Baxter was, in any case, accustomed to *quality*; so much so that he might have described the bishop's study as merely comfortable. But to many others it might have seemed a fitting residence, a natural habitat, for intimidation incarnate.

Sedley himself might have felt intimidated by that study a few years earlier, to the extent that he would have minded each step he took. But he did not feel like that now. He felt that he had gradually gained the upper hand, believing that the fears engendered by the charisma of people and places were the very work of the devil, and that no man and no place should be elevated above his God. You had to speak your mind to anyone, anywhere, irrespective of the authority they wielded and the luxury of their surroundings – if you had a mind to speak at all.

Sedley was well aware that the physical environment into which you were ushered, the very *place*, might itself have a very important role to play in your own moral defeat, perhaps even a defeat abject and absolute. The impressiveness of the Fuehrer's vast and lavish Villa Berghof above Berchtesgaden had been a hypnotic 'softener' for visiting dignitaries whose countries were about to surrender, almost unawares, to the Nazi yoke; so splendidly did the Villa Berghof fulfil its function, for who could have imagined that such heinous dealings could take place in such polished and tasteful surroundings? To enter through the portals of that fine place was to embark upon the road to humiliation and degradation; the stage was set to invite one to believe that reasonableness would prevail; which indeed it *would*; well, *some* kind of reasonableness, *some* kind of logic – invariably the kind that some dignitaries found much to their distaste, the sort of logic that extracted their souls and fed them to the dogs; but the die had already been cast – and the very Villa itself had had a hand in that. The very charisma of the Fuehrerprinzip owed much to its surroundings, as even the most cynical and disapproving of observers attending the Nuremberg Rallies could readily have testified. And at Auschwitz they walked to hell through well-tended gardens and to tunes from 'The Merry Widow' and 'Tales of Hoffman', while that macabre musical ensemble itself consisted of inmates of the *Vernichtsungslager*!

But Sedley did not feel intimidated by the splendour of the bishop's study or the ornate immensity of his house or gardens. If intimidation of this kind had ever been a charm capable in standing between Sedley and freedom of expression, it had dissolved away, acted upon by the acid of man's repeated and unforgiveable inhumanity to man, as though his perception of all the base and interminable errors of mankind was of such intensity that it would not suffer such charms to work and had at last deprived them of their magic, of their power to constrain and inhibit.

~ ~

There was a small fire burning in the grate to dispel the evening chill, despite the fact that it was mid-summer. The bishop, a tall, large-framed, rotund man in his mid-60s, eased himself into one of the large armchairs next to the fireplace, while gesturing to Sedley to take the other opposite him. Despite the amiable gesture, the bishop's large, round face was expressionless, while his bulbous green eyes gave him the appearance of some tropical tree frog – not sinister, perhaps, but inscrutable. As Sedley glanced at the fire he noted that it was log, not coal. Not quite the same kind of fire that burned, according to Uncle Alan, in his great-grandfather's grate, but it was enough to remind him of his uncle's narrative, for the old man had reproached Alan for wanting to save the world single-handedly, for the attempt to put self-interest too far to one side; the old man had tried to tell the stubborn youth that even saints must eat and drink and that sustenance does not always grow on trees and that, when it does, the trees on which it grows invariably belong to someone else whose permission to eat therefrom can't be taken for granted. The old man had appeared to be angry with him – no doubt afraid for Alan's future.

Judging by what Uncle Alan had told him, Sedley's great grandfather wouldn't have been found dead in a place like this. Sedley smiled faintly at the thought, but not faintly enough to be missed by the bulbous green eyes of the bishop.

'Yes. Yes, nothing like a log-fire to warm the spirits – talking of which ...' said the bishop, stretching forward to fill two glasses which, together with a fine crystal decanter, stood on a small elaborately carved wooden table between the two armchairs. Sedley shook his head and waved his hand. 'No? Alright. You don't mind if I do?'

'Mind you,' the bishop went on after pouring himself a glad of sherry, 'it's a bit rich to have to light fires in what's supposed to be the middle of summer! No, we don't seem to be blessed with a friendly climate ...'

'Or a very predictable one,' Sedley put it, assuming that it was probably necessary to say something, anything, to help the preliminaries along. Sedley understood that he was taking part in a ritual, the small talk and the niceties coming first, followed in due course by the stuff and substance. He was in no hurry.

'Quite. Quite,' returned the bishop, smiling with the minimum of facial contortion. 'I must confess I'm not a lover of winters, yet some people seem to yearn for them. No, give me a summer, even a bad one, every time.'

The bishop spoke gently and quietly, but with the intensity of an academic philosopher intrigued by an unexpected puzzle. He had recently read the biography of a trusted and respected citizen who had been found guilty *in absentia* of spying for a foreign power, and the wretched fellow had been quoted as saying that he actually enjoyed the severe winters of the country to which he had defected. This for the good bishop was proof positive that the fellow was a lunatic through and through.

'Winters! Wind! Sleet! Ice! – and the barrenness of everything. I know it gives us the summers to look forward to – but it's rather sad to see the trees leafless, don't you think?'

'I couldn't agree more,' said Sedley, who couldn't have cared less.

The conclusion of these absurd preliminaries was reliably indicated when the bishop planted his sherry glass on the small table between them, took a deep breath and, with a sigh, reclined into his large armchair.

After explaining what had occasioned this cosy *tete-a-tete*, namely the adverse publicity given to Sedley in the press both locally and nationally, the bishop frowned and nodded slowly. 'What ... what I find intriguing, if that's the right word, is the suddenness of it all. I mean, there was no hint of this sort of difficulty before ... er during your Curacy. What's brought it all on – that's what I'd like to know, quite frankly. Oh, you needn't worry! This isn't an inquisition. For goodness sake, don't think you're on trial or anything of that sort! No, no. It's rather embarrassing for us both – I fully understand that; but I trust we can get to the bottom of things and resolve the whole thing to our mutual satisfaction.' He sounded like a moral tutor, determined to get to the root causes of his student's misdemeanour in the most civilised manner possible.

'I'm sorry, but you make it sound as if we're about to discuss the onset of some curious disease.' Sedley smiled through this sentence, but it wasn't easy.

'Disease? I didn't mean to suggest anything of the kind. Problem, issue — yes! Look, you're not the first to speak his mind plainly from the pulpit — and not the last, I sincerely hope. But, how shall I put it? — well, there's speaking one's mind and there's speaking one's mind.'

'One speaks one's mind, or one doesn't, it seems to me,' said Sedley, still trying to smile.

'Look, the issue is this. The kind of publicity you've been generating just won't do. It can only succeed in damaging the Church, not to mention you're own standing within it.'

'You mean I might be given the push?'

'Oh, you know better than that,' laughed the bishop with a wave of his hand. 'We bishops don't carry the clout we once had, which is probably a jolly good thing. In any case, I have no wish to see you unfrocked!' He laughed again. 'No, it's far better, far more civilised to talk things through. But as I said, this is no inquisition.'

'Then why did you tell me to come?'

'Asked. I *asked* you to come.'

'Why did you *ask* me to come?' Sedley was not arrogant, but he was not going out of his way to be deferential, either — a disposition which did not fall within the compass of the bishop's experience with more minor members of the clergy, and he found it somewhat unsettling.

'I've already explained that! There are certain things which require clarification. Surely, you would agree? And once we've got to the bottom of things, perhaps I can offer some advice, some guidance and ...'

'But get to the bottom of what? You see, you still speak as though there's a problem here that emanates from me, that I'm responsible for — and I don't think I can accept that.'

'Just trust me,' sighed the bishop, as though he was now firmly of the opinion that this was going to be a long, hard haul, longer and harder than he had either expected or wanted. 'If we trust each other, we can stop pussy-footing around. Now, you do trust me, don't you? Good. Now, perhaps we can speak man to man.' He paused. 'Every man should have the honesty and the decency to speak his mind, to say what is in his heart, and this duty is particularly pressing for a man of the cloth. A man of the Church has no option but to speak the truth as he sees it, because that is what God *demands* of him. Now, that's settled! Let's move forward from there.' He paused again. 'On the other hand, we have no option but to live with what we have here on earth, warts and all, just as a craftsman must make the best use of the tools at his disposal. The Church is, and always has been, in a precarious position – but perhaps, yes, I agree, more precarious now than ever before, what with the overwhelming growth of mediocrity and ... well, we men of the Church are obliged to observe, how shall I put it? – a certain *decorum*, a certain *protocol. NOW!*' (the bishop uttered the word loudly and sharply and with all the zeal of a man whose pre-eminent reputation stands or falls by his being correctly understood. '*NOW!* Please note what I'm *not* saying. I am not saying that a man of the Church should at any time go so far as to suppress or distort what he believes to be right and true in the sight of God, to compromise what he holds to be sacred. What I *am* saying is that he should strive to appease his conscience while at the same time paying due regard to what I have, admittedly clumsily, referred to as the rules of decorum. After all, there is nothing either perverse or mysterious in any of this. As Christians, we must learn to speak the truth with some discretion, with some, one might say, *humility.* Humility is of course a virtue loved by God, is it not? – which is just as well, I may add. Because our survival, the very survival of the Church itself, depends largely upon our success in observing these rules of decorum. Now, I'm sorry, I know it sounds like a lecture. I didn't mean it to. I'm well aware that I've said nothing you don't know perfectly well already. I've only meant to be helpful. Forgive me if I've sounded rather patronising, but ...'

'Thank you for your concern.' The bishop's use of the word 'appease' had rubbed him up the wrong way – it seemed to show that the two men were and were not speaking the same language. 'But perhaps you can tell me what it means to "speak the truth with discretion"? The effect of this question was to put a full stop to the bishop's attempt to refill his sherry glass.

'Well ... well, I merely mean that we should not seek to use our calling as some kind of party political platform. *That* is not our function. We are not *politicians!* And that is not *seen* to be our function, either. And we must be careful how we are perceived by others – yes, it's a matter of *perception.* And if you think this a limitation of our function, surely you'll agree it's a most salutary one? Suppose, for example, a man of the Christian Church started to hold forth on what *he* saw as the virtues of Nazism, or something equally reprehensible ...'

'Then he would *not* be a man of the *Christian* Church – Christianity and Nazism are poles apart.'

'Yes. Yes.' snapped the bishop. 'Yes, that wasn't a very good example. But suppose he believed that Christian scripture justified it – justified Nazism.'

'Then he'd be wrong. Wildly wrong. Demonstrably wrong. And it would be hard to understand how he got as far as the pulpit in the first place – hard to understand how he ever managed to reconcile his politics with the Christian ethic. He may call upon God, but it would be a different God, the *wrong* God, because the only God worthy of being loved is the God of Love himself – all other conceptions of God are bogus, and ...'

'Quite. Quite!' sighed the bishop. 'Look,' he went on with a large intake of breath, 'you're making it rather difficult for me.'

'With respect, you're making it difficult for yourself.'

'Look here, do you not accept that there are certain rules of decorum to be observed? You see, all I'm saying is, you've used some pretty strong language, and it just won't do, just won't work. Party politics must simply be left to the politicians ... but I'm more than prepared to hear your side of it, of course.'

'I agree, *party* politics, in the narrow sense, must be left to the politicians. But I can't possibly say the same about *politics*! In your own example, if a man of the Church started to express Nazi sympathies, it would be up to us to expose him as a fraud! It would not be possible for the Church to allow it to pass muster. But when you speak of rules of decorum, there are precious few rules, in my opinion, which don't in the end compromise the truth. Well, the Church is in serious decline and, as I see it, the time has come to speak bluntly. The time has come when anything less than total frankness strikes me as a lie. In politics, the Church must exercise moral authority according to the Christian ethic, and it's time that this ethic was clarified and reasserted, and to do this it's necessary to strip away all the inessentials – and we must do this before the Church has passed the point of no return, having been replaced by political creeds posing as religions, creeds that are anathema to the values that we have come to regard as ...'

'Inessentials? Creeds? Oh dear, this *is* strong stuff. You're forgetting that we live in the *real* world – yes, we live on earth, not in Heaven, and we must cut our cloth accordingly.'

'Christ lived in the real world, too. Did he speak in half-truths? But the Church has been speaking half-truths ever since the crucifixion, with all the superstition about the Life Hereafter, and more recently it has adopted an all-out policy of appeasement towards religions which make little provision for love, let alone give it pre-eminence.'

'The Church is in a precarious position – yes, I've already said that myself. That's because it exists in precarious times. That is why we must exercise discretion. You perhaps know these words of Saint Augustine: "There may be some light in men, but let them walk fast – walk fast, lest the shadows come"? If the Church should openly call into question the beliefs of other religions, religions that are, moreover, practised in our own society and that have become, for better or worse, part of the fabric of our society, you might very well expect social disunity, conflict and tension that could easily ...'

'But don't these things exist already? Social disunity, conflict and tension?'

'Yes, but it wouldn't be difficult to paint a much darker scenario.'

'You are simply making a case for appeasement – and I carry a contrary brief.'

'Tell me again', said the bishop, after a pause, 'just how do you suppose the Church can secure its own salvation?'

'By refusing to speak half-truths. By the explicit abandonment of superstition and bogus gods. By outright condemnation of social injustices. By flatly refusing to condone the kind of hypocrisy and appeasement that have assumed the guise of political correctness. By pointing the finger of reproach, whatever the source of calumny may be – whether it emanates from a murderous mindset like Nazism, or from a duly elected Government of whatever political persuasion. By refusing to be pigeon-holed and cajoled by politicians who are simply smarting from just censure. And ...'

'Yes, yes. Well, I'm glad to hear you're not accusing our duly elected Government of Nazi sympathies,' interrupted the bishop, who had heard enough to last him a lifetime in this world, and an eternity in the next.

'But if the Church refuses to be outspoken, then by its own silence and inaction it's performing the function it was to be given under the New Order of Nazism – keeping the people quiet, stupid and dull-witted. But the irony is that the Church is in decline *precisely* because it refuses to be outspoken – people have lost faith in it!'

'Well,' sighed the bishop, after a long and pregnant pause, 'you're eloquent enough, I'll say that for you. It's no wonder the press has found something to prattle about. You've caused quite a stir, and I can see why.' He nodded slowly, as if for emphasis, smiling with unsmiling eyes; and he seemed to be addressing his sherry glass on the table before him, which he had forgotten to refill.

'Well,' he went on, picking up the sherry glass, filling it and placing it down again, 'I asked you here in all good faith, and I'm as anxious as I think you are to preserve that good faith. Now, in the first place, there is much in what you say, yes, that's right, I think there is! It's quite clear that you've given these matters – I mean, principally, the role of the Church – some very serious consideration, and you've arrived at some definite conclusions despite your comparative youthfulness, perhaps because of it. And ...' here he sighed again, '... And I've given you a good hearing. I've heard you out patiently and generously, though I say so myself. And I repeat that I do not disagree with much of what you say – at least in principle. No, perhaps you will listen to me with the same courtesy. Good. Good. Now, first, I would ask you, as it is my *Christian* duty to do, to consider the harm that you may be doing both to yourself and to the Church. Oh, the Church is resilient enough – yes, it's resilience has been proved over the centuries. But of you, I'm less certain. No ...' he waved his hand, 'no, I'm not asking you to write letters of apology to the press, or anything of that sort; perhaps it's better to let sleeping dogs lie – their second bite might go deeper than the first. No, but you might at least temper your feelings somewhat in future, so then the damage may be minimised and, in the course of time, this ... this whole business will blow over. Obviously, your present position cannot be sustained. You'll need to regain the trust of your parishioners, and there I think you'll have your work cut out for you. Even so, it seems the only reasonable course. You have a duty towards your parish, and that duty can hardly be served if you alienate your parishioners, that much I think we *can* agree upon! Of course, you must ask yourself whether you wish to continue with your ministry – and I can't answer that one. But I remind you again that we live in the *real* world, which has been called a jungle, and a human jungle it certainly is, where those who would devour you also have the power to do so without so much as a single cry of protest voiced in your behalf – or none that is audible. Tell me this, are you prepared to let them have their way?'

'Suppose that question had been put to Christ, or to Socrates, or ... or to a priest with the courage to preach Christianity in the Third Reich? And suppose they'd taken that advice and backed down. Would you now think as much of them? They wouldn't be the *same* people at all, and they wouldn't recognise themselves either – and wouldn't the enemy have had his own way, too?'

'You seem to have an answer for everything – but in fact you're only exaggerating the issues and distorting them. And you're not Christ or Socrates, and ...'

'No, because I'm not allowed to be!'

'We seem to be going round in circles,' sighed the bishop. 'Look, understand my own position. On a personal level, man to man, I truly sympathise with your position. But I must speak for the Church, and the Church must be seen to be responsive to criticism – responsive and responsible.'

Sedley inwardly despaired of the support to which the bishop had timidly referred and which, here and there, seemed to be half-promised. His words were like inept paper planes, launched with forethought and perhaps genuine enthusiasm, but never managing to reach their target, instead falling in crumpled heaps in inaccessible places.

'Let's discuss another strand in this matter – which again is important for the Church we both represent irrespective of any personal misgivings which we may or may not have. I mean, the Life Hereafter, which I understand you deny. But this is something which has surely held the Church together and still does – a keystone, as it were. Perhaps you'd prefer to call it a prop – but take that prop away and what do we have left? What have we to offer? Is it not the cornerstone of the Christian Ethic – the hope that underlies it? Because without it, that ethic will come to nothing. The Church has had to weather the storms of ... well, of the development of a scientific outlook, shall we say? and interest in the whole idea of the Life Hereafter has simply fallen away, at least in the minds of many. Even so, it's a faith in something beyond science, however irrational you think that is, that serves to sustain the Church – and of course other religions, too. It sustains whatever support the Church still has left. But if you dismiss this as so much superstition, and if you are considered truly representative of the Church, then you are depriving the Church of its very foundations – its very rationale – its very soul, if you like. Surely you see that?'

'I can't accept that. The way forward must be to establish a role for the Church that is entirely compatible with what you call the scientific outlook and the stringency it demands in terms of evidence and scientific method. Besides ...'

'Others! Others don't see it in that way! You talk down appeasement – but what you're talking about is the appeasement of science! Science is not all there is. And those who look to the Church for comfort, for succour, will not thank you for attempting to deprive them of hope in the Life Hereafter. Where is your compassion? Where is your vaunted love? Who will stand by you? What will you offer them? A morality? A new political party, perhaps? One which has the Sermon on the Mount as its core set of values? Well, then the Church simply becomes one party amongst others, losing its identity, its whole being – and its *mystery*. Or is there no place for mystery, no place for magic? And what the mystery does for Christianity it does also for other religions. Without it, you will simply have competing factions.'

'The Church may promise what it likes, so long as that promise doesn't compromise its own ethic, because that ethic is the true centrepiece, the true cornerstone, as you call it. Already the Church is faced with disintegration. People have lost faith in it. But not because of their scientific outlook, but because they correctly see that the Church is not fulfilling its own ethic! The Church must assert the absolute primacy of this ethic before it loses all credibility. The essence of that ethic is Christian love – and if love constitutes a political party, then so be it.'

'Oh dear! I doubt very much whether people are ready for a Christianity devoid of ...'

'A Life Hereafter? No, people *are* ready! There can be no incentive for love other than love itself. The Christian message addresses itself to the *betterment* of life, not to its *prolongation*! People are quite ready to accept Christ as a moral teacher worth listening to, rather than as some kind of salesman specialising in the Life Hereafter – whatever that means. That message must stand by itself – it must not be degraded by being presented as some kind of carrot. Doesn't the growing secularism itself suggest that people are ready for a radical reappraisal of what you call the *foundations* of Christianity. People have rejected superstition, and because they fail to see the ethic elevated to its proper heights, they have lost faith in Christianity altogether. Of course, if you say that the *Church* isn't ready to reject superstition, well, that's something else ... perhaps it all boils down to a question of courage.'

'You set yourself upon a course that is sure to alienate other Faiths, causing no end of social upheaval! And I don't think you've quite grasped my point!' said the bishop, finally picking up his glass of sherry, taking a much-earned sip and replacing it on the table. 'In the first place, you can't expect the Church to rally round you unequivocally. You can't seriously believe that everyone thinks as you do! You may take it from me that you will not find others as sympathetic as I have been – there aren't that many good listeners around, you know – it takes a large heart to be a good listener. There again, your own parishioners have turned against you, by all accounts. All these placards and slogans and demonstrations! It really is too much! Now suppose there are more placards, slogans, demonstrations – your very own parishioners, the very people you are supposed to take under your spiritual wing – suppose they continue to turn against you, to demand your head on a platter? You talk of credibility, but your own credibility is in grave doubt! And because you are supposed to represent the Church, its own credibility stands to suffer – the Church must protect itself, so might you not expect it to offer your head, or at least to turn a blind eye while it's cut off? That would be reasonable, wouldn't it? – a logical consequence? The Church has no wish to play Herod to the daughter of Herodias. At the same time, can you reasonably expect it to sacrifice its parishioners, however wrong or misguided you believe them to be, and lose its own credibility in the process – the credibility by which you apparently lay such great store?'

Somehow the logic to which the bishop referred had taken a wrong turn. For what the Church counted as its credibility was not the kind of credibility that Sedley wanted it to possess; he wanted it to consist in its moral authority divested of what he regarded as mere superstition. He half perceived this when he sensed that the debate had turned full circle and had to be started all over again – but he didn't feel up to the task a second time; in any case, it was too much like heads beating against walls.

'If I were sacrificed ...' Sedley began.

'Look,' said the bishop, with the longest sigh he had yet produced, 'I am trying to offer the soundest possible advice. I say once again that we live in the real world. Of course, there are powerful interests that wish to keep the Church in the place they have assigned to it. But whatever place that is, it is better than no place at all; and half-truths, however unsatisfactory we find them, are better than no truths at all. Are we not required to be as gentle as doves and as wise as serpents. And wisdom dictates that we offer the truth in a somewhat milder form than you would like to see it offered. Remember again those words of Augustine – you would do well to do so frequently. What exactly is the *whole* truth? Indeed, sometimes a lie is preferable to what you would call the whole truth. You would have people accept the stark truth that there is no life beyond the grave and that we must love one another with no incentive but love itself. I suppose you would say that love, like virtue, is its own reward, and that we should all do good unconditionally, and that it's enough to preach the Sermon on the Mount repeatedly. Unconditional love and unconditional goodness! But you are forgetting the *real* world. My dear Sedley, if you wish to preach the whole truth, you may find it most damaging to the continued existence of the Church. If error keeps the Church alive, if only *half* alive, I for one am prepared to subscribe to it.'

'Even if it compromises the teachings of Jesus Christ?'

'Look here, Sedley, life, *real* life, is at very best a compromise! Better to have a Church that is tolerated than no Church at all! What's more, it just isn't true to say that the Church is ineffective in political life. Does it not influence? Does it not guide? – by its very presence – even if that influence, that guidance, isn't as direct or as loud as you would like it to be? No, what for you is a misguided compromise is in fact a stark necessity!'

'On the contrary. Is it at all conceivable that Christ would have chosen compliance and appeasement to save Christianity? Is it at all possible to save Christianity by *compromising* it?'

'Well, at least Christ had a Church to succeed him. The Church is nothing save the goodwill of those who compose it; if *that* is lost, the *Church* goes with it.'

'And I believe that the Church is as good as the morality that lies at its foundation. Compromise that foundation and the Church is already lost – like a headless chicken, running around as yet unaware that its head has been cut off. I think we may thank God that the Church is not all there is – that there are still individuals who are prepared to say what the Church ought to be, rather than acquiesce in what it is.'

During the short silence that followed, the slow, heavy tick of the grandfather clock beat time in the air, though whether like the drums of war or the pulse of new life was hard to say.

'Ah, well … there it is,' the bishop said, slowly. 'We've come a long way in a short time, and I think we've cleared the air a little, although on essential points we must for the moment agree to differ.' He seemed almost lost in thought, as though the words came from some place deep within. He seemed unable to manage a smile, not even the trace of one.

'There is …' he continued, after taking a large sip of sherry, '… there is just one other matter which I had hoped to be able to omit. But we have spoken candidly, and I feel now it would be remiss of me to hold anything back. Yes, the matters we have been discussing are somewhat complicated by ... well, I think you'd best read it yourself.' He handed Sedley a letter which he had taken from the inside pocket of his jacket. He gave Sedley a few moments to read it. 'Now, I'm quite sure ... Of course, I *know* there can be no substance in this whatever ... but ...'

'But this is outrageous!' said Sedley, looking up sharply. 'To think that anyone should stoop so low to suggest that ...'

'Yes, quite. I understand.' said the bishop, sympathetically.

The bishop had been the recipient of two letters – one containing the petition, and one other. The letter with the petition had appealed to him on doctrinal grounds in the hope that he would exercise a restraining influence on Sedley's 'excesses'. The second letter, which the bishop now handed to Sedley, had been put together with the greatest respect for anonymity. It alleged that Sedley's wife had deserted him, and even went so far as to suggest a viable cause, namely that the company Sedley was keeping consisted of an 'undesirable element' whose sexual inclinations could never be countenanced by those of 'Christian conscience'. Reading between the lines proved all too easy. The implicit accusation might easily have been inspired by the appearance of the Andersons in church at the time of Sedley's last sermon, by the fact that they had been seen shaking Sedley's hand warmly and had been the only attendants to do so, and not least by the fact that wild rumours had been circulating for quite some time regarding their sexual preferences. In the absence of rumour surrounding the brothers, their appearance in church would have been a mere anomaly, and the handshake itself might have passed without significant comment. Certainly it would have been the flimsiest grounds on which to base an innuendo of homosexuality, let alone paedophilia. On homosexuality, which was not in any case a criminal matter, and on paedophilia, which was, the letter was not at all explicit, it being considered sufficient to hint that all was not what should be expected of a vicar of the Christian Church, just enough to indicate a level of dissatisfaction as to Sedley's moral credentials. The letter was more than enough to fire the imagination of anyone out for Sedley's blood. It sought simply to fan the flames – a useful adjunct to the petition.

'You can appreciate,' said the bishop, nursing his sherry glass, 'why I hesitated to show you this at all. Rubbish though it undoubtedly is, I ...'

'So why did you show it to me at all?'

'Oh, to prove a point, I suppose. It's the product of a mind bent on doing you the utmost possible harm, and the Church by implication, if the Church should wish to turn a blind eye to your, shall we say, "transgressions" wouldn't you say?'

'It must be treated with the contempt it deserves,' barked Sedley. 'I wouldn't want to give it any credence by addressing it at all, I ...'

'Silence in the presence of Pilate, you mean?' the bishop interrupted, with a wave of his hand. At the same time, it does have some bearing on the deep waters in which you have unhappily plunged yourself – and possibly the Church with you. It complicates matters. If the author or authors of this piece of nonsense should decide to write to the press ...'

'They'd have a libel suit on their hands!'

'Yes, no doubt. Unless, you treated it with a wall of silence – in which case, that very silence might be taken as an admission of guilt – your not wanting to air your dirty linen in public. Tricky, is it not? On the other hand, should you take the matter up ... Well, the newspapers are fighting libel suits every day of the week – it's nothing new to them. They would take the view that there's no such thing as bad publicity in publishing – they thrive on bad publicity – the worse the better. Oh, not forgetting that they have the financial and legal resources to fight their ground! No, you would either stand alone – or the Church would stand with you and receive a bad press for it troubles. The Church cannot afford a bad press. The press would be on to a winner, whatever the outcome. You could never come out of it smelling of roses. Even in the most unlikely event that you won damages, you'd stand to lose everything else. Whatever is said, whatever is done, whatever is proved or disproved, is really quite beside the point. Why? Because a thing like this *sticks*. What you may prove to a court's satisfaction will nevertheless linger outside it. You would be stained for the rest of your life. And this is especially bad for a man of God, for men of God are required to be more than innocent – they are expected to be beyond all possible reproach – and so much so that others dare not point a finger. In *this* case, however, someone has certainly dared. And if they dare write to me, I see nothing to stop them writing to the newspapers. They have made no explicit accusation? True! But then, they don't *need* to. Their dissatisfaction, the very idea that they need proof of your moral credentials is enough. Doctrinal issues have already been aired against you, raising questions as to your fitness as a vicar of the Christian Church – and no they are impugning your *moral* fitness for the task.'

'Are you suggesting ...?'

'Nothing. I suggest nothing. Perhaps I'm too old to make suggestions – I might hope a little too wise, but I'll reserve that judgement for others. No, it's up to you. You must do, or not do, whatever you think best. The Church can hardly embroil itself in accusations made against particular members of its clergy. If we set a precedent, there'll be no end to it – no, the Church must be seen to be impartial. Otherwise, the Church might get itself too involved in the question of homosexuality, and in a society which is increasingly homophobic that would damage its credibility. The fact that we now live in a society that has not yet relinquished its hold on homophobia can only make your own position more delicate – people are just as adamant to point the finger at you now as they would have done a decade ago when perhaps we were beginning to leave that form of bigotry behind.'

'Ah! But how do you explain that? How have we gone into reverse? Is it not for the reasons I have already set out? – the refusal of the Church to speak out against such bigotry? The decline of the Church? The rise of religions which fill that vacuum with values contrary to those that form the very essence of the true Christian message of love and tolerance? Doesn't *truth* mean anything anymore? Doesn't it have a bearing on anything at all?'

'In the *real* world? Oh, very little, if any. You see, the attack upon you intellectually will be inseparable in the public mind from the attack upon your personal and moral integrity. No, the public at large will make no distinction, with the result that you will be discredited in all ways. The Church, insofar as it manages to maintain a stony silence, will doubtless weather the storm – the assumption being that the Church cannot, in all reasonableness, be held responsible for the waywardness of every Tom, Dick or Harry who decides to don a surplice and carry the Good Book. But you, Sedley, would be thrown to the lions – not of course because the Church *wants* it that way, but because it will have little option but to let it happen; and why? – oh, simply because the Church must exist in the *real* world!'

'By the way,' the bishop continued, after catching his breath, 'I ... I had thought of placing this ... this letter, into the hands of the police. But even they, perhaps least of all *they*, could guarantee a watertight enquiry, and you can't afford a leak. And even if the author were caught and charged, would you bring an action against him? That would be like handing the whole thing over to the press at the outset. Shall we? ...' The bishop held the letter over the fire in the grate. Sedley nodded almost imperceptibly, and the bishop gave up the letter to the hungry flames, saying, 'That, I have no doubt, is where it deserves to be.' He sat back in his armchair and returned to his sherry.

The ticking of the grandfather clock gained, once more, a temporary ascendency in the silence that followed, before the bishop drained his glass and inquired whether Sedley would be staying for supper, a question to which the answer was a foregone conclusion to both. The bishop, following all the rules of polite protocol down to the very last, announced in sympathetic tones that Sedley had much to consider, but that, if necessary, he would make himself available at a moment's notice should he, Sedley, feel the need of further counsel in this altogether unfortunate affair.

~ ~

Sedley had indeed much to consider that night and in the dark days that followed, alone for the first time in the vicarage.

The bishop had not been unreasonable. On the contrary, he had been eminently reasonable. That was something at the same time galling and intriguing – the fact that someone you can't manage to reach can nevertheless sound supremely reasonable. It was rather like the endless 'conferences' between the whites and their red brothers on the plains of Midwest America, at which the former spoke much, if not exclusively, while the red men waited for evidence that their own case had been properly understood. They had a long wait, and are perhaps still waiting, and the damage has been done. Yet there is no doubt that those corpulent white grandfathers had considered themselves most reasonable – 'Damnably reasonable, sir!' In any case, once you granted the concept of the so-called *Doctrine of Manifest Destiny*, according to which God had given rights to the strong over the weak, the right to conquer, occupy, plunder, subjugate, profit, multiply and prosper – well, once you granted that, everything else seemed to follow. Likewise, once you granted the constraints imposed upon you by the *real* world, everything else seemed to be a lost cause.

Yes, the bishop had been most reasonable. But that didn't make anything easier. Sedley felt he had been invited to play a game, the kind of game he would never have played if it had been entirely up to him. Of course, he could have chosen not to play it – but then he would have been denounced as unreasonable – as were the chiefs of the red men of the plains. The game he had played with the bishop begged the question in his own mind whether the 'Christian Conscience' referred to in the letter was the same for its author as it was for the bishop, and the same for the bishop as it was for him; if they were different, could they all be called 'Christian'. The word 'Christian' was at least unclear round the edges, as was the word 'God' – even worse, Sedley was uncomfortably convinced that there were different Gods, and that some of them were decidedly unworthy of the respect they were shown. He and the bishop spoke the same language, and perhaps they both felt that there were limits to the places to which language could get them, though perhaps the limits were not the limits of language but their own – such matters were imponderables. In any case, Sedley was left with the feeling that language alone could not get them together to the same place at the same time, that there was a gulf between them that no amount of talk could bridge. He had been made to feel that the difficulties of the situation were obvious – too obvious to stand in need of much argument. It's as though the bishop had known everything Sedley had wanted to say, but also knew a lot more that Sedley did not know – was the bishop a more reliable source of guidance than Sedley wanted to give him credit for? Perhaps there was more wisdom in what the bishop said than Sedley wanted to admit – perhaps he should consider more carefully. Sedley decided to take more time to sort things out in his own mind. But there were other things to ponder. Did the bishop really believe in the Life Hereafter, for instance? or did he consider it a superstition, albeit one that should lie undisturbed? Sedley concluded that the bishop was simply not telling. Sedley reproached himself for not putting things on the line and asking the bishop straight out whether he really believed in it or not. But then, he probably wouldn't have been given a straight answer – but the uncertainty of his response did seem to suggest that there was more to the bishop than might appear at first sight. Again, the bishop hadn't asked him directly whether the veiled but obvious innuendo of homosexuality had anything in it; was that because he genuinely believed it was no more than a further attempt to discredit him in the eyes of the more bigoted of his parishioners, or was it because he couldn't have cared less one way or the other? Such questions were the natural outcome of Sedley's considerations. He had found the bishop's overall responses uncomfortably inscrutable, so much so that he decided to abandon conjecture altogether and stick with what remained.

What remained was the conviction that the Church would not rush to his rescue. The Church, no more than the woman you married, could take responsibility for what you think or believe – for your bedrock beliefs. You were left alone with your convictions, whether they were right or wrong. But if these convictions were of any value at all, it was up to you to defend them. This was no more than he knew already; and what he had received from the bishop was only a confirmation of what he already knew. Yet, what he had received was much more than that – he had received the *shock* of confirmation; and ultimately, that shock only served to strengthen his resolve to stand his corner. Because it was down to individuals in the end. What was the institution of the Church, anyway? What was a bishop? Only a man. Why should you expect from a bishop anything you could not equally expect from anyone else? A bishop was just as fallible, just as enlightened, just as reliable, just as wrong, just as misguided, just as foolish as anyone else. Knowledge of the Christian God was not something that could be derived from Office, even if that Office seemed at first more relevant than any other. It seemed to follow that to know about God you might just as well ask a butcher as a bishop – which was not an insult to bishops, but an observation about what the Christian God was, namely Love. Anyway, wasn't Jesus a carpenter? That's why it was down to individuals. If you don't know what love is, no one else can tell you.

But although he was shocked, he was not embittered – not towards the bishop. There was something larger, much larger, at stake; much bigger battles to fight. He felt he was up against the Devil, but since people misconstrued the word 'Devil' as much as they did the word 'God', he decided that it would be ill-advised to announce that he was doing battle with that two-horned, red-faced beast. For Sedley, the word 'Devil' simply designated the antithesis of Love, nothing else. He would need to watch his words, otherwise he might be considered quite insane. With the care he needed to exercise over his choice of words, Sedley was rubbing shoulders with the *real* world once more, whether or not he was in a mood to acknowledge the fact.

And although not quite insane, Sedley was certainly stretching out over a limb, as his thinking showed. Any temptation to talk about the Devil was his attempt to come to terms with the fact that a seemingly unbridgeable gulf stood between him and the bishop, a bridge not dissimilar, for all the bishop's reasonableness and sympathy, to that which existed between himself and Charles

Baxter — or, for that matter, between himself and Julia. Did the gulf exist elsewhere? Everywhere? Was he entirely alone? But such thinking was where madness lay, and he should do his best to avoid that.

The bishop was no Fuehrer, nothing like *the* Fuehrer, who had fashioned the Fuehrerprinzip into a ruthless instrument of governance. But was it at all possible, Sedley began to wonder, that the bishop could unwittingly be helping to nurture and sustain the Fuehrerprinzip, with all the intimidation that the principle implied? No, the idea was ... well, absurd. But then, all that *talk*, and all for *nothing*! Yes, it had all been a ritual, from beginning to end — a play acted out, whether or not the actors had meant a word of it, containing no surprises along the way or at the end, and leaving the audience, who had expected something of quality, in a state of shock; just a ritual, one that belonged to the duties and paraphernalia of Office.

Sedley felt more alone than ever before, and was sustained only by a mental picture of the agony of the Crucifixion, and by the muted gratitude of the righteous; the righteous of the past, present and future; the righteous, dead and yet unborn.

Chapter Seventeen

Of Doves and Serpents

Cometh the day when the dove will sleep, and the serpent will awaken to have its say, though in the shadowland its bite is muted, for neither dove nor serpent is to the shadows truly suited.

~ ~

Sedley felt like one who had been advised by his lawyer to settle out of court due to the hazards of litigation or the defects of his case. The bishop had suggested backing down or at least stepping back and adopting a policy of wait and see. But Sedley was convinced that his position could not possibly have been stronger. He was, after all, a man on a mission, and he was ready to risk it all. He believed that there was nothing to back down or step back for, just as you might naively suppose that since you are innocent there is nothing to hide and nothing to fear from the long arm of the law.

The bishop seemed to believe that the world in which they lived was an element within which Christianity might be a force to be reckoned with provided something called 'decorum' was properly and adroitly observed. Sedley, on the other hand, held that, if Christianity were a fish, the sea in which it now swam and had been swimming in for centuries was simply too polluted to sustain it as a credible ethic. Christians had to purify the waters of which the sea was composed, cleansing it of superstition and of inferior religious mindsets which competed with it and threatened to swallow it whole and spit it out lifeless. The process of purification was hardly consistent with subservience to decorum, since it was part and parcel of this process that decorum should be challenged forcefully and overridden

The bishop had spoken of the gentleness of the dove and the wisdom of the serpent. Doves and serpents now began to figure in Sedley's thinking, too, and would become a dominant feature of his imagery in the dark and disturbing hours that lay before him.

Christianity, and therefore the Church that sought to embody its moral teachings, was defined by the imagery of the dove. Doves were gentle things,

things of peace, things that cooed, things that bore the olive branch in their beaks. They were not hard and stubborn things. Not things of contest and confrontation.

Serpents were not gentle things. They were cunning, they carried venom in their bite, they sank their fangs deep into their prey; or else they encircled their victims, meaning to suffocate them; either way, they were instruments of violence and death. Wisdom might of course be attributed to the serpent. But the serpent was concerned above all with its own survival – survival at all costs. And survival at all costs seemed to imply so many negatives: the willingness to inflict pain and death, to be cruel, to be merciless. And yet, these negatives were the armoury of wisdom. Yes, the armoury, for were they not the cutting edge of wisdom; for what use was wisdom that remained merely an idea, one with no practical consequences? After all, it was agreed that it may on occasion be necessary to be cruel to be kind; which is why the defence of Christianity, of the essential Christian message, would require the rules of decorum to be challenged and, when found wanting, to be abandoned; the serpent would need to bite!

Indeed, the dove and the serpent were inextricably linked together – as it were, two sides of the same coin. The dove of Christianity could not even make sense without the serpent of Christianity. If the dove was love of mankind, the serpent was hatred of man's inhumanity to man. So you could not imagine the dove without the serpent, the serpent without the dove. A man who loves Love must hate Evil; his love was the dove in him, his hatred the serpent in him. What sense was the dove without the serpent, what sense the serpent without the dove?

Whether this kind of reasoning was entirely reasonable, or no reasoning at all but merely a piece of sophistry, Sedley managed to give it some sense, and the sense he gave it functioned as a goad to action and further resolve. He decided that if there was no room in the Church for the serpent, then there could be no room for the dove, either. Without the serpent, the Church was no more than an institutionalised amalgam of ritual, full of cant and hypocrisy, bereft of meaningful conscience, just a creature indistinct and forlorn, at best a flowery design with no function other than that of pleasing the eye; and when it ceased to please the eye, it really had nothing of value to offer. If the Church of Christ was no more than a dove cooing innocuously in its nest, courting the affection of all and sundry, feeling lucky to be allowed to live at all, presenting no real challenge to anything outside itself, then it was simply part of the very *status quo* which it refused to challenge; it did not stand apart from the *status quo* and therefore did not, *could* not, call it to account. Whenever it attempted to challenge the *status quo* it would be counted an act of betrayal, since it would be challenging that to which it belonged. If the bishop believed that the gentleness of the dove implied subservience to the rules of decorum and that such subservience was consistent with the role of the serpent, Sedley had convinced himself that it was entirely inconsistent, and that the Church had to abandon the decorum and speak out loud and clear against hatred and intolerance and injustice, whether these evils emanated from within the Church itself, or from Government policy or from rival religions; then and only then could it justify its own existence and be truly called the Church of Christ. Sedley was in no doubt. For him, the day of the serpent had arrived, ad not a day too soon. Either the serpent struck, or the Church would die – or perhaps it was dead already and should now rise like a phoenix from its own ashes. If God was simply another name for Love, it was not that God was dead, only that He was not given much of an opportunity to assert Himself. He existed only on the periphery, and God could never be permitted to exist only on the periphery – it was only right that he should not. God, being what God is, should be given the biggest say. Why, even Charles Baxter would agree if the matter were couched in terms that he might possibly comprehend. Managers might rightly complain that they must be allowed to manage; what then of the Manager Supreme? Did He not have a supreme right to manage? Yet, his office staff were unreliable, shiftless and quite unmoved by the plaintive cries of those they are paid to serve. A manager deprived of communications, of office and subsidiary staff, could hardly be expected to function effectively. Likewise, the God of Love had little chance to make his presence felt. No, God was simply not allowed to do the job that was required of him. God was not all-powerful! He needed permission to function, air to breathe, a soil in which to grow, the correct ambience – which is why God could be alive and kicking in one place and quite dead in another. And so Sedley's thinking was that the circumstances were not right, that they had never been right, but that much could be done to improve them, and that, until this was done, God could not be God, not at any rate a *Christian* God – which is to say, of course, that the God of Love represented nothing unless he were empowered to do so. Sedley would conduct his own crusade; the die had already been cast – but now there was resolution in abundance. There was no doubt in his mind what the Church should do; but the Church was no more than those, from the highest to the lowest, who composed it; and all those who composed it were deficient in the requisite courage to do what was needful; but he was resolved not to share in this deficiency.

~ ~

The bishop had been quite right in thinking that the author of the letter raising questions concerning Sedley's marital difficulties and possible sexual leanings would communicate the same to the national press; such questions were based on conjecture as distinct from fact, and therefore insufficiently strong to stand alone, but in the context of the general dissatisfaction with Sedley's standing amongst his parishioners, they were more presentable and seemingly more supportable. The bishop's error consisted merely in his misjudging the speed of events. For while he was committing that worthy epistle to the flames, a similar letter was already being scrutinised by the editorial staff of the newspaper in question and was subsequently weaved into the kind of article that would inevitably minimise Sedley's credibility and, according to its success in so doing, would also increase the circulation figures. Next morning, Sedley's standing as a vicar of Christ was more questionable than ever. It was clear that the letter to the bishop had been part of an overall strategy. In the event, therefore, nothing had waited upon the bishop's receipt of the letter. It had not been a warning, but, at best, a signal of worse to come; it was merely one broadside amongst others, the cumulative effect of which was to bring this troublesome priest to heel, and to do so most effectively by bringing him down once and for all. In the same way, Sedley's conversation with the bishop had been a calculated waste of time, since no change of heart on Sedley's part was either expected or even wished for; it was merely one step amongst others. And no one amongst the parties involved thought the strategy unreasonable. Sedley's opposition had decided that things had already gone too far, and it was out for blood. The opposition judged, correctly, that Sedley would brook no challenge from either Church or parishioners to his conception of his ministry, but that he would, on the contrary, defend it with the utmost vigour, being immune to reason and the simple dictates of common sense.

The article that emerged into the light of day like some mischievous elf out of sack, was not, once again, front-page news. The Church and its ministers had long been the subject of criticism and the butt of jibes and innuendo, and little that was alleged of this nature could aspire to hold the public interest for long. Sensationalism of this kind was not new, and, although both indifference and hostility towards the Church had gathered momentum in recent years, this was not a noticeably stimulating instance of it. Neither did the article go so far as to make an unequivocal allegation. It merely sought to 'raise questions of some concern on matters which at least cast some measure of doubt as to the suitability of certain members of the clergy to represent the fundamental tenets of the Church.' Even so, the words 'sex', 'domestic upheaval' and 'perversion' appeared in the text and, since they were to be found in the context of doctrinal issues, the reader might have been easily forgiven for thinking that deviation from accepted doctrine and a lack of domestic harmony went hand in hand, or even stood together in the relation of cause and effect. It placed two and two before the reader and invited him to miscalculate – a possibility which the bishop had foreseen. The article seemed at least to be suggesting that where there was one sin there were undoubtedly others in attendance.

And, again as the bishop had sagely predicted, the implicit message was that the Church itself should immediately and unambiguously disassociate itself from doctrinal deviations and members of the clergy whose lives were less than spotless by either bringing them into line or, if necessary, unfrocking them. The unmistakable message was that Sedley's ravings could not possibly be allowed to compete with the received teachings of the Church. And since it was assumed that the Church was the very embodiment of Christianity, Sedley's position could not possibly be confused with Christianity, either.

~ ~

Not long after Sedley's tete-a-tete with the bishop, Julia called the vicarage to say that she would be coming to pick up some of her things. Since she had her own key, the call was unnecessary. Yet, even at this late stage she was testing the ground. Despite the fact that Sedley had not attempted to contact her, or perhaps because of it, she was still toying with the idea that he had had sufficient time to think things over and decide to mend his ways. And so, the call she made was curt and cool and designed to remind him of what was at stake – a further goad towards a more amicable settlement and possible reconciliation. Her heart wasn't in it; but the scales against him still needed to be tipped further – if ever so slightly.

Tipped they were, and most amply. For she encountered the article on the train, having innocuously bought the newspaper to help pass the time. The whole thing seemed providential, because she rarely read newspapers further than the front page. She could hardly contain herself during the journey. If she had suffered embarrassment over the question of Sedley's political excesses, open discussion of their personal affairs was the straw that would break the camel's back and cause it to die on the spot. Until now things had been held in the balance with a thin shred of hope. But now the issue was finally decided. She was incensed, and she now had the further problem of how to make it from the rail station to the vicarage and back without being seen by the same gossipers and rumour-mongers whom she had quickly come to know and to despise. She found herself making irrevocable decisions, only to rescind them in the next instant. First, she meticulously rehearsed what she would say to him. Then she decided not to return to the vicarage at all but to catch the very next train back without so much as leaving the station. But, finally, she returned to her rehearsal. She would blame him for the article, which held their private lives up to ridicule and which made it possible to read between and behind the lines in such a way as to throw doubt on her ability to perform her marital duties fully and properly, and the possible perception of gross inadequacy was something she naturally found particularly distasteful and deeply offensive. In view of all this potential humiliation, the era of the ultimatum was finally laid to rest, having been usurped by the angry farewell.

Which is how she found herself standing before him, once again brandishing a newspaper. He was spared all the polite preliminaries. She spoke in a series of exclamations, decorum blown to the four winds.

'This beats everything! Our private life is ... is common gossip! It was bad enough before! But now I take a taxi and just hope I'm not recognised! What a mess!' She threw the article into Sedley's lap – she had found him sitting in his armchair and he hadn't even bothered to get up to greet her. 'I just can't live with that!' she went on. 'And I won't waste time asking you what you intend to do about it, because I daresay you intend to do absolutely nothing at all! And,

and ... to think I was prepared to smooth things over ... to try and see things from your point of view! But I just can't take this! It's just too late! Adam? Do you hear me? It's just too late!'

'You're quite right,' he mumbled. He seemed totally relaxed, making no attempt to move, let alone stand up. Julia remained standing, and she wouldn't have sat down, even if begged and implored.

'What?'

'I agreed with you. Yes, it's too late.'

'You just don't care, do you? You don't care about *me* at all! But you never have, have you? It's just as well we don't have children, because you wouldn't care about *them*, either, would you?' The truth is, as she reported to her sister later that same day, she just didn't know *what* to say – so she said anything, provided it sounded sufficiently cutting, sufficiently devastating. But then he said things which drove the final nail into his own domestic coffin.

'And everyone that hath forsaken houses, or brethren, or sisters, or father, or mother, or wife, or children, or lands, for my name's sake, shall receive an hundredfold, and shall inherit everlasting life.' Almost as bad as the words he uttered was the fact that they were said vacantly, half-mumbled, as though he were addressing himself in a dreamlike-state, or as though thinking aloud. An observer might have been forgiven for thinking him under the influence of either the bottle or an opiate, or simply ill and stultified by a heavy diet of prophylactics. 'Matthew, Chapter 19, verse 29,' he added, equally vacantly. Perhaps he didn't mean to be cruel. But the result was explosive.

'Now I've heard everything!' she said, accompanying her exclamation with a cynical nod, as if the words were directed entirely at her and her alone – and as if to suggest that now, at long last, the truth, the whole truth, was out. 'I should've listened to your father! Oh yes, he told me I'd have to have a lot of patience with you! I didn't understand him, but I do now! You know, I thought he was jealous – jealous of his own son. But now I know! Now I can understand him – I understand exactly what he meant. And he was right! It was the closest anyone came to telling me to watch out. And it wasn't so much what he said, either. No, his look was enough – quite enough! Even *he* knew I was on to a bad thing – your own father! He's practically disowned you – and I finally see why! The irony of it all! Here you are quoting stuff from the Bible – preaching the Gospel to others. Talk about people in glass houses!' She paused, and then, with a final flourish, concluded her series of exclamations with, 'What the hell am I doing here, anyway – in this bloody madhouse?'

She made a swift and temporary exit upstairs from the living room to pack some of her best dresses, followed by a permanent exit through the front door, which she slammed with an enthusiasm which shook the house from top to bottom. Not even the vicarage, innocent bystander though it was, could escape the strictest censure.

Yet, of course, both her exit and the manner of her exit had been entirely reasonable. In fact, Julia had been as reasonable as the bishop, both in what she had said and in what she had done. Julia and the bishop had at least that much in common, that there was no faulting their reasonableness. And they were severally convinced that what they both had in common separated them neatly from Sedley.

The ease Sedley had felt in the bishop's study, his indifference to its ornate richness, would have been quite inexplicable to Julia. Placed in such surroundings she would have been deeply engaged in the process of silent, inward judgement-making; and her judgement-making would have entailed her wishing to copy this or emulate that. Not that she would have found nothing to criticise in this or that painting or statuette, but criticism would, in complete accordance with the rules of decorum, have been kept very much to herself. She might have felt able to praise or to criticise, but she would not have felt indifferent. She would have undoubtedly commented on some of the art work. She was enchanted with display. Her common-sense approach to such matters was that if something was beautiful then it was fully entitled to be displayed and admired. Beauty hidden in a box was not a virtue. Such a belief had much to commend it. It was perfectly, perhaps even profoundly, reasonable.

Little wonder, then, that she considered her spouse perfectly, perhaps even profoundly, unreasonable. It was not that he disliked art or thought it unimportant, but he simply refused to subscribe to the culture of display; he had, she thought, the odd belief that when people displayed pictures or talked about books it was not because they wanted to share the beauty of art or literary endeavour, but because they wanted to draw attention to their own importance as exhibitors or literary judges. This idea Julia thought boorish and unjustifiably cynical. After all, a picture is painted to be seen and a book is written to be read, and there was little point painting and writing unless what was painted was displayed and what was read was discussed. Her reasoning was a paradigm of logic, and of course the bishop would have been the first to agree. It was a world of difference – this difference of perception between Sedley, on the one hand, and Julia and the bishop on the other. Like the bishop, Julia had a dove-like conception of Christianity, so much so that the serpent hardly had a look in. Wisdom she might have attributed to the reptile, but she would have deprived it of its venom and its bite. Julia and the bishop saw the Church floating listlessly in the same waters, neither questioning nor opposing the pollution in which it vainly sought to survive but merely obeying the rules of conventional ritual, a ritual embedded in and emanating from the unquestioning acceptance of what Sedley saw as conventional respectability.

Sedley was dissatisfied with mere convention. He likened it to the behaviour adopted in semi-formal gatherings in Fellows' Gardens in Academia, where you stood around in groups of three or four, listening to the garbled muttering of trivia from each member of the group in turn, mutterings which invariably consisted of potted autobiographies – or potted biographies, elsewhere called gossip – and the ramifications of climate change. Quadrilles were performed almost unconsciously, as each participant stood now on one foot now on the other, dancing to tunes of banality and sheer boredom: one step forward, one step back, one step to one side, one step to the other; 'All together now – in and out we go'; circles were described, too – first clockwise, then anticlockwise, and everything to the measured beat of conventional mumbo jumbo which claimed to pass for genuine communication. Everything would proceed in strict obedience to the rules of decorum, until a third or fourth glance at your wristwatch permitted you to announce your departure, on the pretext that you had a train to catch or someone to meet; a lie, certainly, but one which allowed you to abandon the quadrille for the saner music of the streets outside – saner, though far from sane. On one occasion, Adam had actually taken one step too many back in his attempt to extricate himself from the quadrille and was later reproached by Julia for his unsociable behaviour; she had had to make excuses for him, pretending that he was feeling ever so slightly unwell, which he was, and needed to answer the call of nature, which he didn't. Julia could not, of course, be faulted in taking him to task, for the common ruling is that either you should not attend such functions at all, which is socially unreasonable, or that you should deviate from acceptable behaviour only when strictly constrained to do so, namely when in the act of dying, and then only with the utmost respect for decorum; no, as always, Julia had been perfectly reasonable. There was a time, now long past, when tobacco might have relieved the boredom of the quadrille, but since smoking in public places had become a social taboo of the first magnitude, punishable by ostracism, if not legal action, such a balm was no longer available; and since it was unseemly to get too high on alcohol, there was nothing for it but to grit your teeth, gird your loins and face the music.

An academic social gathering of this sort was no place for the serpent; on the contrary, it was the natural home of the dove. Neither Julia nor the bishop saw a place for the serpent other than its reputation for cunning, mistranslated as wisdom; and the 'wisdom' of the serpent functioned as little more than an excuse for the total passivity of the dove, a passivity that Sedley perceived as defeatist. As he saw it, moral defeatism could not be allowed to result from an appreciation of the great enormity of the task in hand; on the contrary, and rather paradoxically, defeatism followed from the failure to understand just how enormous the task really was; because the *enormity* of the task was indistinguishable from the *importance* of the task, and you could not shrink from the task simply on the grounds that it was important. Further, the enormity and the importance of the task were indistinguishable from the *urgency* of the task. He believed that a failure to understand this was a failure of perception; from this failure of perception, a defeatism followed that was contrary to the very essence of the serpent.

Sedley now had more time on his hands to consider these things. He was alone, but he supposed that he had always been; no one can die for you when your time comes; but no one can live for you, either. Living and dying are done alone, anything else is an illusion. If these thoughts are diseased, the virus had plenty of time to gather force and to twist itself into all kinds of ugly shapes, like entangled vines hardened by neglect, difficult, and then impossible, to separate and adjudicate. He considered how quickly illusions can dissolve away and leave you standing without so much as a staff on which to rest your weary bones; dissolve away, like a dream on waking; shared hopes, shared dreams, shared ambitions, shared disappointments – all gone. Gone! – But then, perhaps they had never really existed. Not long ago, he and Julia had shared everything, as though they were both inseparable, joined as one; he had been her shadow, and she his. But, no. It had all been illusory – nothing but a grand illusion! Everything he experienced now was his alone. Everything that happened to Julia was hers alone. Different things were happening to different people – people as different as chalk and cheese.

If he was alone, it struck him now as something he had always known. But it was sometimes difficult to believe the things one knew – just as we all know we must die, yet the way we live seems to suggest that we don't really believe it. He had always known that your own dying was something that you necessarily had to do for yourself and that no one could share that experience. Yet, it was hard to believe that your own dying had to be done alone; somehow you seemed to go on in the conviction that it could be a shared experience – as absurd as the idea that someone else could live your life for you, too. Yes, but it was almost as if marriage offered you an alternative, showed you a way out, so that you would never have to die alone when your time came, because you could do it with someone else, together in the darkness, together in the deep and eternal darkness of death – as though death itself could be postponed or not even apply, as though you could save each other from its clutches, or as though there could be no such thing as being alone in death, as though the *privacy* of death could be eliminated. Not only this, but you might believe also that marriage meant that someone else could also live your life for you. Yes, there were many sides to marriage. This was the comfortable side – but all too comfortable, and nothing more than a web of illusion. More importantly, you might even entertain the idea that although marriage entailed some obligations, it might yet free you from your obligations to your God – if you had any God at all.

Sedley thought more about Jack, about what Jack had said – fragments and sentiments. If only you could believe, not simply know, that dying was a private experience and that death was the end of your game, it might imply a kind of freedom – the sort of freedom in comparison with which all other kinds would pale into insignificance; it might undo a kind of paralysis, the kind that comes from dependency, dependency on others. Death was not only final; your death was also *unique*; after your first death there would not come a second; and realising this might also be a kind of release. It would mean, for example, that if what you truly valued was sufficiently important to you, it would be worth standing up for, because if you didn't, you would never be able to return and stand up for it again. There was no second-time-round. What greater incentive could there be when you considered the finality of death? Was it not the realisation of the finality of death that lay at the very root of Love and of Conscience? There was one chance and one chance only; the mistakes of the past, once made, could not be unmade; so, too, in life – opportunities wasted could not be brought back. Once a man was dead, there was no bringing him back for a second try; no bringing him back to reverse one's trespasses against him. So you had to get it right first time round; at least you had to try, and try your damnedest. That was the incentive for trying – the fact that there was no second time round; the best incentive imaginable for doing your utmost. The finality of death highlighted the overriding importance, the supreme primacy, of Love. It struck Sedley as absurdly ironic that the metaphysics of the Church promised more than one time round.

Armed with such tortuous, logically questionable and diseased thoughts, Sedley felt a freedom he had never known before, a freedom to stick at nothing and to be thwarted by no one in the exposition and the defence of what he perceived to be Christian Love. It was important to go as far as he could, and if that meant losing Julia, whom he had never in any case possessed, then so be it; all he would be losing was an illusion, and that was painful, but it was also a step towards an ultimate kind of maturity, for it was no real loss at all. Was he abandoning Julia, or was she abandoning him? Just who was forsaking who? No one was forsaking anyone! In any case, blind loyalty didn't appeal to him. Their marriage should have been one of hearts and minds, and anything less than that was no marriage at all. Loyalty had to be sighted, not sightless, and it had, above all, to be morally supportable. Loyalty, devotion and adoration didn't seem to depend on whether Love was supreme in your scale of values. Eva Braun had been devoted to her Fuehrer; if that was adoration, then she had adored him for what he was, and what he was could not have been separated from what he valued and his own devotion to the Fuehrerprinzip, with all its theoretical and highly practical implications. She had even become suicidal when separated from him. Yes, she had been devoted to him, alright. And she had not only married him at the eleventh hour, but had been prepared to die with him. Why? Because she had been prepared to die *for* him. Why? Because she could not have lived without him. Was that love? Was it fascination? Blind infatuation? Madness? A *kind* of madness? Would knowledge of the holocaust and countless other atrocities have made any difference? In a much lesser but equally pertinent strain, Libby Custer had refused to give even a casual hearing to any accusations levelled against her husband for alleged atrocities committed both on and off the battlefield. She could not have entertained the thought, the very possibility, that her beloved General was anything less than lily-white. And had she entertained the very possibility, she must have decided that she couldn't live with it, and brushed it to one side, to gather dust as a purely academic hypothesis. Both Custer and the Fuehrer, each devoted to the Fuehrerprinzip, were idolized by their spouses, like children by doting parents. That was loyalty. Was it also love? Sedley found it hard to decide whether men are loved because of what they are, or in spite of what they are; yet he could not distinguish between what men are and what they value most, and if what they valued most fell too far short of what Sedley considered to be Love, then either the love they received was misplaced or it was not love at all, but simply a species of infatuation, and either way it seemed to make little difference.

No matter. Sedley was in no mind, and in no heart, to desire either the love, whatever that was, or the loyalty of an Eva Braun or a Libbie Custer. Which was just as well, for it was not at all forthcoming. He was never to enjoy the assurances and the benefits, however fragile and questionable, of such an allegiance. He assumed he was being rejected for what he was, for what he had become, for his refusal to be anything other than what he was. He was not being loved 'despite everything'; he was not being loved at all, on any level; no species of love was directed to him. In rejecting him, she was rejecting the whole man, his very essence, all of him and everything his life meant to him.

Such was Sedley's state of mind during his ponderous walks in the garden of the vicarage, where the stillness of the cypresses now seemed oppressive and where each blade of grass seemed ranked in hostility against him, standing to attention in silent opposition, waiting for the order to commence the attack against him and his infernal conception of Christian Love, whatever it was, and where the stricture 'Those whom God hath joined together let no man put asunder' had grown hollow. Which God was meant in this stricture? If there is a plurality of Gods, Julia's God was different from his. You had to be true to your God. She was true to hers. He was true to his. Did God mean different things for different people? Certainly it meant different things in different religions – there was no doubt about that. And if everyone was wrong and he was right, what else could he do after saying as much and putting his case? For everyone was wedded to his God and would not let go. That was the pity of it – the tragedy, if the God they held onto was undeserving of worship, was evil, wicked. Had Julia married him in the hope of changing him for the better, of converting him to a belief in her God? She had not succeeded. But it was far more likely that it was a case of mistaken identity – she had married him thinking him to be someone other than he was, so that everything that had happened subsequently was merely a process of discovery, a discovery that you had been wrong all along – yes, that's it, a case of mistaken identity.

Julia, in her heart-to-heart sessions with her sister, had her own story to tell. She believed herself to have been as solid as a rock throughout their marriage. If anything had happened to change him, nothing had happened to change her. Adam was the one who had deviated from the straight and narrow. Her faith in him had changed – that much she was more than ready to admit; but, after all, what could be more reasonable than that? She believed herself to have made an unfortunate miscalculation and was anxious to implement a policy of damage limitation by getting out fast. He was now unchangeable; if she had thought otherwise, she would have been fooling herself, and she had allowed herself to be fooled long enough. She had been wrong, she said, to think that in a marriage you could weather any storm with tact and reason; a marriage was as good as the partners involved in it, and if one of them was intractable and impervious to common sense and reasonable argument, well there was nothing to be done. She had read a story about a little boy who thought that a big ship's engines could be turned off or on at a moment's notice and that the ship could stop and start in an instant. Well, it wasn't like that. And it wasn't like that with people, either. And it certainly wasn't true about Adam. He wouldn't even grind to a halt, let alone change in an instant, with the application of a little common sense and reasoning. And it wasn't so much that you could grind your principles to a halt; it was much more that your principles would grind *you* to a halt, as they had ground Adam to a halt, because whatever it was he believed in, it wasn't allowing them to make any progress, wasn't allowing them to achieve anything; it only put a full stop to their aspirations and ambitions, and Julia had aspirations of her own that she was determined to fulfil. But she had been required to accept Adam for what he was – and it was just unreasonable to expect her to do that, simply because the expectation was itself unreasonable. 'I just can't live with that!' she had said. He was too intractable; but in life you had to be a chameleon, changing your colour depending on where you happened to be standing; but he was incapable of doing that – and so he was incapable of getting on in life, and incapable of allowing her to do so as well. Quite naturally, and because she was a most reasonable listener, Julia's sister found her narrative perfectly plausible and logically faultless.

They both had their stories to tell; Julia told hers to her sister; Sedley told his to himself. They occupied different worlds on the same planet; these worlds could not be straddled, nor was it possible to step from one into the other.

He had once explained to Julia his dislike of ice-cream vans with their nursery chimes. As a small child, he had watched his grandfather being driven away to hospital in an ambulance; the old man was soon thereafter to die in his hospital bed. But Sedley had watched from a distance as his grandfather was helped into the ambulance, and had been unaccountably too embarrassed to step forward and kiss his grandfather goodbye. He was never to see his grandfather again. Thereafter, the sight and sound of an ice-cream van was associated with feelings of guilt for not having given his beloved grandfather a farewell embrace.

Julia had smiled politely at the story, as the rules of decorum might be said to require. But Sedley was convinced that, subsequently, whenever Julia heard the chimes of an ice-cream van, the pain it caused him never once occurred to her, perhaps because she had forgotten the story altogether, and he was equally convinced that it was the kind of story that should not be forgotten – not if the person you had related it to truly loved you.

Yet, forgetting was reasonable. After all, we can't be expected to remember everything we've been told!

However, in Sedley's world, the dove and the serpent were two sides of the same coin. Julia could not understand the serpent in him, because she could not understand the dove in him. It was the dove that bade the serpent strike, and the bishop had had as much difficulty understanding that as she did. Sedley ruminated on the story of the ice-cream van, which was yet another strand in the rope that he was making for his own neck. He was left with himself and what he valued, and what he valued was incontrovertible. The serpent would have its say, because it had to have its say; there was no alternative, because no alternative made the slightest bit of sense to him. Sane or insane, Sedley had made his bed and would now have to lie on its hard base.

Chapter Eighteen

The Twilight Zone

Between hill and valley, light and shade, stand decisions yet unmade, for resolutions are hard to keep where, in the twilight zone, every step becomes a leap.

~ ~

There are those who hold that God is inconceivable, that it is impossible to form a conception of God. Sedley would have given them very short shrift and dismissed the claim as so much superstitious and sloppy thinking; he might have appealed to what philosophers call 'objectification' – the fallacy of attributing physical existence to an idea. But perhaps the best that can be said of Sedley's conception of God is that it was convoluted beyond repair. The dove and the serpent were two expressions on the one face of Sedley's one, true, unique God. The face that smiled upon the compassionate was also the face that frowned upon the hard-hearted. The God of Peace was also the God of War, the war waged against evil by uninhibited Christian conscience; the war of outspoken criticism and, whenever necessary, the war of passive resistance. Those who love must also be those who wage war; war against hatred, against intolerance, against man's inhumanity to man. The God of Reconciliation must also be the God of Confrontation; and confrontation would end when inhumanity ended, and inhumanity would know no end as long as humanity itself existed. If the establishment of God's kingdom here on earth was not to be regarded, except by the naively optimistic, as an achievable, final and complete possibility, it had at least to be an ongoing process of construction and reconstruction – without end, but also without irrevocable interruption and final stagnation. Interrupt it and it would stagnate. If it stagnated, light would give way to dark, and the Christian God would be interred and forgotten; and if the God of Love were interred and forgotten, civilisation would be buried with Him, for the God of Love was irreplaceable, and His uniqueness, the fact that no other God could compete with Him, was the one hope left to mankind.

But the God of Love could neither kill nor maim; and since He carried no weapon of destruction, he was, in this sense at least, defenceless against those who did. For his anger derived from love, and He would sooner cease to be than hurt a single hair on the head of the meanest of his human flock. For how could the God of Love, who shed tears for the poor and homeless, for the sick and the deprived, the weary and the heavy-laden – how could such a God as this take up a sword of steel and wield it like an incensed tyrant? Violence was not permitted. That was not the kind of serpent God was; it was not the kind of venom the serpent carried. On the contrary, the serpent was bound to denounce evil in all its forms. How could it, then, indulge in them? Its venom, like a magic potion, sought only to restore life where there was death, to bring order out of chaos. Love was the one weapon in the armoury of the God of Love; a weapon he would wield tirelessly and infinitely; and the only blood that might be shed in His name was one which sought to preserve His very existence – a war of self-defence against an eternal darkness that threatened to descend with each generation of men. The serpent of the God of Love was not to be confused with the vipers He set Himself against.

It was the serpent that named those generations of vipers to their faces; that shook with rage; that chased the money-lenders from the temple; that reproached his would-be followers for having eyes that did not see and ears that did not hear; that battled with Satan in the wilderness and overcame him, the same Satan who tempts men with wealth and power, yet not the power of love; that had the courage to preach a morality that could find little root in the ambience that surrounded it; that had the fortitude to stand before Pilate without so much as a whimper, strong in his innocence and his sense of right. It was the serpent that did these things, and it was the dove that stood between the serpent and the viper, ensuring their eternal and essential dissimilarity.

Sedley's God was a Father, with a father's love, and a father's anger. He loved, and because he could love, he could also rage. But he could never be indifferent, for indifference was a mark of the cold grave, in which nothing counts. Neither could he harm his children, nor see harm be done against them. Yet, his only weapon was Love.

Sedley's God was a loving Father; of this he had no doubt. Of his earthly father he was not at all so certain. If his conception of his heavenly Father was convoluted, that of his earthly father was at best indistinct and at worst unfavourable. James Sedley, to whom Julia Sedley should undoubtedly have harkened before tying the matrimonial knot, did not occupy his thoughts at all during the good Reverend's last days in that most reasonable and respectable of parishes. This lack of interest was mutual, for neither did James Sedley dwell deeply or sympathetically on his offspring, except to reflect that fathers are all too often creatures upon whom the sins of their sons are visited. Obstinacy was perhaps a quality shared by both father and son, though it was not necessarily one that had been handed down, if only because little or nothing seemed to have been handed down at all. Obstinacy, like love, is a house of many mansions; it may take different forms and be rated differently in different men: in one a virtue; in another, a vice. Sedley and his father were certainly not obstinate about the same things. They had drifted apart somewhere in the misty ether of Sedley's childhood, and they were destined never to shake hands over the Great Divide that is believed to separate one generation from another.

~ ~

James Sedley sat at the breakfast table giving an occasional flick to the cuffs of his recently dry-cleaned jacket, while he watched Judith Sedley pouring him his second cup of tea with the ritual dedication of a domestic slave in ancient Rome.

'You shouldn't really wear your jacket at breakfast,' said the Roman, meekly.

'It hasn't come,' he mumbled. The Roman continued pouring. 'The newspaper,' he went on, 'it hasn't arrived. Still, it's just as well. The less I see of newspapers, the better.'

'I'm worried sick about him,' Judith mumbled in return, as she replaced the teapot on its stand on the heavy pine table and covered it with a tea-cosy in a rich floral pattern.

'Worried? Don't tell me you're worried!' he replied, giving one of his cuffs a sharp rebuke. 'Does he worry about *you*? He certainly doesn't worry about *me*! Just what *does* he worry about, that's what I'd like to know! You should've been there – in the office! ...'

'I know. You *told* me. But ...' Judith's contribution died in its foetal state. Even in the least liberal of households, the life of a domestic in ancient Rome could not have been much worse when it came to getting a word in edgeways. There were no 'buts' when James Sedley had the floor, as his colleagues in the office had discovered to their cost.

'Oh, it came to a head. I was determined to bring it to a head, I don't mind admitting it. "Look here," I said, "We all know what's in the papers. And I can tell you now, it's no doing of mine. I can tell you now that, son or no son, this whole business turns my stomach. I wash my hands of it – totally! Religion and politics, if that's what it's all about, don't mix – never have and never will. He goes in for the Church, and then, instead of making a go of it, he starts criticising this and that, alienating everyone in the process, and causing discontent – and, and embarrassment, too, for his parents." Oh yes, I had it out with them alright – I wasn't going to sit in that office with all that staring and whispering – not that they were whispering about me, mind you – but you never know, do you? No, I could read what was in their minds, so I set the record straight – just because he's my son and wears the cloth, doesn't mean I have to agree with everything he says and does – in fact, with him it's just the opposite – always has been. I've yet to agree with *anything* he says or does! "No blame can attach to you, James," they said, damned hypocrites! Mind you, no reference was made to the *other* thing – they wouldn't dare! Yes, you know what I mean! But who in his right mind could bring himself to mention that kind of *garbage* – no wonder his marriage is in trouble! I told you, didn't I? I told you! "Just wait," I said, "Just wait" – well, there you are! Proved right again – though I take no pleasure in it, no pleasure at all. But there's no doubt about it, if it wasn't for the respect I've been at pains to build up over all these years ... well, I'd find myself out on the street, and quite right, too. So don't tell me you're worried! I won't have it – I won't have any of it!'

After that, and feeling quite unable to follow it, all the Roman domestic could do was sigh with resignation, while James Sedley sipped his tea and placed his cup carefully in the saucer without so much as a twitch of nerves. He always drank the best tea out of the best bone-china cups. No mugs for James Sedley, for he was a man of custom and discernment. Judith could not fault him on his choice of tea. For her part, she had bought the tea-cosy to match the tea-set, and it all looked very nice.

For all that, James Sedley did not believe what he had said. Or, at least, he did not believe more than half of it. This diatribe against his own son would not have convinced anyone sufficiently sighted to see beyond the veneer of human emotions. It did not convince Judith Sedley, either. Oh, yes, he believed what he said about religion and politics and that his son shouldn't meddle with the fundamentals of the Church he purported to represent, though he had never troubled to think such things out and was hardly about to start now. But his heart was not truly set against his own son. He did not want to see him humiliated by the press or ousted from the Church. Nor did he desire to see any rift between his son and Julia. Most important of all, he did not wish to sustain any unpleasantness between himself and his son. But his true feelings were not permitted to see the light of day. It was easier, instead, to follow the herd and bark with the dogs, and to follow the line of the divide that had seemed to crystallise between him and his son since Adam's puberty.

And so, James Sedley managed to suppress what he knew to be true, to hog-tie his better instincts and allow his tongue to wag incessantly on themes that repeatedly hid from view his deeper feelings of attachment − time and again regurgitating the foolish, ill-considered commonplaces that are the daily diet of the selfish and the unwise, of the timid and those who live in fear; he seemed to be protecting himself from a meaningful acquaintance with beauty, as though the dove were either a shameful or a fearful thing.

Perhaps Judith Sedley understood her husband better than he understood himself, and perhaps this was why she was content to allow her spouse to rattle on in this pathetic, tedious and unimaginative strain without confrontation. Of course, she was by nature anything but confrontational and certainly not amply endowed with the spirit of the serpent; nevertheless, she understood far more than she was ever given credit for. She knew that her husband's tirade consisted merely of words and that words are not always reliable vehicles of what they purport to express. They were merely words which he would either live to regret, if he lived long enough, or, worse still, would never allow himself to regret, although he lived to be as old as Methuselah. But they were words which were not born in the heart of the man who spoke them; they were words he did not mean but was content to mouth by proxy or in lieu of what his heart longed to say − perhaps because they were simpler and because he had never learned to do anything but mouth; and that was why he was good at clichés, which in turn gave him a fluency of speech, a seemingly inexhaustible supply of useful and appropriate phrases, a veritable reservoir of nice bits and pieces − his mouth the tap which controlled the flow and which could turn on or off at will; it merely required the trigger of a routine exercise of will and a habit of judgement culled from a wealth of routine experience, and the package was complete. It was a package of conventional wisdom that allowed everything to be expressed in conventional terms, everything according to the accepted norms of decorous living; a package that was indispensable to the proper exercise of *authority* and *self-assertion*. For James Sedley was no stranger to the hypnotic power of the Fuehrerprinzip. He was not one to restrain himself with an air of false modesty should the occasion warrant sterner stuff. So good was he in the provision of sterner stuff that those who once heard him out were not easily disposed to hear him out a second time. A phrase like 'I can tell you now that ...' intermingled with 'I can tell you that now!' and interspersed with 'I can tell you that for nothing!' and 'That's where I stand on the matter' or 'I prefer to speak my mind' (or even, on occasion, 'I'm a simple man'!) would invariably do the trick. Such phrases gave him an irresistible air of authority and served to guarantee not only fluency in the delivery of his opinions but their very rightness and moral rectitude into the bargain.

'I phoned him yesterday,' said Judith Sedley, cautiously, as James Sedley made at last to move from the breakfast table, only to sit down again.

'I mean, does he care about anything at all?' he went on, regardless. 'Let's face it, he's never cared about us. Not me. Not you. I can tell you that now! And his own wife – what about *her*, for goodness sake? He *married* her, after all!'

'I wanted to see him, but he kept putting me off,' said Judith as she adjusted the tea-cosy and her spouse bull-dozed on, for he was a bull-dozer second to none.

'Not that I've ever been able to take to her, as you very well know,' he said. 'All the same, you'd expect *him* to have some feeling for her, wouldn't you? I can just imagine how she feels with all that garbage churned up in the press! No, he doesn't set much store by her. Typical! Damned irresponsible! Oh, he's got ambition alright. Trouble is, it's the wrong bloody sort, he just wants his name in the papers and doesn't care how many apple carts he upsets in the process. Anything to get his name in print and he's managed *that* alright! And he's had the audacity to accuse me of wanting to get on in the world. Well, at least I've got something to show for it. And what's he got? He wouldn't listen to me. He wanted to be a vicar, and he ends up with an empty church, and even that'll be taken away from him before very long – mark my words! And you say you're *worried*? Humpf – he's obviously not worried about anything – or anyone! Can you give me one good reason why *we* should worry?'

That last question was profoundly silly, because the answer was all too obvious. The patter continued. But since that question had had its source in the great depths of a sea of paternal emotion, it left its mark, and the patter was, just for a few moments, less fluent, less self-assured. Those moments were like windows into some finer place, some garden where flowers grew unhindered by weeds, and where birds sang in a blue and cloudless sky.

'He's ... he's lost everything ... everything. If only he'd explain himself and ... and apologise, or ... But he's not much good at that – not much good at doing anything, except offending the people he should look up to and respect.' Self-assurance had returned, and James Sedley was off again, the windows having been shut tight once more against those emotional depths that would now remain unplumbed. 'After all, I'm still waiting for an apology myself, and there's a fat chance of getting one, so what respect can he have for anyone else? – Government, Church, his so-called flock? Good God! – he's just as much a juvenile delinquent as those ... those ...' (he was thinking of those 'animals' who had attacked his garden wall and brought it tumbling down, but couldn't quite bring himself to use the word) '... no, if he wants to martyr himself, that's *his* lookout! It's all down to him, from first to last!'

The patter finally ended and the bulldozer came to a grinding halt. The wall-mender, the clock-winder, the cuff-flicker had temporarily exhausted his repertoire of stock phrases to fit standard responses and was left with his own question ringing in his ears. No wonder he sought the comforts of routine, of a stubborn attachment to order and well-trodden ways. He rose from the breakfast table, and with his customary 'I'll be late', suddenly increased pace, as if driven by sheer and irresistible habit. He strode into the hallway, peeked into the long mirror, flicked his cuffs, brushed down his trousers with the palms of his hands, snatched up his executive, polished-leather briefcase, which shone as seductively then as when it had made its first appearance into the world of commerce, and marched with precision down the immaculate garden path, without so much as taking one backward glance.

As for Judith Sedley, her thoughts that day focused more on what she believed her husband and son to have in common rather than on what separated them. She reckoned the common denominator to be obstinacy, a stubbornness born of unconsidered habit in the one, and of much-considered conviction in the other. She was helpless, and she felt it. She could merely stand and watch while one went one way and the other went in the opposite direction, just like Julia and Adam, who were also going their separate ways. It seemed to her that, whatever the outcome, Adam would push things to their limits, which he was indeed determined to do. Or else, he was being pushed. Either way, Judith Sedley had plenty to worry about. For she was a mother, and a mother is always significant by her individuality, for no one else could have conceived and given life to Adam Sedley, and so she was stuck with him, by nature and the depths that nature dictates. She tried, for the most part in vain, to console herself with the memory of her last telephone conversation with him and the jaunty, resilient tone he had displayed, or affected. She resorted to the surface of things, gripping it fast, lest she slipped down into quite unfathomable depths from which there could be no easy climb back. And so, she reckoned, Adam and Julia had something to work out, and that was fair enough; no, hardly unusual in marriage; and as for the article in the press and all the noise some people seemed to be making about it, well, it was best to close your eyes and ears, because, if you did, it might just all go away – yes, because it was just so much flotsam that would eventually sink under its own silly weight. Besides, Adam knew what he was doing, because he was no one's fool; he was deep, was Adam, and she remembered bits and pieces he'd told her about Socrates – yes, he was *deep* – and a mother had to be consoled by that, if little else.

Meanwhile, James Sedley spent that day as a martyr to blissful routine, except that his unanswered question persisted in answering itself all day long: Adam was his *son!* – an ungrateful one, perhaps; confused, perhaps; offensive, perhaps; but his *son* all the same. Your son is not like other men, by virtue of his being your son. On the other hand, a son is a man – a man like any other man: as fallible, as confused, as silly, as offensive – well, a complex of all the virtues and vices that make men what they are. Adam had a lesson coming, and it was only right that he should learn it, and, if necessary, the hard way. It might even be considered a fatherly duty to allow that lesson to be learnt, even if it entailed a bloodied nose; in fact, a father might even rejoice in the fact that his son was about to learn the hard facts of life, of the *real* world. And, the way things were going, that lesson was sure to mean a bloody nose at least. And as for his son's marriage, he hadn't expected much to come of it anyway; it had been a false start, and life is full of those. If they did break up, it was probably the very best thing that could happen to them both; it would certainly not be the first time for things like that to happen;

it would not be the first time for a marriage to be short-lived. Even marriages that were allegedly made in heaven involved at least a few twinges of regret along the way. Come to that, even James's marriage left a lot to be desired and begged the question as to why he hadn't ... But, no, it was too late, and too odious, to go into all that – yes, the least said the better. No, the fact was that Adam was in the process of learning about the *real* world, and the process could be very painful. Was it really too much to say that he should be brought to his knees before he could learn to walk properly? No, certainly not! No doubt Adam would eventually come to his senses, and then he might even begin to place more trust and confidence in his father, just as he did when he was a toddler taking his first uncertain steps, or as he did when as a schoolboy he tried to understand his father's explanation, albeit impatiently rendered, of how the banking system worked, or his explanation of how lucky he was to have been born where he had and not in some godforsaken foreign land where they knew not the meaning of democracy and failed to grasp the advantages of advanced culture and the blessings of common sense. He might have spared time grudgingly for his small son, and this he almost regretted, but at least Adam had given him the respect that a father, albeit a very busy father, deserved; and perhaps that respect would be forthcoming again – if the lessons about the real world were well and truly learnt.

Throughout that day, James Sedley thus comforted himself with the thought that if God was in his Heaven, as He certainly was (if only because he could hardly be anywhere else), and all was right with the world (or at least that part of it in which the Sedleys were blessed to inhabit), Adam would eventually come to his senses, and all would be sweetness and light. It was only a question of time, of waiting for the proverbial penny to drop. And the pennies had to drop before the pounds could be gathered. If all went well, therefore, Adam would come to him, like the return of the prodigal son, with or without Julia, with or without the prospect of doting grandchildren. With luck, a fresh start might be sighted on the horizon, despite the darkness in the valleys below.

If his thoughts that day contained a grain of self-reproach and a spark of optimism, these things were reserved for himself. To Judith he served up the usual dish of offended pride, injured feelings and hopeless resignation.

James Sedley was not well read in Scripture. And it is not likely that he thought much, if at all, about those parts of it that were as familiar to him as the rhyme of Humpty-Dumpty. Words like these:

He that loves father or mother more than me
Is not worthy of me: and he that loves son or daughter
More than me is not worthy of me.
And he that takes not his cross, and follows after me,
Is not worthy of me.
He that finds his life shall lose it;
And he that loses his life for my sake shall find it.

Was Christ someone who set himself up above all others, a supreme egoist. Was he not an evil Pied Piper, attempting to charm sons and daughters away from their parents, contrary to nature, contrary to the natural love between parent and child? A con-man. An evil charmer if ever there was one!

If love is a house of many mansions, James Sedley had locked himself in the basement and thrown away the key – or so Adam Sedley was prepared to argue; for it all turned on what James Sedley regarded as love, what it *meant* to him; if love was an attachment born of possession, it was not the love that Christ had preached; Christianity implied that possession had to be widened and ownership shared. After all, the exhortation was to '*Our* Father which art in Heaven', not '*My* Father which art in Heaven'. It was easy to love the things you felt you possessed, the things you felt you had a proper claim to. But the love that derived from possession was inevitably something that resisted a shared ownership, and was therefore confined and confining, restricted and restricting, cringing and creeping – for that was its very nature. It was a question of whether you could break the circle of possession or, at least, enlarge it to infinity. Christ had asked who his father and mother were. James Sedley, enjoying a self-imposed exile in the basement, might well have understood this to indicate no more than a temporary loss of memory.

If Adam Sedley wished to widen the concept of possession to infinity and his father to restrict it, little wonder they were obliged to agree to differ. Adam Sedley once offended his mother by telling her that if he suspected her of murder he would have no option but to hand her over to the police, that her status as his mother would not prevent him from doing so. He believed that his God could not be bought off – not with money, and not with the affections he held for someone else, not even his own mother. He told her that his commitment to his God was absolute, that his God would not permit him to save his own mother by sacrificing someone else's, and that she would not be permitted to save him from the jaws of a lion by throwing someone else's child into the mouth of a crocodile, that this would be like trying to buy God off, which was not on. And if it were a question of 'having to choose', what then? But, he said, the idea of 'having to choose' might entertain moral philosophers but could have no possible application. Judith Sedley could not, quite rightly, make much of this at all. At which point he simply said that it was not permitted to love your parents or your children more than God, that to serve God rightly blind loyalties could be nowhere on the agenda. It didn't mean, he went on, that you should *dis*honour your parents, only that they could not hold a monopoly over your affections. Love of Adam Sedley's God entailed taking a much wider look around; the net was thrown further afield than one's immediate affections but, at the same time, included them. It was a question of objective judgement and evaluation. If Adam Sedley was a true child of his God, James and Judith Sedley could not be exempted from judgement merely because they were his parents; likewise, Julia could not be exempt simply because a matrimonial contract had been witnessed and signed. They, like everyone else, lived in the same world, under the same heaven, subject to the same temptations and to the same judgement and censure. The rain would fall on all alike. On all upon whom the sun shone, too.

Judith Sedley was confused by her son's attempt to explain his God. She thought the fault was hers; for her son was *deep*, as deep as the ocean; and he had read about Socrates. But she could not help but think that God was a little on the cold side for denying any primacy to a mother or a father or a son or a daughter, and nothing that her son tried to add or take away served to clarify anything or provide much consolation. She simply smiled and nodded, not fully realising how convoluted her son's conception was, and not feeling equipped to offer any challenge. She was left wishing that her son had been able to place her a notch or two higher on the pedestal of familial affections; she felt a little let down.

Perhaps James Sedley did understand his son sufficiently, albeit very vaguely, to fear the consequences of a head-to-head confrontation with his son's God. He was not a man to tolerate a place on the periphery – he either played first-fiddle or nothing at all. Christ taking first place was a threat to his position in the hierarchy of filial affections. As he saw it, every step his son made towards his God was a step away from himself; one step away was one step too many; it was a betrayal. If his son's God demanded absolute loyalty, a head-to-head, not with God, but with his son, was inevitable.

Convoluted or not, defensible or not, that is how Adam Sedley defined his God; that is how he understood Matthew, Chapter 10, verses 37-39, which no doubt explains why he didn't spend much time considering either his father or his mother in their roles as parents, and why he never consulted them or sought comfort from them. And if his father had imprisoned himself in the basement of his affections, there was little his son felt he could do about it, for loyalty for its own sake did not fit well with a commitment to Sedley's God. Loyalty for its own sake had not been forthcoming from Julia, either; otherwise she would not have abandoned him so quickly and so soon. But he convinced himself that he was glad, because he would not have known what to do with it had it come blindly. He neither wanted it nor expected it from his parents, either. And were he to allow his mother to visit, it was likely that she would come more blind than sighted; which is to say, she would have come as a mother, not as an equal.

The convolutions of Sedley's thoughts outdid the convolutions of his brain. He reckoned that his wish to be worthy of his God necessitated taking up the cross of Christ; that he must necessarily be prepared to lose his life to find another. Questioning meant losing; questioning was painful; questioning whether relationships between humans, and deeply valued by them, were all equally valued in the mind of his God, and finding perhaps that they were not. It was the pain of the wilderness – the cerebral wilderness; the wilderness in which Christ himself had confronted Satan, for that wilderness was not a place but a state of mind; and it was not a state of mind to be at all envied. Yes, questioning meant losing; but you could only lose what you possess; and if possession was a sickly, creeping thing, then you could only lose what was sickly and creeping – and that was no real loss at all, for it would be like losing a disease, and who in their right minds would not want to lose that? Besides, there were some things you only *thought* you lost, because you never really possessed them in the first place – like the love of a woman, which was not there in the first place; you would only be losing an illusion; possession in such a case would be no more than an illusion; and so losing would be an illusion, too; in fact, what you called a 'loss' was only a confirmation that you never really had it all along! – and you can't lose what you've never had! The Reverend found this thought deeply consoling, and also deeply wounding; it was a bitter-sweet piece of reasoning.

But while a vicar may lose wife and parents and still remain at his post, to lose his congregation and the goodwill of his parishioners and the very Church he represents, and still expect to remain *in situ* is, by any standards, unreasonable. Even Uncle Alan would have conceded the point – Uncle Alan, who had conceded very little that belonged to convention and the common run of things.

~ ~

Sedley found himself walking down the aisle of an empty church on what was to prove his last Sunday in the commuter land, as his black, leather-soled shoes clapped and clopped on the cold stone floor and over a brass memorial to the fallen of forgotten wars. He ascended the pulpit and opened the large, black embossed bible at a page marked with an imposing bookmark. He paused, and was about to close that mighty tome, when a voice rang out from the shadows of the back pews.

'Go on! I'm all ears!'

Startled, Sedley looked up. Jack was leaning forward out of the shadows, doffing his tattered hat in affectionate greeting. Sedley smiled, and returned to the Good Book.

'I read from Matthew, Chapter 5, verses 43 to 48:

"You have heard that it has been said, love your neighbour, and hate your enemy. But I say to you, love your enemies,

bless those that curse you,

do good to them that hate you,

and prey for them that spitefully use you and persecute you,

that you may be the children of your Father which is in heaven:

for he makes the sun to rise on the evil and on the good, and sends rain on the just and the unjust."'

Sedley closed the Good Book, slowly descended, walked up the aisle and sat down beside Jack, who gave him a quizzical look, with his head leaning to one side.

'And is that all?' asked Jack, after a pause. Sedley smiled.

'Well, many would say I've said quite enough already. So I suppose I'd better stick to the well-trodden text and let that speak for itself, don't you think?' Sedley spoke this last part in a mock whisper, no doubt intending sarcasm.

'Quite right', said Jack, 'We wouldn't want them in convulsions of fear, thinking you're asking something from them, now would we?'

'They don't want lectures.'

'Not if they come from you, hey?'

'Not if they come from me.'

'What did you expect?'

'I don't know what I expected.'

They sat in silence for some moments.

'What do you intend to do, then?' asked Jack, leaning right back in the pew and jerking the peak of his hat down over his forehead and folding his arms over his chest, like some old ranch-hand snatching 40 winks in the noonday sun.

'Any suggestions?' said Sedley, half-heartedly.

'Well, I suppose you could join me on my hill.'

'There are no hills around here,' said Sedley, with a laugh – it was strange to hear laughter in those surroundings.

'Oh, no. There *are* hills. It's just that you don't see them – yes, perhaps you're not ready yet. You know, it's amazing how few people ever do get to see them. Now, don't tell me you're one of those who never get to see the hills!'

'Hills are not for me,' said Sedley, not knowing, or for that matter caring, what the old fellow might mean, or whether he meant anything at all.

'Well, you're not making much progress here, are you? Time to move on, I'd say.'

'People who are sick need a physician, don't they?'

'Physicians need the co-operation of their patients, and it looks as though yours don't want to be healed. Well-trodden ways – you said so yourself, remember? They're not interested, maybe because they don't think they're sick at all, or maybe the prescription charge is just too high. No. You're wasting your time here. Yes, wasting your time. Time to shake the dust!'

The old man nodded sagely and got up. His hat readjusted, he shuffled up the aisle towards the heavy doors, and turned. 'Time to shake the dust!' he repeated, with another nod; and then he shuffled out of sight, and out of Sedley's life for good.

~ ~

Apart from the unexpected reappearance of Jack, Sedley's last Sunday in that parish seemed unremarkable, but, then, endings are often precisely that –

unremarkable; even death, surely the most remarkable event in life, frequently comes upon us unawares in the most natural of circumstances – a stark and impertinent intrusion upon the familiar run of things, one that jolts us out of ourselves and makes a lasting impression; no wonder we hide in the thickets of routine; familiarity is said to breed contempt, but it also shields us against unwelcome guests.

In the hours that followed Jack's exit, Sedley entertained his options, which, for all his cerebral deliberations, proved non-existent. The thought occurred to him that he might write a long, explanatory letter both to the bishop and to the press, not to exonerate himself, for he felt there was nothing to excuse himself for, but as a letter of resignation. Such a letter would amount to a final, last-ditch attack upon what he considered to be the opposition. If he was to go out, and that now seemed certain, he would go out with a bang, one that would resound in the rafters of the Establishment, both Church and State, and one that would at least raise questions in the minds of all those, of whatever religion, who clung to the superstitions that, in his view, constituted a grievous barrier to the stark truth that this life is all there is and all there ever would be – a barrier that stood in the way of the realisation that life is sacred because it is unique and irreplaceable, that man's inhumanity to man, of which war is merely one instance, is a clear expression of the will of a satanic conscience, and that the true meaning of any worthwhile scripture is the stricture to be good and to be tolerant of all but intolerance. Yes, he wanted to go out with a bang – not that any bang he was capable of making would have stood much chance of achieving what he vaguely imagined, for settled opinions are in the habit not simply of remaining where they are but of forming even deeper roots; once questioned, entrenchment becomes the order of the day, for ranks close and the ramparts are more rigorously defended than ever. But, he mused, a letter would at least make him feel better, it being a parting shot over the bows – the least he could do, and the most he could *possibly* do.

The prospect of writing such a letter did not, however, survive scrutiny. He believed that there was little of value to be said that had not been said already to the bishop and to his parishioners; and as for the press, the least he said now the better, for they were sure to make more of it than could justifiably be made; the press were less interested in making martyrs than in breaking them, and it should therefore be treated with a contempt best in a vow of silence. A letter, any letter, seemed too conciliatory, however uncompromising its tone.

The hiatus between popular fallacy and Sedley's God was just too great and too deep to be summed up in a letter; a letter would have persuaded no one who was not already disposed to be persuaded, and he did not wish to preach to the converted. And as for preaching to the unconverted – well, it would have been like attempting to persuade Adolf Hitler to allow a self-determining Jewish State within the boundaries of the Fatherland itself, or trying to get a similar deal for the Palestinians in Israel; no, it would be an infinitely harder task. Surely, then, Jack was right. If something really is mission impossible, it's time to shake the dust off one's feet. But *was* it really mission impossible, after all?

Sedley decided against writing the letter.

What about resignation? But no one had so much as asked him to resign, let alone forced his hand – at least, not explicitly. But then, how explicit had it to be? And besides, a shepherd without a flock was as redundant as a politician without supporting votes. Jack's remark about it being time to shake the dust from his feet was more a reminder of the obvious than a new avenue of approach. What can't be cured must be endured, and what is obvious cannot be denied. It was indeed time to shake the dust from his feet. Which meant that resignation, with or without a letter to go with it or announce it, was definitely on the cards and no doubt had been from the very outset – it had been destined, fated.

So, what beckoned? The wilderness? Jack's hill, whatever *that* was? He would be leaving one wilderness for another. Perhaps the wilderness he would be leaving for would be more palatable than the one he would be leaving behind. Perhaps life on 'the hill' had at least the virtue of simplicity, of honesty, of clarity. You would know where you stood. On the other hand, it was one thing to know where you stood, and quite another to want to stand there. If Sedley was indeed a man on the shore, beckoned by Christ himself to step into the sea and walk on the water towards him, to leave the safety of the land for the uncertainties of the boundless ocean with its tempests and rolling waves, he was quite sure that challenge were not to be found on the hillside – for running for the hills would be an abdication of the very mission he had set himself. No, the challenges that his God enjoined were not to be found on the hills of life, but deep down in the valleys – the valleys which teemed with life, perhaps not the most pleasant forms of life, perhaps not even hopeful life, but *life and the living* nonetheless. Those on the hills did not need to be taught the ways of Christ; those who lived on the hills did not need to be taught Sedley's God, for they knew him already;

Christ the physician had not come to heal the people on the hill, but to cure the sick in the valleys. Sedley's sense of mission was intense once again; it was a question of making sense of his life, of the path he had chosen, and it seemed to have little meaning without a sense of mission, and that entailed challenge. No one had said it would be easy, but even the rockiest ride was better than no ride at all – if you really did want to get places. And you had to *want* it – you had to want to get from one point to another, you had to want it *badly* enough. And if you did, there was no sense talking about resignation, or anything remotely like it. That would be defeatism, and you had hardly begun the journey! You had to get down to the valleys; the hills were no option. Socrates had chosen the market place, not the palaces of kings, and not the wilderness. If you truly wanted to *live,* then you had to choose *life,* not something that wasn't even second-best. Uncle Alan would have been the first to agree, for he lived in the valley of life, and he had contested and he had questioned, and he had taken little at face value, and he had known beauty – in short, he had *lived*!

And so, Sedley resolved to stick things out. He was not at all sure what that might mean. But it did not mean writing letters of explanation, for amongst the shadow people letters of explanation were indistinguishable from begging letters of apology. And it did not mean packing his bags and leaving quietly by the back door, like some town marshall leaving before sun-up, when 'the boys' were supposed to hit town to gun him down. There would be no High Noon for Adam Sedley. He would not pack his bags at all. He would stay exactly where he was until removed by force. He would remain *in situ,* and at the vicarage, which was his home, until the bailiffs were called in. And as for his parishioners and his flock, he would continue to write his sermons. He would be ready at all church services; and if the church was empty he would nevertheless wait the whole session through before returning home. In a phrase, it was to be business as usual. After all, he would simply be doing his bounden duty, for if a church is the house of God, it was only right and proper that it should be maintained and made fit for guests – if and whenever they should decide to come visiting. His Father's house may be deserted but Sedley himself was not prepared to ring the curtain down upon it. He would make his stand. And as for shaking the dust off his feet, he had already done that. He had done it by his invective, by making his ground as clear as he was able to make it and then standing upon it. And now, it was natural and it was important to continue to stand upon it.

Yet doubts still lingered and worried him, like shadowy figures on street corners in the dead of night. There was, after all, something attractive about life on the hill, about total abdication by throwing in the towel and shaking the dust off his feet. It seemed easier to leave than to stand his ground; but it was easier to stay than to leave now only to return later. There should be no sign of panic or fear, nothing that could possibly be interpreted as playing into the hands of the opposition. He would simply bide his time, uncertain of everything, save the superiority of his God over all others. It was the nebulous, uncertain, untried nature of it all that dogged his steps as he paced slowly round the vicarage garden; yes, he would walk under the cypresses which stood tall and now strangely menacing amongst the shadows of evening, as he mused this way and that and bided his time. But what was life without hope? It was the twilight zone in which certainty about the nature of his God was the only beacon.

Chapter Nineteen

A Wink and a Nod

But is it not good that the wheel should turn, that light follows dark and day follows night? For should it not turn, what becomes of the fight? Forever lost for the want of a turn – for the want of a voice and a scream from the hills.

~ ~

The encouraging sentiment that a life worth living entails hope was tapped out, like morse in motion, by Sedley's jaunty step that same night when, slightly less than an hour to midnight, he decided to get some fresh air – at least that is what he told himself, although the air was just as fresh in the vicarage garden as it was elsewhere, and certainly as fresh as it was in the darkened streets of his parish, where the very houses were as somnolent now as their occupants.

He walked out of the protective confines of the vicarage with a decisive step, as though he had made a rendezvous with Hope itself, having arranged to meet the amiable fellow under the brightness of a street lamp – out there, there where the world was, the *real* world, where challenge was to be found in all its formidable abundance; out there, where, unchallenged major cuts having been made in the provision of social services, street lamps were not so plentiful, or at least none that worked.

As he walked, he thought over and over again of Jack's parting words, and of the way the old fellow had looked at him. Sedley wondered whether Jack had merely been putting him to the test when he said that it was time to shake the dust; if so, he would have failed had he agreed to abandon his ministry.

He walked down clean and uncluttered streets near the church, past well-maintained houses in quiet roads, with neat, well-kept gardens on either side. The strong scents of honeysuckle and rose were still unmistakable, lingering long after the blossoms had said goodnight; and expensive cars gleamed in the occasional streetlamps, in driveways set well back from the pavements. And silence reigned ominously all about, like the heavy, unalterable silence of the grave. Not that Sedley was normally susceptible to morbid imaginings; but on this occasion it was scepticism and doubt, not to say cynicism, that began to bite harder on the heels of hope than ever before, attacks which he had to fight off at every turn, like a man in flight dodging the spears and arrows of his pursuers.

Was Christ to be found in such places? Was he to be heard there? Seen there? How could he be heard and seen in such places as these? Was this the world where Christ lived, was this the kind of life? Certainly this was where the challenge was. Oh, there were challenges elsewhere, too – greater challenges by far. But there was challenge in abundance here, too. For this was the world of the shadow people, as Sedley had for a long time called them and thought of them in what most people would have considered to be a somewhat unreasonable, not to say diseased, state of mind. The shadow people – beings who, to all appearances and at a distance, seemed to be creatures of substance with an adequately reasonable grasp of the requirements of civilised life, but who were, on closer inspection and with a different, deeper, set of criteria, little more than shadows in the land of the living, bound to one another by greed, gain and the fear of material loss, unable to pose questions let alone provide answers. It was they, both here and the world over, who had inherited the earth at the expense of the meek. See a shadow and you had every right to infer a thing of substance that formed it. Alas, not so with the shadow people, for they were shadows through and through; to come to know them was to come to know no more than shadows; and to speak to them of truth, love and beauty was merely to see one's very words float, crumple and fall to the ground without ever having reached their destination. The effort to know them better could only end in bitter disappointment of a kind that one could never get used to, or shrug off, or put down to experience and forget.

Had the shadow people been creatures from another planet, they might have been easier to live with; but they were as much of *this* planet as anyone else. They were of this planet and they hid in the shadows of their possessions – their gleaming cars and ideal homes, their well-kept gardens, their immaculate driveways. Being themselves mere shadows, they nourished themselves with the assumption that possessions were far more than they seemed and things to be achieved and cherished. They feared the loss of their possessions above and beyond all other loss, and even the loss of one another was counted a loss of possession, as if to suggest that it was possible to *possess* a fellow creature. They could not let go and were charmed into paralysis, living their lives on the surface of things, not because they were fearful of depth but because they were incapable of conceiving it.

The shadow people believed they had worked everything out, on a scale of calculated profit and loss; they had early acquired laptops and smart-phones on which to compute at home their incomings and outgoings and could, at the touch of a button, have at their command a map of accounts accurate to the penny and inclusive of every detail. For to know your accounts is to know all, or at least all you need to know; the shadow people lived strictly in accordance with the need-to-know principle, having indeed originated the precept. The primacy they gave to profit and loss was, in principle, not unlike the importance so many religions attached to the Life Hereafter; for the Life Hereafter might be conceived as a kind of loss-adjustment, in which losses in this life might be compensated for, and excesses penalised in the life to come.

The more Sedley ruminated in this bleak and insane manner, the more his pace quickened, as if with the unconscious desire to leave the land of shadows as quickly as possible for some place where ...

But no sooner had he turned a corner than he found himself on the fringes of the land of the care-nots, where the streets were littered with consumer throwaways – screwed up soft-drink cans, candy-wrappers and such like. At least the shadow people had had the inestimable decency to hide their waste away, out of sight and out of smell, in trash cans, and were doing much recently to persuade everyone else to follow suit, so that they might clean up the land for the benefit of ... well, just who was to benefit, other than the shadow people themselves, was not so clear; evidently their efforts had cut no ice with the care-nots. Sedley now walked down littered streets, diminutive gardens – not so much gardens as plots of clotted earth and unkempt open graves for trash.

Sedley was careful to distinguish between the care-nots and the have-nots. The care-nots were almost invariably have-nots, but not all have-nots were care-nots. The care-nots made light of such ideas as law and order. They were not organisers; neither were they organised. Their lack of respect for what the shadow people called 'law and order' was a constant source of irritation to the latter in their attempt to so order their lives that the least possible harm might befall either their possessions or them as possessors. The shadow people clung at least as tenaciously to law and order as they did to their other creations, for without law and order what would become of them and what they possessed? Since their identity was defined by what they possessed, to have lost their possessions would have meant losing themselves! Law and order was all about protecting the *status quo*, not about breaking new ground. New ground was essentially threatening, and no one likes to be threatened. Anything which was seen to threaten preservation and conservation offered the prospect of an untamed jungle. Consequently, the domain of the care-nots was the breeding-ground of James Sedley's 'animals' – those who would make regular nightly excursions into the shadow zone to break down garden walls and hurl bricks through the windows of garden sheds.

The care-nots and the shadow people held each other in contempt. Yet their existences were mutually sustaining. Without the care-nots, in what self-glorification could the shadow people bask? Without the shadow people, on whom could the care-nots vent their frustrations? Naturally, the care-nots despised law and order not for what it was in itself, but merely because the sword of justice was wielded by the shadow people. Had the care-nots themselves been permitted to deploy the weapon, who knows to what heights respect for law and order amongst them might have soared?

In Sedley's mind, the existence of the shadow people and the care-nots, and their inevitable contempt for each other, were sure to keep his God out of their affairs, well away at the periphery, where he could do no real harm.

Was Christ to be found here in the domain of the care-nots?

Sedley was dismayed. Was there nowhere his God might get a foothold? But here was *challenge*. Right here, here in Sedley's own backyard. Yet, it was hard. It seemed like the challenge one might pose an acute claustrophobic when presenting him with the prospect of life in a concrete igloo, or an agoraphobic with that of life on the plains of Montana.

Sedley did a u-turn and quickened his pace again, having decided to return to the vicarage by taking a short-cut across a forlorn piece of common land that straddled the domain of the care-nots and that of the shadow people – a piece of land that had suddenly and without consultation become far less common than it had been for centuries past, being now destined for the developers who were bent on converting half of it into an off-site parking-lot for a proposed mini-mart.

~ ~

As he was leaving the erstwhile commons for the better-lit streets beyond, he heard scuffling, shouts and what seemed muffled cries of pain to his left and felt compelled to investigate, urged forward, no doubt, by the dictates of a Christian conscience, being a conscience as sure-footed as a mountain goat and as fleet-footed as a cheetah. His first thought was that it might be a mugging which he might be instrumental in preventing. The odds were very much against his making much of an impression on the assailants, but he felt duty-bound to meet the challenge – he had to do his best with the resources at his disposal, albeit such resources were far more spiritual than physical.

He therefore made a detour towards the fray but could make out very little apart from shadowy figures in combat. Giving a shout of protest, he ran forward and, in doing so, brought down upon his own head the frenzied violence of two rival gangs of youths – just the kind of uncharitable creatures James Sedley had seen fit to baptise 'animals'. Slashed with a knife, he felt a searing pain across his neck and left shoulder; then he was struck with a heavy object; he fell to the ground where he felt the penetrating thuds of kicks targeting his head and abdomen. Lying there in the darkness he was to become oblivious to all the hits he received, but not before his face touched the earth and he was reminded once again of the smell of mother earth after all those years since Zulu Hollow. Zulu Hollow flashed through his mind as quick as lightning, and it was the last image to do so.

Sirens and flashing roof-lights sent the young and mindless tornadoes scurrying into the safety of the darker shadows, down secret paths that led to pitch-dark caverns of repose in which they might hide from the light of day and evade the long arm with which the law is so often and so erroneously credited. The police had been alerted by someone fond of dreaming and angered by the commotion which prevented them from doing so. A police car screeched to a halt, revealing Sedley's crumpled and bloody body in the headlights; he was not recognised for who or what he was — it was simply another body drenched in its own blood. And just another corpse, for wherever he woke up, it was not in the land of the living; he had given up the ghost in the ambulance that hurried him to hospital, 'having sustained,' the police informed the press the following day, 'severe blows to the chest and back, and deep lacerations to the face and neck.' Since the perpetrators of the crime had not be seen, several inferences were possible: Sedley had somehow been the victim of a random knife attack by youths spoiling for fun; or perhaps he had become involved, as in fact was the case, in gang rivalry; and rivalry would almost invariably have involved drug-trafficking; or it might have been a premeditated attack by a person or persons unknown bearing grudges; this latter was played down by the police, possibly for fear of being accused of Islamophobia, since it was by now a phobia gathering some momentum, and because press coverage had managed to link Sedley's name with it as a possible contributor.

Sedley's demise was perhaps even less than a nine-day wonder. When Christ was crucified at least he was hoisted high for all to see and was given, in the language of the media, the highest possible profile. His executioners did not run away, and the crime was perpetrated in broad daylight; nothing was hidden from view, and no part of the procedure was diluted, omitted or denied. If Christ had to die a violent death, his was perhaps a masterly stroke of publicity. And Socrates had had his trial, which the young Plato had attended and would make much of for the rest of his own life, giving his old friend and mentor the maximum possible publicity. At the other end of the scale of values, Adolf Hitler's departure in his bunker would have dwarfed the efforts of the most talented of fringe dramatists and will probably continue to do so for centuries to come.

But the reportage of Sedley's demise was a most commendable piece of containment and damage limitation. Suffice to say, it did not make front-page news, even in the local press. The manner of his passing became an object-lesson, the police stressing that members of the public should be far more wary and should certainly not interfere in situations with which they are ill-equipped to deal, for law-abiding citizens were no match for armed thugs on the rampage and ready to commit the damndest atrocities without the slightest provocation; it was stressed that however noble the motives of right-minded members of the public may be, they should at all times leave policing to the police and law and order to those who know best. No mention was made of cuts to police funding, which were so severe that it had fast become quite a novelty to see a policeman on the streets, and at night never at all. Nor was any space devoted to the very possibility that the assailant might have had political or religious motives; as it so happened, Sedley had been caught up in gang-rivalry, a problem which had for some time been infiltrating into the more respectable suburban commuter land and its immediate environs from inner-city areas, and was spreading like a cancer; even so, this was mere conjecture, and no proof was available – it was therefore a most convenient scapegoat in the armoury of damage limitation given the absence of proof to the contrary.

And so, if James Sedley had been right about his son, if all Adam Sedley wanted to do was to get his name in print and leave his name to posterity, here was a botched-up job if ever there was one! – with nothing but a final, flat obituary, saying more about the requirements of good policing than the efforts of the good Reverend to renounce the metaphysics of the hereafter and plead the case for the kingdom of God here on earth. After an unimpassioned account in the local press, no more was heard of the Reverend Sedley. Neither the world at large nor his insignificant parish seemed any the better for his having existed. No, there was not even one ripple on the surface of those muddy waters. The wheel might have turned, but not nearly far enough.

~ ~

Sedley's demise, therefore, left everything the same as he had found it. Sedley might have been intrigued, to say the least of it, by the very sameness of everything. Had he been blessed with a periscope in his grave, or binoculars in heaven, he would surely have remarked on the sameness of everything. It had not been the showdown he might have expected. He had gone out, not with a bang, but something rather less than a whimper. Had he been a firework, he would have disappointed the crowds on the fifth of November. He was, in a word, forgotten. The cypresses in the vicarage garden were the same as ever, standing tall, stately and unshaken by events; the grass still grew green and upwards and the birds still sang. And even that part of the common where Sedley had made his last stand looked none the worse and none the better for the blood that had been spilt upon it; within a day or two children returned to the spot to play there, and lovers consummated their passions there at dusk, while warring gangs continued to roam its perimeters on the lookout for cheap and deadly thrills and to settle scores. The traffic of commerce lumbered on, and the language of common sense blundered on: the same form of life, the same talk, the same tone; like a still-life which the artist had attempted unsuccessfully to improve and which had been rejected and now outlived him, as if to mock him.

Sedley's headstone had little to say beyond his name and the year of his birth and that of his death – apart, that is, from the well-worn phrase 'In Loving

Memory', carved into the stonework in unashamed irony. Judith Sedley suffered the intractable pain of loss to a depth that only a mother can feel, until an increasing senility, nature's balm, drew down a curtain of vague memory and, finally, forgetfulness on the stage upon which we are all fated to strut and then strut no more. As for James Sedley, he continually blamed himself for his lack of success in persuading his son to join him and settle for a life of commercial endeavour; the nature of his son's own endeavour was never clear to him, largely because he never gave it the cerebral attention it deserved; instead, he went to his grave nursing a guilt complex, a condition that persistently missed the point.

James and Judith Sedley spoke little together after their son's demise. Breakfasts were not what they used to be; James Sedley had to be content to make his own and send himself off to the office, and all without a monologue to reaffirm his territorial rights, for Judith Sedley spent more time in bed and was reluctant, she said unable, to get up. It was just as well; he didn't feel like talking and therefore spoke less, and he was soon to lose the ability. On the verge of retirement he was found dead in a train compartment, on the train that was taking him to the office on what had every appearance of being a normal day. It was indeed a normal day, for everyone except James Sedley himself and those immediately affected by him. 'Poor old Jim, and just ready to retire, too,' was the stock phrase in the office. Otherwise it was a very ordinary day, the same as any other. Though not quite the same. After James Sedley's passing, the antique clock to which he had devoted such loving care and attention ran down and was never rewound, not at least in that household. (It eventually found its way back to the antique shop where James Sedley had found it and was bought by a young couple 'starting out', who were looking for something reliable but refreshingly different from the modern mass-produced digitals, something special, something old, something of quality, something that might form a focal point in the living room and become a subject of conversation with friends.) And although the garden wall was not subjected to further attacks, it crumbled of its own accord through neglect and old age, as though it had pined after its caretaker and died of a broken heart.

So it was that Judith and James Sedley faded smoothly and unremarkably into eternal obscurity, like third-rate actors in third-rate plays, who drop out of theatrical currency unnoticed and simply cease to be.

It might have been something of a consolation to record an eternally heart-broken Julia Sedley, bemoaning her loss, regretting her hasty departure and clinging to her wedding photographs amid sobs of contrition; however, her own composure was regained with astonishing rapidity after only a few weeks' stay with her sister, and she eventually carved out a career in interior design, having given up the ambitious idea of becoming a female version of Vincent Van Gogh.

Sedley's burial rites were conducted by the very incumbent who was to succeed him. But what an incumbent was he! – not at all the kind of replacement that Sedley would have endorsed; quite the contrary! This was a gentleman who would discharge his office in the very best tradition of his predecessors, Sedley apart. He was every bit a John Burgess, a veritable chip off the old block, who would, in turn and in due course, retire, like Burgess, to a pier seat in some respectable seaside resort where, by then, the ghost of old Burgess would be stalking the promenade reciting well-worn scripture in dry and hollow tones. He would retire, taking with him the blessings of his parishioners and, if he played his cards exceptionally well, a gold watch to measure the chilled hours and minutes for which seaside resorts are notorious.

The new incumbent's inaugural sermon was of a nature to inspire unyielding confidence in his suitability for the task ahead, which consisted in shepherding his flock through the wilderness of life in preparation for the life beyond. There was much in his sermon which spoke of gratitude for wife, husband, children, house, job, car, peace and security – though not necessarily in that order. Gratitude was the theme – gratitude which that congregation knew well and was not of a mind to withhold. He might have been likened to a quiz-show host, who, before telling contestants what they stood to win next in the Big Money Game, would remind them of what they had already won, perhaps to put them at ease, perhaps to spur them on to even greater efforts. This was obviously an incumbent who knew his flock, and a flock who understood its incumbent. There could be no crossing of wires here, no awkward misunderstandings, no challenges, no show-downs, no compromising tete-a-tetes with the bishop. Charles Baxter and the lady of enormous proportions were thrilled, firmly believing that they were once again properly represented and properly cared for by a man worthy of their respect and most worthy of the cloth he wore. And the gentleman with the red carnation was at last redundant. With the arrival of the new incumbent, the serpent had, for the foreseeable future, taken a back seat, and so, with it, had the dove, which was replaced by a parrot of respectable parentage and fashionable plumage, both pleasing to the eye and unoffending to the ear.

And so it was business as usual for Charles Baxter and the lady of enormous proportions, both of whom won the instant admiration and attachment of the new incumbent; they resumed their places on the finance committee, which they dominated with the rich blessing of the new incumbent, who was, like his predecessor, eternally grateful for all the efforts they made to ease his burdens and light the way ahead. So grateful was he that he even permitted the lady of enormous proportions to offer frequent advice on the substance and tone of his sermons and to furnish insights into the deeper meaning of Scripture; and out of this grew a Bible Study Group which, naturally, the good lady chaired, and thus it was that she became a never-fading source of illumination to the entire parish, which mourned her eventual passing with great ceremony and floods of tears. It is hard to say who learned more from this good lady's divine inspiration – the new incumbent or the good lady herself; consequently, of course, it is hard to say who learned less.

All in all, it was quite remarkable how quickly Sedley's incumbency had been locked away and put out of sight, together with all its dust-raising and muck-raking episodes. As the lady of enormous proportions put it, they could now continue with every expectation of peace and plenty in the years to come, for it was, she said, as though a whirlwind had passed that way, or something which had been mistaken for a whirlwind – she could not for the life of her decide which; but it was, she went on, more like a nightmare, which, however unpleasant when experienced, is soon forgotten on waking and fades away entirely by breakfast; it was all, she advised, to be put down to experience, as all nasty things should be, and could not be allowed to disturb the continuity of decent, respectable life.

Apart from such glib commentaries, no one saw fit to jibe at Sedley by name or vilify him further now that he was gone. The line 'the living, one wise man has said, delight in speaking of the dead' might have much to commend it; but it did not apply to Adam Sedley, presumably because the very mention of his name would evoke memories too discomforting to entertain. There might have been some who believed that the deceased was morally improved by his own demise, or that mutilation of corpses was not really the done thing, but these more generous sentiments were unexpressed, at least in public. But in any case, there was little point in flogging dead horses; and what was true of horses was true of vicars – indeed more so, because further flogging would only serve to prolong the life of all that nonsense Sedley had spouted about religion, politics, the life hereafter and the moral inferiority of competing religions. It was time to bury it all with Sedley once and for all. In short, the feeling was that the show must go on.

Those who believed that the show was not worth staging in the first place tended to stay home. The Andersons stayed home. In fact, they were never seen again by those who had been the loudest in remarking their unprecedented appearance in church. Never again did the Andersons darken the doors of that great edifice; they remained very much at home in their farmhouse during their candle-lit winter nights, dreaming of childhood Christmases, or of the world as it was, and of the world as it should be.

Much to the relief of Charles Baxter and the lady of enormous proportions, Jack was never seen again either, and was soon to leave those parts for his 'hill', never to return. There was no further talk of him. He was, as it were, erased from the canvas. It is to be wondered how that old fellow bade his final farewell to the land of the living. Perhaps he never made it through the hard winter that was to follow – or perhaps it was a summer when he finally made his exit, with his back to a tree and his hat shading his eyes from a world towards which he had felt a lifelong ambivalence; or perhaps he curled up on Mother Earth one spring, face down on the green grass, breathing in for the last time the aromas of antiquity, much as Sedley himself had done on the common. Or perhaps he expired on the wings of a laugh, or with a smile on his lips. This we shall never know – except to say that there is little doubt as to his fondness for the 'hill' to which he had repeatedly alluded. Did he imagine it a real place, and was it so? If it really was a hill of earth and grassy slopes, he would surely have been found there in eternal repose, his slow shuffles having bent the grass to the music of the sheep, that simple, distant, mournful bleating that is the mark of summer.

Meanwhile, the old man was determined not to end his days in the commuter land of green suburbia; he would leave it, but first a detour must be made *en route*. He and Adam Sedley might have agreed that they lived in a world of shadows. It was not many days after his interment, however, that a very real shadow fell over Sedley's grave – that of the old man, who, having bared his head, bent down and rearranged the few flowers, which, though still alive and blooming, had been displaced by the playful breezes of midsummer. But Jack Barker's eyes were far from tearful. He placed something at the base of the headstone; and then he stood up and listened for a few moments to the strains of the hymn

'Abide With Me', which were rising and falling from the church nearby where the new incumbent had just concluded a most comforting sermon. He replaced his crumpled hat and adjusted it, and then, pausing to give a last benign glance at Sedley's headstone, he smiled unmistakably, and, with a wink and a nod, turned aside and ambled out of the cemetery, jauntily doffing his hat to an elderly lady whom he passed at the rusted, wrought-iron gate; she made her way to Sedley's headstone and placed some flowers there, discarding, as she did so, a piece of wood without noticing what had been rudely inscribed upon it – the words *Dis Manibus*, to the Gods of the Shades, the dedication customarily inscribed on Roman tombstones in antiquity.

At a very different time and in a very different place, Sedley's 'epitaph' might have been spoken from the mouth of a Lakota Sioux Medicine Man: 'Wakan Tanka, Tunkashila, *onshimala*' – which may be very loosely rendered, 'May God Save Us All!'

~ ~ ~ ~

BV - #0009 - 021219 - C0 - 234/156/16 - PB - 9781780916026